CINDER & SORROW

ESSAERISTS WAR
BOOK TWO

NICHOLAS TAYLOR

Cinder & Sorrow

Essaerists War Book Two

Text copyright © 2025 by Nicholas Taylor

This is a work of fiction. Names, places, characters and events portrayed in this book are fictitious and are a product of the author's imagination. Any similarity to persons living or dead is coincidental and not intended by the author.

ISBN-13: 978-1-938387-21-0

www.NicholasTaylor.co

My grandfather has not been alive for some time now, but there isn't a day that goes by that I do not feel his influence on my life. He was always a source of wisdom and encouragement, and he was never afraid to let you know when you could improve. He was famous in our family for the Seven P's: Proper Prior Planning Prevents Piss Poor Performance—a saying that I have inflicted on my own family numerous times. I'd like to think that he'd say I used the Seven P's in this book.

Pops, this book is dedicated to you. Thank you for all that you did for me.

PRONUNCIATION GUIDE

Characters

Mariokos (mar-ee-O-kos) | Xavieno (za-VEE-e-no)
Fioralba (fee-o-RAL-ba) | Caelwen (KAYL-wen)
Valfric (VALF-rik) | Wulfgren (WULF-gren)
Treftune (TREF-toon) | Biankara (bee-an-KA-ra)
Aelric (AYL-rik) | Ilara (I-LAR-a)
Ilfthandor (ILF-than-dor) | Nefeli (ne-FE-lee)
Thraindel (THRANE-del) | Durnara (DUR-na-ra)
Gaelrik (GAYL-rik) | Garethor (GAR-eh-thor)
Kernvald (KERN-vald) | Durgard (DUR-gard)
Yrthorn (YR-thorn) | Aresio (a-RE-see-o)
Theoliano (thee-o-LEE-a-no) | Alessandros (a-les-SAN-dros)
Damianello (da-mee-a-NEL-lo) | Helioz (HE-lee-oz)
Erastos (e-RAS-tos) | Luciakos (lu-see-A-kos)
Geraldox (ger-AL-dox) | Isaios (i-SY-os)
Pandros (PAN-dros) | Feliciano (fe-li-CHEE-a-no)
Bergthral (BERG-thraal) | Hildrana (HIL-dra-na)
Fernwen (FERN-wen) | Eira (E-rah)
Mirthgar (MIRTH-gar) | Osthorn (OST-horn)
Aelwyn (AYL-win) | Branrik (BRAN-rik)
Alaricth (AL-ah-rikth) | Tirwalden (TEER-wal-den)

Countries

Gwenthari (GWEN-thar-ee) | Lysandrian (ly-SAN-dree-an)

Ulfgarath (ULF-ga-rath) | Wulfharboria (WULF-har-bor-ee-a)
Valfarans (VAL-fa-rans) | Eirfrosti (EYE-er-fros-tee)
Rothmornian (ROTH-morn-ee-an) | Wyrdrunir (WYRD-roo-neer)

Places / Things / Misc

Essaerist (es-SAY-rist) | Essaeris (es-SAY-ris)
Essaerite (es-SAY-rite) | Essaerithon (es-SAY-ri-thon)
Valfglidea (VALF-glee-dee-ah) | Wolxaran (Wulks-ah-ran)
Holtstag (HOLT-stahg) | Treowholt (TREE-oh-holt)
Duskell (DUSK-ell) | Holtkern (HOLT-kern)
Dionisiana (dee-o-nee-SEE-a-na) | Dionisio (dee-o-NEE-sio)
Hroldenfell (HROL-den-fell) | Bryndraught (BRIN-drawkt)
Ulfgard (ULF-gard)

PART ONE

CHAPTER I

Valfric's owl moved closer to the city of Hroldenfell. He'd expected it to be intercepted by one of the Lysandrian Essaerites, but it hadn't been. There were birds in the sky, but he suspected that they were real ones and not Essaeris. It was mostly ravens and crows and other scavengers, but many had gone to roost for the evening, though Hroldenfell glowed with light.

After the initial surprise and horror of seeing the city's wall come down and watching the Lysandrian soldiers stream inside, slaughtering the people he'd grown up with, Valfric had moved into a calm anger and resentment. It reminded him of stories he'd heard as a child, from when his people had sacked and razed towns and cities; except this time, it was his people it was happening to. He wondered if it looked the same now as it would have back when his people were strong and were doing something like this to someone else.

He suspected that the razing of a city looked very similar, regardless of the army that was doing the razing. The owl moved closer and dropped down in the sky, able to make out figures as they scurried or moved below.

The initial chaos of the battle had subsided somewhat. There still seemed to be pockets of resistance inside the city, but they were dwindling. Each pocket was slowly losing to Lysandrian forces, and Valfric had watched a handful of Essaerites move around the city, helping to crack fortifications in the few remaining buildings that hadn't been taken yet.

Much of the city was burning or had already burned to the ground. Hroldenfell hadn't had many stone buildings prior to this and had been mostly a composition of wooden structures and tents. That was gone now, and he knew it would never come back.

As the owl neared the ground, he was able to see the countless forms of the dead. It was a collection of men, women, and children. Both free and slave were slain, and he suspected that if the owl could smell, its nostrils would be filled with the stench of burning flesh. As it was, the owl could not smell, and he didn't feel any inclination to change that.

He was feeling numb as the owl continued to circle the city, as he made an assessment. He'd assumed that everyone would be killed, but they hadn't been. Many of the people were left alive. He had seen plenty of the things that he'd expected to see when a city was taken. There had been the pillaging, killing, torment, and rape that he'd expected to happen, but not quite to the extent he would have thought. Now, many of the living residents of the city were being put into groups, watched over closely by the Lysandrians.

Also, he could see processions of soldiers going into the buildings that weren't ablaze, pulling out belongings and piling them up under the direction of other soldiers. It was an odd sort of thing to see. Valfric had taken part in many things just like this. He'd helped take settlements and caravans. There was always the divvying up of spoils. Some of those spoils would be property of some sort—gold or silver or trinkets, livestock, and of course, the living, which were some of the most valuable.

But he had never seen it done in such a calm and orderly fashion. The soldiers moved, following orders from their leaders, gathering whatever they were to gather and then bringing it to wherever they were told to take it. It was like they were doing normal work. After all, this was a job for them, which Valfric supposed he couldn't quite fault them for, as it had always been a job and a trade for him as well.

It was just jarring seeing somebody else do it, and he had to admit, doing it better.

The groups of people inside the city also seemed to have an order to them. None of the groups were too large or too small; they seemed to be just the right size for a group of soldiers to manage. And it appeared that the legions were only keeping those that were able-bodied or young. The rest were dead.

Some of the newly captured people of the city were being made to carry the dead and pile them up to burn. Again, the order to it was horrifying and awe-inspiring at the same time. In all his time raiding, Valfric had never thought of the dead; they lay where they were slain, they were no different than anything else that didn't have value.

Some of the groups had been brought out of the city already and were in or around some of the Lysandrian camps. It was while inspecting one of these groups that he saw it. On occasion, a handful of people would slip away and dart into the woods. Sometimes the soldiers would follow them, but surprisingly often, they didn't. Instead, the soldiers kept their focus on the larger groups of people. There had also been a smattering of horses and groups that had made it out of the city right after its fall. Some of those had died on the Lysandrian counter-fortifications, but a handful had made it through, though the number was small.

He pulled his mind from that of the owl and looked over at his friends. They all looked tense. They hadn't seen what Valfric had seen, but they had heard him describe what was going on, and he could see curiosity and concern in all of their eyes.

He caught the hint of fear in Ilara's face from time to time, but it seemed to be mild. Aelric was looking at him with a hard expression.

"What are the bastards doing?" he asked.

Valfric shook his head slowly. "They're gathering the spoils," he said, though his tone was monotone.

"And?" Aelric asked. "What's wrong?"

Valfric sighed. "Nothing. It's just... we've always been the ones doing this, you know," he said. Thraindel looked at the ground and nodded, and he saw Ilara's expression tighten. Aelric's face looked resigned.

"I see," Aelric said, and Valfric could hear the sorrow in his voice.

Valfric spoke in a rush, "But they're not like us. There's a kind of order to it," he said, unsure of how to explain what he was seeing. "They haven't killed as many as I thought, but the night is young, and there's still a handful of places inside the city that seem to be holding out."

Ilara looked up at him. "Do you think they'll make it? Through the night at least?"

Valfric shook his head. "No, I suspect they'll fall within the next hour or so. However, there have been some people that have escaped."

This seemed to perk Thraindel up. "People have escaped?" he said, and Valfric could hear the tell-tale sign of excitement and optimism in his friend's voice.

"Yes," Valfric said. "It appears that several have made it out. Not large groups, mind you, but some have. Some of them left right when the city fell, but there have been a few that have been in groups that the Lysandrians have taken back to their camps. I've seen a handful slip into the woods here and there. Some of them look hurt," he pointed out.

"And the Lysandrians?" Aelric asked.

Valfric shook his head. "They've gone after a few, but not as many as I would have thought. I can't think of why that would be."

Aelric looked thoughtful, but it was Ilara who answered. "Why would they need to? They've taken the city. They have the entire area. So what if a few new slaves get away?" she said, and he could hear coolness in her voice. "It's not that they don't want everybody. It's just... well, think about how many times we've left a stray animal or cart or something behind," she said.

She was right. They had done that on many occasions. When they raided a settlement, there would always be a handful of items that they missed, and they'd never cared. Why would the Lysandrians be any different? Who cared about a handful of people that would probably die over the next few days or would be collected eventually?

And that was the other side of it, wasn't it? That they would be collected eventually. Valfric knew all too well that there were many Lysandrian patrols in the area. People would need to move fast to get a safe distance away from Hroldenfell. But even then, where would they go? What would they do? They had nothing to bring with them. No food, no clothing, no supplies. Nothing. And he realized that's why the Lysandrians didn't care. Because many of those who left would come stumbling back towards the city at some point out of desperation, or they would simply die. And for those that didn't, they didn't matter. There were too few of them for it to matter to the Lysandrians.

But to Valfric, it might be different.

"We should help them," he said.

"We should help them?" Aelric repeated.

Valfric shook his head. "Yes, we should. They are our people. We should help them. We can help them get clear of the area. And we're going to need everyone we can if we're going to be able to resist the Lysandrians in the future."

This last part seemed to resonate with Thraindel, whose eyes hardened. He stood. "Valfric's right. We're going to need every man and woman we can to resist these people."

For her part, Ilara looked unconvinced, but she nodded. "Very well. I suppose we will need everyone."

She looked over at Aelric, who just shrugged. "Fine. I'm in," he said.

Breaking camp was relatively easy, as they hadn't set up much of a camp to begin with. With as many Lysandrians as there were in the area, Valfric and all the others had been hesitant to have too defined a presence. It had meant little to no fires or tents, with them spending the night sleeping on the ground covered by blankets or makeshift tents that Valfric would use Essaeris to create if it looked like the weather was going to be poor. It wasn't the worst that they'd ever had, and Valfric remembered many times when they had slept directly on the hard dirt of the forest floor when they had been younger and first cutting their teeth. Still, it wasn't exactly an enjoyable experience either.

Once they were done with camp, Valfric felt the Essaeris inside of himself. They were going to need more scouts if they were to do this, to watch for Lysandrians and also to find the people that needed help. The problem was going to be what kind of Essaerites to create and how many.

After pausing for a moment, Ilara said, "What's wrong?"

He opened his eyes, looking at his friends. He never asked them for help or suggestions when creating Essaerites, but now he realized that he was a bit out of his depth. He could create Essaerites that were weapons and all sorts of things—but what to create for a situation like this?

He didn't know.

His initial gut reaction was to create as many wolves as he could. They had exceptional hearing, eyes, and senses of smell, which would help them find people. However, Valfric could only create four or maybe five of them, and that would mean that he wouldn't be able to use his Essaeris to create anything else.

Most of the people they had seen had been on foot. Those on horseback were getting a good distance away from the city, and while Valfric and his party had a handful of extra horses with them, he knew they wouldn't be able to take many. Should he create Essaerites that would be able to carry people?

He answered Ilara's question, "I don't know what to create," he said.

She cocked an eyebrow, and he saw her somber mood break for almost a moment. "Really?"

"Really," he said.

Thraindel laughed and looked to Aelric. "Our time has come to an end, my friend."

Aelric snorted, and Valfric glared at him. "What?"

Ilara was the one who answered. "Don't you know, Valfric? It is the end of the world," she said, in all seriousness.

Valfric gave her a flat look. And she went on, "It is. You don't know everything. You don't know what to create. Oh, it's one of the signs. The gods have spoken of this day," she said.

She looked at Thraindel, who nodded solemnly. "Yes. Yes. Once Valfric does not know everything, or admits that he does not know everything, the world must surely come to an end."

To Valfric's annoyance and amusement, Aelric decided to play along with it. "I do think I heard this tale as a child," he said. "Soon we shall be in Ulfgara's halls!"

He felt tension rolling off of him.

"Fuck you all," Valfric said.

"Is there time for that?" Ilara asked. "I mean, I guess we have a few seconds probably, before the world ends. That should be enough time for you, shouldn't it be?"

Thraindel laughed, and Aelric chuckled. Valfric just shook his head.

"Fuck all of you. But honestly, I'm not sure what to create," he said.

They all got serious.

"Well," Aelric said, "Normally you would create wolves, but why don't you want to do that this time?"

"I could," Valfric said. "They're great for scouting, and we might need them for defense. But they also take a lot of Essaeris. And it might not give us the ability to find as many people or to see threats as far away."

"I take it the birds you usually use won't work," Ilara said, her tone back to business.

"They could, but the forest is thick here. I like the idea of something on the ground. I'll still keep a few hawks and owls in the air, but I don't know," Valfric said, unsure, for one of the first times in his life.

"What other small animals could you create that would be able to help us out?" Thraindel asked. "The only thing I could think of would be hares or rats or something like that, but I don't think they'd be able to move fast enough to cover any ground."

Valfric sat on a large rock on the edge of their camp.

"Yeah, I could do that, but you're right. They wouldn't be able to move very quickly," he said.

Ilara was looking down at the ground, deep in thought.

"Don't know that I've ever seen you think this hard before, Ilara," Aelric said.

She smirked. "Well, at the risk of sounding like I'm quoting Valfric, fuck off," she said.

"How small can you make the wolves?" she asked. "I've seen you make little puppies and dogs before."

Valfric perked up. "I can; they take a whole lot less Essaeris. I could create some smaller Essaerites that are like wolves, but closer to the size of a dog, maybe almost like a fox."

As he thought about it, the more he liked the idea.

"How many of them can you create?" she asked.

This brought him up short. Valfric could create a lot of little animals. The problem would be creating ones that were advanced enough to do what he wanted them to do. He grimaced.

"If I want them to be smart enough to do what we want," he said, "maybe six or seven. In a few hours, I might be able to create up to eight."

As he said it, he could see it in their faces. For the first time, he could see it. There wasn't surprise so much; they all had a pretty decent idea of his abilities, but was it disappointment he detected?

They'd all come to appreciate how powerful some of the more experienced and older Essaerists were. That wasn't Valfric. They knew this. He was a young man. He wasn't some old man who was more of a walking skeleton than a person. But they'd also seen more. They'd seen Lysandrian Essaerists that had to be relatively close to their age. And the Wulfharboira girl they'd battled had appeared younger than Valfric. She was a Gwenthari just like him, but her Essaerites had been so advanced and powerful. The others had seen it, but they hadn't truly appreciated the way he had. Her large cats had torn through his Essaerites, and she had three of them, and still had enough Essaeris left over to create some kind of suit for herself—something he hadn't really seen or heard of before, at least hadn't heard of in someone as young as she was.

Normally, he would have been able to chalk it up to saying that she was exceptionally advanced or powerful in some way, but he knew better now. She wasn't more powerful than he was, necessarily. She was just better. She didn't appear to be as good as the Lysandrian Essaerists, but Valfric wondered if that would change in time, if they were training her and teaching her to be just like them, because while he hated to admit it, they were better than he was, by a lot, and he knew the others were thinking the same thing.

There was an awkward silence that was starting to fill the space. None of them wanted to say it. They still respected Valfric, he suspected, and they knew that he was more powerful than they were, to be sure. But the days of Valfric being the strongest, most powerful bully there was, were clearly at an end, and they had never really been a thing to begin with. They'd just been lucky that they hadn't come up against somebody who was stronger from the word go.

He felt shame. These people depended on him. They followed him. He was their leader. They put their lives in his hands, and in a way, he felt like he had let them down. He tried to shake the feeling. He wouldn't show weakness. He wouldn't show them that he was feeling ashamed. That's not what a warrior did. A warrior was always strong, was always confident, was always ready for the next fight.

"I'll start with six," he said, "then, energy permitting, I will create more, but I also need to leave a lot of my power in reserve," he lied. "To make sure that if we run into any problems with the Lysandrians, I'll have something."

This seemed to track with the rest of them, and their looks of concern melted away. After all, it made sense, didn't it? Why would Valfric put all of his power into these things that were going to be searching for something when they might need his abilities if they got attacked? He needed that confidence, and so did they. It was the same confidence that they had whenever they raided —the confidence that they could do things that others couldn't because they had Valfric with them. Tonight would be no different.

"Give me a bit," he said.

Valfric closed his eyes and breathed in and out, feeling his Essaeris build and swell. As it bubbled up to the surface, he felt it rush out of him. Next to him, a wolf, slightly larger than a fox, came into existence. Valfric opened his eyes and looked down at it. It was good enough. He had used these before to keep their settlement safe from small predators. It had been years since he had used these types of Essaerites, but in the early days, they were the best that he could muster.

Even though it had been years, he felt a small sense of nostalgia as he looked at the Essaerite. Its eyes were not as good as the ones that he created now. He could alter them, but he wasn't sure that that was strictly necessary. The ears were still good, and the nose was excellent. Being an Essaerite with a strong sense of scent was one of the first things that he had mastered, finding that it was useful with body types like wolves and other dogs. When he was young, he had taken the corpses of wolves, dogs, foxes, and coyotes and used his Essaeris to feel them out, to learn how they worked, to sense them, and to recreate them. He thought himself a genius at the time, but he had learned years ago that this was how most Essaerists learned—that you mimicked the things that were around you.

And while the eyes were good enough, he decided to make some small tweaks to them. He replaced the eyes with something similar to what he used now that had much better vision at night, and he suspected that they were going to need it. He created a few more of them, feeling his Essaeris take a hit, but it wasn't completely depleted. If there was a benefit to using Essaerites that he had created before, it was that they took less energy from him, and they were something that his mind and power remembered, each one becoming a little bit easier to create. In a way, he almost kicked himself for not having used them and refining them over the years.

They weren't going to be effective in combat. Any man could take them out. But he thought back to all the times that they would have been handy when looking for trouble or looking for targets.

"They're not as cute as the puppies you create," Ilara said.

He smiled. Valfric was exceptionally good at creating puppies. He had found them to be one of the most useful diversions there was. Unfortunately, a puppy was too small to really do anything useful now.

She knelt down in front of one and scratched its ears.

"Do you want me to have it hump your leg?" Valfric asked.

She looked up at him. "Could you?" she asked, animated. "I bet if I close my eyes, I won't be able to tell the difference between you and it."

He heard a snicker from Aelric and a laugh from Thraindel. He smiled.

"Fuck you," Valfric said.

But she looked at it more critically, and then Aelric said, "This actually could be useful for us in other ways."

"How so?" Valfric asked.

"Almost none of those people have anything with them, which means no food either." He said, "And I'm sure the Lysandrians have cleared most of the large game out of the area, but smaller game?"

Valfric nodded. "I hadn't thought of that," he said.

They'd used his wolves plenty to find hares or other small game in an area in order to feed themselves, but they were almost overkill. They were too strong, too powerful. Not that that was necessarily a problem, but Valfric would need to find a lot of small animals in order to feed people over the next few days. More than the four or five wolves he could create probably could find.

But with a small team of smaller animals like the ones he had now, they might be in luck. He felt better about what they were doing.

"You're right," he said. "Alright, let's do this."

————

Valfric felt exhausted as he brought the last few people into camp. The sun was starting to rise on the horizon, and he wondered how long it had been since he'd last slept—or since he'd last had a good night's sleep anyway. Those had been hard to come by as of late.

He looked around their camp. Ilara, Thraindel, and Aelric were back. With them was a group of people. Some of them were laying on the ground trying to sleep. Others sat against trees alone. A few cried. Others were hurt. But all of them had the same look of dejection or surprise on their faces.

He'd been disappointed with the number of people they had been able to find. He thought they would have been able to find many, but it appeared most had scattered, going in any direction they could. And now that it was light out, or getting to be light out, he knew the Lysandrians would start searching the area.

And while he wanted to sleep, he knew they had to move. He called out to the people.

"I know you're all tired," he said. The gathered people looked over at him. "But we need to move. The Lysandrians will be coming soon."

One woman looked at him and spoke, her voice tired and scared, "You're an Essaerist, can't you protect us?"

He grimaced, feeling a sense of shame come back.

"From some, yes, but not from everything. And the Essaerites that I had to create to find all of you are not strong. They're meant to find things. And I don't think it's wise for me to test myself against four legions," he said.

A few people nodded numbly. The foolishness of standing against four legions was not lost on them.

He put the handful of children they had, along with some of the food, on the horses, and the group began to move out, heading north, away from Hroldenfell.

As they walked, the sun rose above them, turning into what would normally have been a pleasant day. But Valfric wasn't feeling anything pleasant. He was feeling exhausted. Everyone knew this was just the beginning. They would need to find food and shelter and everything else, and they'd have to keep on moving, because sooner or later, the Lysandrians would too.

Ilara came up next to him. She had done so well over the evening, just as she always had, but he could see a slight tension in her eyes.

"Tired?" he asked.

She glanced over at him and shrugged. "I suppose, but I don't really feel it. I feel pretty awake, actually. You?"

"I'm exhausted," he said, "but a lot of that's probably from the pull on my Essaeris."

She looked over at him and then back forward again, as if trying to think of what to say.

"Ilara, what is it?" he asked.

She huffed. "Nothing. Just..." She paused. "Nothing is all. Just thinking about these people, I guess."

"I can understand that," he said.

She looked over at him.

"But can we?" she said. "Can we really understand?" Her voice was low. "After all, we may not have been the ones who had done this to them, but..."

"None of this is our fault," he said, feeling a sense of defiance.

She waved her hand in dismissal. "I know that." She looked at the people. "But we've been the ones to cause this before, haven't we?"

"That was different," Valfric said. Though part of him knew he was wrong.

She looked at him in disbelief. "Was it?" Before he could answer, she shook her head. "I'm sorry. I don't know what I'm saying. I guess maybe I'm more tired than I thought."

He brushed the conversation aside in his mind and wrapped his arm around her shoulders as they walked. "I think we all are, but we'll make camp soon, and we'll get some shut-eye. And those cute little Essaerites of mine should find us some dinner."

She smiled. "I suppose that works. I suppose they are kind of cute."

"You told me they were cute earlier," he said.

"I don't remember saying that," Ilara said.

He laughed. "Of course, you didn't," he said, and he continued walking along.

CHAPTER 2

Bergthral looked out at the vast openness before him. The warm sun shone on his face, heating his chest and shoulders. He breathed in deeply through his nose, taking in the scent of the sea before him.

He stood atop a small cliff that overlooked the ocean. The horizon was open and seemed to stretch on forever, but he knew that just past it lay Eirfrosti. In the air above the water, he could see all manner of birds circling around, searching for fish.

Below him, the surf crashed against the rocks of the cliff face. Behind him was the forest. His eyes scanned the horizon for anything noteworthy—not threats, just anything of interest. He thought he caught a small glimpse of a fishing boat off in the distance, but it was hard to tell.

As he watched the waves, he felt himself relax and calm. He enjoyed starting his day this way, standing on the cliff all by himself, taking in the sea and the sounds around him. It had a meditative effect that he found to be centering and useful for the day.

Next to him was a giant Essaerite that roughly resembled a bear. The current version of it wasn't as large as what he could create, but it was what he normally had around. That wasn't to say it was small; the creature could rip someone limb from limb if need be, and it was menacing to most. Its legs were slightly thicker and more muscular than those of a regular bear, and its neck was just a little bit longer. The jaws were wider and deeper, with the inside being metal.

If you saw it at night as just a silhouette, you might think it was a bear. But during the day, you only noticed the resemblance in shape and silhouette alone. It was very obviously anything but an animal.

It had larger ears than regular bears, and those ears were presently swiveling around, listening for anything they could. Its eyes were comparable to Bergthral's, but its nose was far superior to any human's.

Above the nose and along the forehead was metal. It didn't have fur; instead, it was covered in overlapping scales that resembled armor. They were made from a material that Eirfrosti Essaerists had developed—a cross between ceramics and metal. It was extremely light and very hard-wearing.

Each scale was roughly the size of a man's thumbnail and matte black. Along the edges of each scale was the deepest of blues. Atop the animal's shoulders, he had a rough shape of a saddle in case he wanted to sit on it, though he didn't prefer traveling long distances on the Essaerite. Its gait was a little too rough, in Bergthral's opinion. The paws were larger than those of a regular bear and had more dexterity. The claws were retractable, similar to a cat's, and he could change them to whatever he wanted. Typically, they were about six inches long and made of sharp black metal.

It was incredibly powerful and intimidating, and he always had it around. This had been one of the lessons he learned from his wife, Hildrana, so many years ago. She was an Essaerist as well. Except whereas he was from Valfarans, she was Eirfrosti, and with her came all the knowledge of her people. The Eirfrosti were Gwenthari, but they weren't like the Wulfharborias, Valfarans, or Ulfgarath. They were their own kind of people, and in many ways, Bergthral thought they were far more advanced than other Gwenthari.

One of those areas of advancement was in Essaeris. His wife had apprenticed under a master Essaerist when she was growing up, and she would have had an apprentice too, had she not chosen to marry Bergthral and move away from Eirfrosti. She hadn't shared all of her knowledge with him, as they were sacred guarded secrets for the Eirfrosti, but he knew enough that he might as well have been an Eirfrosti Essaerist. The Essaerite next to him was a testament to that. For the Eirfrosti, Essaerites needed to be special. They needed to be advanced, and they needed to be worked on. They tended to be kept around if it was an Essaerite that was used regularly.

With each day the bear was around, it required a little less Essaeris. There were limits, of course, but it also made it easier to create and maintain. Most Eirfrosti Essaerists had some type of Essaerite like the bear that was always with them. It was a very effective form of protection, and their appearances made a statement, which was also common among the Eirfrosti. But the bear was far more than a blunt instrument that could kill. It was strong and could carry things. It could also be harnessed to pull a cart or plow through a field. In this, Essaerites also had to be multi-purposed. They had to be a benefit and an aid, not just an art piece or weapon.

He turned and walked down a small path that led to a narrow beach, where a stream ran from the forest into the ocean. A few boats were lined up far back from the water's edge. Bergthral rarely went out onto the water. He didn't mind it, but fishing wasn't something he enjoyed, and when he did fish, he used Essaerites for it, again thanks to his wife.

He and his bear walked into the forest and were instantly engulfed by trees. The air was heavy with the smell of moss and dirt, along with the scent of spring flowers that had been in bloom for some time now. The air was rich and wonderful, and shoots of golden light dappled the forest floor. He walked along at a steady pace, his mind going through the tasks he needed to complete for the day.

As he exited the forest, he was met by the sight of green fields, with several small cottages dotted throughout. Bergthral's settlement was small but a tight-knit community, one that he was proud to lead. He traipsed along until he reached his home. It was partially dug into the ground, with a steep thatched roof that rose high overhead. He could see smoke curling out from the chimney.

Outside, Hildrana, his wife, stood. She looked at him and smiled. Hildrana had long, straight black hair as dark as coal. Her skin was a bright white that almost seemed to glow, like that of all her people, and her eyes were a vivid blue. Her figure was lean and lithe, and in Bergthral's opinion, she was the most beautiful woman to have ever lived, and who possibly ever would live. But as she had reminded him, men in love tended not to see things clearly and were a little on the stupid side.

He walked up to her and wrapped his arms around her waist, pulling her in tightly. She embraced him back, and he kissed her.

"How was the ocean, my love?" she asked.

"It was good," he said, releasing her. "Where's Fernwen?" he asked, referring to their daughter.

"She's inside," Hildrana said.

"Do you have her working on something?" he asked.

His wife smirked. "I have her working on a few exercises, yes. Do you need her for something?"

Bergthral shook his head. "No, I'm fine, though I'm sure she would prefer it if I had something for her to do."

Hildrana laughed softly. "Oh, I'm sure she would."

It was difficult for Essaerists to have children, and Bergthral and Hildrana had almost given up on their chances at parenthood until Hildrana became pregnant with their daughter, Fernwen. What had been even more unlikely was that Fernwen was born an Essaerist. To Bergthral's and Hildrana's knowledge, and to all the knowledge of the Eirfrosti, there was nothing that could guarantee that someone would be born an Essaerist. They were extremely rare, and it didn't seem to matter if your parents were Essaerists or not. So it almost never happened with Essaerists.

So when Fernwen showed signs of Essaeris, they had been shocked and elated. Hildrana began the process of training her daughter in the way of her people. While her oaths could not allow her to fully train her husband, Hildrana was not so hindered with her own daughter, and Bergthral had no doubt that Fernwen would become a very powerful Essaerist someday, just as her mother was.

Before he could go in and see his daughter, he noticed a man approaching his home. As he looked, he could see he was of average height, middle-aged, and had a long blonde braided beard. Bergthral smiled and walked out to greet him.

"Durnhart, how are you?" he said warmly.

Durnhart smiled and reached out his hand. Bergthral grabbed it, shaking it, and then pulled Durnhart in for a half hug.

"I'm doing well, my friend. How are you?" Durnhart said.

"I'm good. What brings you to these parts?" Bergthral asked.

Durnhart grimaced. "Nothing good, I have to admit."

Bergthral frowned. "Come in and tell me about it, then," he said, waving Durnhart into his home.

Bergthral motioned to the table, and Durnhart sat down. Hildrana grabbed a pitcher and poured all three of them mugs of Bryndraught. Durnhart took a long pull and sighed.

"Thank you," he said.

"Of course," Hildrana said. "So what's the news?"

"I told you about the rumors that Lysandrian was attacking Ulfgarath in the south," he said.

Bergthral and Hildrana nodded.

"Turns out those rumors were true," Durnhart said. "They just took out the city of Hroldenfell."

He waited for Hildrana or Bergthral to respond, but neither did. Bergthral racked his mind. He hadn't heard of the city before, but that didn't mean much. He didn't venture deep into the south, near the Lysandrian borders.

"I'm sorry, I haven't heard of that city before," Hildrana said.

Durnhart took another drink. "I'm not surprised. Eirfrosti rarely make it down that far," he said. "But the city's gone nonetheless. The Lysandrians razed it to the ground."

Bergthral sat back. "They razed it," he said, surprised.

Durnhart nodded. "Yes, they did. It's burned to the ground now. Everyone was either killed or enslaved. They were hit by four legions."

Hildrana looked concerned now, and Bergthral felt his own concern rise in his chest.

"That's concerning," Bergthral said. "Four legions? How many is that?" he said to himself.

"Around twenty thousand men," Hildrana supplied.

Durnhart glanced over at her. She shrugged. "Growing up, I learned a lot about Lysandrian," she said.

"Well, twenty thousand is the number I've heard," Durnhart said. "I've also heard it's closer to fifty thousand, and other rumors say it was five thousand. But the most I hear is around twenty thousand, mostly from people who have had experience trading with the Lysandrians before."

"Fifty seems a little high, and five seems a little ridiculous to take out a city," Bergthral said.

"Are they stopping there?" Hildrana asked.

Durnhart shook his head. "I don't think so. The legions have continued to push north. They've been there for a while. Hroldenfell isn't exactly a border town. It was on top of a hilltop, and it was more of a fortress," he said.

"I would have thought we'd have heard about it being under siege," Bergthral commented.

"It wasn't under siege for very long," Durnhart said. "Apparently, they were able to bring down the wall. I've seen that wall before, mind you. It was a big stone wall. They brought it down, and soldiers streamed right into the city. Once the wall was down, it was over within a night."

That was very disconcerting—that the Lysandrians were able to bring down a city wall and then subdue that city so quickly. Ulfgarath weren't known for being weak. In fact, in Ulfgarath, they prided themselves on being warriors. And though they had been shrinking over the last few generations, he knew most of the people were strong and capable. That the Lysandrians were able to overtake a city so quickly gave him pause.

"Everyone's meeting in Kernvale," Durnhart eventually said.

Bergthral raised an eyebrow. "Everyone? From everywhere?" he asked.

Durnhart shrugged. "I suppose not everyone. Just settlement leaders. I thought you should know. Your voice carries a lot of weight around here."

"Why would this pertain to us?" Bergthral asked.

Hildrana echoed his statement. "Unless you think that the Lysandrians plan on coming this far north," she said, in disbelief.

Durnhart shrugged. "I don't know what they're going to do. I'm just passing on the message as far as that goes. I think people are wondering if we should go and help the Ulfgarath, or," he trailed off.

Bergthral sighed. "Or take advantage of it."

Durnhart looked chagrined. "It is our way."

"Sometimes," Bergthral said.

He didn't particularly like the idea of turning Ulfgarath's problems into a raiding opportunity. Though raiding wasn't exactly Bergthral's thing to begin with. That was also something he could thank his wife for. He had a much more Eirfrosti mentality on the world. They raided, and they were powerful, but it was rare that they raided, and it was usually the acts of the more opportunistic of their culture.

Hildrana looked at him. "What are you thinking, Bergthral?"

He smiled. "I should be asking you that question."

She rolled her eyes, and he couldn't help but grin.

"You know it's true. I'm a blunt object. You, on the other hand, my love," he said.

She snorted. "You're an unstoppable force. But, to answer your question, I'm thinking you should go to this meeting. I don't think it's wise for us to take advantage of this and raid in Ulfgarath lands," she said. "There's no reason to aggravate the Lysandrians and make ourselves a target for them.

"And there's also a chance that Ulfgarath won't lose. If they win, and we've been raiding them," she said.

Bergthral nodded in agreement. "Yes. Then they will be that much more likely to seek retribution."

He looked over at Durnhart, who just laughed. "Nobody cares about my opinion," he said. "But if it's up to me, I don't think we should bother with it at all. There's no point in us going and fighting and dying just to risk a few riches. But then I'm also a lazy merchant," he said with a smile.

"You're anything but lazy," Hildrana said. "But thank you for the news."

Bergthral took a long drink of Bryndraught. "When is the meeting?" he asked.

"In a few days' time," Durnhart said. "I recommend leaving today or tomorrow at the absolute latest."

Bergthral sighed. "Very well. I suppose I should get a few things packed up then."

Durnhart smiled. "Wonderful. Let me know when you're ready to leave."

CHAPTER 3

The Bear Essaerite swayed and jostled underneath Bergthral as he crested a small hill and looked down at the city of Kernvale. Next to him was Kerngar from his settlement and Durnhart. Behind him, a few other men from his settlement had decided to make the trip. Some had a little business to conduct in Kernvale, but most were curious to hear the news and see what was going to happen in the southern lands with the Ulfgarath and Lysandrians.

The road was muddy, and the bear's paws slipped slightly as it moved. The others were on horseback, but Bergthral preferred to ride his Essaerite. It was part of its purpose, after all, and it made a statement—something his wife told him was always important for an Essaerist to make.

He could tell the day was going to be warm. The night before, it had rained, covering everything in little glistening beads of water. He breathed in deeply, enjoying the smell of the forest and the dirt road. He knew it wouldn't be long before they would be in Kernvale, and all he would smell was the scents of animals, waste, people, and fish.

Kernvale sat at the water's edge, nestled at the end of a natural harbor. Before him, he could see the ocean, dotted with fishing boats. Kernvale was also the city closest to the Eirfrosti coast. As such, you could find a lot of Eirfrosti in Kernvale. It was one of the few places where they were relatively common, as most people from Valfarans didn't like the Eirfrosti, though Bergthral could never quite understand why.

They slowly drew closer to the city's whitewashed stone wall. Along the tops, Bergthral could see the occasional guard watching anyone approaching the city. He noted a few of them stop and look in his direction. It wasn't every day that an Essaerist came to town, and it was rarer still when an Essaerist arrived with an Essaerite that looked like Bergthral's—one that screamed of his Eirfrosti tutelage. It made people uncomfortable.

But Bergthral was also a known entity. He was well-respected by many in the area, and most knew him and his Essaerites. So as they approached the city gates, the main guards only nodded at their party as they walked through. Once past the gates and inside the city proper, Bergthral was assaulted by the sounds and sights of Kernvale.

All around him were buildings with weathered stone and stucco walls, their surfaces mottled with moss and cracks. The roofs, a patchwork of thatch and dark slate, sagged in places, hinting at years of repair and neglect. People wended their way through muddy streets, their clothes a kaleidoscope of hues and shades. As they neared the center of town, he saw inns and shops lining the streets where people lived. The center of the town had markets dotting around it, where merchants shouted for attention as Bergthral and his group passed. Many of the people of Kernvale were fishmongers, but other merchants were present as well. You could find jewelers, slave traders, or whatever else you could imagine.

Bergthral glanced at their wares, noting what was popular and what was unpopular, mostly out of curiosity. He had never been a trinket or bauble person. He had pretty much everything he wanted, and anything he found that he did want, he could create with Essaeris easily enough. And indeed, because of his ability and his wife's ability to use Essaeris, their settlement was far better off than most.

His bear slowed its pace as it wove through the crowd. By and large, people moved out of the way, even though Bergthral was known by the leadership and some of the townsfolk. People didn't exactly want to be in the way of a giant Essaeris bear. He thought that was understandable, but the Essaerite was also a source of curiosity, and people gathered around to see it or pressed closer.

Bergthral always found it amusing when some people tried to avoid the bear while others pressed closer to see it. Watching the two groups collide and try to work past each other in frustration always made him smirk and chuckle. He probably shouldn't enjoy it, but there was something about it that he found amusing.

Next to him, Durnhart grunted, "Fuck, I forgot what a pain in the ass it is moving through a city with you in tow," he said, good-naturedly.

Bergthral looked over at him and smiled. "I thought you liked the attention," he said. "Doesn't it help you with sales?"

Durnhart rolled his eyes. "Perhaps knowing an Essaerist does, yes, but making it through a town," he said, waving around, "it's a fucking nightmare. These people don't know if they should be mesmerized by that atrocity you're riding on or if they should run in terror." Then, looking at Bergthral's face, he chuckled. "But I dare say that's what you enjoy the most about this, isn't it?"

Bergthral couldn't help but smirk. He shrugged. "It might be a little entertaining," he said.

Durnhart laughed. "That's what I thought."

In the center of town was a large building with stone walls and a high roof. It was where the meeting would take place. Bergthral dismounted and joined the others as they walked through the front doors. He had been in the center of many settlements and common buildings, but the one in Kernvale always seemed more like an inn to him.

The inside of the building was warm and lit only by candles and fires. He could hear the loud commotion of men and women talking, chairs scraping against the floor, and plates clinking on tables. People sat around drinking and eating, some in the wide open and others in the corners or in dim, secluded places, as they discussed business in low tones.

Bergthral's eyes swept around the dimly lit room, taking in the rough-hewn tables, the flicker of candlelight dancing off scarred wooden beams, and the low murmur of conversation punctuated by the occasional clink of a mug. The meeting would officially be in the evening, but Bergthral knew the real meeting was going on right now. In the small groups and discussions that were being had, by the time the actual event came around, there would probably be very little in the way of conversation that would go anywhere.

So, he looked and noted those who were speaking and those who were not. Around him were the heads of many settlements and towns. Almost every single one of those settlements and towns was much larger than his own, but he still had a seat at the table.

Something that occasionally drew the ire of some of the others, particularly Tirwalden. He caught the man's eye. Tirwalden was older than Bergthral and had long flowing blonde hair with a bald patch and a long beard. His face was scarred, and his nose was bent and crooked from the number of times it had been broken throughout his life.

Tirwalden and Bergthral did not see eye to eye, ever. Tirwalden's settlement was just to the southwest of Bergthral's, and their relationship had always been contentious. Bergthral's parents and Tirwalden's parents had hated each other as well. Bergthral suspected there was nothing more that Tirwalden would like to do than wipe Bergthral's settlement off the face of the planet. But that wouldn't be something that would be happening anytime soon because, even though Tirwalden's settlement was large and had many good warriors, they weren't about to waste their lives on a handful of people—and Bergthral knew that's what his settlement was, a handful of people. It had grown over the years, but it would never be large; it would never be a threat to most settlements in the area. However, a thorn in their side it could be. With two Essaerists, nobody would risk attacking them. It wasn't worth the reward.

Tirwalden's eyes narrowed as they met Bergthral's, and his lips twisted in a grimace of distaste. Tirwalden also had a lot of problems with Bergthral's choice of spouses. He was firmly in the camp that the Eirfrosti were bad, and that their Essaerists were evil and used dark powers that no one should use or touch. There had been many occasions when Tirwalden had referred to

Hildrana as being a witch, and he had insinuated that Bergthral had likewise been infected by her malignant abilities, as so clearly apparent by Bergthral's Essaerites. But Bergthral did his best to ignore Tirwalden and instead focused on the matters at hand, which were finding people and discovering everyone's thoughts and plans for the future.

For his part, Bergthral had zero desire to engage with anybody in the Ulfgarath lands, be they the Ulfgarath or the Lysandrians. So he spent his afternoon speaking to everyone he could. He discovered there were two general consensuses: one was that the people of Valfarans should take full advantage of Ulfgarath's weakness and raid as much as they could down south.

There was, of course, a lot of merit to this; there was wealth to be had in the Ulfgarath lands, and with them being otherwise occupied with the Lysandrians, it was unlikely that any settlements or cities would band together to try and deal with the Valfarans as they came in. They certainly hadn't done a good job of stopping the Wulfharborias from encroaching on their lands over the last couple of generations.

Bergthral was aware that the Wulfharborias had been raiding and moving into Ulfgarath lands aggressively for some time now, and it seemed that the Ulfgarath were unwilling to come together to stop the threat. It was a fair assessment that they would likewise be unwilling to band together to do anything about Valfarans as they came in, but Bergthral wasn't sure at the same time.

The next leading school of thought was that the Ulfgarath should be left to themselves and completely ignored, instead focusing on their own lands and their own deeds. Some had even gone so far as to say that there would be value in settlements and cities working together and unifying, in case the Lysandrians decided that once they were done with Ulfgarath, they wanted Valfarans as well. Bergthral thought this was a much more sensible line of reasoning, but he suspected that it would not win out in the long run.

Perhaps settlements would be unwilling to raid in Ulfgarath lands if for no other reason than some of the people would need to travel great distances, but he found it unlikely that his people would somehow gather together and make a stand. After all, many of the settlements here had raided each other in recent years.

And he knew exactly what the thoughts of some of the more influential leaders would be. Leaders like Tirwalden. Bergthral knew exactly what the man would want. He would be sending men to raid the Ulfgarath lands—of that, Bergthral had no doubt. Tirwalden's settlement wasn't so large and wealthy by happenstance. And while Bergthral did not care for the man, he could not deny that his tenure over his settlement had seen them grow in size and wealth. Bergthral knew the people in Tirwalden's settlement loved and respected him, even if Bergthral knew that he was a hateful ass. But wasn't that the case with most great leaders? Weren't they all hateful asses?

Night had come, and people were beginning to gather in the center of the building. None of the merchants from earlier in the day were still inside; instead, it was just the representatives of settlements and towns gathering around. In the periphery, some of the people who had come with them were listening and waiting. With them was Bergthral's group. They all gathered around, waiting to see what would be said.

An old, wizened man walked into the center of the room. As he did, conversations grew silent, and all turned their attention to him. He cast his gaze around the gathered leaders, looking each in the eye.

"Tonight, we gather to talk about what the people of this land will do," he said, and despite his age, his voice was strong and loud. "We have all heard of the fate that has befallen the Ulfgarath city of Hroldenfell in the south."

Before he could speak further, Tirwalden stood and spoke, "What of it? What do we care of the fall of a city far away in a land of weaklings?" He looked around the gathering. "Unless we are here to talk about plans to raid those lands?"

"We are here to decide *if* we should raid those lands," the older man said, his tone agitated.

Tirwalden laughed, "Surely you jest? Why wouldn't we do it?"

"Because weakening the Ulfgarath only helps the Lysandrians," Bergthral said as he stood.

Everyone in the room looked at him; some looked like they agreed, but many did not. Tirwalden had made a lot of headway during the day.

"Why do we care if we help weaken the Ulfgarath for the Lysandrians so long as we come home fat and happy?" Tirwalden said.

People grunted their approval.

You've lost this argument, Bergthral thought to himself. The people here had made up their minds on what they were going to do before they'd even gotten into town. He could see that as he looked around. No, this meeting was not about deciding if settlements wanted to raid or not; it was deciding who was going to be going with whom, and for those who weren't going to Ulfgarath, it was for them to decide which of their neighbors might be easy pickings as soon as raiding parties left.

Tirwalden went on, holding up a finger, "Oh, unless it's something else. Perhaps Bergthral here would like those of us in Valfarans to not become stronger and to not add to our wealth."

Bergthral scoffed, "And why would I want that, Tirwalden?"

Tirwalden grinned, "So we are weaker than your masters to the north."

Bergthral felt his anger rise, but the old man spoke, "Enough!" He eyed Tirwalden. "I'll not have any of that in my hall, Tirwalden. We are not here to talk about the Eirfrosti."

Tirwalden's face reddened. "Why? Because you are in their pocket?"

The old man stared daggers at Tirwalden. "As much as yours, Tirwalden. Unless it wasn't you buying armor from an Eirfrosti merchant not an hour before this meeting?"

Everyone looked at Tirwalden, who simply scowled. The old man nodded once. "That's what I thought." He looked out at everyone. "Now we will have this conversation as leaders and not asses. Each settlement gets their chance to speak."

———

A FEW HOURS LATER, A TIRED AND EXASPERATED BERGTHRAL SAT NEXT TO DURNHART.

"It could have gone worse," Durnhart said.

Bergthral took a drink of Bryndraught, trying to clear his mind and frustrations. "Could it have?"

Durnhart took a drink of his own Bryndraught. "Yes, it could have. A split decision is about the best that people on your side could have hoped for."

Bergthral grunted and took another drink. He supposed he couldn't argue with that. Only some of the gathered settlements would raid the Ulfgarath lands, but none would be banding together.

"It's a mistake," Bergthral said.

Next to him, Durnhart shrugged. "Maybe, maybe not."

Bergthral looked over at Durnhart. "Are you going to raid the Ulfgarath lands?"

Durnhart shook his head and laughed. "No, of course not. I'm no warrior. You know that," he said, taking a drink. "But I'll find a way to profit off of it, I'm sure," he said, giving Bergthral a toothy smile.

Bergthral shook his head. Next to him, a chair scraped on the floor, and a man sat down. Bergthral looked over, seeing Kerngar. He could see the man was conflicted.

Bergthral sat up. "What is it?" he asked.

Kerngar looked at him, then down at the table, and then back to him again. Bergthral sighed; he thought he might know where this was going.

"Out with it," he said.

Kerngar's face flushed. "Some of us don't agree with your stance," Kerngar said haltingly.

Bergthral raised an eyebrow. "I'm sure. Would you like to enlighten me about this disagreement?"

Kerngar looked more uncomfortable, but like he was trying to steel himself. "We respect you as the leader of the settlement—"

Bergthral cut him off. "But you're going to do whatever the fuck you want, aren't you?"

Kerngar's eyes lit up. "Why shouldn't we?" he asked.

Bergthral felt his anger flare up, but he pushed it down. "You should do what you want," he said. "So what is it that you want to do?" he asked.

Kerngar looked a little surprised that Bergthral hadn't pushed it more. But after a moment, he seemed to accept that and went on. "Some of us are going to raid the Ulfgarath lands."

Bergthral wanted to forbid it, wanted to tell them that they were being stupid. But what difference would it make? It would make none. He knew that. These men were young, confident, and bold. They wanted to test themselves, and they wanted to earn riches and respect. He couldn't fault them for that. And he couldn't honestly stop them from doing that as well. Just because he thought it was a bad idea to raid the Ulfgarath lands didn't mean that it actually was. And he had to remind himself of that.

Bergthral took a long drink of Bryndraught and set his cup down on the table. "So when are you leaving, and whose group are you joining?" he asked.

"I thought you would have fought me more on it," Kerngar said.

Bergthral shrugged. "You're a free man to do what you will, and just because I think it's a bad idea doesn't mean that I'm right. So when are you leaving and who are you going with?"

"We'll come home and head straight out. A few of us found a few raiding parties," Kerngar said, and then quickly added, "none of them with Tirwalden."

At least there was that. Had they said they were joining up with Tirwalden, Bergthral would have been legitimately concerned that when they came home, if they came home, they would try to take over the settlement.

He took another drink of Bryndraught. "Very well then, that's your right, and I suppose as long as you're not with anyone from Tirwalden's settlement, I can't argue it," he said.

Kerngar scowled. "I'd never join up with that piece of shit."

Bergthral smiled. "Glad to hear it," he said. He put his hand on Kerngar's forearm. "I truly wish you the best of luck down there and the happiest of hunting," he said sincerely.

Kerngar nodded. "Thank you, and thank you for being so easy about this. I was worried you would forbid us from going."

Bergthral laughed. "And would you have listened?"

"Yes, of course we would," Kerngar said quickly. "If you ordered us not to, we wouldn't go."

Bergthral felt a bloom of pride in his chest for the man before him. He smiled. "And you would have resented me for years to come," he said.

"Unless you were right, then we might be thankful about it," he said with a lopsided smile.

Bergthral laughed. "I suppose that's true, but," he said with a sigh, "I would rather you make your own decisions and your own mistakes than resent me for mine."

Kerngar nodded. "Thank you, and we will accompany you back home. After all, we have a lot that we have to gather and say goodbye to our families," he said.

Bergthral smiled tightly. "We'll be leaving in the morning, but you have the rest of your evening to enjoy all that Kernvale has to offer," he said, "and if you're going to be going out raiding, I would certainly enjoy the comforts of home and a nice town before you go out onto the road."

Kerngar grinned. "Oh, I certainly plan on enjoying myself this evening," he said.

Kerngar stood and walked away. Bergthral looked over at Durnhart, who was giving him a questioning look.

"Out with it," Bergthral said.

"Sending some of your best fighters away," Durnhart said, letting it hang in the air.

Bergthral shrugged. "Tirwalden's doing the same, and between Hildrana and I," he said, and shrugged. "I'm not worried about it." He glanced over at Tirwalden. "Not that I don't think that fuck wouldn't mind putting a knife in both of our backs if he had the opportunity."

CHAPTER 4

Mariokos stirred beneath the heavy blanket, the warmth clinging to his skin as his eyes fluttered open, adjusting to the dim morning light. Caelwen shifted slightly in his arms as she slept. He smiled, debating whether to go back to sleep or not, but decided against it. The days had been getting warmer, but the evenings were still cool, so they had kept sleeping under a blanket. Now it was a little too warm in the mornings, so he reached out with his Essaeris and released one of the blankets on top of them. As it vanished, a linen sheet settled over him, cooling his skin.

He also felt a warm lump between him and Caelwen. The lump moved, and he looked down.

"Sorry, Treftune," he said, looking at the Valfglidea. He had apparently been on the blanket, and Mariokos hadn't noticed. He suspected Treftune wasn't thrilled about being woken up by having his bed disappear from under him. His hand came out from under the sheets, and he ran his finger up the little Valfglidea's head, between his eyes and ears. Treftune's eyes closed, and he made a little contented sound. His fur was soft and a gentle blue this morning.

He noticed that Treftune liked to sleep being blue for some reason, though sometimes he was yellow, red, or brown. But he noticed that the Valfglidea seemed to be blue when he was in a good mood or relaxed. Mariokos didn't know if it was indicative of the species or if it was just something that Treftune did.

Treftune rolled onto his back and stretched out, and Mariokos smiled, rubbing his belly. Caelwen gave a muffled sigh and nuzzled into Mariokos's chest. He turned his attention back to his wife, looking at her sleeping form. She had been such a surprise. He certainly hadn't expected to be married off while at war, but it had been the best things about the whole experience. Her eyes cracked open, and he ran his fingers through her long, fiery red hair, brushing his thumb along her cheek.

"Good morning," he whispered.

She smiled softly and nuzzled into him more.

"Good morning," she said.

Her arms wrapped around him and gave him a squeeze. He kissed her forehead, and her eyes opened wider. He tilted her chin up and kissed her lips gently, holding the kiss for a moment. It made for such a nice start to the morning. He felt her hand move up his arm and neck as her fingers moved through his hair, gently scratching his scalp. He sighed and closed his eyes in contentment. He kissed her again, looking into her eyes, feeling his heart melt just a little bit. She could get a thrill out of him without even trying. He kissed her again, and she deepened the kiss. He felt her move, positioning herself, molding herself to him in a seductive, sleepy way.

Treftune chittered and jumped off of them, disturbed by the movement.

He couldn't help but chuckle a little bit. He broke the kiss with Caelwen, and she gently but firmly grabbed his chin and pulled it back to hers.

"He'll be fine," she said and kissed him again.

He smiled as he kissed her, and his hand moved up her back, caressing her. He cupped her breast in his hand, feeling its soft yet firm flesh beneath his fingers. He ran his thumb over her nipple, feeling it harden and hearing her give a soft sigh.

They continued to kiss, and their tongues met, swirling around each other. Mariokos felt himself fully awake now, and he gently pushed Caelwen onto her back. His lips traveled along her jaw and neck, feeling her soft skin under his lips. Her breathing became deeper, and he felt himself getting aroused. He kissed up her neck and nibbled her ear, his thumb still gently circling around her hardened nipple.

He was looking forward to being up early. As he moved on top of her, he kissed her again, looking forward to exploring her body with his mouth. He looked into her eyes, seeing them bright and excited, and then he heard it—the sound of a horn. It blew again, the cadence familiar, announcing an inevitability that no one in the Legion could avoid.

He felt disappointed but resigned. He began to shift, and Caelwen's grip tightened around him. He saw her eyes narrow.

"I'm going to fucking kill him," she said, her voice not sounding seductive or lustful or tired, just confident, certain, promising.

He couldn't help but smile. He kissed her. "You can't kill the men who sound the horn that it's time to get up," he told her for what felt like the millionth time.

"Why not?" she asked. "Are they particularly good fighters? I don't think anyone would blame me. In fact, I think I might be the hero of the camp."

He rolled off of her and laughed. "You know they don't choose the position," Mariokos said.

"But they follow the orders, don't they?" she said, rolling onto her side. Treftune was chittering more and moving around, wanting breakfast.

The horn sounded again, and he saw Caelwen's eyes move to the crack in their tent. He couldn't help but laugh. "No killing anybody for waking you up," he said.

She looked at him. Her eyes were still narrowed, but they lacked the ferocity that he had seen in them before. "Are you trying to be added to the list?" she said. "Don't think that I'll be willing to spare you on account of some of your talents," she said with a bit of a crooked smile.

He felt his heart flutter again, but he also laughed. "Really? I don't know if I believe that," he said.

She snorted. "Well, maybe you should prove yourself just to be sure."

He laughed. "You know I can't. We have to get up."

Her eyes narrowed in thought, and for a moment, he was concerned. Not that she was going to kill him. He didn't think she would do that, but just whatever she was going to do next.

She smiled softly, and her hand moved between them. He felt her soft fingers wrap around his shaft, and he groaned.

"Are you sure, my love? You can't stay in bed for just a few moments longer?" she said, her voice husky and seductive.

He groaned. "Caelwen, this is so not fair."

She kissed his neck. "I mean, I just want to be with my husband. Is that so wrong?" she said softly into his ear.

No, it wasn't wrong. His mind fought. He knew he needed to get up. He needed to be ready. He needed to go have breakfast with his squad. But the movement of her hands was so wonderful.

She kissed down his neck to his chest. "I want to show you how much I love you," she said, "how much I appreciate being with you."

Her voice was soft and seductive in a way that he thought might drive him out of his mind.

"Just think of what I could do with these lips," she said, pressing her lips to his chest for just a few moments.

"Caelwen, you're going to get me court-martialed, I swear," he said.

She looked up at him and smiled.

"I suppose just a few minutes," he said.

She grinned and ran her fingers through his hair. "Very well, but..." she bit her lip, "duty calls, and who am I to stop the progress of the legions?"

She gave him a quick peck on the lips and then stood up.

He groaned.

"Oh, not funny," he said.

"Neither is being woken up every morning at the crack of dawn by some cunt with a horn," she said. "All you had to do was let me kill him, that's it. You didn't even have to do it, and you could be enjoying yourself right now, and everyone else in the Legion could be asleep and warm, enjoying whatever dream it was that they were having."

He stood and shook his head, but he couldn't help but laugh a little at the same time. Caelwen was so different from a Lysandrian woman. She had a lot in common with some of the women that he had known, but there was something about her that seemed freer in a way, and more unencumbered.

He reached out with his Essaeris and created a tunic that he pulled over his head. He saw her do likewise, though instead of a tunic, she created a dress. She had done well with slipping into some of the trappings of Lysandrian life. She dressed like a proper Aristolios woman, and even though she didn't necessarily act the part, she certainly looked it.

Her dress was creamy with blue accents of silk; to everyone, it would be apparent that she was an Aristolios and not some mercenary or merchant. There would be no denying it. In many ways, she played the role better than other Aristolios women when it came to appearances. And every day, Caelwen created her outfit, something that Mariokos had been happy she had taken to.

Of course, on that note, Caelwen had taken to every single lesson that he, Xavieno, or Fioralba had given her. He'd been amazed at how quickly Caelwen had picked up everything, and he suspected she was now at the point where she was just as powerful as any fully trained Lysandrian Essaerist was, if not very close to it.

He released their sheets and bedding, and they went out into the morning light. All around them, the camp was a flurry of activity as men got ready for the day. He could smell fires being started so that squads could cook their morning meal.

Caelwen had taken to joining Mariokos with his squad every morning for breakfast. It wasn't common for a wife to do this, but it also hadn't been extremely common that Mariokos continued to eat with his squad for morning and evening meals once he'd been married. For most Aristolios men, when their families were with them, that was who they dined with.

But Mariokos thought it was important to meet with his squad and to be with them. He also thought it was good for Caelwen to build a relationship with them as well. They walked over to where his squad's tents were. A fire was burning, and Caelwen had a stump Essaerite that was busily cooking breakfast.

His squad had taken to her relatively quickly, and he suspected much of it had to do with the fact that she had an Essaerite that cooked them breakfast every day, and that she had a wicked sense of humor that any soldier could appreciate. Even Erastos had warmed up to her, though he still seemed to hold the belief that every other Gwenthari was swine and trash and should be killed.

Mariokos and Caelwen joined them and sat down. The men were passing around plates that had bread on them. Mariokos took a piece of bread and tore into it. Treftune, for his part, was going from man to man, looking up at them expectantly.

He started with Erastos. He looked up at Erastos, and Erastos sighed, tore off a piece of his bread, and handed it to Treftune. "Dominaro," he said. Treftune gobbled down the bread, chittered, and moved on to the next.

Helioz likewise gave Treftune a small chunk of bread and said, "Dominaro." And Treftune repeated the process with Luciakos.

Treftune stood in front of another man in the squad, who looked down and sighed. "Why do we have to pay tribute to this little thing?" he said, looking up at the rest of the squad.

Helioz clapped the man on the shoulder. "Because that is the way it works. You can pay him, or he can steal from you, which we know is far worse," he said.

"So because we don't want to be stolen from, or bitten," the man added, giving Treftune a glare, "then we have to pay him off every day?"

Luciakos nodded. "Yes, it's much like when we take a town or a city; they pay tribute to us. That is what we do with Dominaro here." The men had taken to calling Treftune "Dominaro," which was the honorific for someone who was higher in station than you were.

Mariokos thought that the little Valfglidea must have known that the word was special because Treftune puffed up every time one of them called him it, and Mariokos found it amusing to no end.

Luciakos added, "And besides those berries that he brought us the other day—"

The man nodded and tore off a piece of bread. "This is true. Sorry, Dominaro," he said to Treftune.

Treftune ate the bread, chittered happily, and scurried off with his bushy tail flicking behind him. It was true. Treftune brought the men a lot of berries and treats, sometimes in the form of mushrooms that he found, or other little tasty tidbits. He'd become almost a mascot of the Legion. He spent his day with his Essaerites, jumping around from man to man, either getting food, giving food, or having his ears and belly scratched.

Mariokos had found it amusing, as he was pretty sure that unless he was with the squad, everyone else only saw one of the Essaerites. Still, he must have full sensation through his Essaerites because he seemed to enjoy it when an Essaerite's ears were scratched just as much as his own. It also meant that if someone was mad and tried to attack one of the Essaerites, Treftune was, of course, safe, though most had given up on trying to stop the Valfglidea. Instead, they'd learned that if you paid him off, he would bring you treats and keep you entertained. So, he was now "Dominaro" to just about everyone in the Legion.

Almost on cue, several other versions of Treftune showed up, swooping down from some of the tents. They went to one of the plates and opened their mouths, disgorging a large group of berries.

The men of the squad all gave Treftune thanks and plucked some of the berries off the plate. Eating them, "he's really good at finding some of the best ripe ones," Erastos grunted.

"That he is, and those truffles he found the other day," Helioz said, shaking his head.

The real Treftune crawled up Caelwen's arm and wrapped around her neck. She scratched under his chin, and Erastos looked at her, then looked back down at the ground and said, trying to hold his voice even, "Some strange things have been happening as of late," he said, and looked up at her.

She looked at him confused. "Like what?" she said.

"It turns out a few of the men have been tripping on the road," he said.

She cocked her head. "Tripping? Okay, how's that strange?"

Mariokos noticed Helioz and Luciakos smirk and look down.

Erastos went on, "The thing that's funny is they've been tripping on rocks and roots and things that nobody else is seeing on the road. A few of them have reported even seeing," Erastos paused, trying to think of what to say, "monsters in the woods, and then they trip, or something of that nature. But nobody else sees them," he said.

Caelwen looked at her meal. "That is odd," she said, sounding confused.

Mariokos thought he knew where this was going. Erastos was looking at her. "Yes, very confusing. You know what's the most interesting part of all?" he said.

"What's that?" she asked sweetly.

"All of these men are the same ones who wake us up every morning with the horns," he said.

Caelwen looked at him, her face scrunched up in curiosity. "That is so bizarre," she said.

Helioz and Luciakos were looking away, trying not to snicker. Mariokos could tell that it was taking Erastos some effort not to smile and not to look anything but serious. He nodded. "Yes, it's very bizarre, isn't it? I wonder what could be causing it. And why those men?"

Caelwen shrugged. "I don't know. It's a mystery. I mean, they do us this wonderful service every day of making sure that we don't have to worry about sleeping," she said sweetly. "I wonder if it's things they're making up, figments of their imagination," she mused. "Perhaps caused by guilt?" She looked up and thought.

Erastos shook his head and chuckled, and he looked over at Mariokos. "I don't know if I should tell you sorry or not," he said to Mariokos. "But I don't think I would get on her bad side, though," he added.

Mariokos smiled. "Oh, believe me, I'm well aware of that," he said, shooting Caelwen a sidelong glance.

She merely smirked and went back to her meal...

———

Caelwen noticed Fioralba approaching.

"Good morning," she said, looking over at Fioralba.

"Good morning," Fioralba said, smiling softly.

Caelwen noticed that Fioralba looked tired and haggard. There were circles under her eyes, and she seemed to be holding herself a little differently. It had been creeping up as of late.

"Are you doing okay?" Caelwen asked.

Fioralba smiled tightly. "I'm fine, just tired is all. The pace we've been moving at," she huffed.

Caelwen understood. The Legion had been moving at a hard march, which meant making twenty-five miles a day. They also hadn't spent more than a night in one camp since they had started moving. Even Caelwen was getting a little tired of the pace.

All around them, the camp was being torn down, and Caelwen, along with the rest of the support caravan, were readying their carts. For her, she turned her attention back to what she'd been working on.

Fioralba walked up next to her. "Making a cart?" she asked, sounding a little confused.

"Yes," Caelwen said. "Wulfgren had to give his cart to someone else from my settlement when they broke theirs, so I needed this. Thank you for letting me use yours this whole time," she added.

Fioralba smiled. "You can still use it if you want," she said.

"Thank you, but I'm fine," Caelwen said warmly. "Really, there's a lot of things I have to put on it, and I should have my own anyway," she explained.

Fioralba looked at the cart critically. It didn't have any wheels on it yet. Caelwen had only gotten the wood for it the other day and had been using an Essaerite to carry it around as she had been constructing it. Presently, it was mostly a flat surface, though it had some feet on it that she had built that allowed her to keep it level and somewhat off the ground. It was slightly longer than the cart that Fioralba and Xavieno had and had a few other modifications that Mariokos had helped her with.

"Doesn't it need wheels?" Fioralba asked and smirked.

Caelwen laughed. "Yeah, I'm going to make those soon," she said. "But until then," she gestured.

She flexed her Essaeris, creating some wheels. She created some Essaerites to fix the wheels in position and then another Essaerite at the front that would pull the cart along. It was one similar to what Fioralba used. Caelwen had found Fioralba's Essaerites and the way she looked at creating them to be extremely useful.

Fioralba looked at it and smiled in approval. "Looking good," she said. "Why is it so big?"

Caelwen sighed, brushing a loose strand of hair behind her ear as she picked up a crate. The rough wood of the crate bit into her palms as she lifted it. "These," she said, as she picked it up, there was the sound of scurrying from inside. She set it on the cart.

Fioralba peered at it. "Oh, the rabbits you've been talking about," she said.

"Yes, the rabbits," Caelwen huffed. "Without my brother having a cart to carry them on, I have to do it. But they need more space," she said. "It was fine when we first had them and there was only a couple, but they've been breeding," she explained.

"Aren't you planning on slaughtering some of them and selling the meat?" Fioralba pointed out.

"Yes, we are," Caelwen said, "but my brother was able to purchase a few of the other breeding pairs that some of the other people from the settlement had. Turns out they're a bit of a pain in the ass to cart around with you," she said.

"And your plan?" Fioralba asked.

"I'm going to create a cage for them to move around in with Essaeris and alter it over the next few days and then build an actual permanent one and keep it on the cart," she said. "The whole cart's designed so I can keep it level and haul these things around."

Fioralba nodded approvingly. "I dare say before too long you're going to be making more than Mariokos," she said.

Caelwen grinned. "Before too long," she said. "What makes you think that I'm not already?"

Fioralba raised an eyebrow. "Off of the rabbits?"

Caelwen shook her head. "No, off of foraging," she said. "I have some Essaerites that are in the area foraging for mostly mushrooms and other fungi right now, like truffles," Caelwen said. "But with how fast the Legion's been moving, I've had to use hawks and owls to transport some of those other Essaerites around," she said.

"Not bad," Fioralba said. "So what, selling it to merchants?"

Caelwen nodded. "Yep, selling it to merchants and sometimes the soldiers. I've been making a decent amount of coin off of the truffles," she said and smiled. "But I figure soon some of the medicinal herbs that I'm used to using will be growing in the area, and I can finally stock up on some tinctures and other things of that nature," she said.

There was a sound of a horn indicating that the caravan was going to begin moving soon.

"Shall we?" Caelwen said.

"We shall," Fioralba said and smiled.

Caelwen saw Fioralba create an Essaerite that she would ride on. It was two-legged, similar to the one that pulled her cart, except it had a padded seat on it. As it came into existence, she saw it wobble and its left leg buckled. It fell over, and then Fioralba released it, swearing softly. Caelwen was surprised; she'd never seen any of Fioralba's Essaerites struggle before.

Fioralba huffed and created it again; this time, the other leg buckled. She could see the other woman's embarrassment. Caelwen created two Essaerites just like it. "It's fine. I'll create some," she said.

Fioralba looked over at her, her eyes tight for a moment and then softened. "Thank you," she said. "I'm just so..." She was at a loss for words.

"Tired?" Caelwen said. "I get it. It's fine. Don't worry about it. Honestly, with how much you've helped me out, I feel obligated to do stuff for you. Please, let me take care of your transportation for the day."

Fioralba nodded and got on her Essaerite that Caelwen had created. The caravan was beginning to move, and they shuffled into place and began moving up the road at a speed that Caelwen did not care for. It'd have been fine if she would have been on horseback or just on a regular Essaerite, but with a cart and so many people, it had become a pain in the ass and meant that there were dust clouds that swirled around them all day long, clogging their noses, making them sneeze and cough.

"Why are we moving at this pace again?" Caelwen said.

Fioralba leaned over conspiratorially. "Rumor has it we're heading off some Gwenthari."

Caelwen looked over at her. "Heading off some Gwenthari?"

Fioralba nodded. "A large group is heading up towards the north. The Legion's moving to cut them off so they can't join up with one of the cities that's up there," she replied.

"What city is it?" Caelwen asked.

Fioralba lowered her voice so that others couldn't overhear them. "I'm not sure this is correct, but I heard it's called Ulfgard," she said.

Caelwen's eyebrows went up. "Ulfgard is no small city," she said, "and it's not going to be as easy of a take as Hroldenfell."

She had still been slightly awe-inspired and horrified by what had happened at Hroldenfell. She'd expected the city to hold out much longer. It had been a fortress, after all, but it hadn't, and it had not gone well for those who had resisted.

But she pushed it from her mind. That was war. And she knew if the tables had been turned and it had been Gwenthari outside of a Lysandrian fortress, the results would have been the same, if not worse. She'd been surprised in many ways. Yes, there were many horrible things that had happened in Hroldenfell, but not as many as she would have suspected. There had been killings, burnings, people turned into slaves, but much of it lacked the brutality that she would have expected from her own people. It was brutal, yes, but not as much. And she wasn't sure what to make of it.

As the caravan moved, she took in Fioralba, noticing how tired she was. "Not getting a lot of sleep?" she asked. She smirked. "Xavieno keeping you up at night?" she said suggestively, trying to make Fioralba laugh.

Fioralba blushed a little and then chuckled. "Maybe," she said. "What am I saying? Maybe? Of course he is!"

Caelwen smiled. "Well, that's fun, right?"

Fioralba grinned. "It is, yes. But I'm also tired of the pace that we're moving at—not just that Xavieno always wants it," she said. "I don't know if Mariokos's like that. I don't think he is. Our friend that he was with back home, Biankara, didn't seem to think that Mariokos was that way."

Caelwen smiled. "Oh, he has his moments," she said, thinking about how much she had enjoyed toying with him that morning. "But I take it Xavieno is a little bit more so?"

"He's your typical Lysandrian man and soldier," she said.

"Oh?" Caelwen said with a raised eyebrow.

Fioralba nodded. "Yes. Yes, it's all about being a man and being ready for battle and all that other shit," Fioralba said and laughed. "And it's fine. Honestly, it's not like I don't enjoy it."

"But a little tired?" Caelwen said.

Fioralba shrugged. "I guess, but we don't stay up that late or get up that early. I don't know. I think it's just the pace that we're moving at; it makes it stressful for some reason," she said, then changed the subject. "How are you and Mariokos doing?"

Caelwen shrugged. "We're doing well. I enjoy him a lot. I have to admit I'm surprised by that," she said.

"I'm happy he found you," she said, "and I've enjoyed having you around too, even though you're a barbarian," Fioralba added.

Caelwen laughed. "It's always good to have barbarian friends."

CHAPTER 5

I t hadn't been a full day's march when the legions finally came to a stop for the day. Mariokos was appreciative of the shorter journey. They'd been on a hard march for so long, and they'd covered a vast distance in that time. Now behind him, the legion was working on setting up camp, as were the other three legions that were part of the expeditionary force. For his part, he walked forward to a table.

They were in an open area, surrounded by fields and patches of forest. In front of him and the table was the Ilfrun River. The river ran north and eventually emptied into the ocean. It started in the high peaks to the southwest of them. In this part of the land, the river was wide. Its currents were relatively slow compared to much of the southwestern sections, but it was deep. As he approached, his gaze swept out to the horizon, seeing the far shore in the distance.

There were groups of men standing at the table, all gathered around one man in particular. Aresio was in Mariokos's legion and was the head engineer of the legion. He was widely considered to be one of the best engineers in all of the legions in the empire, and as a result, tended to be the head engineer for the expeditionary force.

He was older, with grey creeping up the sides of his brown hair. Mariokos liked him. He was no-nonsense and good at what he did. As Mariokos approached, some of the other engineers turned, looking at him, some of them recognizing him.

Aresio looked up and waved him over.

"Sir," Mariokos said as he approached.

"Good, I'm glad you're here," Aresio said, not wasting any time with pleasantries. "As you can see, we have a river that needs crossing."

Mariokos looked down at a piece of paper that was on the table. It was fairly straightforward. The Ilfrun was wide, as indicated on the paper, and it appeared to be deep. Aresio explained, "Looks like the river is ten to fifteen feet deep in some of the deepest parts, and this is the narrowest spot for a few miles. It looks like it's just under a thousand feet across."

Mariokos nodded, waiting for instructions.

"We're going to build a bridge, but the currents and the depths could make it a little bit more tedious than normal," Aresio said, though his voice didn't reflect any signs of concern. He started pointing up along a different section of the map that was to the north. "We're going to need to use barges to drive in piles. I need you to command all of the Essaerists to help with this," he said.

Mariokos nodded. "Of course. What do you need us to do?"

He was surprised that he was being put in charge of all the Essaerists. He suspected that he would have to give Xavieno a few orders, and it made sense that perhaps Fioralba and Caelwen might be involved, but if it was all the Essaerists, that would mean those from Aeterna as well. Though there was only one that was in the Legion, technically, and his wife. Still, he was surprised.

"The barges," Aresio said. "The piles need to be put in exactly the correct places. Normally we would use small boats to anchor them, but I'm thinking your lot will be better for it. I need you to create anchor systems all along the river to hold the barges in place, and they need to be precise. We're also going to need help with some other construction work, but this is what I want your primary focus to be.

"Once the work gets underway, we're going to be using your team to help move the barges along quickly from place to place," he said.

Mariokos nodded. "What's our timeline?"

"As quickly as possible," Aresio said, "but I would like to see this done in the next week to a week and a half. A lot of it will depend on what we can source in the area and what the riverbed looks like, so I want you to get Essaerites in there quickly to figure out what we'll be going up against," he said.

Mariokos nodded. "Understood."

"Good," Aresio said.

———

Xavieno walked with Caelwen and Fioralba up to Mariokos, who was standing on the banks of the Ilfrun River. He went and stood next to his friend, looking out at the water. The current was moving slowly, and it relaxed him as he looked at it. The other shore was far in the distance, but he knew this was one of the narrower spots of the river in the area.

Next to him, Fioralba breathed in. "That is one big river," she said.

Caelwen spoke. "The Ilfrun runs all the way up to the sea," she said. "It's like this for most of the way, though. If you go to the southwest, I understand that it thins out where it originally forms, but other rivers join it," she commented.

"Have you ever seen it before?" Mariokos asked her.

She nodded. "I have. But it was a long time ago. So why are we here?" she asked.

Why indeed? Xavieno thought. He looked to Mariokos. "I saw you meeting with the engineers, so my guess is we're crossing this," he said.

Mariokos nodded. "Yes, we are. The Gwenthari have a group that's to the southwest. They're moving up north towards Ulfgard. I think the legions mean to cut them off," he said.

"By crossing here?" Caelwen asked, surprised.

It made sense to Xavieno.

Mariokos explained, "Yes, we're going to cross here."

"It's going to take boats a long time," she mused. Then she looked at everyone as they all chuckled.

"What?" she said. "Is it not going to take a long time with boats?" she asked.

Mariokos put his arm around his wife's shoulder and gave her a squeeze. "We aren't using boats. We're going to build a bridge," he said, looking at the river.

She chuckled. "Very funny. So are we supposed to help build the boats or what?"

Fioralba spoke. "He's not joking."

Caelwen looked over at Fioralba and then back at Mariokos. "You aren't?" she said.

Mariokos smiled and kissed the top of her head. "Nope, I'm not. We should have a couple of Essaerists coming from Aeterna shortly. Aresio put me in charge."

This tracks, Xavieno thought; it'd be easier with Essaerists to do some of the work. And Aeterna was the only other legion that had any.

"Wait a second. I still want to come back to you being serious about building a bridge across the Ilfrun. It has to be, what, a thousand feet across?" she said.

Mariokos nodded. "Something like that. Though my guess is it's closer to nine hundred and fifty, but let's say a thousand feet for the sake of argument."

"And how is that faster than finding another way to cross or using barges?" Caelwen pressed.

Mariokos shrugged. "It'll only take us a week or a week and a half to build the bridge, and then we'll be back on the move again. If we were to go to the southwest, it would take us weeks."

Caelwen gaped, and Xavieno found her expression amusing.

"Haven't we taught you what the legions are all about yet?" he teased.

She looked at him and then back at the river. "The camps, yes, but are you all seriously crazy enough to build a bridge? It's not going to work—not that fast, at least," she said.

Mariokos grinned. "Oh, it'll work, and it'll certainly go that fast, if not faster. All of Aresio's timelines are assuming just legionnaires. We've got Essaerists with us," he said. "Look, it's not going to be that bad. It's going to be like a lot of bridges. It's just temporary; it'll be timber. It only needs to get the legions across once and maybe twice if we need to retreat," he said.

"Yeah, and it needs to be over a thousand feet long and in however much water that is," Caelwen said.

"We think ten to fifteen feet in some of the deepest parts, but I have some Essaerites out checking it now, so we should have a better idea soon," Mariokos said.

Caelwen's gaze sharpened, her eyes narrowing as she muttered something about being in a group of insane people.

Xavieno grinned and patted her shoulder. "And you're one of us now; doesn't that feel good? To be part of the crazy group," he said.

She rolled her eyes. "Yes, it's wonderful," she said.

Xavieno saw two people approaching them, and next to him, Fioralba tensed just slightly. They knew Isolara and Kyrillos, of course, though Xavieno knew this would be Caelwen's first time meeting them. They were a couple of years older than Mariokos and Xavieno and were in the Emperor's Legion.

Isolara was beautiful, with long wavy hair and bright green eyes. Her body curved in all the right places, and she was wearing a dress of the style of all the upper class. It was perfect and exquisite in every way, as was everything about Isolara. She was talented, and even though it was frowned upon for women to engage in any form of combat, she was an Essaerist, and that made her unique. Xavieno knew that while she did not take part in battles, her Essaerites were the personal protection for the Emperor during a battle.

Her husband Kyrillos, on the other hand, was known for his battle prowess. He was also the reason why Fioralba tensed just slightly. If Kyrillos respected you, he was fine and enjoyable to be around, but if he didn't, then he tended to disregard you. And for Kyrillos, respect was earned by being an exceptional Essaerist or warrior—and though Fioralba was exceptional, she didn't distinguish herself the way those on the front line did or the way his wife did.

For his part, Xavieno enjoyed Kyrillos.

He had short, wavy brown hair and deep brown eyes. He was very handsome, and Xavieno had always had a bit of a thing for him, something he knew went both ways. The first time they had met, the flirting between the two had resulted in Isolara and Fioralba building a fairly decent friendship off of ridiculing their husbands.

He supposed he could understand that. Xavieno smiled as Kyrillos and Isolara approached. Kyrillos smiled at him, his eyes moving up and down Xavieno, and Xavieno did likewise. Next to him, he saw Fioralba smirk, one that was mirrored in Isolara's expression.

"Isolara, Kyrillos," Mariokos said, approaching the two. Kyrillos smiled at Mariokos and reached out his hand, shaking it. Isolara smiled and gave her greeting.

Mariokos went on, "I believe you know Xavieno and Fioralba," he said, and Isolara rolled her eyes.

"Yes, we do, but we do not know this person," she said, looking at Caelwen.

Xavieno noticed Caelwen, not so much tense but looking at the other two Essaerists calculatingly.

"And who is this?" Kyrillos said.

"This is my wife, Caelwen," Mariokos said, beaming down at Caelwen.

Isolara nodded and greeted her warmly, holding out her hand, and Kyrillos seemed to look at her quizzically for a moment.

"Are you the one with the cats?" he asked after a moment.

Caelwen nodded. "Yes. I assume you saw them in Hroldenfell," she said.

He nodded. "I did. Brutally efficient," he commented, though Xavieno could tell they were not enough to earn Kyrillos's respect, and he was about to blow off Caelwen.

Xavieno spoke up. "You should see her Essaerithon," he said. "The thing is fucking terrifying."

He saw Caelwen smile. "Thank you."

Kyrillos perked up. "You have an Essaerithon as well?"

Xavieno went on, "Yes. Caelwen turns herself into a tree with this animal skull. She can take out horses and whole groups of men," Xavieno said, seeing this earn Caelwen a look of approval from Kyrillos, and Xavieno added, "Honestly, Kyrillos, I think she could probably even take out yours."

Kyrillos's head tilted to the side, his brow furrowing as curiosity flickered in his dark eyes. Isolara mirrored his reaction, her gaze sharpening with quiet intrigue.

"Do you really think so? Or are you just trying to get a rise out of me?" Kyrillos said.

"No, he's being serious," Mariokos said. "The thing was damn impressive before she caught up with the Legion, but now—" Mariokos shook his head in pride at his wife.

"It's not that much better, and they're trying to build me up much more than I am," Caelwen said.

"No, they're not. They're just being honest," Fioralba said, accusatorially. "You'll have to excuse Caelwen; she likes to be underestimated."

This got Isolara's attention. "Smart girl," she said. "So you can create an Essaerithon that Xavieno here thinks can take out Kyrillos's."

Caelwen shrugged. "It might. Yours was that one with all the arms and the blades in Hroldenfell, right?"

Kyrillos smiled happily. "Yes, that was it."

Caelwen nodded. "It was very impressive. I don't think I was able to see anybody do any damage to it," she said.

"It's very difficult for them to do."

Xavieno spoke. "He is not kidding. Kyrillos is one of the best Essaerists in the empire. Beyond being talented, his Essaerithon is near unstoppable, though I think yours could stand a chance."

"Thank you," Caelwen said, her cheeks blushing a little bit.

"And in combination with those cats," Xavieno said and whistled.

Kyrillos's eyes widened in surprise. "You can create your Essaerithon and the cats?"

Caelwen nodded. "Yes, I actually created it around the idea of being able to use both at the same time," she said.

Xavieno saw Kyrillos smile. His assessment of Caelwen was high, and Xavieno was happy to help with it. He nodded. "Well, then I'm glad you're on our side," he said. Kyrillos turned to Mariokos. "And I dare say I've been underestimating you for years," Kyrillos said. "My apologies."

Mariokos raised an eyebrow, and Isolara answered for Kyrillos, "The walls of Hroldenfell. We always knew that you were a powerful and capable Essaerist, but your specialties are not in combat, so they're not something that we really see, you understand," Isolara said.

Kyrillos spoke, "but seeing that wall come down," he shook his head. "I'll admit, I put most of my focus on Essaerites that are good in direct combat, that can take out troops and cavalry and minor fortifications, but after seeing that, I've begun to realize that there are other ways to be powerful, and I would be lying if I said I wouldn't be terrified to be in a fortress and have you on the other side," he said.

Mariokos smiled tightly. "Thank you for the compliment. It means a lot coming from the both of you," he said. "But I suppose we should get on to what we're here for."

"Yes, we should," Isolara said. "I assume we're going across a river," she said casually.

This made Mariokos chuckle. "Yes, we are. We're going to be building a bridge," he said, and then glanced over at Caelwen. "Something I've been told by someone very special to me is insane."

"That's because it is insane," Caelwen said, "but I've given up on trying to convince you Lysandrians, so let's hear it. How are we building a bridge across this giant river?"

Kyrillos and Isolara both smirked.

———

CAELWEN TOOK IN THE OTHER ESSAERISTS. WHILE SHE THOUGHT IT WAS INSANE TO think that they could build a bridge across the Ilfrun in the time frame that they were given, she also realized that she had underestimated the Lysandrians since she had first seen them, and she wasn't sure if that was a wise idea to do anymore. So she decided to tell herself that if they said they were going to build a bridge across the Ilfrun in a week, then that's what they were going to do.

With her mind made up, she turned her attention back to her husband. She was happy seeing him in charge. He seemed to do well with the responsibility, and she was glad to see that the Essaerists from the other legion seemed to respect him, something she suspected was not easy to achieve. She wasn't sure what she thought of the other Essaerists, for that matter.

Isolara seemed pleasant enough, and her husband—well, she wasn't sure what she thought of him. Perhaps it was that Kyrillos came off as being above others that Caelwen didn't like, or maybe it was the way that he obviously looked down on Fioralba that bothered her. Caelwen had to remind herself that she didn't know anything about the other people and the relationships that they had with others, though she was grateful for Xavieno. She was fine with being underestimated, but for some reason, this seemed to rankle Xavieno, Fioralba, and Mariokos.

"So do you have any ideas for how to anchor the barges in the river?" Kyrillos asked.

Mariokos grimaced. "I have a few ideas. The problem is going to be the riverbed."

He held out his hand and created an Essaerite. It had four legs and looked like it was made out of stone. Coming out of the back of it was a large spike that curved, and on the front, there was a hook that Caelwen assumed you could attach a rope to. All of them looked at the Essaerite.

"That looks pretty straightforward," Isolara said.

"It is," Mariokos said.

"But it won't be able to stay secure in the riverbed," Caelwen said as she looked up at Mariokos. "That's what you're thinking, isn't it?"

He huffed. "Yes. Some of the riverbed is loose rock. These might hold, but they might slip if the current's too strong for the barges," he said.

"We could make them heavier," Fioralba pointed out.

"We could," Mariokos said.

"That won't work," Isolara said. "We'd end up using all of our Essaeris just on the anchors, and I'm sure the Legion needs help with something else."

Caelwen agreed. She thought, working the problem over in her head. An idea came to her. "Well, what if we tried something a little different?" she said, and all of them looked at her.

"A little differently from what?" Xavieno asked.

"You Lysandrians only think in stone and metal," she said.

Kyrillos chuckled. "And what do Gwenthari think in?" he asked.

She smiled softly. "We think in living things, in flesh and sinew, and in plants," she said. She held out her hand, feeling her Essaeris run down it. An Essaerite sprouted into existence. It was similar to ones that she'd used in the past to catch hogs, though this one was different. It had four legs made out of vines and branches, and in the center of it was a stone.

"Alright, what's your plan?" Mariokos asked.

"The problem is the riverbed's being loose, right? This can get around it," Caelwen explained. She made an alteration, creating a hook at the front for ropes to attach to, and a small vine that came out of the back.

"It doesn't look very big," Xavieno pointed out. "We're going to need something heavier than that to anchor," he said.

She resisted the urge to roll her eyes. "I know it's small, but you see, whereas Mariokos was using a spike, this will be using roots. Here, let me show you," she said. She went and fetched one of the soldiers, asking them to bring her a rope. They did, and she tied it around the hook, then sent the Essaerite scuttling into the river. As it hit the water, she felt it get pulled a little downstream, and its root feet twisted and clung to the riverbed, pulling it along.

After it had gone ten or fifteen feet, she had it settle in. The little bit of vine coming out of the back and some from the feet started growing their way into the riverbed, moving down and deep, winding around, and gripping. After a moment, she looked at the others. "It's anchored," she said. "It should be able to hold a lot of weight."

Xavieno didn't look convinced.

"I don't know," Kyrillos said.

"Sorry, Caelwen, I'm not sure on this one," Xavieno said.

She looked over at Mariokos, who simply shrugged and gave a small smile. The others might have been doubting her, but she very much doubted that he was. She handed Xavieno the rope. "Fine, then give it a tug," she said.

He sighed.

"What, unless you don't think you're strong enough?" she said.

"I'm strong enough," Xavieno retorted.

He pulled the rope taut and started to pull. It didn't move. He looked over at her and pulled again. Nothing. "You're not making it heavier," he said.

"No," she said. "This is significantly lighter than the one that Mariokos created, and we should be able to create a lot of them, but I want you to prove me wrong. Come on, give it a pull," she said. "Like you really mean it."

She heard Fioralba and Isolara chuckle. Xavieno pulled again. He pulled on it hard, his face furrowed and covered in sweat.

Kyrillos went up and joined him. "It's one thing if it can resist one man," he said, pulling on the rope. The two of them grunted and heaved.

Caelwen could sense the strain on the Essaerite, but it wasn't a lot. The two continued to pull and decided to create a few Essaerites that were like legionnaires who joined in pulling on the rope. Still, nothing moved. There began to be some conversation between the two of them and a little bit of bickering about who wasn't pulling hard enough or who should be pulling more. She noticed Isolara come up next to her. The woman was watching with amusement.

"It does seem to be very effective," she said.

"It'll hold," Caelwen said. "I suppose I should let it go," she said.

She felt Isolara's hand on her arm. Caelwen looked over at her. Isolara shook her head. "Oh, no, no, no, dear, we're not going to be doing that," she said, and looked over at Xavieno and Kyrillos. "I'm not giving up this entertainment."

Caelwen felt herself grin. "It is kind of fun to watch, isn't it?"

"Yes," Isolara said. "The big strong men being bested by a little woman," she said with a grin. She looked over at Caelwen. "I think you and I will get along just fine."

Caelwen smiled. "I think we will, too."

Mariokos walked over to them. "How long are you going to keep these idiots at it?" he asked.

Isolara shrugged, and Caelwen looked at him. "How long would you like?" she said.

He looked over, hearing the other two grunt. "I don't know; this is enjoyable."

Fioralba came up. "I say the next time they're all pulling as hard as they can, you just release the whole Essaerite," she said.

Isolara cooed. "Yes, we'll watch them fall on their asses," she said excitedly.

Caelwen's smile curled slowly. Once Kyrillos and Xavieno were pulling at their full strength, with a flick of her mind, the Essaerite in the river vanished, and the rope went slack. The two of them crashed onto each other, rolled for a moment in frustration, and then looked over at Caelwen, both glaring. Both of them looked at their wives, their glares softening.

"I think we've been played, old friend," Kyrillos said.

Xavieno huffed and got up. He held out his hand for Kyrillos. "Yes, I dare say we have been."

CHAPTER 6

Mariokos felt the pull on his power out in the riverbed. It had taken them a little while to get used to the Essaerites that Caelwen had come up with, but he had to admit they were extraordinarily effective. They had them running across the river along the bed, both north and south of where the bridge would be, allowing the barges to be tied perfectly into place as they drove in piles.

The crisp morning air carried the scent of damp soil and fresh leaves, making the mornings feel sharp and nice, while the cool evenings made for easy sleeping. Overall, he enjoyed the area they were in. The landscape was beautiful. There was green all around, and the air was fresh and clear. Behind him, the various camps worked on clearing the forest to build barges or parts of the bridge. He turned his attention back out to the river. Several barges drifted into position, their hulls moving through the current as men shouted and strained at the ropes to guide them into place. They were large, with pile drivers positioned on them, along with the piles in question.

Each of them had several sets of pulleys and wheels that were attached to the ropes leading into the water to the Essaerite anchors that held them in place. On top of the barges, massive treadwheels creaked and groaned as men marched inside them, straining against the weight to drive the pulleys and winches that hauled up the heavy pile driver weights. Along the riverbed, he had another Essaerite for each of the barges. This one's job was rather simple. It would help position the tip of the pile when it went into the riverbed and ensure that it was moving in smoothly and consistently.

This was something that the legion was used to doing, but the Essaerites made it easier and faster for them. The piles were mostly being constructed by legionnaires. There weren't any trees in the area thick or sturdy enough to serve as piles, so teams of legionnaires worked steadily, fashioning the necessary piles themselves. Behind him was a symphony of sound and activity. On a barge, they were moving a pile into position.

He focused on the Essaerite beneath the river's surface. The water was murky, but it could still see. Mariokos looked through its eyes, watching as the pile slipped down, moving towards it. The pile hit right in front of the Essaerite, and it walked over to it, using large gripping pincers and arms to move the tip of the pile exactly into position. Once it was in position and held, Mariokos waved at the men on the barge. The weight on the pile driver moved up and then came down. It thunked on the top of the pile with a large clunk. The Essaerite in the water saw the pile drive into the riverbed a little bit. The weight began to be lifted again, and again came down. The pile went a little bit deeper.

This would be his life for the next few days. He would help as the piles were initially driven into the riverbed, and then he would move the Essaerite over to another location. After they'd been started, he didn't need to monitor them as much, but still, the work would be tedious; yet somehow, he enjoyed it.

He knew other Essaerists found this work to be boring and tiresome, but for Mariokos, he lived for it. They were creating a bridge. He had played it off as if it wasn't a big deal when Caelwen had first voiced her amazement at it. In so many ways, she was right and wrong. It was a bridge like many they had built, just a temporary one. It was just longer than those they had built before. But it was its length that made it so special. Never had he heard of the legions crossing a river the size of the Ilfrun and doing so in such a short time frame. He was a part of something that would be in the histories for years to come.

The driver went up and thunked back down. Again and again, slowly creating a cadence. He moved the Essaerite over to the next pile and guided it into position. Again there was the thunk as the pile began to be driven into the riverbed. He sighed and smiled. There were far worse ways to spend a nice day.

———

CAELWEN CLOSED THE LID TO THE RABBIT ENCLOSURE ON HER CART. "THERE," SHE SAID.

"Finished?" Fioralba asked.

Caelwen nodded. "Yes, I'm finished," she said, and smiled, "it'll be nice not to have to use Essaeris to house these little things anymore." And she meant it.

The cage didn't take up much of her power, but it was still taxing and a waste. The new one was set up to handle multiple generations of rabbits and should give her and her brother plenty of room for growth.

Fioralba looked inside the cage. "It's too bad they're so cute," she said.

"Why, would you prefer it if they were ugly?" she asked.

Fioralba shrugged. "A little. I feel bad when I have to eat something cute," she said.

Caelwen chuckled. "You don't have to eat them," she pointed out.

Fioralba tisked. "But I do; they're so tasty," she said. She looked at the cage. "Sorry, little guys."

She saw Fioralba tense a little bit, her eyes narrowing. Caelwen looked in the direction that Fioralba was looking and saw the source of the frustration. Ilfthandor and Wulfgren were approaching. Fioralba moved, turning her back to them, and looked intently at Caelwen.

"Remember your place. You're an Aristolios," Fioralba said.

There had been some conversation around this. Ilfthandor was becoming increasingly frustrated with his place in the Legion. As in, he didn't have a place in the Legion; he was just part of Caelwen's old settlement. Men from the settlement worked for the Legion and got paid, and at some point in time, Ilfthandor would have lands that he would be able to move to. But it wasn't that time yet, and the settlement still had a lot of work to do. So he thought of himself as still being in charge.

The thing was, Ilfthandor wasn't in charge anymore. He might have been in their settlement, but he was nothing in the Legion. As he neared, she could see that irritation and frustration were apparent on his face. For his part, Wulfgren looked resigned, if not a little put out. She'd be happy to see her brother at least, but she could care less about seeing Ilfthandor again.

Caelwen ran her hands over the fabric of her dress. Today, like so many days, she had gone with a dress that was what other Aristolios women in the Legion wore. The fabric was soft and breathable, and she had to admit she found them enjoyable to wear. She'd never given too much thought to attire when she had been younger. It wasn't that people didn't care about how they looked, but she hadn't put the same thought into it that the Aristolios seemed to. She also didn't have the same exposure to the fabrics that she did now. Though the dress was created with Essaeris, she'd been shown and given swatches of every type of linen, cotton, and silk there was, and she'd learned how to recreate all of them, and do so in a myriad of colors. It meant that every day she could wear something that fit her mood and was also brand new, with the fabric always being soft and nice on her skin.

"Uncle," Caelwen said as he approached.

"I'm surprised you even know who I am anymore, Caelwen," Ilfthandor said as he walked up to her.

She sighed and gave him a knowing look. "We spoke just the other day. Are you getting senile in your old age?"

She saw his face redden with anger. She looked over at Wulfgren.

"Wulfgren, how are you this morning?" she asked.

He gave a tight look over at Ilfthandor and sighed. "I'm fine. It's nice being stopped for a little while," he said. "So what is it that you guys are doing in the river? I heard you're building a bridge."

"We are," Fioralba said.

Wulfgren glanced out in the direction of the river and shook his head.

"Alright, I guess by this point, I shouldn't be surprised by anything the Lysandrians do," he said.

"Enough about talking about some stupid bridge that won't be built," Ilfthandor said. "Caelwen, you and I need to talk."

She sighed. "What do we need to talk about, Uncle? Who wronged you this time?"

"You and your brother? For your information," Ilfthandor said.

Caelwen raised an eyebrow. "Okay, what did we do?" she asked, her voice flat and emotionless.

"You have not been paying me tribute or proper respect," he said. "Wulfgren here seems to think that he is somehow better than me and doesn't need to listen to what I tell him to do, and you for that matter," Ilfthandor said. He waved at Caelwen. "Look at you. In that dress. In this camp. Walking around like you're important. And like you're a Lysandrian. Who do you think you are?"

She cocked her head to the side. "I am Lysandrian. Remember? When you married me off, I became Lysandrian. For that matter, you're a Lysandrian as well, as is Wulfgren and everybody else from our settlement. And what are you talking about tribute? Why would I pay you anything?"

He flared up. "Because I am the leader," he said. "You owe me tribute. I know you've been selling these rabbits and everything else that you find. I should be getting a part of that," he said, crossing his arms.

The look on Wulfgren's face told Caelwen that this had been a fairly regular conversation that he'd been having with Ilfthandor, and she suspected that it had only been because Wulfgren had been dealing with Ilfthandor that Caelwen hadn't had to address this particular issue.

She lifted her jaw a little. "I owe you absolutely nothing," she said, "and nor does anybody else from our settlement. We are part of the Legion now. You need to understand that. And for your information, Wulfgren works for the Legion. So he takes orders from them, not from you, and he is above you."

Ilfthandor's eyes lit with fire. "What do you mean? He's above me?" he growled.

"Simple," Fioralba said, cutting in, "Wulfgren is Caelwen's brother. When Caelwen married Mariokos and joined the Legion, she became an Aristolios. Her brother, when he became Lysandrian because he was Caelwen's brother, became a Citizano. Your settlement joined the Empire, but you're only Caelwen's uncle. That means that you're a Subaltero; ergo, Wulfgren is above you, and Caelwen most certainly is," she said with flint in her voice.

Ilfthandor looked like he was about to say something that he would regret.

Caelwen spoke. "Ilfthandor, this is the way it is. I do not owe you anything. Wulfgren does not owe you anything. You need to learn this. And for the record, if you are not happy with where we are, then you shouldn't have dealt in poor faith with everyone around us, which is what forced us to leave our home in the first place." She said, "but after what happened at Hroldenfell, I would say we are pretty lucky that we're part of the Legion."

"I'll echo that," Wulfgren said. "This is a far better life."

Ilfthandor looked between the two of them. "We wouldn't have had that problem. The Legion isn't moving in that direction. And I will not take any lip from you. If you think you're above me, you have another thing coming," he said.

She narrowed her eyes. "Ilfthandor, watch it. This isn't like how it used to be."

She saw his face turn a deep red, and she saw his hand flinch. For a moment, she thought he was thinking about hitting her. Maybe he was. When she was younger, he had done it plenty of times, but he hadn't dared to do it since she had come into her power. At any rate, it wasn't going to matter.

She heard the gruff voice of Mariokos's sergeant, Erastos. "What do you think you're doing, you fucking idiot?" he barked, stepping between Caelwen and Ilfthandor.

He looked daggers at Ilfthandor, and Ilfthandor backed away. He was right too. Erastos was everything that every legionnaire wanted to be. He was strong, capable, fearless, and tough. He was also mean as hell.

Ilfthandor was about to speak when Erastos spoke. "What the fuck do you think you're doing, you stupid fucking barbarian? Do you have any idea who she is?"

"She's my niece!" Ilfthandor said.

"No, she's an Aristolios, and her husband is part of my squad, which means he's one of mine, which means she is too. Not only are you not going to hit any of my people or do anything to any of my people, but if you are dumb enough to do anything to an Aristolios woman, you'll be lucky if you only end up a slave," Erastos said, his voice hard and fierce.

She saw Ilfthandor's eyes widen, and then he glanced over at Caelwen and then back to Erastos, and then he backed up a bit.

Erastos spoke again, his voice still stern. "I don't know what the fuck you were before all this or what you think you are now, but you need to understand this is how the Legion works. You are a fucking Subaltero, and you are lucky to be a Subaltero. You have a chance at an actual life in the greatest Empire the world has ever or will ever know, and you are lucky enough to have a niece who's an Essaerist and an Aristolios. I would do everything I could if I were you to stay in her good graces because sooner or later, this war is gonna end, and you're sure gonna want to have someone like her on your side," he said. He turned back to Fioralba and Caelwen and smiled tightly at both of them. "Good morning," he said and walked off.

Caelwen was in shock. She'd always thought that Erastos didn't like her, and maybe he didn't, but as he had said, Caelwen was an Aristolios, and Mariokos was part of his squad. She looked over at her uncle. "Any questions," she asked, he glared for a moment and then glared at Wulfgren and stalked off.

Wulfgren smiled and whistled as he went. "I like Erastos, even if I'm a barbarian."

She laughed. "You've always been a barbarian."

Wulfgren walked over to the rabbit cage, peering inside. "It looks good, Caelwen. I'd have never thought you to be a carpenter," he said.

"Well, my husband's rather good at it," Caelwen said. "He's been able to help me with a lot of it; I've learned a lot from him."

Wulfgren nodded. "Yeah, you got a good one there," he said. He looked over at Fioralba. "Sorry about my uncle."

Fioralba shook her head. "Nothing to be sorry about. And I dare say after Erastos, I don't think you're going to have to worry about him mouthing off to you again anytime soon."

Wulfgren grinned. "I know, that part's kind of nice." He looked over at his sister. "So?"

"So what?" she asked.

He looked back at the cage. "So what's the plan for these?"

She rolled her eyes. "You're really planning on making a go of rabbit farming, aren't you?" she said.

"Why wouldn't I? They have great margins, and it's easy to do, especially when your sister's an Essaerist and basically does all the work for you. But she still remembers that I'm an equal business partner," he said.

She snorted. "How could I ever forget that we're equals in this, even though I do seem to do all the work?" she said, narrowing her eyes playfully. She sighed, "but we have been able to sell a few of them, and I dare say that the pelts will be worth a lot come winter."

"Yeah, I think we'll be able to do pretty well then," Wulfgren commented. "And after the war, they'll be great," he said.

After the war. That hadn't been something that Caelwen had given a lot of thought to. She sucked her lip.

"What is it?" he asked.

She shook her head. "Just thinking about after the war; it's not something I've given a lot of thought to. We were in our settlement, we were driven out, we joined the legions; I just haven't thought much about the future," she said. She looked over at Fioralba. "What will happen after the war?"

Fioralba looked inside the cage, watching the rabbits move around. "Well, we'll go back home."

"But where is home?" Caelwen asked.

"Dionisiana," Fioralba said. "I think you'll like it there. It's a lot of rolling hills and green fields. There's a lot of wine produced there," she said with a smile.

"I suppose that's good," Caelwen said.

Wulfgren perked up. "Do you think there's a market for rabbits?"

Fioralba chuckled. "I'm sure there's a market for rabbits, Wulfgren," she said, placatingly.

He nodded. "Good. We can't go someplace where there's not a market for rabbits."

Caelwen rolled her eyes. She was silent for a moment.

"What is it?" Fioralba asked.

She shrugged. "I guess just thinking about not going back to where I lived before. I knew I was never going to. Once we left, we were leaving. And I know I'm Lysandrian now, but still," she said.

Fioralba nodded. "Right. Lysandrian isn't necessarily home," she said. "But it will be. Someday. I promise you'll like it."

"I'm sure I will. It's just something I need to get my head around. What will we do when we get home?" she asked.

Fioralba shrugged. "Whatever you want. Being part of the legions, and being the rank that our husbands are, and that they are Essaerists, part of that agreement means that they'll get lands. You'll have a fairly large plot of land to do with as you please. You could farm, or you could do other things." She looked at Wulfgren. "Like having your brother live there, who's a rabbit farmer," she said. "I'm sure your neighbors will find that amusing."

Caelwen chuckled softly. "Oh, I'm sure they'll find plenty about us amusing."

She thought about it. It didn't sound like a bad life. "I suppose I can live with that," she said, "even if it means having to keep Wulfgren around."

Fioralba smiled. "You could always leave him with wherever your settlement ends up," she said.

Wulfgren stood up and shook his head. "Nah, then I'd have to raise the rabbits on my own. I'm not going to do that, and there's no way that Caelwen's going to miss out on making some coin."

She smirked. He had her there. She wasn't going to miss out on it. Indeed, the fuzzy little creatures were proving to be quite profitable. The Legion had plenty of livestock that it brought with it, but the rabbits grew faster, were cheaper and easier to maintain, and they provided something different. Along with Caelwen's ability to forage, she was pretty sure that soon she'd be making more than Mariokos, something she'd be sure to remind him of.

CHAPTER 7

Ice-cold water soaked Valfric's tunic as he stumbled his way through the stream. On his shoulders was a young child who wasn't making the task any easier for him. They had spotted the small group of people not too long ago. Valfric and his team had already crossed the small stream, and they were now helping the others. These weren't the first groups they had seen as of late. Many were fleeing the lands around Hroldenfell and to the west, where Valfarans' raiding parties were reaching into Ulfgarath territory.

He felt his feet slipping along the rocks of the stream. The water was moving quickly, and the streams were getting deeper and faster as all the snow from winter melted up high in the peaks. The stream he was crossing now would continue to move north, joining with other streams until it eventually dumped into the Ilfrun. From there, it would continue to the sea. The territory was dense with forests, steep mountains, and rocky crags, with difficult paths winding through them. The routes they took wound around, taking far more time than if the land were flat. It was frustrating, but Valfric knew the Lysandrians would face the same situation when they moved into this land. So it was a wash.

The kid continued to squirm on Valfric's shoulders, almost slipping off. He reached up, stopping the little boy from falling, and in the process, his foot slipped on one of the rocks in the riverbed, twisting his ankle.

"Fuck," he grunted, then corrected himself and continued moving forward. "Stay still," he said.

The kid said something about being sorry, but it didn't sound like he was strictly paying attention. For Valfric, this wasn't exactly a pleasant experience, but for the kid, he was on an adventure and was being carried across a stream that, to a small child, probably looked like a raging river. On the bright side, the water was cold enough that it numbed Valfric's legs and ankles, so he wasn't sure if he'd actually hurt himself or not. When he got out of the river, he set the boy down and looked over to see Aelric and Thraindel completing their crossings as well.

Thraindel was carrying a heavy bag, and Aelric had two kids on his shoulders that he was ferrying across. People from the group were helping across horses and mules that were laden with what few belongings the people had with them. Ilara was tending to their horses and otherwise making sure everything was going in an orderly fashion. On second thought, Valfric wasn't sure how Ilara had gotten out of having to help anybody across the stream.

As Aelric set down his cargo, he looked over at Valfric and Thraindel and spoke softly, saying, "I liked it better when we were the ones doing the raiding."

Valfric grimaced. "It was a little bit easier, wasn't it?"

Thraindel nodded. "Yeah, and I always thought we had it kind of hard, you know, risking our lives to steal some shit." He looked at the people who were checking to make sure they hadn't lost anything on the crossing. "But I think this is more of a pain in the ass."

Valfric agreed. This was definitely more of a pain in the ass. They could have stolen from these people, but what would the point have been? Nothing they had was of any value. And even if they wanted to take them as slaves, how would they be able to manage so many? It just wasn't feasible. And they all knew that there were bigger problems at hand.

Valfric found the leader of the group. He was an older gentleman that everyone with him seemed to look up to. "Alright, is that everything?"

The man looked over at his people, seeming to do a head count. He smiled and nodded. "Yes. Thank you so much for your assistance." He said, reaching out, taking Valfric's hand and clasping it. "I don't know what we would have done without you."

Valfric felt himself smile. "Oh, you would have managed it, I'm sure. It would have just taken you longer," he said. He squeezed the man's hand and let go.

"You don't give yourself enough credit. I wish there were more people like you," he commented.

This made Valfric feel a pang of guilt. Out of the corner of his eye, he saw Ilara flinch a little bit. They hadn't heavily raided in Ulfgarath territory, but they had some, and he knew that throughout most of his life, if he had come upon a weak group like this, he would have taken advantage of it. But that was from a time when weak groups were a rarity. Now they were the norm.

Valfric shook his head. "You're too kind. Would you care to join us? I guess I should ask, where are you heading again?"

The man looked serious. "We're going to head north to Ulfgard. I think it's the only place that's going to be safe, honestly," he said.

"We've been hearing a lot of that," Aelric said. "Everyone seems to be heading to Ulfgard. We are too."

The man's mood brightened. "Are you? Well, if we're not an inconvenience, we would love to travel with you. Have you seen many others like us?"

"Yes, we have," Ilara said.

"Too many. And honestly, we're surprised," Valfric spoke. "I was expecting to see people from the south and east, near where Hroldenfell was, and where Wulfharboria has been moving more and more into Ulfgarath territory, but I've been surprised to see how many people from the west have been moving," he said.

The man's expression darkened. "It's the Valfarans. It started not long ago. We've always raided back and forth with them, you see, but the raids have changed; they've increased in cadence, and we've been seeing more and more of them." The man shook his head. "Our settlement lost its best warriors, and we had to flee. If you can believe it, we used to be strong."

"I can believe it," Valfric said. "How many people in your settlement have died?" he asked out of curiosity.

The man's expression darkened further. "Over half the people in my settlement are dead," he said, his voice sounding hollow. "Some of them from raids, but others from disease or from other issues. When we started losing people, it was harder to take care of livestock and crops, and unfortunately, that's how these things go," he said. "I'm sure the gods have a plan for us. I just don't know what it is."

A plan indeed, Valfric thought. He was curious what the gods thought of all this. They had to be watching. They always were. But what were they making of it? Did they want the Gwenthari to be pushed to the brink of extinction by the Lysandrians? Was this a punishment for not remembering who they were? Valfric wasn't sure.

"We should get moving," Valfric said.

The man nodded. "You lead the way."

They began picking their way through the woods, following roughly trod paths that switched back and forth as they went down the hill. When they got to the base of one of the mountains, they walked along a very narrow valley and then started up another thickly wooded hill. The area was difficult terrain, and Valfric was sweating and breathing hard when he noticed that something was amiss.

The sounds of birds chirping had stopped. He looked around, feeling his hair on the back of his neck prickle. Instantly, the others recognized something was wrong, though the group they had found still were talking amongst themselves.

Valfric walked towards the tree line, staring into it. He reached out to the wolves that he had in the area, feeling, sensing. One of them breathed in deeply through its nose. "Fuck," he grunted.

A group of people exploded from the tree line on the other side of their group. Valfric called out, "Attack!" He said, "We're under attack!"

The people they had found seemed confused, but he didn't pay them any attention. He reached down into his power and created a sword and shield. He ran forward as the group approached. He registered the look of shock on a man's face as Valfric created the weapons, and he slammed his shield into the man, sending him sprawling. He ducked down, dodging a spear from another man, and Valfric stabbed forward, plunging the blade into the man's gut. He called out and screamed, his breath leaving in a whoosh. There were more people now, and Valfric's wolves were there, growling and howling, taking the attention of the raiders away from the humans. Out of the corner of his eye, he saw the people in the group engaging with a few raiders, though he couldn't spare much attention.

One of his wolves lunged at somebody, clamping onto their arm. Another grabbed onto the person's other arm and pulled. Ilara ran forward and stabbed the person in the chest. The wolves let go, and she spun, moving to the next foe. Valfric lost himself in it, but it was over almost as quickly as it started. He heard Aelric cut down one more person, and Valfric looked around, feeling his face and body splattered in the blood of others.

Valfric kicked the corpse below him, making sure that the man was dead. He peered down at him, seeing him covered in blood. He looked around. Their little group appeared to be okay.

He sent his wolves out, circling the area, looking for anything they could. They sniffed the air, looking for danger. Everyone roved around. He heard Thraindel swearing behind him, and he turned to look, seeing a cut on Thraindel's arm. Valfric felt his heart pick up, and he moved over to his friend.

"You okay?" he asked.

Thraindel's teeth were gritted. "Yeah, it's fine, it's just a flesh wound," he said. "Fucking hurts, though."

"Let me look at it," Valfric said. Thraindel held out the arm. It was just a flesh wound, but it was bleeding a lot and needed to be cleaned out. He looked over, seeing Ilara covered in blood.

She quickly shook her head. "I'm fine. No one got me," she said.

"As am I," Aelric said, coming out of the woods.

He too was covered in blood. Valfric turned his attention back to the group they had been traveling with. They were all cowering together, and the few men had swords and spears. He had seen a few of them engage with the raiding party, and they had fought admirably, but there weren't very many of them, and they had to stay close to their families. He saw one woman with a bloody dagger, and in a way, this made him more disturbed. Not that she had fought. There was nothing wrong with women fighting. In fact, in Valfric's opinion, they should fight. No, that the women of this group fought and defended themselves was good. It's what Gwenthari women did. And that seemed to be something that their people hadn't forgotten.

No, what bothered him was that these people were competent. They were capable, and they fought just as well as anybody in Valfric's old settlement would have. And they'd been driven out by the Valfarans. And this was what was left of them. This was concerning on so many levels because it meant that the strong were also now being forced out. And that was something that Valfric hadn't expected.

"Are you alright?" he asked the group.

They nodded. The man who was their leader said nobody was hurt. "How are your people?" he asked, "and thank you for defending us. I had no idea that you were an Essaerist," he said in amazement.

"We're fine. Thraindel got hurt, but he should be okay," he said. "And you're welcome."

Valfric didn't comment about being an Essaerist. It wasn't something that he was open about. It wasn't that it was something that he thought should be hidden. He just knew if somebody was untrustworthy and thought his people weak, they would act. If they knew he was an Essaerist, they wouldn't, which could mean that they could put themselves in a situation of being around people they could not trust and not knowing it. Valfric would much rather have somebody try a sneak attack on them and fail than not know they were with people that could slip their throats in the night.

A woman from the settlement was walking up to Thraindel. She was holding a rag in her hand. "Come here, let's get you tended to," she said.

"I'll be fine, thank you," Thraindel said.

The woman came up to him and took his hand, looking at his arm.

"Really, I'm..." he started.

"Oh, shut it," she said.

Valfric smiled. The woman was older and had probably been bullying around injured people her entire life. Thraindel looked over at Valfric, who shrugged. "I wouldn't argue with her if I were you."

Thraindel sighed, and the woman began dabbing at the cut. "Let's get it cleaned out and wrapped. You don't want it to fester," she said.

Thraindel sighed again. "Yes, ma'am," he said, following her over to her cart.

Valfric looked over at Ilara, who grinned. "It's fun seeing stuff like that happen, isn't it?" she said.

"That it is," Aelric said.

They all looked out to where the raiding party had come from.

"They managed to get close," Thraindel said.

"How did your wolves not sense them?" Ilara asked.

Valfric's jaw tightened in irritation. "They were downwind, and with this fucking terrain, it was a nightmare to spot them coming at all. They got lucky," he said. "I'm going to have to keep a couple of the wolves closer in case something like that happens again, and see what I can do to scout the area more," he said.

They nodded. "Don't stretch yourself too thin," Aelric said. "There's a lot of people in these forests, and a lot of them are desperate."

Valfric nodded. "Yes, I'm well aware of that. Desperate people do dumb things."

"And dumb people and dumb things could get us killed," Aelric said.

They made camp for the evening. Well after the sun had set, Valfric sat holding his hands out over a fire. Next to him, Ilara was finishing up her dinner. The wolves had managed to find a deer in the area. It had been an easy kill for them and meant that everybody would have a full belly for the night. It also helped to ease some of the fear and tension. Thraindel had been tended to and was getting along well with the newcomers. They seemed to have taken him in, and Valfric's group, for their part, were doing the same.

They needed to find a new settlement, even if it pained him to think that. Perhaps these people would be that settlement. From his tent, Valfric could hear Aelric snoring, and he looked over at Ilara.

"You've been quiet tonight," he said. She was looking down at the fire. "Ilara," he said.

She started a bit. "Oh, sorry," she said. "Yeah, the food was fine."

He laughed and bumped into her with his shoulder. "I didn't ask you about the food. I said you've been quiet tonight."

She looked a little abashed. "Oh, well, sorry," she said. "Yeah, I guess I have been."

"Why?" he asked.

She looked back to the fire, and after a moment said, "Just thinking about life is all."

"And what are you thinking about life? I never took you to be a philosopher before," he taunted.

She glared playfully at him. "I'm many things. You just don't know them," she said.

"Come on, talk to me," he said.

She looked at their little group. "This, this is what I'm thinking. Our settlement is gone. They're dead."

"And we weren't there for it," Valfric said. "I feel guilty about that as well. But I'm thankful that all of us are alive."

She sighed. "I'm thankful that we're alive too. We tried. There's nothing that we would have been able to do, and I know that. It's just, this whole thing is awful. And these people," she said. "We know what it's like not to have a home now. We know what it's like to be afraid. And to be on the run."

She looked over at Valfric, her expression dark and concerned. "How many times were we the reason for this?" she asked.

He raised an eyebrow. "What do you mean?"

She looked back at the people. "This, them. How many times were we the reason why people fled or were afraid or watched their loved ones die or suffer at our hands? You know what would have happened if we would have lost today."

He did know what would have happened to them. He felt a pit in his gut. "It's the way of the world," he said.

She shook her head. "Is it? I'm not so sure anymore. Part of me can't help but think that this is all happening because the gods are punishing us," she said.

"Because we are weak," he said.

"Yes, because we are weak. But not weak the way we thought."

"Then weak how?" he asked curiously.

"Weak in that we used our ability to fight and to hurt and to do all those things, and we did it for our own gain. We did it for the fun; we did it for the riches. We didn't do it to protect," she said, her voice dejected. "We didn't do it to build up our people."

He didn't know what to say. A small voice in his head told him that she was right, that the gods were mad at them, that they were being punished.

"I'm not sure what to say," he said after a moment.

She shrugged. "What is there to say?"

"So does this mean you're not going to fight anymore?" he asked, trying to lighten the mood.

She smiled. "No, it doesn't mean that at all. It just means that the reason why I fight and kill will be different," she said. "I'm not fighting for money or riches or slaves or accolades anymore." She looked over at the people. "I'll protect them, I'll protect you and Thraindel and Aelric, but I'm just not sure that I can be the one that makes people afraid and terrified anymore... I'm sorry," she said after a moment.

He put his hand on her shoulder and gave it a little squeeze. "You have nothing to be sorry for, my friend." He stood from the fire. "I'm going to go to sleep," he said. She nodded. "Do you want to join me?" he asked.

"No, I'm going to stay up and keep watch," she said.

He nodded and slipped into his tent.

CHAPTER 8

Fioralba released a bowl that she'd been using for breakfast. It was mid-morning, and she was ready to get on with the day. She stood and made her way through the camp. There were a few legionnaires around, but by and large, the only people in the camp were merchants and other support personnel, along with spouses and families of those few legionnaires who were allowed to bring their families with them.

She walked through the camp and out the main gate. The legions had been heavily engaged in construction. The areas surrounding the camp were an assortment of workstations as men worked. She followed a now well-worn path towards the Ilfrun. She could hear the water running as she approached. Standing along the banks was Caelwen. Fioralba came and stood next to her.

"Good morning," Fioralba said.

Caelwen glanced over at her. "Good morning," she said softly, and then her gaze returned back to the bridge.

It was about half finished now. In the next few days, it would be done, and then the legion would be on the move. Fioralba smirked.

"Still can't believe it?" she asked.

Caelwen shook her head. "Seeing is believing, isn't it? But, no, in a way I don't." She looked out over the bridge, inspecting it critically. "Even when I decided that maybe it was possible that this could be done, I expected the bridge to be shabby and rickety, thrown together haphazardly."

Fioralba raised an eyebrow. "Because the legions do so much of that?"

Caelwen laughed. "I know. But still, my mind just couldn't wrap itself around it. And here we have this," she said, pointing at the bridge.

It was far from being rickety or shabby. It was the polar opposite of that. While this bridge would likely be temporary and only be here for a few weeks or maybe a few months, it was still constructed to a high standard. All the piles had been driven in perfectly and were exactly where they needed to be. Atop them was the rest of the bridge's construction. Their craftsmanship was far from lacking, but that was the legions, wasn't it? They never did anything halfway. Even a camp that would be destroyed or burned down the next day was built to exacting precision. The bridge was no different. She knew at some point, when the legions moved across it, it would be solid and firm, and there would be no concern from anyone as they walked across.

They were joined by Isolara. Her long, flowing hair framed her beautiful face, and she regarded Caelwen and Fioralba warmly. "Good morning, ladies," she said.

"Good morning, Isolara," Fioralba said.

"Good morning," Caelwen said.

"Do you know what the plan is for today?" Isolara asked.

Fioralba wasn't sure, but Caelwen answered. "Mariokos has a few assignments for us to complete. But the bridge is moving along. It's ahead of schedule. He thinks a large part of that was the help we provided with the Essaerites along the riverbed."

Fioralba nodded. "They were extraordinarily helpful. And very clever," she said.

Caelwen shrugged. "Thanks," she said, though her tone sounded more like she was just trying to be polite.

Fioralba had learned that Caelwen didn't seek accolades. She didn't seem to care if people thought she was good or bad at what she did. In some ways, she almost seemed to prefer being underestimated, like it gave her an advantage. But for Caelwen, solving a problem was just that—solving a problem. It didn't make her better than anyone else. It was a very unique thing, in Fioralba's opinion, and was one of the things that showed more than anything that Caelwen was not Lysandrian.

In Lysandrian, one sought distinction by being excellent at something, being wealthy or powerful, beautiful or cunning. One was always trying to prove themselves to others, trying to show just what they were. It didn't appear to be that way for Caelwen, and she thought maybe it was something about being a Gwenthari, but another part of her thought it could just be Caelwen. The woman was incredibly practical in almost all things.

Caelwen spoke. "We're going to be helping some of the carpenters, from my understanding, but I don't know much about it. I think the work will probably be pretty easy."

"What makes you say that?" Fioralba asked.

Caelwen shrugged. "Because the carpenters know what they're doing. We don't necessarily, but we can provide strong Essaerites and things of that nature."

"So the work that slaves would normally do," Isolara said with a smirk.

Caelwen shrugged again. "I suppose, and I know the Legion has plenty of slaves, but the more help, the better, right?"

Fioralba noticed Isolara's smile.

"There really is no work that is beneath you, is there?" Isolara asked.

Caelwen looked a little taken aback by the question. She shook her head. "Should there be? If something needs to be done, it needs to be done," she said simply and wandered off.

They followed Caelwen, and as she had promised, they were going to be doing grunt labor, or more importantly, their Essaerites were going to. They were to create Essaerites that would be moving around raw timber to different stations where it would be cut up and turned into boards and planks for the bridge.

Caelwen and Isolara created their Essaerites that moved off. Fioralba reached inside herself, feeling her power seem to fight her just a little bit. *That's odd,* she thought. This had been happening as of late. She forced through the moment, and the Essaeris inside of her bloomed and came out of her in a rush. An Essaerite that was supposed to be two legs with a clamp on the front that could grab the trunks of trees and pull them came into existence, but the clamp was misshapen and odd. Fioralba felt her embarrassment rise, and she released the Essaerite. She created it again. This time, the clamp was correct, but the Essaerite's feet had an issue with one of its toes.

"Is there something wrong with the foot?" Isolara said next to Fioralba.

Fioralba felt herself blush. "Yeah, I just, um, yeah," she said, then released the Essaerite and created it again. This time, it came in correctly.

"There you go, got it," Isolara said.

Fioralba felt herself blush even deeper. "Yeah, I don't know what happened," she said. Then she felt her irritation flare up. "Actually, I do. I'm just tired. I've been struggling with it. I'm sorry," she said, her voice a little firm.

Isolara raised an eyebrow. "I didn't mean to offend you, and you have nothing to be sorry about."

For some reason, this irritated Fioralba more. "Oh, I see. It makes sense that I couldn't create a basic Essaerite. My mistake," she said, her voice icy.

Isolara looked at her intently for a moment, cocking her head to the side. "Why are you being defensive about this?"

"Why are you being patronizing?" Fioralba asked.

Isolara gave a small smile. "You haven't figured it out yet, have you?" she said.

Fioralba felt her anger rising. "Figured out what?"

Isolara sighed softly. "I'm not trying to make you angry," she said.

"Then what are you trying to do?" Fioralba asked.

Isolara looked a bit at a loss for words and said, "Just to confirm. Do you know you're pregnant?"

"I'm what?" Fioralba said. "How could you possibly—" She stopped.

And as she stopped speaking, her mind seemed to stop with it. Things started clicking into place in her mind like the pieces of the bridge out in the river before her. She had been struggling for a few weeks now. Her Essaeris just had been fighting her, something it had only ever done on one other occasion that she could think of in the recent past.

Isolara nodded softly. "You didn't know you were pregnant," she said. Then she smiled. "Congratulations?"

Fioralba looked over as Caelwen was walking up.

"What's wrong?" Caelwen asked.

"I'm pregnant," Fioralba said.

Caelwen looked a little surprised and nodded. "Okay, that's good. Congratulations. You and Xavieno wanted a child, right?" she asked.

Fioralba nodded, her anger gone. Her eyes were filling up with tears. "Yes."

Caelwen looked confused. "Then why are you crying? I'm sorry, I don't understand," Caelwen said.

Isolara came and put her arm around Fioralba. "She's only just figured it out," she said.

Caelwen nodded. "Ahh. What gave it away? Are you late?"

Fioralba did some math in her head. "I am, but I started having problems with my Essaeris before." She trailed off.

Caelwen looked confused. Isolara explained. "When Essaerists are pregnant, our Essaeris fluctuates and is unreliable. Even using Essaeris can be dangerous for a baby," she explained.

"I didn't know that," Caelwen said, shocked.

"Why would you? You've told us you didn't grow up around other Essaerists," Isolara said kindly.

Fioralba looked over at Isolara. "I really am pregnant, aren't I?" she said. "That's why I've been tired, why I haven't felt good, why I've been irritable, and my Essaeris..." she said, feeling a slight sense of horror. "My Essaeris hasn't been acting correctly."

"And it's not a good idea for you to use it, either," Isolara said. "Now that you know, you have to use your Essaeris sparingly. Yes, you have to use a little every day; otherwise, you'll feel it build up and make it feel like you're going crazy, but only the bare minimum," she said. "And you know it's not going to be reliable."

Fioralba nodded. This was something she did know. The further along she got, the less reliable her Essaeris would become, and they had found that women who tried to use their Essaeris during pregnancies oftentimes caused the pregnancy to have issues, especially in the later stages.

"Good for you, Fioralba," she said, "I'm so happy for you."

Fioralba smiled. "This is good news, isn't it?"

"It's very good news," Caelwen said. "This is something that you and Xavieno want."

Fioralba nodded. "You're right. This is good news. This is a good thing. Just surprising," she said. "After our last, well, after the last time," she said.

Isolara patted her arm. "This time might be different. Just take it easy and don't use your Essaeris," she said sternly.

Fioralba nodded. "Right, I won't."

"And you might want to tell Xavieno," Caelwen said.

Fioralba laughed. "Yeah, that might be a good idea, isn't it?"

Later that evening, Fioralba sat by the fire as dinner cooked. They'd been eating with Mariokos and Caelwen, but the latter had made sure Fioralba and Xavieno would have privacy. Also, something that was new for her was it was a pot that Caelwen had created that sat bubbling by the fire.

Xavieno came striding up to her, and she felt a small hint of nerves as she stood.

He hugged and kissed her. "Good evening, Bellisara."

She smiled and kissed him back. "How was your day?"

"Fine," he looked around. "Where is Caelwen?"

She took his hand. "It's just us tonight."

He turned his attention to her, a look of concern crossing his face. "Is something wrong?"

"No, nothing's wrong. In fact, there's something great," she said, feeling herself start to smile. "I'm pregnant."

He stared at her as her words sunk in. She saw so many emotions cross his face before it rested on happiness. "You're sure?"

She nodded. "I'm sure. It's why my powers have been acting up, and I've been tired and moody..."

His hands were at her waist, and she could see joy in his eyes. "You have been moody, to be sure," he mused.

She smacked his arm, and he grinned and kissed her. "This time will be different," he said as he held her.

She nodded. "This time will be different."

———

VALFRIC'S HORSE STUMBLED ON THE SLICK ROAD, ITS HOOVES SLIDING THROUGH THE MUD as it plodded forward. He was cold and drenched. It had been raining for several hours. Not a hard rain, mind you, but a steady drizzly one that had everything slick with water, including the road, which had turned to mud. All around, he could hear the sound of horses' hooves coming out of the mud with slurping, slopping sounds and the calls of people as their wagons got stuck in the muck.

It didn't help that there were so many people on the road traveling on it while it was wet. Their little group had been joined by others and still others until there was a steady stream of people along the road. Off to his left, he could hear the roar of the Ilfrun as it ran quickly beside them. They were still in a relatively rugged area, and the road switched around on itself as it followed the river's path, but it wasn't as bad as it had been a few days ago. They were generally heading north now, moving to a spot where there was a bridge that crossed the Ilfrun.

It wasn't advisable to try to cross the river oneself as it was deep and quick-moving in this area, and the bridge they were headed to was one of the last ones for days as the river continued to move fast and went through more diffi-cult terrain. Then it would widen out until it got to the point where it wasn't practical to build a bridge, and instead, you had to use barges to cross it— something that wasn't practical for this many people.

The Ilfrun had always cut Ulfgarath in half. It created a difficult or near-impossible barrier that armies and trade struggled to move past. There were roads running on either side up it all the way to the coastline that were rich for trade and agriculture, but it made it difficult for armies. Part of Valfric wondered if Lysandrian would stop at the Ilfrun. If they would reach its banks and move to the south and move to the north, but otherwise decide not to mess with it. He wouldn't blame them. It wouldn't be the first time in history that that had happened. But a larger part of him thought that the Lysandrians would be overconfident, that they would find some way around the river, prob-ably by taking the same path that Valfric and his company had, as it was shorter and faster than moving up to the coast to take ships.

Or maybe the Lysandrians would opt for barges to cross, though he doubted it. It would take forever for one legion to cross, let alone four. And to what end? On the other side of the river was all of Ulfgarath. Yes, they had conquered Hroldenfell, something that still shook him, but Hroldenfell was just one city, and it was far from being the largest. Now, the Lysandrians had largely conquered an area of Ulfgarath that wasn't as densely populated as others. As they moved north, even if they didn't cross the Ilfrun, they would see steeper and steeper resistance.

The hawks that he had in the area made him question just how far Lysan-drian could make it. On both sides of the river, the groups of people were massive. Many of the parties were camped out, waiting out the rain, but they would start moving again, and there were still many on the road. There were thousands of people more than he had ever seen, and as his hawks traveled around, there seemed to be no end to them.

"I fucking hate this weather," Thraindel grumbled next to him.

Valfric looked over. Thraindel's arm was healing well, and he glanced down at it.

"How's the arm?" he asked.

Thraindel looked at his arm. "It's fine," he said.

"I agree with you," Valfric said. "I fucking hate this weather too. Well, I should say I hate this weather when I'm on the move," he amended.

Thraindel smiled knowingly. "Yeah, it wasn't so bad at home when it gave you an excuse not to leave the house, was it?" he said.

Valfric shook his head. "It could be kind of nice. And you knew it'd make everything grow and smell good," he said. "But now I don't think the smell is gonna happen. Now, if anything, with so many people and animals on the road..." Valfric suspected that as soon as the sun came out and started warming everything, the smell could be rather awful.

Aelric and Ilara were with them too, all of them on their horses, their eyes and heads moving around looking for threats. The threats were everywhere, but nowhere at the same time. They had seen a handful of scuffles, but most people were just moving in an orderly fashion. Everyone had the same destination. They were all going to Ulfgard, and nobody had anything to spare, so there was no point in fighting and stealing from one another.

Up ahead, Valfric could see a group of people all clumped together.

He moved one of his hawks into the area, seeing the bridge. It was small, not very wide, and looked like it had seen better days. But it went over the Ilfrun River, and there was a steady stream of people crossing it. Part of him had considered the idea of destroying the bridge after his group had gotten over it as a way of slowing the Lysandrians down. They would find another way to pass, or they would move to the southwest and then head back north, but it could cost them days or even weeks.

He reconsidered that now. Though the bridge looked like it had seen better days, it was mostly stone, and he knew that there were people coming from miles behind them. He couldn't destroy the bridge, even if he'd wanted to. So instead, they came to a stop and waited until they were able to shuffle forward and go across it. As he did, he was deafened by the sound of the river as it ran under them, and he felt slight unease as the horses clomped along on the slippery stone.

Once they were on the other side, he felt himself calm, and after a bit, the rain started to slow until it eventually came to a stop. He thought about stopping and building a fire, but there were too many people, and it would be difficult. So, instead, they kept moving until the land opened up a bit, and they came into a field that was dotted with tents and campfires burning. Their group angled to an open patch and came to a stop.

Valfric got off his horse and looked around. He had changed his Essaerites. They no longer looked like wolves but instead looked like dogs, and he had six of them as opposed to his normal four. He had found that most people didn't respond well to wolves. He didn't blame them, and their animals doubly so didn't like them. So, with everyone around, it seemed easier to go over to dogs. People accepted them and didn't find them suspicious. It gave them a little bit less of a defense, but it also gave them some more warning, and the dogs were far from ordinary.

He told the group of people that they had been coming with to set up camp, and everyone listened to him without any question. Out of the corner of his eye, he saw a group of men approaching them. He turned. One of the men was older, with long, braided hair and a beard. His blue eyes took in Valfric critically. Valfric squared his shoulders as he approached the small group.

"Good afternoon," he said.

"Afternoon," the man said.

"The name is Valfric."

"I'm Osthart," the man said. He looked over at Valfric's party. "These yours?"

Valfric glanced back and then looked back to him and nodded. "Mostly, yes. Some that we've been traveling with along the way. Why?" Valfric looked over the man's shoulder. "Are those yours?"

The man nodded. "Yes. It's my settlement. I don't want any trouble."

Valfric shrugged. "I wasn't planning on starting any. Were you planning on it?" The man eyed him, and then after a moment seemed to relax.

"Alright. You seem fine. That's a lot of dogs you have," Osthart said.

One of the people from their group called out, "He's an Essaerist!" It was a young boy who just seemed excited about it. Valfric resisted the urge to groan. The man looked at him, his eyes more critical again.

"You're an Essaerist?"

Valfric did sigh this time. "Yes, I am." To prove his point, he created a small bird on his shoulder and then released it. The men on either side of Osthart shuffled a little bit. "Is that going to be a problem?" Valfric asked.

The man shook his head. "The opposite, in fact. It's good to have an Essaerist around. Why the dogs, though?" he asked.

Valfric shrugged. "Because horses don't like wolves."

The man chuckled. "I suppose that's fair enough. We have dry wood if you'd like some for a fire."

Valfric nodded. "That'd be most welcome, thank you." He waved over some of the people, telling them to go get some of the wood. There were some perks to being an Essaerist, and he suspected this man saw it. If he could play nice with Valfric, then that meant they'd have an Essaerist with them. That was more security for his settlement.

The man waved Valfric over to his tent, and he came over and sat next to a fire.

"What have you heard?" Valfric asked.

Osthart shook his head. "Nothing good, obviously. How could there be anything good in these times?" he said with a huff. "But, from what little we have heard, Lysandrian is still on the other side of the Ilfrun. But I haven't heard much other than that. Apparently, they're up north, but the river's wide there. I'm not sure why they're camping out."

"Perhaps, before making a push to the north or the south," Valfric said.

Osthart nodded. "Seems like as good a guess as any, but maybe they'll stop at the Ilfrun. I wouldn't be surprised. Still, we're going to Ulfgard. You?"

Valfric nodded. "The same."

Out of the corner of his eye, Valfric noticed slaves moving about doing work. One of them caught his eye. Her hair was a dark auburn that was almost brown. She had a slight Lysandrian look to her. And for a moment, he thought she was Lysandrian. But on a second glance, he realized she wasn't.

"You seem to have a lot of slaves," he said. "I'm surprised. Most people haven't had them."

Osthart nodded. "Yeah, well, most people waited until they were completely driven from their lands, didn't they?"

"You didn't?" Valfric asked.

Osthart shook his head. "No, we didn't. We saw what was coming, and we left. We may have picked up a few things along the way," he said.

Valfric couldn't help but smile. "A little light raiding?"

The man chuckled. "One does what one has to," he said. "But not much. Still, having the extra labor is useful."

"I'm sure it is. Unfortunately, our settlement was in Hroldenfell," he said.

Osthart shook his head. "Was it as bad as they say, or were you not there? You must not have been if you're here," he said.

Valfric shook his head. "We were there. Unfortunately, the city was surrounded before we were able to get inside. Then once the Lysandrian camps were there, there was no getting in," he said. "We saw the whole thing happen. The whole city is gone," he said darkly.

"Well, then I guess we know why it's important to get to Ulfgard and fortify it," Osthart said.

"That is truth, my friend," Valfric said with a smile. "Thank you for giving us some wood," he said, and then added, "if you'd like, you could tell me where your camp ends, and I can make sure that I have a couple of dogs that rove around to make sure that nothing happens," he said.

Osthart smiled. "Well, that would be wonderful. Thank you."

Valfric's mind reached out, and one of the dogs came up to him. "Have this man trace your camp with the dog," he said.

"Thank you again," Osthart said.

They stood and clasped hands, and Valfric walked back to his camp. It was already set up by the time he got there. He stretched his arms above his head. "It's good to come home to a house that's already set up."

Ilara looked over at him and glared. "Yes, funny how you make it back as soon as everything in camp is set," she said.

"It is a mystery, isn't it?" Valfric said. "Hmm, can't figure it out though."

She chuckled. "Everything alright with the neighbors?" she asked.

He nodded. "Yes, I think they'll be fine."

"Good," she said and looked around.

"You look like you're in a better mood," he said.

She shrugged. "I don't know, I guess it's the knowledge that we're not going to lose," she said.

He raised an eyebrow. "Did you think we were going to?"

"After I saw Hroldenfell," she said flatly. "You can't tell me that you didn't think it too."

He sighed. "No, you're right, but what has changed your mind?" he asked.

She gestured around. "Look at this, just in this group right here, there has

to be what? Thousands of people, men and women, that are all capable of fighting," she said, "and you told me that your hawks saw many, many more."

"It's more people than I've ever seen," he admitted.

"More than there are in the legions?" she asked.

He thought for a moment. "Yes, actually, probably a lot more."

She smiled. "Exactly. They may have been able to overwhelm Hroldenfell,
but that's not going to be the case for this group, and once we make it to
Ulfgard," she said with a smile, "well, I just think this war is about to change
directions."

He felt himself smile. It was good to see her happy and confident. He
nodded and looked around. Seeing the seas of people, he felt his confidence go
up. "I think you're right. Even if all these people are only half the soldiers that
Lysandrians have—which I know is not true because they're all Gwenthari—I
dare say if Lysandrian comes to attack us, they're going to be very sorry that
they did."

CHAPTER 9

Xavieno trudged toward his tent, his steps weighted by the long day. His feet and hands were sore from working, but the bridge was done. He parted the tent flaps and poked his head inside.

"Where's my love?" he said. Walking in, he saw Fioralba sitting on the cot. She was looking down, her hands in her lap. He could see tears running down her cheeks. He instantly felt concern rise, and he went and sat next to her, putting his arm around her. "What's wrong?" he asked. "Is it the baby?" He said, unsure if she would know anything about the child yet.

She looked over at him, her eyes puffy. "Yes... no," she said.

He was confused. "Um, yes or no?" he asked.

She looked back down at her lap. "I think the baby's fine. I'm still having problems with my powers," she said.

His concern deepened. "I thought you weren't going to be using them, other than the bare minimum."

"That's all I have been doing," she protested. "But I can't even do that!" She huffed.

He looked at the ground and noticed it. There was a basin sitting at the base of her feet. Normally, whenever they bathed, they would create brass basins full of warm water that they would use to wipe themselves down with. He could see that it was supposed to be a basin, and probably that it was supposed to be brass. But it didn't look that way. The metal was discolored, and there were holes in it. He picked it up, feeling how off it was. The weight was strange, and the metal didn't feel right to him. It was a very un-Fioralba thing to have happen. His wife was a master at creating materials, far better than he was.

He sighed and placed his hand on her knee. "I'm sorry, my love."

She huffed and wiped at her eyes. "It's okay. I know this is part of it. It's just so frustrating. You get used to your abilities, you know? It's just a part of you, and something that you do, and all of a sudden, it's gone and not doing anything. I know I just have to do things the way everybody else does, but I don't like it, and I spent an hour on that stupid basin."

He cocked his head to the side. Part of him wanted to remind her that she shouldn't be using her Essaeris that much, that it could be bad for her or the baby, but he thought maybe this wasn't the time to say that. So instead, he gave her leg a slight squeeze with his hand and created a basin of his own with warm water.

"Then I will create them for you," he said. "That's only for a few months, and I get that coming from me, who still has their powers to use, that may not sound fair or right, but at least we're in it together."

"Thank you," she said. "And no, it doesn't sound fair, but I also know you can't help it." She smiled softly and sighed. "A few months, provided it lasts that long," she said darkly.

He felt a pit in his gut. "It will happen this time," he said. "I just know it." And he did; there was something deep down inside of him that said Fioralba was going to bring this baby into the world, but he could understand her concerns.

He gave her another squeeze. "I'll be with you the whole time," he said.

But he knew that wasn't entirely true. They were extremely busy. She glanced over at him.

"You'll be in combat," she said. "You know now that we're about to cross the bridge. The days of just marching are going to come to an end, and even if they don't..." she sighed.

It was true. Being pregnant on the road wasn't ideal, but they weren't exactly close to the Empire anymore. But, they did have Caelwen, which was saying something. She had proven to be one of the best healers in the Legion, though her background wasn't anything like that of the Lysandrians. Still, she was sought after, and Xavieno knew she had delivered babies.

"We have Caelwen," he said.

This seemed to make Fioralba feel a little bit better. "We do have Caelwen; that does count for something," she said and smiled. "But I don't know about being on the road for the whole pregnancy." She shook her head.

He hated to say it, or to think it. "Well, perhaps if there is a permanent fort that's settled, soon you could stay there for the remainder of the pregnancy," he offered.

She looked over at him. "Doubtful. How likely do you think that is? And do you think that would be better than being in a camp?" she said.

He shook his head. "No, I know it wouldn't. Forts have more structure, but that's it. It might be less stressful than being on the road," he sighed. "It would be better if you were home," he said, hating the words.

She leaned against him. "And after I deliver?" she said, letting it hang there.

He felt that pit forming in his gut again. That was the real question, wasn't it? Having a baby in a war camp. It didn't seem like the place to raise a child. It was fraught with danger, and there was constant movement. No, this place was not a place for an infant. He glanced over at her, doing the math in his head. They had just found out that she was pregnant.

Essaerists tended to figure it out sooner than regular women because their powers began to fluctuate. That meant that Fioralba had plenty of time to make it home before the pregnancy got difficult. And then, she would be at their home with their families and friends to help. He thought of their friend Biankara and what she would do with Fioralba if she were around. He smiled.

Biankara would not only go to the ends of the world to make sure that the baby was safe and well cared for, but she would keep Fioralba from doing anything at all.

"What you really need is Biankara," he said.

She laughed. "I don't know if that sounds wonderful or horrible. Gods, could you imagine how much she would mother me and boss me around?" she said with a smile, though it looked like Fioralba didn't mind the thought of it.

"And how spoiled would the baby be?" he said.

Fioralba laughed again. "It would be ridiculous." She sighed and looked at her husband.

He felt sad but calm. This was right. Her eyes filled with tears. "It won't be long. Please tell me you won't be gone long," she said.

He sighed. "I still have some time left in the Legion, but that doesn't mean this war will keep going forever," he said, feeling his heart drop and his own eyes fill up. "I'm going to miss you so much," he said, his voice breaking.

She nodded. "I'm going to miss you, too." Her voice was shaky and ragged. "This is the right decision, though," she said.

"It is," he echoed, "even if I hate it."

She took in a shaky breath. "You're going to have to take care of yourself without me," she said.

He smiled. "I think I can manage it."

She laughed. "I'm not sure about that," she said. "But Caelwen can manage you. She's managing Mariokos alright," she said.

Xavieno smiled. "I'll still have them."

Fioralba was thoughtful for a bit. "You need to get an attendant," she said after a few minutes. Or it felt like minutes, but it had probably only been seconds.

He was confused. "A what?"

She looked at him. "You need an attendant. You're an Aristolios."

He scoffed. "Mariokos came out here without one. And I don't have one now."

"You don't because you have a wife. And Mariokos came out here without one because Biankara changed her mind at the last minute. But he's never been married. You have been. And you have a kid on the way." She sighed. "While it seems stupid, this is the role that we play. Biankara has driven that into my head." She said, "Atheonis, if I came home and told her that I didn't insist that you had one..." She shook her head.

He smiled. "So because you're worried about getting some grief from Biankara, I have to get an attendant?"

She smiled. "Not just that." She looked down. "You know how you are. You need somebody."

He looked down at his lap and sighed. "I'll be fine. I have Mariokos and Caelwen to talk to. And if I have any other things that I need, there are plenty of prostitutes in the camp," he said. And it was true. There were roving brothels that came with them.

She looked at him. "You know those aren't safe."

"Lots of men use them," he said. "They're very popular before a battle."

She chuckled. "Yes, I know, and I know it's part of being a Lysandrian man, but you're an Aristolios," she said, putting weight on the word.

He sighed. "I'm an Aristolios," he said, and it was true.

The prostitutes in the camps were not always safe. Diseases did happen, and he didn't like the thought of catching one of those and bringing it home to Fioralba.

She leaned against him. "It doesn't have to be all bad. You could pick a woman or a man. Whatever you want," she said.

He smiled. "I'll keep that in mind." Then after a moment, "Do you have a preference?"

She shrugged. "Not particularly, but it should be someone who's able to take care of you as well. They tend to your belongings, but it doesn't matter. It's whatever you want. They're your attendant, and I dare say the moment I get home, Biankara is going to make me get one anyway, so there's that," she said.

He chuckled. "And what are you going to get?"

She shook her head. "I don't know, and I'm not thinking about that right now, but it's something that you'll need to do once I leave. Promise me," she said.

He sighed. "Fine. I'll get one."

It wasn't a question of money; they had plenty of that. Xavieno was paid well through the Legion, and they hadn't spent anything. Also, with some of his accomplishments, he could easily ask to be awarded a slave after they took an area. It wasn't uncommon for Aristolios to do so, as opposed to receiving the regular bonus that they might get after a battle.

After a moment of thought, he decided that's what he would do. He would take one of those people, not one of the ones that the Legion already had. He decided to change the subject.

"When are you going to leave?" he asked.

"I suppose I should leave tomorrow, shouldn't I?" she said. "After all, tomorrow the Legion's crossing the bridge, and then you'll be on the other side of the Ilfrun. I don't see the point in going back across it again in a few days. There are some merchant caravans that are leaving. I'll join them," she said.

He nodded. "So soon," he whispered. "Not that I disagree with the choice. It's the right choice to make. It's the smart thing to do. Now is the perfect time for it," he sighed.

He leaned over and kissed the top of her head. "But at least we have tonight," he said.

She smiled. "We have tonight. And we have tomorrow morning until I have to leave," she said.

He leaned his head down and kissed her softly. "Yes, we have that. And I'm not letting you out of my arms until then," he said.

She smiled. "Good."

———

MARIOKOS WAS THE DEFINITION OF COMFORT. AS HE LAY ON HIS BACK, CAELWEN CURLED up next to him, her head on his chest, fast asleep. He felt himself stir and opened his eyes. It was still dim in the tent, so it couldn't have been too far into the morning. As his eyes opened, they were met with another set of eyes, eyes that were very close. They were black and beady, on a face that presently had bluish fur.

Treftune's gaze was intent, and his large ears swiveled around. It wasn't the most welcoming way to wake up. Treftune instantly noticed that Mariokos was awake, and he moved just a little bit, just an excited shuffle. *Fuck*, Mariokos thought. There would be no going back to sleep now.

Once Treftune noticed that one of them was awake, it was over. Mariokos thought it was rather hypocritical of Caelwen to get mad at the Legion for waking everyone up when this furry little shit did it plenty of the time. He tried closing his eyes, and Treftune simply chirped. He sighed and whispered, "You're going to wake her up." He said, "We know that's not a good thing."

Treftune chirped again, and Mariokos stroked the creature's head between his ears. He closed his eyes and hummed in contentment. "I don't see why you get to relax," he said softly. He felt Caelwen stir in his arms. *Fuck*, he thought.

They both held very still. Caelwen sighed and seemed to go back to sleep. He breathed out a sigh of relief and eyed Treftune. Treftune didn't look very apologetic and just stared back at him. Mariokos went back to petting the Valfglidea and tried to close his eyes.

He was almost back asleep when the morning horn sounded. Caelwen shifted next to him, grumbled softly, and then yawned.

"Good morning," he said.

Treftune chirped at her, and she reached up, petting him.

"Good morning," she said.

With a sigh, she looked up at Treftune and smiled. "How are you today?" she said, scratching behind his ears.

"You never seem that happy in the morning to see me," he said.

She looked over at him and grinned. "Oh, I'm sorry. Do you need a little attention this morning?" she said.

He smirked. "The horn already sounded," he said.

She smiled devilishly. "We can be quick," she said. "And I know that Lysandrian men have needs." Her tone was almost mocking.

He chuckled, and she moved, straddling him. "You do have needs, don't you?" A smile played at the corners of her mouth, and he felt his heart do a little flip. Outside, the horn sounded again.

"But the—" he was cut off as she ground her hips down against him in the most delightful of ways.

"The what?" she said in his ear, kissing his neck. "I didn't hear what you were about to say."

He was fully awake now and felt his arousal building; his hands went to her hips. "I suppose we do have a little time..."

She nibbled his ear and then sat up. "There's no reason to risk it," she said and tried to get up.

He barked a laugh. "Oh no, you aren't doing that again."

He rolled her onto her back, making her laugh and causing Treftune to jump off them with an annoyed chitter.

———

MARIOKOS CREATED A TUNIC AND STEPPED OUTSIDE OF HIS TENT. HE WAS RUNNING behind for the morning, but he was okay with it. Caelwen was behind him. She had created a dress and was pulling her hair back, tying it behind her head. The camp was in full swing, and they made their way to where their squad usually had breakfast, but Mariokos saw Fioralba and Xavieno.

Mariokos and Caelwen walked up to them. "Morning," he said. "Is everything alright?" he asked. They both looked sad. He instantly felt fear. "Is there something wrong with the baby?"

Caelwen came up to Fioralba, looking at her intently. "Is there?" she asked.

Fioralba shook her head. "No, I'm fine, I'm fine. We just..." Fioralba looked down.

"Fioralba's leaving the camp," Xavieno said.

Mariokos felt like he just had some water thrown in his face. "She's what?"

"I'm leaving, Mariokos," Fioralba said sadly. "It just doesn't seem like a good idea to be pregnant on the road. I can get home in a couple of months and have the baby there. Plus, a baby in the war camp..." she said.

"But we..." Mariokos started.

He was surprised when Caelwen spoke. "That's a good idea."

Fioralba looked over at Caelwen. "I'm glad you agree."

Caelwen shrugged. "I'm going to miss you a lot, but it's the smart thing to do. If it's difficult for an Essaerist to carry a baby, it doesn't make sense for you to try to do that in a camp, and I certainly don't think this is a place for a baby."

It really wasn't something that Mariokos could argue. He sighed. "Be safe on the road," he said.

He walked up to her and gave Fioralba a hug.

"I will, thank you. I'll be fine. I'm going to leave with some merchants today," she said, "before you cross the river."

That also made sense. This was the time to do it. He looked her over.

"Xavieno, are you going to be okay?" he asked.

Xavieno smiled half-heartedly. "I don't think I'm going to have much of a choice, but it's the right thing to do." He put his arm around Fioralba's shoulders. "Even though I'm going to hate every second of it."

She smiled tightly, not looking like she meant it. Caelwen seemed disappointed to be seeing Fioralba go but was taking it the best. Normally, Mariokos would chalk this up to Caelwen not knowing Fioralba as long as Xavieno and Mariokos had, but he also knew that Fioralba was Caelwen's only actual friend in the Legion, so for her, this would be a very lonely time. But she was also incredibly practical.

There were horns sounding, and Mariokos looked back to Fioralba. "I'm sorry, I have to go. You take care of yourself." He leaned in and kissed her cheek. "I'll see you later," he said to Caelwen.

He went over to his squad. As he approached, Erastos looked up.

"Where the fuck have you been?" he asked.

"Fioralba's leaving the camp. She doesn't think it'll be wise for the baby, for them, for her to stay on the road and to raise a baby here. Xavieno and Caelwen agree," Mariokos said.

The hard expression on Erastos's face softened for a moment. "It's the smart thing to do. I hate the thought of losing an Essaerist, and for Xavieno being alone, but with her being pregnant and not being able to use her powers, we're already short an Essaerist, and she's right. Still, don't be fucking late again," he said, but it didn't have the same heart that it usually did.

Mariokos helped with his squad after breakfast as they tore down the camp and readied themselves to cross the Ilfrun. Before she left, Fioralba came by and said a quick farewell to him and then joined her caravan that was heading back down towards the Empire. He watched her go with a sense of sadness and optimism—sadness that he wouldn't see her again for some time, but optimism about the future.

The legions formed up, and the order came to move out. Mariokos stood next to his squad as they walked up to the bridge and began crossing it. As they crossed, his nose was filled with the scent of moving water and clear air. Below them, the bridge was solid and stable. He smirked, thinking about what Caelwen would think of the whole thing. He was sure she had an opinion on it that she would share later, but for the moment, he enjoyed crossing the bridge that she had deemed insane and felt a sense of pride at it because this bridge would go down in history, and he had been part of it.

CHAPTER 10

Mariokos ate in silence with the rest of his squad and Caelwen, the quiet hum of the camp broken only by the occasional murmured "Dominaro" as men paid their daily tribute to Treftune. The smell of smoke hung heavy in the cool morning air, mixing with the distant clang of sharpening blades and the low murmur of soldiers preparing for the march. The rain over the last few days had mercifully ended, leaving the ground dry and easier to march on, which was handy when you had twenty thousand people walking in a line.

They'd been moving along the Ilfrun River, heading south towards a large group of Gwenthari that were heading north towards Ulfgard. The Gwenthari wouldn't make it. Next to him, Caelwen was thoughtful. He looked over at her.

"Something on your mind?" he asked.

She paused for a moment, then said, "Soon we should be reaching a group of Gwenthari, right?"

"Yes," he confirmed.

Everyone in the squad was paying attention to the conversation. She cocked her head to the side. "What am I to do? When we were at Hroldenfell, it was pretty easy; I just helped a little bit. But with a major battle, what am I supposed to do?"

Erastos spoke. "Lysandrian women don't fight, but you're also an Essaerist, so the rules don't exactly apply to you. What would you like to do?"

She shrugged. "Well, what are you going to be doing?" she asked Mariokos.

"It depends," he said.

"Right, on what? In Hroldenfell, you worked on the siege, but you didn't have any Essaerites go into the city necessarily, not at least as part of the main assault force," she said.

Erastos spoke again. "He will most likely be helping with some sort of bombardment," he said, and then, reading Caelwen's look of confusion, added, "When it comes to major battles, we don't tend to put Essaerists on the front line. It's not that an Essaerist's life is worth more than a normal man's life. It's just that they're harder to replace and that their uses are better spent outside of the line."

Mariokos took up the thread. "When we first met, you saw me with Essaerites that looked like legionnaires. That's fine for patrols, and in a pinch, if the legion is attacked unexpectedly, I'll deploy those same types of Essaerites and fight with the rest of the legion. But like Erastos said, in most major battles, that won't be the case.

"What I will probably be doing will be to create a group of smaller Essaerites that will throw darts, spears, or javelins at the enemy," he said.

"They're fucking effective," Erastos said, giving Mariokos an approving nod. Then he directed his words to Caelwen. "You haven't seen the legion in an open battlefield yet. You've seen a small skirmish here and there, but nothing that we'd consider to be a major engagement. You probably will in the next few days. Generally speaking, the skirmishers will go in first and distract. With those groups will be the Essaerites that Mariokos is talking about. While a human might not always hit somebody with a javelin or a spear, his Essaerites always do," he said.

Mariokos spoke. "Yes, they almost always do, and they can throw far more than any human can at a more regular cadence. Then they will typically fall back behind the first line, where I'll either create more javelins for them, or they'll be supplied javelins or darts by the Legion. These Essaerites jump up above the heads of the men in front of them and throw more objects. It's extremely effective," he said.

"But," Caelwen said.

"But it takes most of my concentration," Mariokos said.

Helioz spoke. "That's where the rest of us come in. We're all part of the third line, the most elite, but what we will do if Mariokos is engaged in this way is our squad will stay back. We will surround him, allowing him to crouch down and focus on his Essaerites, and we will protect him. On the surface, it might seem like a waste, pulling some men away from the line, but it's not. He's far more effective on his own, and it's better to keep him safe. You'll see Xavieno's squad do likewise."

Caelwen smirked. "I'm surprised he's willing to do that."

Erastos shook his head. "Not his choice. If you'd like, you can protect Mariokos, but we will still have men assigned to it. Also, they're mostly there to provide a small shield wall in case there are any spears or arrows that come our way."

Caelwen was thoughtful for a moment. "Would it be possible for me to fight with my brother?"

Mariokos was surprised by this. "You want to fight?" he asked.

She shrugged. "No, I don't, but I also don't want those that I care about going in harm's way while I stand around doing nothing. Not that I don't like the thought of just waiting for you to come home so I can make you dinner," she said with a smirk.

He chuckled. "Wait, if you fight, does that mean I'm gonna have to make my own dinner?" he asked.

She bumped her shoulder against his. "So can I fight with my brother?" she asked.

Mariokos looked over at Erastos, who shrugged. "Not my decision, but I wouldn't see why not. Your cats could be useful, but I dare say you're going to want more than just those cats of yours in the fight."

She nodded in agreement. "No, I wouldn't just have them; I would go in with my Essaerithon as well."

Mariokos knew that the squad hadn't seen her Essaerithon in its full form. Xavieno had, and Erastos had, but the others hadn't.

She went on, "Unless you think that that would be better with the rest of the Legion?"

Erastos thought for a moment. "We'd have to ask command what they want, but my guess will be that they'll want you with your brother. Unless you want to be out in front of the main lines where the other Essaerites that are meant for direct combat will be, which doesn't seem like a very smart or safe decision," he said.

"No, it really doesn't," Mariokos said. "Your Essaerithon can take a beating, but there are limits to it."

She nodded. "There are limits."

"Is it as fast as a horse?" Erastos asked.

She shook her head. "No, not at a full gallop."

"The people from your settlement will be mostly on horseback, guarding our flanks and flanking the enemy, but that doesn't mean they'll be going at a full gallop the whole time. Do you think you could keep up with cavalry?" he asked.

She shrugged. "Well enough. And once I'm there, I know the fight won't be moving quick anyway," she said.

Erastos looked thoughtful. "I'll speak to command and let you know before we set out for the day, but I would say keep your Essaeris in check. You might need it," he thought for a moment. "On that level, you might want to start working on those cats now, just in case."

"Do you think we'll be attacked on the road?" Helioz asked.

"I don't see why not. We've seen a few parties, but it's mostly been the Legion taking them by surprise. But there's no reason to think that the Gwen-thari won't figure out that we're here if they haven't already. And they would be wise to attack us while on the move, once the Legion is formed up," Erastos said, shaking his head.

"Yeah, agreed," Luciakos said.

The horn sounded to begin taking down camp, and everyone got up. Mariokos stood and kissed Caelwen's cheek. "Have a good day," he said.

She smiled tightly. "You too."

He sighed. "It'll be okay," he said.

"Perhaps," she said. "But you're not the only one that I have to worry about. Still, be safe and be smart."

"You too," he said.

———

SWEAT BEADED ON VALFRIC'S SKIN UNDER THE BAKING SUN, BUT THE HEAT FELT ODDLY good. The sun warmed his skin, begging his muscles to relax. As they rode along, on one side of him was Ilara and on the other side, Osthart. He was getting close to Osthart relatively quickly. He liked the man and the way he ran his settlement, and Valfric was pretty sure that when this was all said and done, Valfric and his team would have an invitation to live with the rest of Osthart's people. It was something he fully planned on taking advantage of if the opportunity arose.

Around them were hordes of people, all of them traveling along. To the right was the Ilfrun. It was widening at this point, but not as wide as it would be up north, and it was also fast-moving, making it difficult or impossible to cross, save for a handful of rope bridges that would dangle between two rock faces on either side of the river whenever it narrowed a bit, but nothing that any group could move through, and certainly nothing that could move through with carts or animals.

Next to him, Ilara had her eyes closed with her face tilted up towards the sun. As she smiled, she more than anyone seemed to be happy that the rain had gone.

"Are you having a nice little nap?" Valfric asked.

She chuckled. "No, just enjoying the sun," she said, looking at him.

He grinned. "Hopefully it will be nice for the next few days," he said.

She squinted up at the sky. "I don't see a cloud up there, so I'd say that's a pretty safe bet. It's been a little warm in the evenings though," she mused.

It was the middle of summer now, and that was to be expected. Valfric turned to Osthart. "When this is all said and done, are you going to stay up by Ulfgard?" he asked.

Osthart shrugged. "Maybe; we might go back to our old settlement, though. It's good fields, good lands." Then he said, "We probably wouldn't have had to leave if we had an Essaerist around." He eyed Valfric.

Valfric cocked a smile. "Probably not. Is that an invitation?"

Osthart chuckled. "Maybe it is, maybe it isn't," he said, then sighed. "But I don't know what we'll do. I'm not even sure how much my settlement will stay together, to be honest with you. We'll be so much further north than we were before once we're in Ulfgard, and with all of the shit going on with the

Valfarans." He shrugged. "It's hard to say. Chances are we'll all scatter to the wind, but that's how these things go."

This was true; this was how things went. Communities changed and shifted. They hadn't always, but Valfric knew that it had changed in the last few generations. Up ahead, he saw some dust being kicked up, and he started to hear a commotion.

"What the fuck is it now?" Aelric grumbled next to Ilara.

They were coming out to an area that was flattening out and turning into a field. The river wound around it, creating a bulbous area with some trees and small hills on one side.

"Probably some more people squabbling over where to make camp for the night," Ilara said.

Osthart grunted. "It's only midday; what the fuck is wrong with them?"

Valfric shrugged. "Summer days slow people down."

Osthart grunted again.

"I'll see what it is," Valfric said.

His mind reached out to one of his hawks and had it move up the mass of people until it got to the front of the group, seeing where the commotion was. "Odd," Valfric said. "I don't see..." And he trailed off.

"What is it?" Ilara asked.

"I can't fucking believe it," Valfric said, his tone flat and disbelieving.

"You can't believe what?" Ilara asked.

He came back into his own body and looked over at them. "Lysandrian," he said.

"Lysandrian?" Osthart said.

He looked over at him. "Yes. Lysandrian. The legions, they're here."

Osthart scoffed. "Ahead of us? No, you must be mistaken. It's not a funny joke to play."

Valfric felt the blood draining from his face. He saw it on Ilara, Aelric, and Thraindel's faces as well. They knew that Valfric wasn't lying. The commotion was getting louder. Osthart tensed. "They're here?"

"How many?" Aelric asked.

"I'm looking," Valfric said, feeling his heart begin to pick up.

He felt a pit forming in his gut. "Ulfgara, how is it?" he muttered. "It must be all of them," he said. "I see standards for all four legions." Valfric paused, looking around. "They know we're here. The columns are breaking up. They're forming into ranks," he said, his voice urgent.

He pulled himself back into his body. He could see the concern in everyone's eyes.

"Well, fuck," Osthart said. He began shouting orders to his people.

Valfric turned to his group that had been following him. "Lysandrian is ahead of us. Prepare yourselves," he said.

His team instantly sprang into action. They stopped their horses and took off their packs, grabbing armor and weapons, readying themselves for the fight. Valfric released a couple of his hawks, saving the Essaeris so he could pour it into his wolves. Essaeris crackled through Valfric as he reached out to the dogs, their forms twisting and lengthening under his command. Fur darkened and muscles thickened, nails hardening into claws. The wolves made horses nearby skittish and move around, but they didn't have any time. The enemy was too close.

For his part, Thraindel looked excited now. As he strapped his sword around his waist, he said, "This is going to be a bloodbath."

"Yes, it should be," Valfric agreed.

"We outnumber them by a lot," Aelric grunted.

"We outnumber them two or three to one at least, but probably four or five to one if I'm not mistaken," Valfric said.

That was true; they did greatly outnumber the Lysandrians. Valfric calmed himself. He was only feeling worried and afraid because they'd been taken off guard, but the legions would have been just as taken off guard as the Gwenthari were. That meant that that part was evened out. Neither had the element of surprise. It was going to come down to a numbers game, and Valfric grinned.

Lysandrian did not have the numbers.

Osthart was shouting more orders now, and Valfric turned, seeing him in armor getting up on his horse. Valfric got up on his. All around, people were doing likewise. They may not have been an organized army, but they were a large one, and they were a capable one. And whereas Lysandrian only had the legionaries that actually fought, their support train didn't do anything. That was not the case for the Gwenthari. Every man and woman would be fighting. Yes, the major non-combatants would be in the back, but they would hardly be defenseless. Valfric flashed a fierce smile at his team, excitement boiling up inside him, and turned back to Osthart.

"It looks like we might not have to go to Ulfgard after all," Valfric said.

Osthart grinned. "No, it looks like we won't be."

CHAPTER II

Mariokos heard Erastos and Theoliano barking orders over the general din and commotion of the Legion as they formed up. He was in his full armor, along with every other Legionnaire in the Legion. They'd spotted the Gwenthari, who were amassing in preparation to attack. From the handful of Hawks he had in the area, he could see that the Gwenthari vastly outnumbered the Legions, but that wasn't going to matter because the Gwenthari weren't the Lysandrian Legions.

Mariokos had underestimated their individual skill before leaving his homeland, but he knew that in large-scale battle, it wouldn't matter. The Legions were professional, they were consistent, they were well-drilled, and they had brilliant military minds leading them. The Gwenthari knew they were heading into a slaughter. They were just confused about which side was going to be the ones slaughtered.

Erastos came up to Mariokos. "Projectiles," he said.

Mariokos nodded, understanding. He closed his eyes, feeling his power inside of him bubble and turn. He had been building it up all day in preparation for what was coming. They had known that they were probably going to have him on projectile duty, and as such, he hadn't created any Legionnaires. His power rippled out of him, and around him, small Essaerites came into appearance. They had spindly legs and were shorter than a man, but they had long arms that were powerful and able to sling javelins and darts at speed and accuracy.

Horns sounded, and he opened his eyes, joining the ranks of the third line. They moved into position on one end of a field. His heart hammered in his chest. He wondered what Caelwen was going to do. He suspected that she was already helping her brother, who no doubt would be wrapping around the

Legions to attack the Gwenthari from the north, or at least to keep them
hemmed in to prevent them from being able to flank the Legions.

But one could never tell. After all, from what the Hawks could see, Aquilae
wasn't on the flank. From south to north, it went Gladii, then Aeterna, Aquilae,
and Vindicis took the north. So it was possible that Wulfgren and the people of
his settlement would not be used to flank, as Vindicis had plenty of Gwenthari
mercenaries of their own.

Mariokos cleared this from his mind. It wasn't important. He needed to
focus on what he was doing right here, right now, because he was about to be
part of a very large, very bloody battle. And while he was confident that the
Lysandrians would win, he knew there was a possibility, though small, that
they could lose, that they could be pushed back, that he or Caelwen or Xavieno
or any of those in his squad could be injured or killed today. So he needed to
focus, needed to make sure that didn't happen. And the best way he could do
that would be by focusing on his Essaerites and making sure they took out as
many Gwenthari cavalry as they could, because that would be the first order of
business.

It was obvious from how the Gwenthari were forming up. They'd amassed
into a large group with horses at the front. They had so, so many horses, a stag-
gering number of them, many, many more than the Legions did. But while the
horses were a major threat for the skirmishers, they would be less so for the
first line. The Gwenthari were about to see just how effective the Legion could
be. There was a silence over the men, other than the sound of officers shouting
out orders. This was the Lysandrian way.

In the distance, he heard the general roar and rumble of many thousands of
men and women screaming war cries, trying to intimidate the Lysandrians. It
wouldn't work. More Essaeris rippled out of him, and he created more of the
Essaerites. This time, with them, he also created javelins. Each one of them had
ten. He had fifteen Essaerites in total.

He looked to Erastos. "Horses?" he asked.

Erastos nodded grimly. It was a simple enough task. The Gwenthari would
charge. Their cavalry would be coming first, in hopes of breaking the Lysandrian lines, scattering the Legions, and cutting down as many as they could.
For the skirmishers, this could prove to be a problem, and they would likely run
behind the first line before the cavalry could arrive. But what the Gwenthari
were not taking into account was that besides the skirmishers, every single
Legionnaire had a javelin that was just for the purpose of throwing. There
would be thousands of javelins coming at their cavalry, but more than that,
there would be Mariokos's coming at them.

He would focus, and he would target specific animals, dropping them,
sending their riders sprawling and sending other horses scattering or tripping
over them. The Gwenthari charge would lose momentum long before reaching
the skirmishers. And then, once it got closer, the first line would begin their

assault, and they would turn into a solid shield wall after their initial javelins were thrown.

Pikes would be held out, multiple men holding them, keeping them in the ground, making for a deadly wall for the horses to slam into. Then it would be a ground fight. The Gwenthari would be there, their ground forces running up, ready to die, and they would experience the slow, unstoppable movement forward of the Legions.

The command came. In the distance, Mariokos saw the horses of the Gwenthari charge forward. Erastos barked an order, and Mariokos knelt down as Luciakos, Helioz, and Erastos moved in front and beside him, holding up their shields. Others from the squad did likewise, encasing Mariokos in his own protective world.

The Gwenthari were barreling forward, and he sent his Essaerites out with the skirmishers. They weren't moving far away from the first line. They would be there just far enough ahead to be able to throw a few javelins and then run behind the first line. The skirmishers would be useful once the Gwenthari infantry arrived. The horses got closer and closer, the men and women atop them yelling and screaming. Some of his Essaerites caught the form of Xavieno's advanced Essaerites.

Their white granite skin shone in the hot midday sun. Their four arms, each holding javelins or swords or shields, waiting, ever waiting. Lysandrian did not generally charge forward. They didn't need to. The enemy would come to them. As they got closer, Mariokos saw some of the skirmishers throw their javelins. They would miss. They would fall short. And the men came running back towards the first line.

He didn't blame them. After all, they were risking their lives being in front of the Legion. Mariokos was not. As the Gwenthari came closer, he gave the command, and his Essaerites hurled javelins at the oncoming cavalry. Before the javelins had even crossed half the distance of the space, the Essaerites were preparing their next volley. By the time the first hit, the second volley was already on its way, and the third was being prepared.

Mariokos watched as javelins flew and buried themselves deep in the chests of horses. The animals screamed and fell, rolling onto the ground. He saw one man's horse roll on top of him. There was general pandemonium as the horses piled up on each other. Others dodged around, the Gwenthari being very capable riders. More of his Essaerites threw. One volley. Then another volley. And then another. Soon he had them falling back, running behind the first line with everyone else. He could hear the Gwenthari with his own ears. He heard them screaming. He heard the hooves of their horses as they came, but still, he kept his eyes closed, his breathing steady.

His mind flicked out, his power building as he created more darts and javelins. His Essaerites jumped above that of the first line as the cavalry hit. As they did, the Essaerites jumped and threw their deadly payload at the riders, killing more and more people.

———

VALFRIC SAT ON TOP OF HIS HORSE AT THE FOREFRONT OF THE GWENTHARI HORDE. ON either side of him were Ilara, Thraindel, and then Aelric on the other side of Thraindel. The other side of Ilara was Osthart and his settlement. Valfric looked over at him and smiled. The older man grinned. Ilara looked on edge, the way she always did before a fight. Keyed in, ready to go, ready for blood. Thraindel looked like he was about ready to explode with excitement. He could see it in the man's eyes. He lived for this.

Aelric looked the most controlled and calm. His eyes narrowed as he looked at the Lysandrian lines ahead of them. The Legions were almost nearly formed up now, as were the Gwenthari.

"Soon," Valfric said.

Thraindel grinned. "Not soon enough," he said. "I can't wait to work my way through the Legion," he grinned.

Valfric felt his own excitement. "Today will be a day," he said. Ilara nodded, as did Osthart. Valfric felt pride inside of himself. "Today will be the day that our people remember what they are and who they are!"

"That they will," Aelric said.

"Today will be the day that we avenge Hroldenfell!" Valfric said, his voice cold and harsh, thinking of all those that they had known and lost in the city when it had been taken. Yes, he was going to enjoy himself. He was going to relish this, as was every other Gwenthari here. Today, the Lysandrians would find out their place in the world. Lysandrian had seemed to have forgotten it, but they would remind them.

Their army wasn't so much an army as a horde. There were no commanders other than those who led their own settlements. So Valfric didn't know who gave the order to charge. Maybe it was no one; maybe it was just a general feel, but all of a sudden, they all began to move forward. He spurred the horse he was on forward, but he kept his wolves even with the horses. There was no need for them to go out and be killed before the main army even made it there.

He felt his horse pick up speed, chugging along, its flanks expanding and contracting with its breath. Valfric leaned over the animal's neck, bringing himself close to it as it ran faster and faster. The cavalry was separating out from each other, giving a little bit of room on either side. Valfric pulled forward, moving next to Osthart. He looked dead ahead, seeing lines and lines of Lysandrians. They had a shield wall. In front of that shield wall were groups of men that were running around. Some of them were throwing javelins.

Valfric laughed. They wouldn't even make it to them. He did see something ahead that looked different. Men, but not men. They were spindly. He saw them rear back and throw javelins. His eyes widened for a moment as he realized what it was. "Fuck," he yelled. He saw them in the air as little dots on the horizon. And then a second later, his horse screamed as a javelin hit its chest.

Valfric held on tight but felt himself being flung from the saddle as the animal pitched forward and rolled. He saw the ground fast approach him, and he was whipped around. He hit and felt something pop inside of his back. He screamed in pain and then felt the crushing weight of the horse as it rolled. There was more pain. It exploded in his head and his arms and sides and legs.

His mind was fuzzy, and the world swam before him. Everything was blue, and he realized he was looking up at the sky. Pain ripped through his entire body, and he groaned with it. His horse was on top of him, pinning his leg down. He tried to move and instantly screamed, feeling pain in his back. It was like he was being ripped in half. He panted and gasped. He looked around, seeing the cavalry meeting the Lysandrian lines.

More javelins were in the air. Next to him, Osthart was standing up, his own horse dead with a javelin. Valfric reached out with his mind, feeling one of his wolves. The animal darted and jumped up. Osthart's eyes widened, wondering what was happening, and then the animal was hit by a javelin that should have hit Osthart. It rolled on the ground and shook the javelin free. Osthart stumbled away and came over towards Valfric.

"You saved my life," Osthart said.

"Get me up," he grunted.

Osthart's head twisted to the side as they heard a general roar of people. The infantry was here. People came running past, holding shields and swords and axes. They clashed with the Lysandrian lines. Osthart worked, trying to free Valfric.

"Wait here," he said, "we have to push them back."

Valfric felt pain scream through him. He gasped. He tried to turn his attention to his Essaerites, but it was so difficult. The pain was clouding his mind. He could only catch flashes of what was going on. They were near the shield wall, watching as Gwenthari and Lysandrians clashed.

His heart pounded in his chest, though he didn't know if it was from the pain or from the horror of what he was seeing. The Gwenthari were supposed to win. This was supposed to be an easy victory, but that wasn't the case. They were hitting up against the shield wall, and the Lysandrians just pushed them back. Swords and spears came out, cutting people down. And then the Lysandrians would move forward just a little bit. And then the process would happen again, and again. The wall was coming closer to Valfric.

He struggled underneath the horse. One of his wolves was by Osthart. The man was on the ground, having been knocked over. A Lysandrian soldier came to cut him down, and the wolf leaped on the man, grabbing his arm, whipping him around, and allowing Osthart to get up and move out of the way. Where was Ilara, Aelric, and Thraindel? Valfric wondered, his mind racing. As if the thought had conjured them, Ilara and Aelric came bursting out of the fray. Both were covered in blood. Ilara looked like she had hit her head. They came up to him.

"Are you okay?" Ilara asked.

"No," Valfric grunted. "What's going on? Where's Thraindel?"

He saw an expression of horror wash across Ilara's face and Aelric's face harden. "He's gone," he said simply. "Ilara, we need to get this horse off of him!"

"What do you mean he's gone?" Valfric said, and then he screamed as they pushed the horse. Aelric pulled on Valfric's leg, freeing him. Pain shot through him as they tried to help him up. "I can't walk," he said, gasping in pain. "What do you mean he's gone?"

"He's gone," Ilara said, her voice hard. "He's dead."

"What?" Valfric said, in disbelief.

For a moment, the pain seemed to vanish. They had him on his feet and were dragging him back from the front line.

"We need to get back," Aelric said. "We need to get away from the front."

This wasn't possible. Valfric's mind reeled. "What do you mean Thraindel is dead?"

Ilara's voice was thick from effort and emotion. "I mean he's dead. I watched a Lysandrian cut him down."

Aelric took over, "stabbed him right through his chest with a sword," he said, his voice strained. "We need to get back from this. We need to get away from the main fight. How are your Essaerites?"

Valfric tried to clear his mind, but it was so difficult with the pain. Where were his Essaerites? Several of them were down, but he still had one left. "I have one," he gasped.

"Good. Keep it near," Aelric said.

He motioned with his mind, and it fell back. As it moved, it saw Osthart coming along. He appeared to have been injured, but not bad enough that he couldn't walk. The wolf bumped into Osthart and moved its head so that Osthart would follow it. "I found Osthart," Valfric said.

———

CAELWEN FELT SOMETHING HEAVY CRASH INTO HER BACK, SENDING HER SPRAWLING. HER Essaerithon rolled with her inside of it, and she moved out of the way as the horse came down, driving its hooves into the ground. She kicked out at it, pushing it back. She rolled again, getting up.

All around her was a din of commotion and screaming, fighting, and death. The sound of swords hitting each other and horses whinnying and screaming with battle filled her ears even through the helmet of the Essaerite. She swung out with her right hand, hitting the horseman who had knocked her over. Out of the corner of her eye, she saw a man coming from her left, also on horseback. She twisted her right hand, turning it into a fist that crashed into the horse's chest, shattering bone and flesh. The man went down.

She lashed out at others around her. Wulfgren was fighting with the rest of her settlement. Men with ropes and hooks were coming, throwing them, trying to get purchase on Caelwen's Essaerithon, trying to control her. She felt them tug on her, but she was so much stronger. Her feet dug in, roots digging into the ground, and she wrenched back, pulling men out of saddles, spilling them onto the ground.

She moved forward. Swinging her arms, the blades on her forearms cutting through people as she went, she pulled forward into a group of men and women on foot. She sent them sprawling and sailing in a wave of death and destruction. Behind her, her settlement surged forward, joining her.

———

ONE OF XAVIENO'S ESSAERITE'S FEET SLIPPED ON THE GROUND, BUT IT CAUGHT ITSELF. He had it so the ears weren't hearing as well as they normally did; the din of the battle had been distracting. The Essaerite's upper left hand held a sword that it used to cut a woman's skull in half. As the blade hit, it sent blood and bone flying, spattering her horrified companions. They tried to back away from the Essaerite, but they were being pressed forward by the Gwenthari behind them.

Xavieno moved into one of the other Essaerites who was likewise engaged. It too found its footing to be weak, though it was fairing better than the humans around it. Their little section of the line had come to a halt with neither side pressing forward. It was making for a mass of corpses on the ground, and as the blood drained from the dead, it was turning the dirt and grass into slippery mud. The once pristine white of the Essaerite was covered in mud and gore, but it paid it no mind as it moved forward with its deadly work.

A youth came charging at it, his face a mask of determination. The Essaerite kicked him in the chest, knocking him over. The boy tried to roll to get up but was stopped by a spear in his gut. Xavieno didn't hold his attention on the scene to see if the boy was alive or dead. Instead, the Essaerite ripped out the spear and swung it, smashing another enemy in the face. The Gwenthari tried to back away, and the line began to move forward.

———

CAELWEN WAS BREATHING HARD DESPITE THE FACT THAT IT WAS HER ESSAERITHON DOING all the work. She felt a drain on her power. All of her creations had needed significant healing, but the battle was winding down. Two of her cats were pulling on a man, ripping him apart when the order to stop the advance came. Before her, the Gwenthari were retreating, and it didn't appear the Legions were going to give chase.

Once they were a good distance away, she opened her helmet. Instantly, her senses were assaulted with the afternoon's work. The scent of blood, death, and shit coiled its way up her nostrils, but she didn't lower her helmet. Wulf-gren rode up next to her, his face a mask of a man who had no feelings. He looked numb and desensitized to the horrors around them. She was sure she looked the same. He looked over at her.

"You good?" he asked.

"Yes. You?" she asked.

He nodded, "I am. We didn't lose anyone from the settlement today," he said.

That was good. That was why she was here, wasn't it? To protect those she loved. She turned her attention back out to the killing field. People were scattered around on the ground, dying and groaning in pain. With a flick of her mind, she sent her cats to find those that wouldn't make it and give them a quick end.

———

VALFRIC GRITTED HIS TEETH IN PAIN. THE SOUNDS OF FIGHTING WERE GONE NOW, replaced by the moans and groans of the wounded and dying. Aelric was tending to a minor wound, and Ilara was looking into the fire. Osthart was with them. Many of the people in his settlement had been killed.

The man looked back at him. "You've saved my life a few times today," he said grimly.

"You're welcome," Valfric said.

He tried to reach out to his power. He had one wolf left, and he might have had enough energy to create another one if he could just focus. But focus was so difficult right now. Every time he tried to use his Essaeris, it slipped through his fingers, like when he was a kid. It was the pain he knew. He tried to calm his breathing and his mind to create another one. His Essaeris fizzled and popped, but he wasn't able to focus enough to create the Essaerite, and it just appeared as a furry lump next to him.

"Rest," Ilara said. "You need to rest. You're going to need it."

How had the day gone so wrong? How had it all turned out so badly? He couldn't rest. There was no way he could sleep. He might pass out in a while, but rest? That wasn't going to be something he could do.

"Where are the Lysandrians?" he asked.

Osthart answered, "They're building camps, of course."

Ilara's eyes widened a bit. "They're building camps? Like with walls and everything?"

Osthart nodded grimly. "Yes, just like it was any other day," he said, looking at the fire.

"I wondered why they weren't attacking," Aelric said. "I guess it makes sense. They're building a camp so they can deal with us in the morning."

And deal with them they would. To their back was the Ilfrun River. To their front were the Lysandrians. There would be no getting past them. They had them up against a natural barrier. Valfric knew that there were groups of people that were making their way across the one rope bridge that crossed the Ilfrun at this point, but there were tens of thousands of Gwenthari that were here. It wouldn't be possible for everyone to make it across.

Valfric moved up onto his elbows. "We need to get people out," he said, "and we need to hold off the Lysandrians as long as we can."

Victory wasn't something that they were going to get. He knew that now. He had been so foolish to think that it was. They had started the day overconfident with the assumption that they would win, but they hadn't. There had been a few breaks in the Lysandrian lines, but those breaks had been few and far between. Instead, it had just been Gwenthari being killed.

Valfric had never seen or thought anything like it possible, even after witnessing what happened at Hroldenfell. This was somehow so much worse, and he knew it would be even worse tomorrow. He looked over at Ilara. She was looking at the fire, her face blank. He reached out and put his hand on her leg.

"What are you thinking?" he said.

She glanced at him and then back at the fire. "Just thinking about tomorrow," she said, "and thinking about Thraindel."

He still couldn't believe that Thraindel was gone, that he'd fallen in battle, and that Valfric hadn't even been there to see it or to help. He'd been lying under a horse, screaming and moaning in pain. *Pathetic*, he thought.

"I never thought you were afraid to die," Valfric said, trying to bring a little levity to the situation.

She looked at him. "I'm not afraid of dying. I'm afraid of what will happen to these people," she said. And then more softly, "and what will happen to me if I live."

"What do you mean?" Valfric said.

"You know what she means," Aelric said. "You know what will happen. The same thing that happens every time we win," he said.

Valfric didn't want to think about that. No. Ilara, Aelric, Valfric, and Osthart, they would make it out. They would survive, and they would not be taken prisoner by the Lysandrians.

"We can get out," he said, and grimaced as he tried to move. "We can fight them."

Ilara looked at him. "You aren't fighting anybody." She looked over at Osthart. "Neither are you. You're hurt too badly," she said.

Osthart grunted. "I know. Those of my settlement who aren't injured are going to stay and fight, but the rest of us, we're heading across the river if we can tonight. We're close enough to that bridge. On that note. Valfric, is there anything you can do to help?"

Valfric thought. "I can't make rope, not enough to cross that river, but I might be able to help in some ways. I'm not sure. What do you need?"

"We need to make more bridges," Osthart said. "Perhaps some Essaerites could help us. They could swim across the river, carry a rope, anything," he said.

Valfric thought, and then nodded. "I think I might be able to create something. Something that could swim across the river with a rope, then climb up the other side."

The rope bridge was atop a small stone cliff. On the other side of the embankment, there was one that was similar to it. If they could get a rope across, they could build another bridge. He focused on his Essaeris, feeling it sputter and pop, but he was able to create a basic Essaerite. It moved off with Osthart to go try to create something.

He turned his attention back to Ilara and Aelric. "Are you going to stay, fight, and die? Or are we leaving?" he asked.

Aelric looked at him again. "You are leaving. You're too hurt."

"I'm not leaving you two here to die," Valfric said.

"And you won't be," Ilara said. "You're going to be able to use your Essaerites from across that river, but we can't risk having to move you. You know what the pain will do to you," she said.

He felt pathetic and humiliated. He was going to be treated like some common invalid because if he felt any pain, he might not be as effective of an Essaerist. "I'm sorry," he said after a moment.

Aelric shook his head. "For what? You saved people today, and you still killed more people than most did. No, what happened was just what happens in battle. Tomorrow, we will hold the Lysandrians as long as we can, and we will join the last groups crossing the bridge. Or, we might be able to make it if we swim across the river."

Ilara looked skeptical. "The current's too fast. It'll pull you under and drown you."

Aelric shrugged. "Maybe. Maybe not. But either way, this is how it needs to be."

Valfric felt himself slipping out of consciousness, and he tried to keep himself awake. Ilara chided him, "Sleep. You need as much as you can. We're going to need you more tomorrow than we ever have," she said.

So he let his eyes close. If it was for a minute or for an hour, he didn't know, but when he woke again, the pain had subsided a little bit, but still radiated from his back.

Osthart was back. "It's time to get you moving," he said.

"Time to what?" Valfric said.

"We're getting you across the river tonight," Aelric said. "Your Essaerite was able to help create a couple more bridges. People are using them, but we need to get you on the other side, so that way you can rest up and be ready for tomorrow."

"You don't need to move me," he groaned.

Osthart started to picked up Valfric underneath his arms.

"Eira," Osthart grumbled.

Valfric saw a girl come running up. She grabbed Valfric's feet, picking them up. She had deep auburn hair and green eyes. She looked like she could have been in her early twenties or late teens. She muttered something.

"Idiot girl," Osthart said.

Valfric groaned as they picked him up. They began shuffling towards the bridge.

"You don't have to," he said.

"Shut it," Aelric said. "Don't make this more difficult than it needs to be."

Valfric sighed. And they continued to move. As they got to the bridge, Aelric said, "I'll carry him," to Osthart.

Valfric tried not to wince and groan as Aelric began carrying him across the rope bridge. It was tedious work and took a while. There were many people around them, and with each movement, Valfric was sure that he was going to be let loose and fall into the rushing river below. His mind swam with the pain, but soon enough he felt cold ground underneath him.

He panted and looked up at Aelric, Ilara, Osthart, and the slave girl, Eira. Her eyes were darting around, and she looked afraid.

Ilara huffed. "It'll be light soon. We need to get back," she said. Aelric nodded. Ilara looked down at him. "Be safe. Do you have Essaerites over there?"

Valfric nodded. "Yes. I have one wolf, and I'll have another one created shortly," he said.

"That'll do," Aelric said, "or it'll have to do. Osthart, take care of him," he said.

Osthart nodded. "I will." He looked over at Eira. "Tend to whatever he needs, understand, girl?"

She nodded quickly.

Valfric felt his shame rising, and he tried to hold it together as his friends left him. He laid there on the ground, feeling pain radiate from him, in the back of his mind, realizing that he wasn't going to see Aelric or Ilara ever again, and he'd already seen Thraindel for the last time. He just hadn't known when it was going to happen, and coloring it all was the deep and abiding feeling that this was all his fault, all of it. Everything was his doing.

CHAPTER 12

Xavieno faced the vast Gwenthari horde, stretching endlessly before him, mirrored by the legions flanking him on either side. He stood next to Mariokos, Kyrillos, and Isolara. The latter was about to move over to where the Emperor was so she could be his protection. The strategy for the day was different from what they had employed the day before. Instead of Mariokos being on projectile duty, he had his Essaerithon. Kyrillos had his as well, and Xavieno had his advanced Essaerites at his disposal.

Also different today was that Caelwen was not going to be going into the fray herself. Xavieno stood next to Kyrillos, behind him Kyrillos' Essaerithon loomed. It was a monstrosity, with four legs and four arms that ended in blades. It was large and terrifying, cutting and slashing through anything that was around it. Its hide was hardened and difficult to pierce. Xavieno had never heard of anything that had been able to take it down before, though he suspected that Caelwen's Essaerithon could pose a significant threat to it.

Mariokos was speaking with his sergeant, but behind him was his Essaerithon. It was different from what it normally was. Typically, Mariokos's Essaerithon had a host of smaller Essaerites with it that worked as supports, clearing out timber or dirt or anything else as the Essaerithon trenched and did whatever else it needed to. Those were gone. Instead, it had a shell covering it.

This was to make it less susceptible to attack. They had learned that while Mariokos's Essaerithon was ideally suited for creating camps, it was also effective in combat, particularly for what they would be facing today. The Gwenthari had overturned many of their carts and other supplies, building makeshift walls and camps around pockets of themselves. While the Legion would make it through those walls in fairly short order, the entire time the Legionnaires would be under attack from the Gwenthari.

This was one of the areas where Mariokos's Essaerithon would come into play. It would be able to break down those walls and create holes in a matter of moments, as opposed to the time it would take the men to clear them out. It was also why it had the shell on it, to protect it from anything coming at it, though Xavieno suspected that the Essaerithon was relatively robust on its own, as it was designed for heavy construction work.

Kyrillos nodded, and Xavieno looked at where he was looking. Caelwen was approaching. She was wearing a dress that had the cut of regular Lysandrian dresses but was far from being one. The dress was deep greens and blacks with swirling designs and runes. It gave her an exotic look and contrasted with her pale skin and fire-red hair. She looked beautiful and terrifying. She was flanked by her Essaerites.

"That woman is far more capable and terrifying than I would have ever given her credit for when I met her," Kyrillos said next to Xavieno.

Isolara echoed the statement. "She really is."

"I saw that Essaerithon you told us about yesterday when we fought," Kyrillos said, smiling. "And you're right; I think it would stand a chance of defeating mine."

He smiled as he watched Caelwen approach, and Isolara spoke, "Yes, Mariokos has most certainly found himself a formidable wife," she said with a smile.

Xavieno chuckled. "You have no idea."

Caelwen had with her five large cats. Xavieno and Mariokos had been helping her refine them, just as they had her Essaerithon. Gone was their fur, replaced instead by metallic and ceramic scales, making them far more hard-wearing. Xavieno had also helped her come up with a few flourishes on the scales and the head to give them a more intimidating look.

As she approached, she didn't look happy, but she didn't look upset either. Her face was set, resolute with what they needed to do.

"Good morning," she said to all of them.

"Good morning," Isolara said. She turned to her husband and kissed his cheek. "It's time for me to go," she said. She looked at Xavieno and Caelwen and nodded. "Best of luck today."

Caelwen came and stood next to Xavieno; they were shortly joined by Mariokos, who had finished his conversation. She smiled softly at him. "So, go over again what we're doing today," Caelwen said.

Mariokos explained, "It's fairly straightforward. To the north, the Gwenthari have a rope bridge crossing the river. They can't move many people with it, so it's not necessarily a threat, but they won't be pushing that direction. If they're able to make it through to the north, they'd just be heading into wide-open fields where we could run them down. Your brother and other Gwenthari mercenaries are in that area for just such an event," he said. "To the south is where we have a possible risk. If they're able to breach the lines to the south, they'll be able to make it into all of that rugged country around here. They'll be a nightmare to flush out, and I dare say we'll be dealing with small parties attacking supply lines and otherwise harassing us. So most of the Legion's forces are going to be around there. That leaves us with the center.

"We can't exactly have a breach in the lines here, and that is where the four of us will come into play," Mariokos said.

Kyrillos took over, pointing out throughout the horde, "You see these bubbles where they've created little mini camps," he said.

Caelwen nodded. "Yes."

"We need to tear those walls down. We need to get through all of that. Mariokos' and my Essaerithons should be able to handle most of those walls. Mine can kill relatively effectively, but Mariokos' cannot. You're going to need to use your Essaerites to protect his while it's around the walls and then otherwise deal with the enemy. Xavieno, you'll be doing likewise with mine, though again, my Essaerithon should be able to handle itself until it's engaged with the wall. On that side, it will not be able to move through the walls as quickly as Mariokos' Essaerite can."

Caelwen nodded solemnly. "Very well, I can do that. Is there anything else?"

Xavieno was thoughtful. "No, I don't think so. The legions will be dealing with a lot of these pockets too, but we should be helping in the center at least. After those areas are done, I suspect we will be taking care of potential breaches or problems in the line, but today is going to be very straightforward," he said grimly.

And it was a grim feeling. Today was going to be a difficult day. Xavieno had learned that the day before. He'd found a thrill in combat, even in Hroldenfell. There had been something about taking the city, but yesterday had been different. They had been massively outnumbered, yet they had won. By all rights, it had been a slaughter, and today would be even more so. And Xavieno wasn't sure how he felt about it.

He knew Mariokos was also conflicted. Mariokos was so much less violent and war-hungry than Xavieno was. Xavieno suspected that Mariokos's Essaerites had killed far more men and women yesterday than his had. It was odd in so many ways. Mariokos was not the warrior in their group. He was not the one who thought of ways to win in battle, yet his Essaerites, which were predominantly designed for construction, or in the case of the ones that threw javelins as support, were the ones that did the most damage to the enemy.

Likewise, he sometimes wondered what this was like for Caelwen. She went along with everything just fine, as did her settlement. They worked without complaint. But it was their people that were being attacked, wasn't it? Yes, these people were Ulfgarath, but they were Gwenthari. Caelwen understood that she was in a war camp, and therefore she acted accordingly. But he didn't think that she enjoyed it.

He had seen her work with her rabbits and otherwise help out the healers of the camp. She was very adept at it and had different techniques and skills than they did. They were learning from her, and she from them. And she was gaining a bit of a reputation for being one of the most competent healers in the Legion. A reputation that Xavieno very much doubted she cared about because why would Caelwen care about something like that?

Horns and orders began to be issued and sounded, and Xavieno pushed his reverie from his mind and focused on what was to come, on the battle that was to happen. He and Kyrillos would be generally moving to the south, staying in the center but moving towards the south as they went. He waited for the order to come. The Gwenthari were ready. They were waiting. Ranks and ranks of them stood ready to charge the Lysandrian lines, though Xavieno noted the distinct lack of cavalry. So much of that had died the day before or was concentrated along the south. The order came, and the Legions began to move forward. But the Essaerists stayed put. They waited. They were not part of the first wave of this attack.

The first line moved behind the skirmishers as they moved to distract and otherwise harass the enemy. Xavieno watched the skirmishers engage with the Gwenthari. It wasn't much of an even match with the skirmish line. The Gwenthari had an advantage, not only in numbers but in skill and technique. So much of the skirmish line was there to be more like brawlers than anything else, something that worked well for the Gwenthari. But soon enough, the first line had slowly made it to the front, and then it began.

Men pressed against each other and against the shield wall that stayed stable for just a little while, and then Xavieno saw it in certain parts. A group of legionnaires would move forward just a little bit, and the Gwenthari would fall back. Then it happened in other spots. Behind the first line, skirmishers threw javelins and darts at the enemy. With the tight-packed battle, most of those javelins and darts found purchase, and the line began to move forward, step by step, moment by moment.

When the time came, the Essaerists moved their Essaerites down near the front. Xavieno was surrounded by his squad, and he kneeled down, allowing his mind to fully merge with that of his Essaerites. On his left was a pod of soldiers around Kyrillos, and to his right, Caelwen and Mariokos kneeled with Mariokos's squad around them. Xavieno moved into his Essaerites. They were coming up on the first of the makeshift walls. It was piled high with carts and debris, with Gwenthari on top of it with bows, arrows, and spears, shooting down on the legionnaires.

For their part, the Legion was using one of the more classic formations that people knew it by. There was the front shield wall, but the men behind those in the front had their shields lifted above their heads, able to cover the heads of those in front of them. It created a bubble of shields that the Legion moved in, making it so that the Gwenthari's arrows and spears largely didn't find purchase on anything other than a shield.

And the Legion moved forward. When they got close enough, the line parted, and Kyrillos's Essaerithon moved. The Gwenthari surged when they saw the opening in the line, but soon were falling back or being torn to pieces. As Kyrillos's Essaerithon advanced, its four-bladed limbs slashed and cut through people; it didn't matter if they were wearing armor or shields or how thick they were, the blades just went right through them. Right behind them, Xavieno's Essaerites came out. They had far more precision than Kyrillos's, but they weren't quite as effective, Xavieno thought.

His Essaerites moved out and began cutting through Gwenthari quickly. People screamed and ran from them, unable to harm them. Out of the corner of one of the Essaerites' eyes, Xavieno saw that Mariokos's Essaerithon had made it to one of the walls. Its bladed teeth were cutting through the wall quickly, chopping up carts and wood. All around it, warriors died as Caelwen's cats pounced on them, ripping them to shreds and tearing their throats and chests open. It was gory, and it was brutal. Xavieno turned back to his killing. Kyrillos's Essaerithon had made it to one of the walls. It began digging its way through.

Xavieno sent one of his Essaerites over the wall, surprising some of the Gwenthari inside. He cut through them quickly, but he paused on the other side of the wall, for on the other side, he saw that the walls were just bubbles, and inside were the elderly and children, along with only a handful of warriors who weren't on the walls to defend. The makeshift barricades came down, and he watched as Kyrillos's Essaerithon moved through the group with deadly efficiency.

People screamed and tried to flee, but there was nowhere to go. There was nothing to be done. His Essaerite registered a hit, and he looked, seeing that while his other Essaerites were engaged, the ones whose eyes he was behind had just been standing there watching the carnage. He released his control over it, and it killed the man who had attacked it. He tried to shake himself and put his focus back on the fight at hand, clearing his mind and doing his job, though he couldn't help but hear the sound of death all around him. After a few moments, he shut off the sound coming from the Essaerites and instead just relied on what their eyes could see, though he wasn't sure if that was much better.

———

PAIN SURGED THROUGH VALFRIC'S BODY, SHARP AND SEARING. HIS JAW LOCKED AS HIS teeth ground together, the taste of copper flooding his mouth. His muscles spasmed, and he fought the urge to cry out, breathing in ragged, shallow gasps. He'd never felt this much pain before in his life, and he wondered how long it would take him to heal. He tried to shift a little bit. He was lying on a board that was being held up by spindly Essaeris legs. His Essaeris sputtered inside of him. He was unable to hold onto it. His mind was too cloudy with the pain, but he had managed the legs for the board, and he had also managed to split the wolf that he had with Aelric and Ilara, so they each had one with them.

They were near the bridge that went across the Ilfrun. They had told Valfric that the plan was relatively straightforward. They would help as long as they could, but if it appeared that the Gwenthari were going to lose or that they were going to lose the bridge, then they would cross the bridge and join Valfric. He still hated himself for not being down there to help them, but it was all that there was to do.

From where he had parked himself, he could see the battlefield on the other side of the river. It was vast, but it was easy to tell where Gwenthari ended and Lysandrian began. He could see pockets where they had piled up carts and any of their belongings to create makeshift walls and fortifications. He thought it was a good idea. It would slow the Lysandrians down and give people the opportunity to cross the bridge or if they were lucky, to make a breakthrough in the south, where people could flee.

As the battle began, he moved himself into the eyes of his wolves. They were standing next to Aelric and Ilara, and he felt his heart thud in his real chest as his friends were in harm's way, and he was lying on a board on the other side of a river. *Pathetic,* he thought to himself. He tried to focus. He needed to keep his wits about him. The action began as the Lysandrians launched their attack. Ilara and Aelric moved forward with the other Gwenthari, engaging the enemy.

As his wolves moved, he was able to see what they were truly up against. A wall of shields was before them. Other men had shields above the lines of the first men, making all of the arrows, rocks, and spears that the Gwenthari were throwing at them all but useless. They bounced off the soldiers, who moved like one giant animal, ever pressing forward. As the Gwenthari got closer to the lines, javelins and darts came out, some striking people, others falling short or missing. Valfric looked for areas where he could gain access to the shield wall and do some damage, but it was difficult. The soldiers didn't move. They also didn't make any sound, save for the commands that their commanders shouted out. His people, on the other hand, screamed and cheered and otherwise did everything they could to be loud and intimidate the enemy.

Valfric realized that it wasn't going to work. These weren't men that you could intimidate. They were professional soldiers, something that his people had largely forgotten how to be. And as memories from the day before set in, he knew how today was going to go, and it made him feel sick.

He moved into the wolf that was near Aelric. Aelric came running at the shield wall, slamming into it. He sent a man sprawling, and almost immediately, Aelric was having to back up as another legionnaire took the man's place. Swords and spears came lashing out at him, and Aelric caught the blows on his shield, lashing out on his own. Valfric had his wolf launch forward at the shield, but it just bounced off and was pushed away. As the wolf came closer again, a spear came out and stabbed it in the shoulder. He had it back away. It was infuriating.

Why wouldn't these men just come out and fight in single combat, like they had some shred of decency and honor? A voice in the back of his head reminded him that he didn't have any decency or honor either. He'd always taken the advantage, always taken the underhanded way. Why would the Lysandrians do anything different?

Aelric surged forward again, clashing with another man. Valfric grinned as Aelric's blade found purchase, and the man fell to the ground. But in the moment that the man fell and Aelric raised his blade for the killing blow, Valfric saw a spearhead moving in Aelric's direction. His wolf launched forward, trying to stop it, but too late. The spear caught Aelric in the gut. The man backed away, grunting in pain. The wolf grabbed the haft of the spear and ripped it out of the soldier's hand, turning and wheeling on him, trying to attack. The wolf registered several hits from shields and blades. It lost a leg and fell back, rolling. He turned to Aelric, ready to pull him away from the fight.

The wolf limped over, grabbing onto Aelric's tunic, pulling. Aelric was writhing and groaning, blood coming out of his gut. "Come on, hang on, hang on," Valfric was saying to himself.

He could get Aelric away. He could get him near the bridge, and someone could carry him across. But then the wolf registered a hit on its hindquarters, and it dropped, its spine broken. It rolled over, looking. The shield wall was there now. The legion had moved forward. Aelric held up his hands, trying to defend himself as blades came down into his chest and abdomen. "No!" Valfric screamed, his mind snapping back to his own body. "No, no, no." He felt agony tear through him as he moved. His back screamed in pain, as did his ribs. But not as much as his mind and heart. He felt hot tears sting his eyes. "No, no, no," he muttered.

He moved into the other wolf's body. It was also hurt. Next to it, he saw Ilara. She was trying to back away, limping. She dropped her sword as a man hit her with his shield, sending her sprawling. Again, Valfric's wolf moved. But it was too hurt. And again, it was pinned down, its leg pierced by a spear. It whipped around to attack the man who had speared it. And in that time, another man came up and stabbed it in the neck. Valfric felt his mind racing and his heart beating. This wasn't happening. This wasn't possible. No, this was not really happening. The wolf's head lolled over, seeing Ilara on the ground, blood coming from her head. She moved a little but seemed to be unconscious as the Lysandrians approached her. And then, the wolf was killed.

Valfric came back into his body and screamed as loud as he could. Next to him, the slave girl, Eira, fidgeted and worried, mumbling something. Osthart came up to him.

"What is it?" he asked.

Valfric just began to cry and scream.

"Is it the pain?" he said. And then, reading the look on Valfric's face, he saw Osthart's face darken. "I'm sorry. I'm so sorry." His voice was thick.

Valfric couldn't believe it. They were gone. They were all gone. Thraindel, Aelric, Ilara. They were gone. They were dead, and it was because of him.

Through the tears and pain, he looked out over the battlefield, except that it wasn't a battlefield. It was a massacre. The Legionnaires pressed forward, and in their wake was a field of bodies, thousands upon thousands of bodies. He was sure it was a figment of his imagination, but he was convinced he could see the river turning red, running crimson with the blood of the slain, but he knew it couldn't be real. Could it?

CHAPTER 13

Xavieno walked with Alessandros and Theoliano next to him, along with a contingent of other Legionnaires. The air stunk. It was the stench of death—not of rotting meat, no, that smell would come—but of blood and, piss and, shit, and the insides of so many animals and people.

It had been one of the most awe-inspiring things he had ever seen. There were so many who had been killed, so many slain. The Legion had suffered casualties, but nowhere near as many as Xavieno would have thought possible. No, it had been very disproportionate. There were Gwenthari who were left alive. They had surrendered or were injured. They would become slaves—indeed, more slaves than had ever been taken in all of Lysandrian history. The wealth accumulated from the day was only eclipsed by the horror of it all.

Underneath his feet, the ground was soggy with blood. He felt it licking up his sandals and onto his feet, legs, and tunic. He wanted to scrub it away, wanted it to be gone. This hadn't been what he'd expected. He'd expected glory. He'd expected excitement. He'd expected to be the good guy. But that had all started to change, hadn't it? It had changed in Hroldenfell, but he had still held on to hope. Now, looking out at the field of death and carnage, he didn't think he could. Bellamara was supposed to shield him from feeling this, wasn't she? After all, war was her will.

Theoliano hadn't said anything—not that Xavieno had expected him to—but he could see the slight disquiet in the other man's expression. Theoliano was battle-hardened and a good commander, but today hadn't been a battle. Alessandros, on the other hand, appeared smug. He would profit greatly from today, and while it made Xavieno sick to think about, he would too.

There would be bonuses to be paid, and Xavieno had played a critical role. Even if, in the grand scheme of things, he knew the day would not have turned out any differently, he had still played a role. Also, Fioralba had made sure to tell Theoliano about hers and Xavieno's arrangement before she had left, and Theoliano and Alessandros were making sure that he was good for it.

So they were walking up to a group of Gwenthari men and women. They looked bedraggled. Around them were soldiers. None of the people wore any armor or weapons; that had all been stripped away. They were just in tunics, some of them dirty with dirt or blood.

"You can pick from one of these," Theoliano said, "but I'll warn you, most of them are soldiers. There might be others to choose from," he added.

"All of the Gwenthari fancy themselves soldiers," Alessandros said snidely, "unless you want to choose a child or someone who is elderly. You're going to need to choose from one of these if you want a strong, capable slave."

Xavieno walked up to the people, looking down the lines of them. They all looked down at the ground, most of them in disbelief. Many of them had looks of deep sorrow on their faces. Xavieno could only imagine what it was like for them, their families all dead.

Theoliano made comments, as did Alessandros, giving their opinions on who or what he should choose. Xavieno only half-heartedly listened. He didn't want an attendant, and he certainly didn't want it to be one of these people. He didn't want to force anybody to do anything—not after what he'd seen.

He didn't have issues with slaves, and he'd enjoyed plenty of them. It was the way of the world, but he felt like he had taken from these people. They walked up to a woman who was wearing a tunic of red and blue. She looked down at the ground. Her long blonde hair had mud and blood caked in it.

"Look at this one here," Alessandros said, walking up to her.

Her eyes darted up briefly and then back down to the ground. Xavieno stood in front of her. He could see her tremble slightly. As his eyes went over her, he couldn't help but notice that she was beautiful. Her figure was nice, and she seemed to have that exotic beauty that Caelwen possessed.

"Look up at us," Theoliano said.

The woman looked up. Her eyes were a beautiful blue.

"Very nice indeed," Alessandros said, reaching out. He ran his fingers down the woman's cheek and neck. "It's a shame I told the men I wouldn't partake of anything today," he tisked.

Xavieno felt a slight surge of revulsion inside himself. Everyone knew the regulations, but no one seemed to care. It made Xavieno want to choose this woman just to irritate Alessandros.

"Do you know what this is?" Xavieno asked.

The woman looked at him, her eyes fearful. "Do I know what this is?" she asked.

"Yes. Do you know what we are here for?"

Her eyes darted between the men. "I have a pretty good idea of what's about to happen, yes," she said, her voice quivering.

Alessandros chuckled, and it irritated Xavieno.

"And what's that?" Xavieno asked.

The woman looked down. She tried to speak but couldn't.

"Is it the same thing that your people would have done?" Theoliano asked.

She looked over at him and then back down. Xavieno saw her cheeks flush in shame. "Yes," she said softly.

"Have you raided before?" Theoliano asked.

She nodded, and Xavieno looked at her differently. She seemed timid to him, but he suspected that had a lot to do with what she had seen and experienced that day. But he was reminded that she was a warrior, and if she had raided, she had taken part in plenty of atrocities.

"So you do have an idea of what many will experience this evening?" Theoliano said.

"Yes," she said.

"Would you have had a problem with it if the tables were turned?" Theoliano asked.

The woman looked more ashamed. "No," she admitted.

Theoliano nodded. "I didn't think so."

Alessandros's attention was pulled away by some soldiers asking him questions. Xavieno was about to move on, but he couldn't.

"You seem ashamed," he said.

She blushed again. "I am."

"For losing?" he asked.

"No, for everything else," she said.

"We should move on," Theoliano said. "She's nice on the eyes, but she'll slit your throat in your sleep."

"I don't know," Xavieno said.

He walked up closer to the woman and tilted her chin up to look into his eyes. He couldn't tell how bad her head injury was, but she looked to be okay. "How bad is that cut on your head?" he asked.

"It's fine," she said, confused. "Will it matter?"

"It might," Xavieno said. "Look, I'm not going to say that what you think is going to happen to you won't happen to people tonight or isn't happening right now," he said. "It's the world. Those who are living are going to become slaves. That I think you understand rather well," he said. "So here's the thing: I am being awarded a slave for my performance in this battle. I am one of the Lysandrian Essaerists. Do you know what an Essaerist is?" he asked.

Her eyes didn't narrow or tighten in fear; instead, she just nodded.

"So you've known one before then?"

She nodded again. "Yes, I have from my old settlement."

"Do you see those men over there?" he said, pointing to some civilians who were talking to some soldiers.

"Yes," she said.

"The way this is going to work is they're going to buy many of you. Some of you will be taken back to the Empire to be sold. Others will stay here in the

Legion. That or someone like myself might purchase you, or like right now, you could become my slave," he said.

She looked at him intently. The fear was still in her eyes.

"I don't want to have to go through the process of breaking you like those men will do. So I will ask you, do you want to be my slave? You will be my personal property to do with as I please." He asked.

She blanched a little but nodded. "I understand. And if I don't want to be your slave?" she asked.

"Did she just talk back?" Theoliano asked.

Xavieno held up a hand. "Then you'll go with one of them. If you're wondering what you'll become, I don't know," Xavieno said. "You might be a laborer. You might be sold to a brothel. You might be sold to an individual like me. I really can't tell you. So you can take your chances with them, or you can take your chances with me."

She only thought for a moment. "With you?" she said, almost like it was a question.

"You want to be mine, then," he asked. She looked unsure. "I expect loyalty," he said. "Are you going to make me have to do things to you to make you behave? Because if you do, I'm just going to sell you. My wife thinks I need an attendant. I don't particularly want one. So do not make things difficult for me," Xavieno said, trying to make his voice sound stern.

"I'll behave," she said.

He nodded. "Very well."

He turned to Theoliano to tell him that he was going to take her. Then he saw Caelwen approaching. She was back to wearing a normal Lysandrian dress now. She walked up to Xavieno and looked at the woman.

"What are you doing?" Caelwen asked.

"I think I'm going to have this woman be my attendant," Xavieno said.

Caelwen nodded and inspected her. "She's very pretty," she said. Xavieno noticed the woman blanch a little bit more. Caelwen looked at her. "What's your name?" she asked.

"My name?" the woman said.

Caelwen chuckled. "You have one, don't you? Are you confused by the question? You do have a lot of blood on your head. I'll have to take a look at that," she said, her tone almost playful.

"My name is Ilara," the woman said.

Caelwen nodded. "Well, good to meet you, Ilara. Are you going to try to slit my friend's throat in the middle of the night?" she asked.

Ilara shook her head. "No, I won't."

Caelwen nodded. "Well, that's good enough for me," she said.

Xavieno snorted. "Thanks for that thorough assessment," he said and created a slave collar. Ilara's eyes widened slightly as she saw it come into view. It had blue glass beads on it. He handed it to Ilara. "Put it around your neck," he said. He saw Ilara's eyes well up, but she did as she was told and wrapped it around her neck.

The Essaerite changed and twisted, turning into a solid band that fit snugly around her. "Is it uncomfortable?" he asked.

She shook her head as tears streamed down her face. "No, it's fine... Master," she said, almost like she was forcing herself.

"The term is Dominaro," Caelwen said. "For women, it is Dominara. Now, I know that this will be new to you. Lysandrian slaves are different. Did you see that blue that's on your collar?" she said. Ilara nodded. "That means that you are owned by an Aristolios. Aristolios are the highest in Lysandrian society."

Ilara seemed confused. "Okay."

Caelwen went on, "Because Xavieno is an Essaerist. He's an Aristolios. Because I am an Essaerist and I am married to another Essaerist, I am also an Aristolios. Anybody with green glass on their collars means that they're owned by a Citizano. Anybody with red glass means that they're owned by a company or organization." Caelwen said. She looked over at Xavieno. "You have to understand that slaves are very different for Gwenthari than they are for Lysandrians."

Xavieno seemed confused. "Property is property, isn't it?"

Caelwen shook her head. "Yes and no, but Ilara here needs to understand that she does have some rights that do not exist for slaves who are Gwenthari. For example, Xavieno is the only one who can do anything to you. Not even his wife Fioralba can, and because he's so high up in society, you do not have to worry about anybody telling you what to do. There are limits to what Xavieno can do to you as well, though. Those limits are very few and far between," Caelwen said. "But in my experience, Xavieno is a good man. Behave, and you should be fine," she said.

Alessandros was back, and he was looking at Ilara greedily. "I might have to go back on my word to the men tonight," he said.

"Too late, Xavieno already claimed her," Theoliano said.

"What?" Alessandros said, then noticed the slave collar around Ilara's neck. He grumbled and walked off.

Caelwen looked over at Xavieno. "I dare say you saved this woman a horrible night."

"Perhaps," Xavieno said, but he knew it was true. "Alright, come on, Ilara, let's get you back to the camp." He looked over at Caelwen. "Do you mind?" he said.

Caelwen sighed. "Yes, I'll make sure that she's fine and in good condition, and I'll get her cleaned up. I suppose she's going to be mine to watch during the day?" she asked.

Xavieno felt abashed. "You can have her tend to your rabbits during the day," he said.

Caelwen snorted. "Lovely." She looked back at Ilara, then back to Xavieno.

"Well, I suppose we'll see how it goes." Her tone became playful. "Fancy yourself a rabbit farmer, Ilara?"

Ilara looked confused. "What's a rabbit?"

————

CAELWEN WALKED WITH XAVIENO AND ILARA BACK TOWARD THE CAMPS. AROUND HER, she could see the dead and hear the moans and groans of the wounded and dying, along with the sobs of others and the screams of still others. It was disgusting, it was horrifying, and it was everything that was bad in this world. But despite all that, she had no issue with the men around her.

It was odd how she could separate those things, knowing that the Legionnaires were not inherently bad or good people. Even in some ways, she couldn't quite blame the commanders. It had been luck that they had run across this group, but the Emperor had chosen to push forward and had chosen a slaughter. Part of her recognized that made him a bad person, but she also understood that if they had just let the Gwenthari leave, they would have been attacking the Legions in small bands and groups, and that would just lead to more death.

It left her conflicted, though she could see on Xavieno's face that there wasn't as much conflict there—just doubt, shame, and disappointment.

"You did well today," she said.

He scoffed. "If you can call this doing well," he said darkly.

She looked back at Ilara. She was following them but wasn't saying anything. Caelwen couldn't blame her. She had just lost everything, hadn't she? She looked over at Xavieno. "What are you going to do with her?"

He shrugged. "I don't know, whatever attendants do," he said. "What is it that attendants do?"

She chuckled. "You're asking the barbarian?"

He smiled. "Yes, I am asking the barbarian."

She was happy to hear some levity in his voice. She wondered how Mariokos was doing. He was so much gentler than Xavieno was. She knew that he was presently working on the camps. It had just been because Xavieno was supposed to be awarded somebody that he hadn't been there, though she suspected that his Essaerites were hard at work.

They made their way to the camp and walked in. It had been built the day before but was being fortified now. There were also sub-camps being erected where Gwenthari captives would be kept until they could be transported back to the Empire, or whatever the Emperor was planning with them. They made their way toward their tent. Caelwen had pitched hers and Mariokos's next to Xavieno's because they liked spending dinner together, and it was a habit for her. She had also taken to carting around Xavieno's cart with her Essaerites.

As they made it to the tent, she stopped and looked over at Xavieno. "Alright, I'll get her cleaned up and taken care of," she said to him.

"Thank you," Xavieno said. "I appreciate it."

Caelwen nodded. "Of course." She turned her attention to Ilara, who looked slightly confused. Caelwen huffed. "Xavieno," she said.

Xavieno looked confused as he was walking off. Caelwen nodded over at Ilara. Xavieno looked more confused. Caelwen huffed again. "She's a slave. She's trying to behave. Don't make it difficult for her. Do you want her to follow you or stay with me?" she said.

Xavieno shook his head. "Oh, I'm sorry. Stay with Caelwen. Listen to her. If I'm ever not around, listen to her and Mariokos," he said, then nodded and walked off.

Caelwen looked over at Ilara, who looked back at her, then down to the ground. "I know you had a hard day," Caelwen said.

Ilara just nodded. "Yes, Dominara," she said.

"Right then," Caelwen said. "Let's get you cleaned up. Come on into the tent."

She waved Ilara inside her tent, and once they were inside, she looked at her. Her tunic was covered in mud and blood, though Caelwen wasn't sure how much of it was Ilara's or not. But she could smell it on her. "Take that off," she said.

Caelwen reached out with her Essaeris and created a basin full of warm water and a rag. Ilara seemed to move numbly as she removed her tunic. As it fell to the ground, Caelwen got a better look at the woman's body. There were some bruises from the fight, but it appeared that she didn't have any major injuries. Caelwen came up to her.

"I'm going to touch you," she said.

Ilara didn't say anything. Caelwen prodded around in the woman's hair, looking for the cut. She found it. It was a gash, and there was a bump on her head. Ilara flinched a little as Caelwen touched it. "Sorry," Caelwen said. "I don't think it's too bad. You should be fine in a few days," she said. "We'll get you cleaned up, and then I'll create an Essaerite that will cover that cut," she said.

"Yes, Dominara," Ilara said, her voice empty.

"There's a basin with water and a rag in it," she said. "Get yourself cleaned up. This is something you're going to be doing daily, by the way. Lysandrians are clean."

Ilara nodded and began wiping herself down. Caelwen sat on her bed and watched.

She was torn about how to view Ilara. She knew that she was a warrior, and she knew that she had done many horrible things. That was common for warriors and raiding parties. But Ilara had also just lost everyone that she knew.

As Ilara was cleaning herself up, Caelwen said, "I'm sorry. I know today has been unimaginable for you."

"Thank you, Dominara," Ilara said, her voice shaky.

"I assume your Essaerist friend didn't make it," Caelwen said. Ilara looked over at her, confused. Caelwen smirked. "The wolves," she said.

Ilara's eyes widened. "I... I..." she stammered.

Caelwen stood. "Even if he's alive, I suppose I don't expect you to tell me. But I didn't see any of those wolves today. So I'm assuming that he didn't make it." Then, reading the look of confusion on Ilara's face, she added, "Oh, I remember you. I remember when you attacked my settlement when I first met the Lysandrians," she said, her voice a little bit darker. Ilara seemed to back away a little, her eyes full of fear. "You have nothing to worry about," Caelwen said. "After all, I didn't lose any of my people that day, did I?"

Ilara shook her head. "No, you didn't. I'm..." she started.

"It's fine," Caelwen said. "I didn't lose anybody. But that means I also know what you are and, therefore, who you are," she said, choosing her words carefully. Ilara looked down. "I saw your skill and that of your people. And based on what you chose to attack, I dare say that you've killed and hurt a lot of people over the years."

Ilara was still looking down and nodded slightly. "Yes, I have," she said.

Caelwen nodded. "I've done things that I'm not proud of, but I never chose that lifestyle," she said. "So you are extremely lucky," Caelwen said, "because Xavieno chose you. Out of all the people who were captured today, I dare say you are among those who actually have a hard life coming to them. But as it is, Xavieno picked you, and you have an opportunity to start a new life. I would recommend you do a good job."

Ilara looked at her. "You don't seem angry or like you hate me," she said.

Caelwen shook her head. "No, I have no reason to hate you, and I'm not angry. Like I said, we didn't lose anybody, and I understand the way of our people. But I also want to make it very clear to you: you are in the best spot that you could ever be in. Being an Aristolios slave, in some ways, will be nicer than being a normal citizen of Lysandrian. The gods have smiled down on you, so I recommend you don't waste the opportunity."

Ilara nodded. "Yes, Dominara." And then after a moment, "What do I need to do as his attendant?"

Caelwen created a dress with Essaeris. "We'll get you actual clothes, or Xavieno will make some for you, but put this on," she said. "But to be an attendant, you basically just do what he says. You'll set up his tent, make his meals, but most importantly with Xavieno, be a companion. Someone he can talk to. Someone he can enjoy," Caelwen said suggestively, seeing Ilara blanch a little bit, but she nodded.

Caelwen thought of how to make it more palatable for Ilara. "Look at it as an arranged marriage where you don't have to have his children, and once he's back with his wife, you don't have to deal with most of his problems."

Ilara looked thoughtful. "I guess I could look at it that way," she said. "I never thought of it that way," she said after a minute.

Caelwen shrugged. "For you, there's not going to be a lot of differences, honestly. With other men, there would be, but not with him."

This seemed to make Ilara a little less afraid, and Caelwen nodded. She figured this was a concept that the other woman could get her head around. Arranged marriages weren't exactly uncommon in Gwenthari society.

"Were arranged marriages common in your settlement?" Caelwen asked.

Ilara shrugged. "Yeah, the norm. I assumed one day I would be married," she said, "but then I joined Valfric's party," she said, her voice thick.

"So you thought those days were behind you? The days of potentially being someone's wife?" Caelwen asked.

Ilara shook her head. "No. They would have happened sooner or later. Just I don't know," she said.

Caelwen nodded. Ilara put on the dress, and Caelwen looked at her in it. "Good. We'll get your hair cleaned up and everything else. You'll want to always look nice. You're an extension of Xavieno by being his attendant, so you'll have to act the part. The nice part is that even though you're a slave, no one's going to treat you like one. They'll treat you just like an Aristolios woman," she said.

Ilara nodded. "I don't think I understand."

Caelwen patted her arm. "You will."

CHAPTER 14

Caelwen glared at a soldier as he walked past her tent. The young man averted his gaze and walked quickly away. Her eyes remained on him as he disappeared into the distance.

A soft voice came from next to her. "Is that man afraid of you?" Ilara asked.

Caelwen looked at her. This morning, Ilara wore a dress that was white with gold accents, which matched relatively well with her collar, though Caelwen very much doubted that Xavieno had been trying to find something that matched. On closer inspection, she could see that the cut of the dress wasn't exactly perfect. She'd need to talk to Xavieno about it. After all, if she had been able to pick up how to make Lysandrian fashion after only being in the Legion for a short time, he should have mastered it by this point.

Ilara looked better than she had the day she was captured. There was some color returning to her face, and it appeared that all of her bruises had mostly healed, though Caelwen still checked on her from time to time to ensure she didn't have any adverse effects from when her head was cut. Her mood was still understandably sullen and reserved, even though Caelwen suspected that Ilara was anything but a sullen or reserved person, she didn't know if that version of Ilara was still around or not. Xavieno came out of his tent and stalked away, his shoulders tense. He didn't bother looking at Ilara as he moved.

Concern flickered across Ilara's face.

"Is everything alright between the two of you?" Caelwen asked.

Ilara shrugged. "I don't know. I don't know him very well yet," she said. "He seems... troubled," she added after a moment. "Is it his wife being gone?"

Caelwen shrugged. "I don't think so. I think it was the battle. But he'll come around. You'll see. He's very pleasant. And to your point, I hope that man is afraid of me. Not Xavieno, but the one you saw slinking past us," Caelwen clarified.

Ilara looked a little confused. "Did he do something to you?"

Caelwen nodded. "And to you. And to Xavieno. And my husband. And everyone else in this Legion. He has done something to us. And he does it every day. Him and his friends."

Ilara looked more confused and concerned. "And they keep him in the Legion?"

Caelwen nodded. "Yes. My husband says it's his duty, but I think he enjoys it."

Ilara looked even more confused. From behind them, Mariokos spoke. "Ilara, that man is one of the people who sounds the horns that wake us up every day."

Ilara's look of confusion continued to deepen.

Caelwen continued, "It's malicious the way he does it."

Mariokos rolled his eyes. "It is not malicious the way he does it. It's his duty. And he's terrified of you," he said.

Caelwen felt the smallest of smiles cross her lips. "He should be," she said.

Mariokos shook his head. "I know we do this every day. But every day, I still think it's important." He stepped closer and looked her in the eyes, placing his hands on her shoulders. "Promise me you won't kill any of the men who wake us up today."

She thought for a moment, and his expression became more serious. She huffed. "Fine. They live another day," she said sarcastically.

Mariokos nodded and sighed, "I suppose that's all I can hope for. Alright, I need to go," he said.

Caelwen kissed him and sent him on his way. She turned back to Ilara, who still looked confused, but Caelwen thought she might have caught a hint of amusement in her expression. Caelwen looked over at the tents. "Alright, I suppose we should pull these down and get ready for the day," she said.

Ilara nodded and moved over to her tent, beginning to disassemble it. Caelwen was thoughtful. "Why doesn't Xavieno just release it every day? He used to. Or at least I thought he used to. Now that I think about it, maybe it was Fioralba who did it." Caelwen mused.

"I'm not sure," Ilara said. "He's never said one way or the other. I didn't even know this was made with Essaeris."

Caelwen nodded and thought. She made a mental note of it. There was something off about Xavieno, and there had been for a few days. She had hoped that he would just shake his dark mood after the battle, but it didn't seem to be changing. He seemed distracted and wasn't his normal self. Caelwen released her tent. She picked up their handful of belongings, taking them over to her cart. Next to it was Xavieno and Ilara's cart. It, too, had a few meager belongings on it. Fioralba had always kept a smaller cart than Caelwen's since Fioralba didn't have livestock traveling with her. It was one that Ilara could easily pull, but Caelwen felt bad making her do it when Caelwen could just create an Essaerite that could do it so much easier.

She reached inside herself, feeling the Essaeris just beneath the surface. It rippled out in the form of a couple of Essaerites to take care of the carts. Once that was done, she returned to her campsite, seeing that Ilara was almost finished packing everything up. She worked efficiently and effectively, speaking to the amount of time she had spent on the road. As she wrapped up, she carried everything over and put it on her cart, then looked out at the Legion as it tore down the camp.

"It's something else, isn't it?" Caelwen said.

Ilara nodded. "It's something. I'm not sure what to make of it, to be honest with you. When we first saw these camps, we just thought they were because they were near Hroldenfell," she admitted.

Caelwen nodded. "I'm sure that's how most people saw them. Because it was supposed to be a siege, wasn't it? And why would you build something if it was just for a night?"

Ilara nodded. "Even the first night after, well, you know, after I came here, I thought maybe the camps were built the way they were because they were worried that we were going to attack before you beat us, or maybe we were going to be here for a while. But seeing them every day, and this speed," she said, shaking her head.

Caelwen understood those feelings all too well. "I didn't believe most of the things that I saw when I first joined the Legion," Caelwen said. "But now that I've been around it, well, I still don't know that I believe it all the time. And it's nothing like I ever experienced in my entire life. And you're right about the speed. At least we're going at a more casual pace now."

Around them, the camp was coming down quickly, and Caelwen knew it would only be a short time before they would be leaving. If the last few days were any indicator of the future, they would continue to move north, back up towards the bridge that they had built. Caelwen wasn't sure if the plan was to cross back over the Ilfrun or if it was just to transfer slaves and take on reinforcements there. In fact, for all she knew, they were going to destroy the bridge and build a brand new one. It was so hard for her to tell what the Legion was planning on doing. And Command didn't really tell anybody.

Mariokos and Xavieno seemed to know more than most people, but that was just because they helped with scouting, and they needed to know what to look for and what general area to move in. But for the rank-and-file Legionnaires, Caelwen doubted they even had any idea what part of the world they were in at any given moment, nor any idea where they would be the next day.

When the time came, they joined in with the rest of the support caravan of the Legion as they began to move out. Caelwen had created Essaerites for her and Ilara to ride on, and they rode together quietly. Caelwen enjoyed the summer warmth on her skin. The sun was bright, and the air was scented with flowers and grass, along with the occasional wafts of water from the river as they moved along.

Along with the support contingent of the Legion were the captives that the Legion was responsible for. They were behind Caelwen and Ilara, but occasionally they would see them, and Caelwen would catch Ilara watching intently, her expression concerned. One time when Ilara caught Caelwen looking at her, Caelwen said, "I'm sorry, I know this is hard."

Ilara looked back at the road, seeming to think for a moment. "It is... it is difficult, but in so many ways not," she said. Caelwen raised an eyebrow, and Ilara continued, "I don't know any of these people; my settlement is dead, and I've seen captives before."

"So is it just the loss of your friends that has you down then?" Caelwen asked. She couldn't exactly blame Ilara if that was the case.

Ilara was contemplative for a few moments. "I would be lying to you if I said that I wasn't shaken up about that. I had known them my whole life; they were brothers to me, but I also understand that's how war is. And I suppose they are in Ulfgara's halls now, and that's what they always wanted."

"So then what has you looking so concerned?" Caelwen asked.

Ilara blushed a little. "You'll think less of me," she said and huffed, "as if that's even possible."

"I don't think any less of you," Caelwen said. "Come on, spit it out. Our people aren't known for keeping a tight clamp on their tongues."

Ilara smiled softly. "I suppose that's true." She thought for a few moments and then said, "I don't want to be one of them."

Caelwen was confused. "A Lysandrian?" she asked.

Ilara shook her head. "No, one of them. One of the ones with red glass on their collars, or even green glass for that matter."

Caelwen nodded, understanding. "I noticed you didn't say one with blue glass."

"I understand what I am. And I also understand that I'm incredibly lucky to be what I am," she said with a bit of a sigh. "I honestly never thought I would say something like that. But I know that it could have been far worse for me. I certainly deserved it. After all, I've put many, many others through far worse. And here I seem to have relatively landed in it," Ilara admitted.

Caelwen could appreciate someone taking a practical view of their lives. "So, what's your concern, then?"

Ilara sighed. "That Xavieno will sell me? That he'll change his mind? I don't know. So much could go wrong."

Caelwen nodded, understanding. She could see where having an uncertain future would be very disheartening for someone who was a slave. It was difficult enough for someone who was free.

"It seems like Xavieno has been in a dark mood lately. How has it been, just in your tent? Does he talk to you? Does he sleep with you?" she asked.

Ilara shook her head. "I'm viewing it the way you told me to, like an arranged marriage. It made it much more... palatable, but we don't seem to have anything that's like a marriage," she explained. "He creates another bed for me, and I sleep in it, but he's never touched me, and he doesn't talk to me. The few times that he has, he's been polite, I guess, but... I don't know," she said with a sigh.

Caelwen was a little surprised. Xavieno wasn't exactly a reserved person, nor was he someone who would turn down attention from a beautiful woman. "Well, I would say he's probably not going to sell you. That just doesn't seem like something Xavieno would do. He never wanted an attendant to begin with."

"And that's exactly my fear," Ilara said, "that he never wanted one to begin with, or if he gets tired of me, or when this whole thing is over and he goes back home," she said, letting it hang there.

Caelwen hadn't thought about that. What would Ilara's lot be as soon as the war was over and everyone had returned to Lysandrian? While right now she didn't think that Xavieno would sell her, it was a possibility when they got back home. Perhaps Fioralba wouldn't like it and would change her mind, or they would just get tired of someone. She could see where Ilara would go for a high price, and she could also see where that would be very concerning for someone like her.

"Well, then I guess you need to make sure you keep him happy," Caelwen said.

Ilara sighed, "how? I make food for him, I try to care for him, but I don't know how to do any of this shit." She said, a little indignant.

Caelwen chuckled, "you could try rubbing his shoulders, but honestly, maybe you could throw yourself at him a little bit." She said, trying to help. "It may be distasteful."

Ilara sighed, "that's the thing; it's not all that distasteful. He's been respectful, he's been kind, he's easy on the eyes. So it's not exactly like it would be that much of an effort for me to do. If it wasn't for this situation, I wouldn't have thought twice about it."

"So what is it?" Caelwen asked.

"I just worry about what happens if it doesn't work." She huffed. "I'm sorry, I shouldn't be bothering you with this."

Caelwen shrugged, "what else are we going to talk about on the road? We have twenty miles that we're going to go today, then we're going to build a camp, we're going to eat dinner, sleep, and then in the morning, some cunt with a horn is going to wake us up, and we're going to do it all over again."

For the first time since she'd met her, Ilara laughed. "You really hate the horns, don't you?"

Caelwen scowled. "More than you know. Do you not?"

Ilara was still smiling. It was good to see, and Caelwen was happy for it.

Ilara shrugged. "I don't think it really bothers me that much. I was always a morning person."

Caelwen nodded and narrowed her eyes a little. "I knew there was something that seemed wrong about you."

Ilara laughed again. "Did I finally step too far? Have I made an enemy of you?" she asked.

Caelwen nodded. "Perhaps. But you might be able to make it up to me," she said.

Ilara looked at her flatly. "And how is that?"

Caelwen smiled. "Oh, you will be on rabbit patrol today, and when we stop for the evening."

Ilara smiled. "That works for me. I do like the rabbits."

Caelwen smiled softly. "They are cute."

"How do you kill them?" Ilara asked. "I understand the mechanics, but they are really adorable."

Caelwen nodded sagely. "I don't. I make an Essaerite do it. I know it's cowardly, and I normally don't mind butchering something, but I think it's the eyes and the fur. I just..." she sighed. "Even though they're so tasty."

————

XAVIENO SAT FINISHING HIS DINNER, LOOKING INTO THE EMBERS OF THE DYING FIRE. None of them were cold, so after they were done cooking dinner, they had allowed it to burn out. If they needed light, they could always use torches or Essaeris.

He was sitting with Ilara, Caelwen, and Mariokos. The day had been hot, and the march had felt surprisingly good, with the heat bearing down on him, making him sweat, and the constant movement had helped clear his foul mood a little, but it was still there, just in the back of his mind. He had been trying his best to clear his mind and thoughts.

These were core training principles for any Essaerist, and he knew it helped them after combat. He had gone through the exercises several times during the day and was feeling more and more like himself, but it was difficult with Ilara sitting next to him. As soon as he had gotten back to camp, she had been there to tend to any of his needs, though he hadn't had any. After all, what needs would he have when he could just create an Essaerite to do something? It seemed so wasteful to have an actual person do something for him. Still, it had been nice when she had offered to rub his shoulders.

He had relaxed some as he felt some knots come out, while Caelwen had a stump Essaerite that worked on their dinner. They had sat and eaten companionably; Caelwen and Ilara seemed to be building a good rapport, which Xavieno thought was probably good. They were going to be around each other for a long time, and he was thankful that he had Caelwen to take care of Ilara during the day.

But as they finished their dinner, Xavieno didn't feel like talking and chatting with the others. So he sat and looked at the fire, again trying to clear his mind and tension. The marching helped dispel some of the energy, but it was still there. He needed to find a way to work through it.

The others were laughing, and he wasn't paying attention. "Xavieno," he heard.

He looked up, seeing Mariokos looking at him, a half-smile on his face. "Are you paying attention?" he asked.

Xavieno looked chagrined. "No, I'm sorry, I'm not." He stood up, "I think I'm going to go to bed," he said, nodding at everyone. "Good night." He walked off, not waiting for a reply, and went into his tent.

As soon as the flap closed, he sighed. He knew he shouldn't be dismissive of the others, but he couldn't help himself. He knew that Mariokos would understand. He heard the fabric behind him of the tent, and he turned to see Ilara coming in. He raised an eyebrow. "Do you need something?"

She looked at him. "Aren't I supposed to be the one asking you that?" she said.

He couldn't help but roll his eyes. "I don't need anything, thank you," he said.

"I'm sorry, I didn't mean to upset you, Dominaro," she said.

He shook his head. "Just call me Xavieno—please. You don't have to call me Dominaro."

She nodded. "Okay. Xavieno, I'm sorry, I didn't mean to upset you."

He sighed. "You didn't upset me. You're fine." She looked like she was thinking about something. She chewed on her lip as she thought. He sighed again. "Just spit it out. What is it?"

She nodded. "Okay. I'm not sure how to say this," she started, "but I want to make you happy," she said.

He raised an eyebrow. "You want to make me happy?"

She came up to him and nodded, "yes, I am your attendant, and there's not much in the way of attending that you need, but I want to be good," she said, as if she were choosing her words with care.

He felt a slight flash of guilt. "You're doing fine. I'm sorry if I've made you think that you're not."

She shook her head. "No, no, there's nothing that you've done. I'm not doing this right," she said.

"Not doing what right?" he asked.

"This," she said. "This isn't..." She stopped herself.

"What? You can say whatever you want to me," he said.

She looked at him. "This isn't me."

"Okay, then who is it?" he asked, trying not to be irritated.

"This is me trying to do whatever I think this is supposed to be, but I'm not this person."

"What are you, then?" he asked exasperatedly.

"I'm a warrior. I'm confident. I'm capable of taking care of myself and capable of taking care of you, but I don't know how to act," she said, frustrated.

He could respect that. After all, when he had first become an Aristolios, he hadn't a clue what to do, and even after years of doing it, he still regularly messed it up, and Biankara had to correct him.

He softened his expression. "You're doing fine. I know this is a big change for you, and I'm so sorry," he started.

She stopped him, placing her hands on his chest. "I don't want you to feel sorry. I'm just telling you that I'm not good at this, and I don't know how to go about this. So why don't I just try being myself?"

He shrugged. "Okay, be yourself, but maybe not the part where you try to kill me."

He saw her glare playfully for a moment, and in that moment, something seemed to warm between the two of them.

"I wasn't planning on it," she said, "I mean trying to do my duties as an attendant but doing it as me."

He nodded. "Fair enough. So, what is it that you're trying to do?"

She nodded and took a breath. She stepped back, and he saw her release the clasp of her dress; it fell to the floor, and his eyes widened for a moment, taking in her form. At the same time, he felt his heart pick up and do a little thump in his chest. He couldn't stop himself as his eyes moved from her face down her slender neck to her body, her perfect breasts and form, her smooth sides, and the planes of her belly, and down between her legs.

He felt his heart do a little flip again. "I don't think I understand," he said.

She smiled at him, the most seductive smile he thought he'd ever seen any woman give before in his life as she walked up to him. "I want to make you happy," she said.

His brain seemed to have a problem functioning. "Make me happy," he said.

She nodded. "Yes, happy."

"I guess I'm," he started.

She gently reached out, placing her hand on his crotch. He felt a flip in his stomach, and he felt his cock twitch. "Make you happy," she said.

"You don't," he started.

"I want to do this," she said. And she slowly got on her knees before him. His heart began to pound in his chest, and a voice in the back of his mind was screaming and cheering with delight. This was what she was here to do, wasn't it? He felt her tugging at his tunic, lifting it up.

Despite the warmth of the air, it still felt cool as she lifted the fabric. She looked up at him, her blue eyes captivating him. Her hands moved up his thighs, and he felt his mind begin to slip.

"Y-you don't," he started, but his voice was weak.

"But it will make you happy, won't it? Dominaro?" she said.

Erosino, he thought.

Her head moved forward, her soft lips kissing him, driving away all of his sullen, dark emotions. He groaned softly and allowed himself to be swept away from the here and now.

———

XAVIENO LAY ON HIS BACK IN THE DARK TENT. A BREEZE WAFTED IN THROUGH THE FLAPS, cooling him. Ilara lay at his side, her body warm but not in a stifling way. Shame and guilt gnawed at his insides. He knew why she had done what she had that evening. She wanted to please him and do her duty, she was looking for security, and for a slave, what other was was better than pleasing your master?

You've never cared before, he thought to himself. And he hadn't. He'd bedded plenty of slaves over his life; it was almost expected of a man of his position, but all of those had been different. They weren't people whose lives he'd ruined. Or had he?

He glanced down at Ilara's sleeping form. He wanted to push her away, but he couldn't. It wasn't her fault; she was doing exactly what she was supposed to do. He was at fault and had been since he'd stepped foot on the battlefield. *You did your duty,* he reminded himself, but it didn't feel that way.

He tried to push the battle from his mind; what was done was done, and it was the will of the gods. Bellamara had placed the legions there, and that was that. But he still felt like he had taken from Ilara, and he felt shame for it. She shifted next to him but didn't wake up. As she moved, he saw the curve of her body, and his mind went back to that evening. It had been... wonderful. And while he was feeling shame right now, some of the darkness had left for a while, and the ball of tension and energy that he had just beneath the surface was gone. It was like a weight being lifted from him. And wasn't that a good thing? *Maybe,* he thought.

He wished it was his wife lying next to him. She'd know what to say and how to comfort him. *Fioralba,* he thought, seeing her in his mind's eye. He sighed. His shame was gone now that he was thinking about his wife, but in its place was emptiness. *It's better she's not here,* he thought. He was thankful she hadn't been there when the Legion had done what it had. When he had done what he had.

Now the shame was back. Ilara's warmth felt like a branding iron against his side. He wanted to move away but didn't. Instead, he lay there, feeling guilt rip at him until eventually, sleep took him.

CHAPTER 15

The sun was warm on Valfric's skin, and a lovely breeze was coming across the settlement, carrying with it the scent of wildflowers and grass. He sighed and stretched, feeling his back pop nicely. He looked around at all the various cottages and homes of the people he had grown up with. People were out working the fields or otherwise going about their day.

He looked over, seeing Ilara, Aelric, and Thraindel talking and laughing with each other. He couldn't tell what they were saying, but he was happy to see it. He walked up to them, and they looked at him and smiled.

"Such a perfect day," Aelric said.

"It really is," Valfric replied, looking around. "Don't know that I could picture anything better."

"No, probably not," Ilara said with a grin. "But we could maybe use something to drink."

He rolled his eyes. "I'll go grab some Bryndraught." He walked inside his home, fishing around on the shelves for it. He found a large tankard on his table, already full. "That's nice," he said, picking it up. The metal handle was cool in his hands. He walked outside, ready to be blinded by the sun. But there wasn't sun anymore. Instead, the sky was covered in dark gray clouds. *Gods, I didn't think I was in there that long,* he thought.

As he breathed in, he noticed there had been a change in the air as well. He could no longer smell the wildflowers or the grass. Instead, there was something else that had a tang that was almost metallic, a sourness to it like death. Along with the smell, he thought he caught the scent of fire and smoke. His heart picked up, and he looked, seeing that all the houses and cottages of his settlement were gone, replaced by charred remains.

On the ground, he saw the bodies of people lying in blood, the sickly-sweet stench of decay turning his stomach. His breath quickened, heart thudding painfully in his chest as his gaze fixed on the twisted limbs and lifeless faces. He backed up, bile rising in his throat, dropping the tankard with a dull clank. As It hit the ground, he called out for his friends, but they didn't respond. He came running around the side of his house, and lying on the ground were Thraindel and Aelric. Their bodies were cut open, their insides strewn about. He felt panic rising as he saw Ilara lying on the ground as well. She was bleeding, her eyes half-lidded. She was mumbling something.

He came up to her, trying to stop the bleeding. "What happened? What happened to you?" he asked, frantic.

She looked up at him, gazing into his eyes, and he could see the light in them dying. She spoke, but he couldn't hear her. He leaned over, pressing his ear near her lips. Hearing her raspy voice, he asked, "What is it? Who did this?"

Her voice was soft and raspy. "You. You did this, Val...fric," she said, and then she yelped and screamed.

He woke with a start. As he awoke, he felt the pain in his back explode. Next to him, he heard something hit the ground, followed by the sound of angry voices. He looked over to see some of the men they'd been traveling with standing over someone on the ground who was whimpering and crying. The men were laughing. One of them brought their hands up and back down, smacking the woman hard in the face. She went sprawling, and Valfric saw her face. It was the slave girl, Eira.

His irritation rose instantly. "Leave her the fuck alone," Valfric spat.

The men looked over at him. He winced in pain. Eira looked at him, her eyes wide, and she scrambled over towards him.

"Valfric, Valfric," she said, her voice concerned. "Valfric hurt?" she asked, her hands patting his arms.

She looked confused, as if she didn't know what to do, and she probably didn't. There was something wrong with Eira. The same thing that had been wrong, perhaps, with his brother. Though Valfric didn't think it was exactly the same thing.

There was a red mark on her face where the men had hit her, and he could see tears in her eyes, but she just focused on him, trying to figure out what was wrong with him. He laid back down. "I'm fine," he said with a groan. "I'm fine."

"Valfric, Valfric," she said.

"I'm fine." He reached out and grabbed her arm. She flinched a little bit but stopped after a moment. "I'm fine," he said, trying to control his voice. His brother had been like this too, easily excited, and in his experience, speaking calmly seemed to help. So he smoothed out his voice, "I'm fine, Eira." He looked over at the men who had hit her. "Fuck off, let me sleep," he said.

The men grunted something but walked off. Eira was looking at him. "Valfric hurt?" she asked.

"Eira, I'm fine," he said with a sigh.

She nodded and started to walk away. Suddenly he felt bad. "Come here," he said.

She came back over to him tentatively. "Valfric," she said.

He glanced over at the men who had been hurting her and sighed. "Sit with me and keep me company."

She took a seat next to him, sitting quietly. After a few moments, she started humming to herself. He couldn't decide if the sound of it was annoying or not, but he wasn't going to say anything to her. Instead, he just tried to close his eyes and think past the pain. He took a few deep breaths, trying to control it, feeling it subside a little bit. His mind moved between his Essaerites as he checked all of them in the area. Most of their party had scattered, and they were just with a smaller group now. He thought that was probably for the best.

They had been heading through more rugged territory over the last few days, and he suspected that was going to continue. They had to go southwest before they could head north again. They needed to find a safe place to cross the Ilfrun before it became a raging river. Before, he would have consoled himself with the thought that the Lysandrians couldn't cross the river, but now he knew otherwise. For all he knew, they could be hot on their trail and would make it to them soon.

They needed to get moving. He roused himself, and Eira looked over at him. "Valfric?" she said.

"Go get Osthart," he said.

She stood up and nodded, walking off. After a few minutes, Osthart appeared. "Did you send her to come get me?" he asked.

Valfric nodded. "We need to get moving," he said.

Osthart looked concerned. "Did your Essaerites find something?" he asked.

Valfric shook his head. "No. Not yet, but we need to keep ahead of the Lysandrians," he said.

"Assuming they're even coming after us," one of the men who had hit Eira said.

Osthart turned to the man and hissed, "Shut the fuck up." He looked back to Valfric. "I want to agree with him, but I don't think it's a good idea to underestimate the Lysandrians again," he said. He started barking orders for everyone to get up and moving. Osthart turned back to him. "You let me know if you see anything."

Valfric nodded. "I will," he said.

They began moving, or in Valfric's case, he lay on his plank while Essaerites carried him. Next to him, Eira walked, looking around at everything as she hummed to herself. She seemed happy enough, but she always flinched when she saw other people, and occasionally she would rub at her slave collar, revealing raw skin underneath it. She reminded him so much of Gaelrik, and that made his gut twist with guilt. "Tell me about yourself," Valfric said.

Eira looked at him confused. "Valfric? Thirsty? Hungry?" she asked.

He shook his head. "Tell me about you."

She looked confused again. "I'm Eira," she said.

He nodded. "Yes, I know you're Eira, but what else about you?" he asked.

"Eira slave, Eira help," she said.

He resisted the urge to sigh, but he did hear Osthart's voice. "You're not going to get much out of her," he said.

Valfric looked over at him. "Yeah?"

"We picked her up when we were raiding. Something is wrong with her. Her brain's fucked up," Osthart said.

That rankled Valfric a little bit, but he didn't let it show. "I could tell," he said.

"She's simple, but she listens and is pretty good. And some of the guys have fun with her," he said.

That part bothered Valfric. It made him think of other times he'd seen people have fun with others. His mind went back to Yrthorn and his abuse of Nefeli, abuse that Valfric was sure Eira was all too familiar with. For that matter, it made him think of the times that he'd had fun with people. That also made him feel guilty, but he pushed that aside. "She's been helpful for me," Valfric said.

Osthart shrugged. "Good, I'm glad." Valfric winced as he felt a bump. "You alright?" Osthart asked.

Valfric huffed, irritated. "I'm sorry," he said.

Osthart raised an eyebrow. "For what?"

"For this," Valfric said. "For not being more help, for slowing you down."

Osthart laughed. "You haven't slowed us down at all, and you've taken care of yourself. Fuck, for that matter, I wouldn't even be alive if it wasn't for you, nor half of these people. And those Essaerites of yours have kept everyone fed. So you're fine, even if you're milking that injury," he said with a grin.

"Fuck you," Valfric said with a laugh and then groaned.

———

As night fell, they made camp. For Valfric, this meant letting Eira set up his tent. He didn't mind a slave doing work for him, but he hated the fact that they *had* to do the work for him. He'd let them serve him his whole life. It was the way of the world, but he didn't like needing anything.

Before, he'd always just known he was using somebody like they were supposed to be used. Now they were taking care of him, and he didn't feel very good. His wolves were able to find enough prey in the area that everyone was able to eat meat and sat around the fires enjoying themselves. For his part, Valfric stayed on his own, barely able to sit up and feed himself.

As the night wore on, he saw the men from before tormenting Eira again. They were pushing her down to the ground, then telling her to get back up and doing it again. Then they'd hit her and laugh. Now that he could place her sounds, his mind traced back to the evenings since crossing the river. They were all marked by the sounds of Eira, sometimes out in the open like now or from the insides of tents. He felt anger building inside of himself. He had seen this before, hadn't he? Had seen where this led? Though he very much doubted that Eira would or even could hurt anybody, he still felt rage building, and as the men pushed her down and she cried in confusion and pain, he couldn't help but see his father doing the same thing to Gaelrik. As he got angrier, his back hurt more as he tensed his muscles, and after a while, he couldn't take it anymore. With a grunt, he stood and created a crutch for himself to walk with.

He hobbled over to the group. "Leave her the fuck alone," Valfric said. "That's enough!"

The men looked up. "Are you stupid?" one of them asked. "We can do whatever the fuck we want to her," he said. "Isn't that right, honey?" he said to Eira.

She nodded, tears streaming down her face. "Yes, yes," she said, flinching from them.

They laughed, and Valfric got closer. "You're not going to anymore," he said, his voice flinty.

The men squared up with him, and Valfric reached out with his mind, feeling the Essaerites in the area. This was going to turn into a fight, and he realized he was in no shape for it. He would need his Essaerites to do it for him. They would arrive shortly. The men were stalking towards him, and even if he was going to lose, he wasn't going to go down without a fight.

"What the fuck are you going to do about it?" one of them growled.

"I'm going to fucking kill you," Valfric said, his voice cold and icy.

Eira was up. "Valfric, no hurt, Valfric, no hurt," she was saying, trying to stop him. She put her hand out on his chest, keeping him from moving forward.

"That's right, listen to her, Valfric," one of the men said. "Don't be stupid."

He was going to be stupid. There was no way around it. The question was, would they be able to kill him before his Essaerites arrived? Before anything could go any further, Osthart came walking up.

"What's going on?" he demanded.

"This piece of shit thinks he can tell us what to do," one of the men said.

Osthart looked over at Valfric, and Valfric said, "I told him to leave her alone." His voice was cold and brittle, and he didn't stop looking at the men.

"They can do what they want," Osthart said.

"Not around me they can't," Valfric said.

"Do you want to make a bet on that?" one of the men said.

Osthart held up his hand. "Eira is a slave," he said to Valfric, and then he looked at the men. "And Valfric is an Essaerist. Do you dumb fucks really want to push him?"

Valfric looked over at Osthart, his teeth gritted. "I don't care," he said.

Osthart looked thoughtful for a moment. "You really don't want us to bother her?"

Valfric shook his head. Osthart looked at the two men, then back to Valfric, trying to calculate, trying to decide what to do. Then he looked over at Eira and huffed. "This isn't fucking worth it for a slave.

"Valfric, you've saved my life a couple of times over, and you've fed all of these people. You haven't asked for anything in return," he said. And then he raised his voice, yelling, "Listen here," Osthart said. He pointed at Eira. "This slave, this slave belongs to Valfric. Do you understand? She is his property, and if you do anything to his property, you have to answer to him," he said. There were a few murmurs, but people nodded in agreement. The two men just glared and stalked off. Osthart looked over at him. "We good now?"

Valfric felt his anger fading. "Osthart, I didn't mean—"

Osthart held up his hands. "Are we good now?"

Valfric sighed. "Yes, and again."

Osthart stopped him and came up to him, patting Valfric's shoulder. "I was going to offer her to you this afternoon, but our conversation changed subjects. Now I wish I had remembered so this whole affair could have been avoided," he said. "You seem to have a soft spot for her, and we have more people than we honestly need. Again, I owe you so much," he said.

Valfric nodded. "Thank you."

Osthart turned to Eira. "You belong to him now, do you understand, Eira?"

She nodded. "Valfric owns Eira," she said, and walked up to him. "Valfric, Valfric, own Eira, Valfric own Eira."

Valfric nodded. "Yes, I know, I own you, Eira." He winced in pain, and she reached out for him. "I'm fine," he said. "I'm fine. Come on," he said, wandering back towards his tent. Every now and then, he shot a few glances over his shoulder to make sure the men weren't doing anything. They stared daggers at him but otherwise didn't seem to want to challenge Osthart. *That might change,* Valfric thought. As he made it to his tent, he sighed, realizing that now it had to fit two. Eira helped him get inside the tent, and he laid down on the ground, on top of some blankets that he had created.

She knelt next to him and fidgeted. He reached into his Essaeris, feeling it ebb and flow, and with some effort, he created some more blankets. "Here, roll these out. You can sleep on them," he said.

She nodded. "Okay." She rolled them out and laid down on them.

He looked over at her, seeing a few bruises on her face, and he felt sympathy and guilt rise within him. Then his eyes went down to the slave collar that was still rubbing her neck raw. "Come here," he said. She moved towards him, and he created a knife. She flinched for a moment but stayed still as he cut off the collar.

She looked almost panicked. "Valfric, Valfric, Valfric," she started saying.

"It's okay," he said. He reached out with Essaeris, creating another one, this one wrapped with soft fabric. "Here, put this on," he said. Though for some reason, he felt bad asking her to do it. *She's safer as my slave,* he reminded himself. She put it on, and it changed, fitting around her neck. "How does it feel? On your skin?" he asked.

She ran her fingers over it, and he saw her smile. "Soft. Soft, Valfric," she said.

He nodded. "Good." He laid down, feeling his back throb. "Fuck," he said.

"Valfric, why fuck?" she asked.

He looked over at her. "I just hurt, that's all. Let's go to sleep. And Eira, don't talk to those guys again, okay?"

She looked confused. "Valfric, guys?"

He thought about answering and then said, "Fuck it, good night, Eira."

———

MARIOKOS FELT HIS ESSAERITHON MOVING THROUGH THE WATER. THE CURRENTS OF THE Ilfrun moved against it, trying to push it along, but it just dug into the ground. It moved from pile to pile, ripping them from the riverbed, making the bridge collapse and float downstream. They transported all of the captives they had taken at the massacre to traders on the other side of the bridge. Those people were now headed towards the Empire for sale. Further south of them, one of the legions had remained behind to build a permanent bridge across the Ilfrun that the legions could use. Also, the legion from the fort was slowly working its way north, creating better, more permanent roads, establishing supply lines, and ensuring that legions would have everything they needed to move forward.

Caelwen stood next to him, looking beautiful as she always did. She looked disappointed, though. "What's bothering you?" he asked.

She looked over at him. "The bridge," she said flatly.

"What's wrong with the bridge?" he asked. "Well, other than you shouldn't cross it now unless you want to be swept downriver."

She chuckled. "I suppose there's that. It's just when you said that it wouldn't be permanent, and we built it so fast." She sighed. "It's just weird seeing it go. And you seemed so proud of it, and I'm so proud of you."

He smiled. "Thank you. You came up with some pretty useful stuff on it, too," he added.

She smiled softly. "Thank you. So, what do we do now?"

He shrugged. "If I had to guess, we're heading up north towards Ulfgard. But we'll secure parts of the countryside as we go. It's not very far from here," he said.

"It's not going to be like Hroldenfell," she said darkly.

He suspected that she was right. It wouldn't be like Hroldenfell, and it wouldn't be like the battle at the Ilfrun, if you could call it that. Ulfgard would be a fortified city. Unlike Hroldenfell, which had been more of a trading hub that used to be a fort, Ulfgard was still a city. It had fortifications, supply lines, and lots of resources. From what little Mariokos had been able to glean from the Legion's command, Gwenthari from all over the area had been heading there to help build up the city to prepare for the Lysandrians. No, it was not going to be an easy take, but Mariokos knew that it was inevitable. You couldn't stop the legions. They were like the tide or the sun or the seasons. You could resist, but it ultimately didn't matter in the end. As the bridge finished collapsing, he released his Essaerithon.

He noticed Wulfgren had joined them and was looking out at the river. "All of that work just to tear that down, huh?" Wulfgren said.

"There was no reason to keep it. All it could do would potentially help our enemy, and in a few months' time, it wouldn't be safe," he said.

He'd been much more accepting of how things worked than Caelwen had been. Mariokos suspected this was because he had spent time with the legions before and had already gotten over all the shock that Caelwen had to get through. Wulfgren turned to his sister, looking at her expectantly. She glared up at him.

"Are you here to see me as your sister? Or are you here to ask about rabbits?" she asked.

"Why can't it be both?" Wulfgren asked flatly.

She huffed. "That means you're here about the rabbits. Ilara's taking care of them," she said, starting to walk off. Mariokos joined her, enjoying the banter with her brother.

"Well, is she competent at it?" Wulfgren asked, concerned.

Caelwen looked over at him. "Competent at what? They're rabbits, Wulfgren. They eat grass and drink water and apparently have a lot of sex because there are so many of them. I'm sure Ilara can handle it."

Wulfgren looked thoughtful. "I don't know how I feel about this, sis."

She rolled her eyes. "You don't get a choice," she said. "Unless you want to start taking care of your own rabbits."

He held up his hands. "There's no reason to be defensive about it. I'm just watching out for our investment. That you think is fine to let some random slave take care of..."

"She's not a random slave," Mariokos said in Ilara's defense. He didn't know her really, but she seemed fine enough, and Caelwen approved of her, which was all Mariokos really needed.

"And even if she was a random slave, who cares? They're in a cage, eating grass, drinking water, and having sex," Caelwen said, put out. "And she used to be a warrior, and she's Xavieno's. I think we're fine."

"Exactly," Wulfgren said. "She's a killer, and we're leaving our future with a killer."

Mariokos couldn't help but laugh. Caelwen looked at him and scowled. "Don't encourage him."

He held up his hands. "How am I encouraging him?"

"You are," Caelwen said, her eyes narrowed. "Wulfgren, I'm not having this discussion with you. And I do have Essaerites in the area, just in case anything goes wrong."

"That's all you had to say. You just had to say that you had Essaerites in the area. Still, I think I should meet this woman," he said.

Caelwen rolled her eyes. "Fine, you can meet her. You can talk to her and bug her all you want about rabbits," she said.

He nodded as if he'd won some sort of argument. "That's exactly what I'm going to do."

"Fine," she said.

"Fine," he echoed.

Caelwen walked ahead of them, and Mariokos looked back at Wulfgren, who gave him a quick grin. Mariokos chuckled and shook his head. It appeared that no matter how old you were or what culture you came from, you enjoyed getting a rise out of your siblings.

Mariokos slowed down, coming next to Wulfgren. "You're the only one I've seen who can get under her skin that easily... well, other than the men who wake us up."

Wulfgren smiled broadly. "It's good for her, and getting her worked up is one of the purest joys in life," he said, then got serious. "Yeah, she really hates those guys. Even when we were kids, I was afraid when I had to wake her up."

They walked for a few moments, moving into the camp that had already been erected and built. All around them was the flurry of activity that was standard for the Legion towards the end of the day. As they got closer to their tents, Mariokos caught sight of Ilara, standing next to the cart with Xavieno, both of them peering inside.

Xavieno looked over at Mariokos as they approached. There were bags under his eyes, and his mood was still dark, but it seemed to be getting a lot better, with the darkness only coming out every now and then. Though there seemed to be a weird tension between him and Ilara that he couldn't quite figure out. Ilara looked at them and nodded respectfully. Mariokos had gotten her over her using any formal title with him, as had Caelwen.

Ilara looked over at Wulfgren, and Wulfgren said, "Is this the slave taking care of the rabbits?"

"Her name is Ilara," Caelwen said.

Wulfgren shrugged. "I didn't mean it in a bad way." He looked at Ilara. "Are you taking care of the rabbits?"

Ilara looked a little confused. "I suppose I am. There's not much to do," she said.

Xavieno spoke, looking in the cage. "Yeah, they just kind of seem to eat grass all day. Looks like there's some water in there."

"And they have sex," Wulfgren said like he was making a point. "That's why there's so many of them. That's why they're so profitable. I just want to make sure that I'm comfortable with you taking care of the rabbits."

Xavieno looked over at Wulfgren and raised an eyebrow, then looked at Caelwen, who was puffing up.

"Wulfgren," she said sternly.

Wulfgren looked at her, was about to say something, and then sighed. "You're going to threaten to kill me, aren't you?" he said flatly. She just stared at him. He held up his hands. "Fine, no more talk of the rabbits," he said.

"Good," she said.

He smiled. "Great. What are we having for dinner?"

Caelwen huffed.

CHAPTER 16

Mariokos watched as his Essaerithon trenched along the side of a road, creating drainage for it. The Legion had stopped for a few days to build up some roads in the area. They were in wide open fields, and it appeared the roads were poorly maintained or not used at all. So the Legion had paused to widen them and make them more stable, allowing supplies and men to move.

He was fine with the work; in fact, he preferred it to the Legion's famous job of battle. There was something he could enjoy about working on a road. He knew that for generations to come, people would use this.

The Legion had broken up into smaller groups, spreading over a stretch of a few miles to do the road work. The other Legions in the area were likewise out in the countryside, securing resources in any towns or villages that might resist Lysandrian rule. From what he had heard, there hadn't been very many that had done so thus far. It was one thing for a city to challenge an army, but another for a village to do so. It meant that they had plenty of food coming in, and the days were relatively relaxing as far as Legion life could go.

The weather was hot, and he was covered in sweat and dust. He worked alongside Essaerites and legionnaires. He had other Essaerites in the area looking for rocks and anything else that could be crushed and turned into gravel, and he helped spread it around, leveling it out as engineers marked what needed to be done and how to slope the roads.

In other areas, they would build small culverts, allowing water to flow and preventing it from washing out their work. All around him was the sound of men working. He felt something on his back, and his head turned to see Treftune on his shoulder, though he very much doubted that it was the real Treftune, as that one rarely went too far away from Caelwen.

"Hey, little buddy, how are you doing?" he said, reaching up and petting the little Valfglidea.

It chitted and hummed in contentment, then plopped itself down on his shoulder, relaxed. He went back to work, enjoying having the little furball as company. His arms and back were sore as the day started coming to a close, and he headed back towards the camp. His Essaerithon would continue to work until there wasn't enough light for it to function. He considered improving its eyes to give it the ability to work at night, but there wasn't much of a need for it. Aside from trenching along the roads, it would also move along and grade sections before the legions came in and put gravel down.

It sped up the work, making him popular, as men appreciated not having to do some of the harder labor that the Essaerite could handle in moments. Xavieno's Essaerites were likewise engaged in similar activity, though Mariokos knew that Xavieno didn't enjoy it as much. Still, the other man seemed to be appreciating not being on the move or in combat.

His mood had also been lightening over the last few days, and he was almost back to his old self. Mariokos was happy to see it. He had been worried about him, but he had known at some point he'd come back around. Everyone always did. On the surface, it would seem that an Essaerist would be able to recover from a battle mentally much faster than a normal legionnaire. After all, they trained their minds from a very young age to be able to control their powers and emotions, something that made stress easier to handle.

And oftentimes, it wasn't the Essaerists themselves who were doing the battle and the killing. They had a lower risk of being injured compared to other soldiers, and they didn't have to do anything necessarily with their own two hands most of the time, though there had been plenty of times when Mariokos had had to fight, as had Xavieno. But what people failed to take into account was that you were in the eyes and in the heads of all of your Essaerites, all of whom were busily killing and fighting others. So in a way, it wasn't that one of you was fighting, but many versions of you were fighting in a battle. And that could be difficult to wrap your mind around. It had been for him when Hroldenfell had fallen. While it had been a solid victory and something that they'd been ordered to do, Mariokos had still known that it had been him who brought down the walls, and in so doing, brought the deaths of so many.

But he'd also been able to get over it relatively quickly because his Essaerites hadn't gone into those walls to do any of the killing. All of his work had happened before, and by the time the fighting inside started, he didn't have any energy to put into it.

He also hadn't gone in personally. The Legion wasn't about to risk an Essaerist on something that the rest of the Legionnaires could easily handle. As such, while Hroldenfell had been razed, Mariokos had been comfortable back in camp. That hadn't been the case at the Ilfrun River, obviously. His Essaerites had been very engaged in battle. But on the second day, when things had gone so much darker than they had before, his Essaerithon hadn't directly done the killing.

Like before, it was responsible for taking down walls and defenses so that other men and other Essaerites could kill. That hadn't been the case for Xavieno. Also, one of the biggest differences between the two of them was that Xavieno had always been fascinated by battle when they were younger. He looked forward to being a warrior and a hero. He'd wanted glory and fame. But as the war progressed, they had both discovered that the glory, honors, and majesty of battle that they had heard in stories as kids were just that—stories. In reality, it was brutal, bloody, and difficult, and it was hard to find an actual winner in any conflict.

As he got back into the camp, he walked over to where his and Xavieno's tent would be. Though he knew that Xavieno was further away than Mariokos had been, therefore he'd probably be spending the night with the rest of his platoon out in the field.

Mariokos found Ilara and Caelwen around a fire working on dinner. He walked up to Caelwen, scooping her up in his arms and kissing her deeply. She kissed him back, her arms winding around his neck. As they broke the kiss, she smiled.

"How was your day?" she asked.

"It was great. We worked on a road. How about yours?" he asked.

Caelwen smiled, bemused. "I'm glad working on a road was a good day for you," she said. "Ours was fine. It was nice and warm today, and we just did little things around the camp but mostly took care of the rabbits. I had a few Essaerites in the area that were looking for herbs, berries, and fruit," she said.

He raised an eyebrow in anticipation. "Did you find anything?" he asked.

She smiled. "Of course I did." She handed him some berries that he popped into his mouth.

"Ilara, how was your day?" he asked.

She smiled softly. "It was fine, thank you."

They sat and began having dinner, which consisted of boiled oats with some honey. It was a simple meal, but it was common for the legionaries to have, and Mariokos didn't mind it. Caelwen and Ilara didn't seem to care either. Ilara wasn't as practical as Caelwen was, but she wasn't anywhere near as impractical as most Lysandrians were.

It was good to get food in his belly, and he ate quickly until he was halfway done with his bowl and then slowed down. After a bit, he decided to make conversation. "Ilara, are you finding the legions to be okay, at least?" he asked, wondering if this would be a touchy subject or not.

She didn't seem bothered by the question. She shrugged softly. "They're so much different than I thought they would be, admittedly. But they're fine, I suppose," she said, though she looked curious.

"What are you wanting to ask?" he asked after a moment.

"Why are you working on a road?" she asked.

Caelwen perked up. "Yeah, we were talking about that today. Why all this effort on a road in the area?"

Mariokos shrugged. "Easy, really. The road is of military importance and needs to be widened and fortified so that it can handle more traffic," he said.

"But why?" Ilara said. "I'm sorry, I'm not trying to question you, I'm just curious," she said.

He shook his head. "You're fine. Question away. Well, we'll need it for the legions, but also for commerce afterward. This road will lead back to the Ilfrun, to a bridge that's being planned that will be permanent, connecting to a road that will lead back to the rest of the empire," he said.

This seemed to give both women pause. "The rest of the empire?" Ilara asked after a moment.

He nodded. "Yes, the rest of the empire. The Ilfrun essentially divided Ulfgarath into two pieces, given the southern piece is much smaller than the northern piece, but it effectively cut a huge swath of land out and away from the rest of Ulfgarath, save for a few small bridges to the south and some barge networks that I've heard are up north.

"We'll find other places to put in bridges, but this way, this territory will be connected to the rest of the empire. It'll be important for commerce," he explained. Ilara nodded slowly, and Caelwen looked thoughtful. "For some reason, I feel like this is more confusing," Mariokos said.

Caelwen was the one who said it first. "This isn't Gwenthari territory anymore, is it?" she said.

Now it was Mariokos's turn to look confused. "No, it's part of Lysandrian. Did you think otherwise?" he asked.

"Yes," Caelwen said truthfully.

He was a little surprised. "What did you think we were doing?" he asked, not unkindly.

"Well," Caelwen started, "almost like a raid, maybe? I don't know, now that I think about it. But armies move into areas, they take things, and they go back home," she said after a minute.

Ilara nodded. "That's what I thought was happening too. That Lysandrian was moving in, taking out anything that might threaten it, and then taking resources and people back to the empire, just like you would in any other raid."

He understood now. Both Caelwen and Ilara were Gwenthari, and that was the Gwenthari way. You raided, took what was valuable, burned everything else, and then you left.

He shook his head. "No, we're not here to raid. We're here to conquer," he said. "All this territory, it's Lysandrian now. As will be anything else that the legions move through. We aren't just here to take. Well, I suppose we are. We're taking territory, but we're not just here to raid and take this land's riches and head back home," he said.

This seemed to make some sense to Caelwen, though she still looked slightly puzzled by it. For Ilara, though, it looked almost like she'd been hit in the gut.

"Ilara, I'm sorry," Mariokos started.

She recovered and shook her head. "No, don't be sorry. It's just not what I was expecting, is all. It makes sense now. This war had to be so expensive for you, but for some reason, I just had in my mind that this was just a raid. That when this was all over, it would just be the Ulfgarath people, shattered and broken, waiting for the Valfarans to come in, along with Wulfharboria, to finish what has been going on for a couple of generations," she said. Her voice was soft, thoughtful, and sad.

He felt his expression darken. "Ilara, I am not sure what to say," he said.

She sighed. "There's nothing to say." After a few moments of thought, she said, "Maybe this is better. Maybe being under Lysandrian will be better for us. My people have been dying out for so long now. Ulfgarath was such a strong people, but not anymore."

He thought for a moment, then said, "They will be again."

She looked over at him. "How?"

"With the help of the Empire," Mariokos said simply.

"But we won't be us," Ilara said, her tone rough, her hands tightening into fists as she stared into the fire.

Caelwen sighed and looked at her. "Has being us been working?"

Ilara was about to speak and stopped. She looked down and gave just the slightest shake of her head. "Yeah, I guess being us hasn't worked out that well, has it?"

CHAPTER 17

The bowl between Hildrana and Fernwen was a unique one, but in Hildrana's experience, it provided an excellent teaching tool. It was made out of Essaeris, of course, with the outside of the bowl being a pitted black rock. The inside was polished metal, and part of the exercise was to create a bowl that had both these materials infused perfectly together.

Hildrana was holding the bowl on one side, her hands cupped underneath it. Her daughter, Fernwen, held the other side, mirroring her mother's grip. They were sitting in the middle of their home on cushions they had created together. Hildrana was controlling her breathing and focusing, but the bulk of her attention was on her daughter, whose eyes were closed, her face a mask of effort and concentration.

"Breathe," Hildrana said.

Fernwen didn't answer, but instead, her breathing smoothed out.

"Relax," Hildrana reminded her.

Fernwen's expression softened slightly. As it did, Hildrana could instantly see the difference—or more importantly, feel the difference. They were combining their powers for the exercise, with Hildrana creating the bowl along with Fernwen. Fernwen was to read what Hildrana did and the materials inside and try to mimic it on her own. So it made the bowl more of a weaving than anything else. If you could call a bowl a weaving. Hildrana focused on the bowl, feeling the structures that Fernwen was building inside of it, seeing how the rock and the metal connected.

This part of the exercise was easy, comparatively speaking. The rock and metal were not special. The only thing special about the bowl was where they connected, but that was going to change. Hildrana started making slight changes to the exterior, adding in crystals and changing the rock. She felt as Fernwen tried to keep up with her, creating similar structures and materials.

This was all part of the training. You had to be able to create anything with ease. This was common knowledge for most Essaerists. And part of that ease was being able to do it consistently. The more you created something, the easier it was, and the less energy it took. But there was more to being an Essaerist than just being able to make things.

There was the other half of their power. The half that, in Hildrana's experience, many Essaerists neglected to develop past its most basic of states. Early on, Essaerists learned that they could interact with an object, say a rock or a piece of fabric. They could touch it. And if they touched it with their powers, they could figure out what it was made of and how it was made. And then they could mimic it.

This was incredibly handy and useful and could be seen in nature all the time with the animals that could use Essaeris of their own. By being able to mimic something, it expanded what an Essaerist could do. This could be done doubly so if another Essaerist allowed you to get a read on something that they had created.

They could block this, of course, but it was such an excellent training tool. It also meant that young Essaerists could learn on pure items—items that didn't have any variation or were not diluted in some way. So they could get the truest representation of something.

But that tended to be where people stopped trying. They did a basic read on things. And this was, in a way, a tragedy in Hildrana's mind. Her people, the Eirfrosti, had a much different way of looking at Essaeris. It was part of why she was training her daughter in her people's ways now. Though those ways were secret for those outside of Eirfrosti, that was different for Fernwen, because Fernwen was Hildrana's daughter. And if she wasn't brought up and trained in the way of the Eirfrosti, that would be very shameful. So Hildrana worked with her daughter, teaching her how to read. If you could read everything around you, truly read it, down to the most minute detail, the world opened up to you in the most amazing way.

It also made Eirfrosti Essaerists feared amongst the Gwenthari. It was why they had a reputation for being witches. Because they did things that other Gwenthari Essaerists didn't seem to have the ability to do.

Hildrana knew that this was different for Lysandrian. The Lysandrian Essaerists did not learn to read to the same extent that Eirfrosti ones did, at least not all of them. Hildrana was sure that some did, but by and large, they didn't. But they did train their Essaerists, and their Essaerists were more powerful when it came to application. For the Eirfrosti, reading was extremely important. It allowed one to be able to walk around and know what was underneath them, to feel everything—the roots in the ground, the soil, the bugs, the little things that lived in the soil that you couldn't see with your eye.

It allowed you to touch an animal and know everything that there was to know about its body. This had a lot of practical applications. You could, say, detect if there was poison in your food. As such, Eirfrosti Essaerists were notoriously difficult to kill with poison, if not impossible. It also meant that you could look at a piece of meat and see if it was rotten, or you could hold a coin and be able to tell just how much gold or silver was in it.

For her people, this was part of what made Eirfrosti Essaerists power brokers, because they could detect everything. They could detect if a coin was counterfeit or not. They could see the quality of the grain and sense the purity of metals, stones, and even pelts and meats. They could put their hand on a bridge and detect the structure of the rocks and wood that made it and could find structural flaws that could be exploited in battle or repaired in peacetime.

It meant being able to touch a sick person and being able to tell why they were sick. Not necessarily always how to cure the ailment, but almost always how to find it. And it meant being able to find it inside of oneself. Hildrana was more aware of her body than anybody.

Fernwen would be the same. But before you could read those things, you had to know what they felt like with your powers. So, Hildrana pushed her energy and Essaeris into the bowl, altering it and changing it, allowing her daughter to read and learn and mimic so that someday, when it was necessary, Fernwen could do the same for herself.

That day would shortly come when Fernwen would be able to recognize every single poison that had ever been made, and the antidotes for it. And if there was a poison, venom, or some other thing that she hadn't seen before, she would have a better idea of how to counteract it. It would mean that her daughter would know how to avoid people who had ailments that were catching and could not be cured. She would be able to feel inside of herself whenever she had some ailment. It would mean not being cheated by counterfeit coins, or by buying impure merchandise or eating rotten food. It would mean being able to see those who were hurt and knowing how to best help them. And also how to create efficient and effective Essaerites that could do whatever she needed.

These were the gifts of reading.

"Concentrate," Hildrana reminded her daughter.

She could feel Fernwen's Essaeris inside of the bowl. It was straining. This, too, was part of the exercise—building up one's endurance to use their powers. It wasn't an easy thing, and Fernwen was young. Hildrana knew that she was pushing her hard, but no harder than she had been pushed when she was younger. Something that she knew deep down Fernwen relished and enjoyed, even if her husband, Bergthral, sometimes thought it was slightly unnecessary.

He was far more dedicated than most Gwenthari Essaerists, and in part, that was because Hildrana had helped train him, much to the consternation of some of her elders. But he still lacked some of the drive and discipline that the Eirfrosti did. This was no fault of his own. He just hadn't been raised the way they were.

She felt Fernwen's Essaeris failing, and Hildrana pulled away. Pushing was one thing. Sometimes pushing to the point where you could no longer function as well was helpful, but not always. She released the bowl.

"That'll do for now," she said.

Fernwen sighed, and her eyes opened. Hildrana could see the strain in her eyes, though she could also see the determination in them as well.

"Thank you, Mother," Fernwen said, her voice soft and tired.

Hildrana smiled softly. "You're welcome." Fernwen looked at her, reading her expression. "What?" Hildrana said. Fernwen shook her head.

"You don't even look tired," she said. "I know that's the idea," she said, trailing off.

Hildrana smiled, standing up. "And that also means that you know the levels that you can achieve, too," she said.

"I suppose," Fernwen said, standing up. She stretched, loosening her muscles, tilting her head from side to side.

"You're holding tension in your shoulders again, aren't you?" Hildrana asked.

Fernwen nodded. "I've been trying to stop, but when I start getting tired, I tighten up."

"You are new to this," Hildrana reminded her. "It will come in time. You are aware of the problem, and you are trying to fix it. That is all we can do."

Hildrana walked over to the table and broke off a piece of bread from a loaf, handing it to Fernwen. They both began to eat, and Hildrana's stomach rumbled. She'd been too engrossed in the training to pay attention to her own body.

Her husband, Bergthral, came in. He was a tall, muscular man with long blonde hair and blue eyes. He had a beard growing from his face, and his smile always reminded her why she was willing to leave her homeland and didn't regret it.

Fernwen smiled up at her father, who came in and hugged her, kissing the top of her head.

"How are you two doing?" he asked.

"Fine. Tired. I was training," Fernwen said.

"Were you now? I'm sure you're doing wonderfully. You'll be better than me before you know it," he said, making Fernwen smile.

Bergthral walked up to Hildrana and kissed her, and while Fernwen may not have noticed it, Hildrana did. There was stress in her husband's eyes. Hildrana smiled as Bergthral grabbed a piece of bread.

Fernwen finished hers, and Hildrana said, "You should go play outside. It's so nice out."

Fernwen got up, nodding, not needing more encouragement than that. She went running out of the house to do whatever it was that young people did that they thought grown-ups didn't know about.

She looked over at her husband. "What is it?" she asked.

He sat down across from her. "There's news. Not good news," he said.

She raised her eyebrow. "About what?"

"You remember the men that went to raid in the Ulfgarath territory?" he asked.

She nodded. "Has there been word from them?"

"Not from them. But from the people they were with," he said, his expression grim. "They're gone. All of them. Apparently, their group ran into the legions, and it didn't go well."

This brought her up short. "But they were supposed to be raiding the northern sections of Ulfgarath, not the south."

He nodded. "They were."

Hildrana was confused. "Lysandrian has moved north of the Ilfrun," she asked, concerned.

He nodded. "Yes. I don't know much about it; there wasn't much news, but it sounds like everyone was surprised to see them. They were much further north than we thought they would be, and we didn't hear anything from the southern parts of Valfarans, so that means one thing."

"They crossed the river, but not in the south; they crossed where the river was wide," she said.

This wasn't a surprise to her, though it appeared to be to her husband. Growing up, Hildrana knew just how powerful the Lysandrians were. She'd learned about them, as had every Eirfrosti Essaerist. Knowing potential enemies, even if they were far away, was important. And while the rest of the Gwenthari remembered the days when Lysandrian was weak, her people knew differently. She knew they were strong, and she knew that they were incredibly industrious, though she never suspected that they would have the ability to cross the Ilfrun.

She reminded herself that the information that Bergthral received may not have been the most accurate; it was probably second- or third-hand information, but she did believe that the men from their settlement were dead. He was looking down at the table, and she was lost in thought.

After a moment, he sighed. "I suppose there's nothing to do about it. I'm just surprised," he said, his voice heavy.

———

A LIGHT BREEZE WHISKED HEAT AWAY FROM MARIOKOS AS HE MARCHED WITH THE REST of his squad. The legion had been moving steadily for several days, and they had entered an area that consisted of rolling hills with spots of dense forest.

The summer sun beat down on them, though it wasn't as warm as it was in his homeland, so it made the feeling kind of nice. The region that they had been in was beautiful as well, and they hadn't experienced heavy amounts of resistance. By and large, they found two types of settlements or populated areas as they moved: ones that were either fine with turning over control to

Lysandrian without putting up much of a fight, or ones that were abandoned.

The ones that were abandoned seemed to be more common, but not by as much of a margin as Mariokos would have thought. News had clearly spread about the massacre along the Ilfrun River, along with what happened in Hrold-enfell, but for some reason, many of the settlements didn't seem to be as concerned that the same thing would happen to them, or if they were, they'd simply left.

It had been an odd sort of thing. It wasn't to say that the legions hadn't run into some problems. There had been plenty of Gwenthari raiding parties, though Caelwen had told him that she wasn't sure how many of them were Ulfgarath. It was very likely that a lot of them were Valfarans, something that Ilara had confirmed.

She had reported that Valfarans had been stepping up raiding activities in the west following the fall of Hroldenfell. Many of the people that they had been traveling with had been victims of that. In each of the cases, it hadn't been a problem for the legions, and the raiding parties seemed not to be interested in dealing with them. He suspected they were looking for easy pickings.

Pickings that were all around, with the lack of people in the area. When people left towns and villages, it was obvious that they sometimes did so in a hurry. Perhaps they were hiding in the countryside, something he suspected was possible. But more often, he thought they were headed towards Ulfgard or other northern cities, though there were scant few outside of Ulfgard.

However, with their quick movement, it meant that they had to leave many of their belongings behind, mostly in the form of physical wealth, as livestock seemed to go with them. Still, they found plenty of chickens and other animals, but by and large, they found unharvested crops and homes full of goods. It had created a positive atmosphere for many in the legions. They were getting their regular pay, plus there was more than enough loot to go around for anybody who was interested in that sort of thing and little in the way of fighting with beautiful weather.

This would, of course, change at some point, Mariokos understood that, and their leadership seemed to understand that as well—that the easy days of today would be paid for in blood and effort tomorrow. They were coming up over a hill that led into a valley. Mariokos sent some of his hawks ahead to continue scouting the area. One of them popped over the hill and took it all in.

"There's a city on the other side," Mariokos said to the men around him.

It appeared they were reaching Ulfgard. Soon the legion was cresting the hill, and as they did, Mariokos was able to view it with his own eyes. Yes, it was definitely Ulfgard.

It sat at the end of a valley that appeared to go north forever. Ulfgard was atop a hill that, on the north side, had a river that ran along it. To the south were some small valleys that generally led into mountains. But Ulfgard itself was far from what Hroldenfell had been. Hroldenfell had seemed like an abandoned city that had been put back together or some sort of menagerie or hodgepodge of peoples.

Ulfgard was not that. In fact, it looked like Lysandrian cities in so many ways. It had a curtain wall that went around near the base of the hill, and it had several other series of walls as it moved up. He saw lots of stone buildings, not the wood of Hroldenfell. The smoke from many chimneys rose in the air above Ulfgard, and all around it were fields.

The countryside was spotted with homes, and he could see a general line of people moving to the city gates, preparing for Lysandrian. Instantly, the levity and relaxed nature of the legion seemed to change. He could feel it ripple through the men. A tension built, a stress that could only come with an impending battle. And Ulfgard would be a battle, to say the least. This was not going to be like Hroldenfell, where he would be able to easily bore underneath the walls, bringing them down. No, he suspected that his Essaerithon wouldn't be able to bore under these walls. They would be predominantly dealing with rock, and the walls were positioned as such that they would be able to defend relatively easily.

He also very much doubted that Ulfgard didn't have Essaerists. There wouldn't be many, by any stretch of the imagination, but there had to be a handful—probably more than the legions had with them. That would make things difficult for the Lysandrian Essaerists. They wouldn't be able to act with impunity, like they had at the Ilfrun, or like they had by and large over Hrolden-fell, which only seemed to have maybe one Essaerist in the entire group.

Here he knew this would be different. If what they had encountered at the Ilfrun and what they had heard had been correct, anybody who was anybody in Ulfgarath was in Ulfgard, and they were there to make a stand. No, this was not going to be Hroldenfell.

Orders began coming up the lines, along with placements for camps. The legions would move like they had at Hroldenfell, though—slow and purpose-ful. Because while it appeared to be well-defended, Ulfgard did have something going against it. And that was, it was full of people, chewing through limited resources, whereas the legions were going to be coming in and inheriting the valleys. Valleys that looked like they were full of fields ready to harvest, or that would soon be ready to harvest. The legion was not going to have to worry about supplies. They were hitting Ulfgard at the perfect time of year.

If Ulfgard held out for months on end, or even over the winter, the legions would be fully stocked with rations and supplies. They would be able to spend the winter dealing with roads and anything in the area while Ulfgard ate through its food.

And while eventually it might turn into the same thing that had happened at Hroldenfell, it may not. Mariokos wasn't sure. One thing he was sure of, though, was that they were going to be here for some time. As they marched into the valley, he put his effort and focus into building up his power so that he could create his Essaerithon.

His part for today would not be different than it would be any other day, nor would it be for so many of the legionaries. There would be the same amount of men posted on guard duty, with others building the camp, and others foraging. No, today would not be some glorious battle that would go in the history books. That was not how these things tended to go. Today would be rather normal.

And it was, as the legion came to its designated camp, Mariokos created his Essaerithon, which got to work digging ditches and trenches, while his smaller Essaerites assisted in constructing the wall. Soon, the camp was built, and he was walking towards where his tent would be.

He found Caelwen setting it up, along with Ilara. They both looked tense. This was something he could understand. As he approached, Caelwen looked up at him, and he came up to her and kissed her, feeling her lips tight and strained. He wrapped his arm around her waist.

"What's wrong?" he asked.

She looked up at him. "Ulfgard," she said.

He nodded. "Yes, what about it?" he asked.

She glared. "You know what about it. It's not going to be easy," she said.

He shook his head. "No, it won't. But it's not going to be impossible either."

He let go of her, and she went to finish unpacking a few of their belongings as her stump Essaerite worked on dinner. He saw Ilara too. She also looked tense, though he suspected her attention was less about concern for the legions and more concern for those who lived in Ulfgard and the surrounding area. She looked over at him. He tried to look welcoming and kind, but he suspected to her that while she could sometimes forget that he was part of the invading army, she never truly forgot.

"What's on your mind?" he asked her.

She shook her head. "Nothing."

He sighed. "It's okay. What's on your mind?" he asked again.

She sucked her lip for a moment. "What's going to happen to the people in the surrounding area?" she asked.

He shrugged. "Mostly nothing. The army will need supplies, but I don't see any problems unless they resist," he said, understanding just how callous that must sound. He reminded himself that Ilara was not exactly a pushover. She and her settlement apparently relied heavily on raiding for a lot of their supplies. So he suspected that in a way, part of her would be surprised to hear that there wasn't a plan on killing everybody in the countryside. The legions needed them—needed the food, needed the support. If you killed everybody, those that you missed would try to hurt you, and you would just have to work their fields. There was no point in it aside from the fact that in a few years this place would probably be a center of trade as it would be part of the Empire.

"So they won't be hurt?" she asked after a minute.

He wasn't going to lie to her. "Some probably will," he said honestly. "I wish I could say that that wasn't the case. I wish that all of our legionaries followed the rules that they were supposed to, but..." he said, letting it hang out there.

She shook her head. "No, I don't mean... I meant more like command. I understand soldiers will be soldiers, and I am the last person who can judge that. Honestly, most of my people can't judge that. I was more curious about what the orders would be.

"So there's really no plan in killing everybody in the area, or just taking their belongings or turning them into slaves?" she asked.

He shook his head. "No, there's no reason to. We've found that many will work with us. They're just folks," he said, which was something that always surprised him.

Not that the Gwenthari were just folks; that made sense to him. But that it was always a struggle for many of the Gwenthari to understand. Caelwen seemed to get it, but it seemed to be a bit of a struggle for Ilara. He wondered if that was because of her background and that she had spent so much time raiding herself. To her, that was the way of life, but Mariokos knew that even in a society that depended on raiding, more people had to grow crops than those who raided those crops. And that was something that the Empire understood all too well: labor, and how to effectively use it and encourage it. Sometimes, it was with the stick, but oftentimes, that wasn't necessary. The need to feed, clothe, and shelter one's family made for excellent motivation.

He heard someone walking behind him, and he turned to see Xavieno, who, surprisingly, looked to be in a relatively good mood. He smiled as he approached.

"What's the news?" Mariokos asked.

Xavieno smiled. "Just making camp, and I dare say we're going to be here for some time," he said.

He came up and smelled whatever Caelwen was making. "I know it's just going to be boiled oats, but I'd like to think that it'd be something else, you know."

Mariokos chuckled. "It's the life of the Legionnaires," he said. "It's all fine dining for us," he said with a laugh.

Xavieno rolled his eyes. "Fine dining, indeed."

"I do have to say, I miss Fioralba in that way," Caelwen said.

Xavieno's smile softened a little bit. "She was a very talented cook," he said, "and so good at creating Essaerites that tasted good."

Ilara perked up. "I didn't think you could eat Essaerites."

"You can," Xavieno said, "you just can't digest them, but adding flavoring agents, they're very useful for," he said.

Caelwen looked a little chagrined. "I'm sorry, I'm not as good at it as she is."

Xavieno shook his head. "I wouldn't expect you to. Honestly, if I'd taken the time to learn, it wouldn't be a problem," he said.

Caelwen glared a little bit at Xavieno. "Are you saying I'm not good at it at all?"

Xavieno held up his hands. "I did not say that. You know I didn't say that," he said.

She glared at him again, but Mariokos could see the slight twitch in the corner of her mouth. Caelwen was a very good cook. So was Mariokos, and frankly, Xavieno was too. It's just that Fioralba was unusually talented at it, and she had a love for it that Mariokos didn't quite have, Xavieno couldn't grasp, and Caelwen was far too practical to care about.

"But it was implied..." Caelwen said.

Xavieno backpedaled. "No, I was not implying anything."

Caelwen smiled. "I know, I just promised your wife I'd keep you trained."

"Trained," Xavieno huffed, and Mariokos smirked.

PART TWO

CHAPTER 18

They were surrounded by green fields of wildflowers in every color of the rainbow. The air was warm, and the sky was blue with only a handful of white, puffy clouds above them. It would have been perfect if Valfric's back wasn't killing him. The pain had gotten a little better but was still always there. He had moved from being carried to being able to hobble around using a crutch he made out of Essaeris.

Their group had been growing ever smaller day by day as people split off and went their own way. Valfric had purchased a mule from one of the groups leaving. He had given them a deer that his wolves had been able to take down in exchange for the mule. The animal was older, and he didn't think it was the highest quality mule there was, but for the price, it was worth it for the people. They had food and didn't have to care for an animal they didn't need. And for Valfric, he had something for pack.

He could have used an Essaerite for this, but he decided that he wanted to keep his abilities as secret as possible whenever they moved into new areas, so he had the mule. Atop it was an Essaeris saddle with some meager belongings that were also created out of Essaeris. Being able to use his powers consistently was also something that was nice. The pain could occasionally get in the way, but generally, it was something he could push aside. And with the ability to use it more readily, he felt a modicum of sanity come back to him.

He created a stump and sat down on it heavily, with a huff. He created another one, and Osthart sat down next to him, looking over at him.

"You seem to be doing much better today," Osthart said.

Valfric nodded. "I suppose. The sun feels good on my back, and moving seems to be loosening things up, but I don't think I'm going to be running around or climbing trees anytime soon," he said.

Osthart smiled. "The older you get, the less you run and the less trees you climb anyway, my friend," he said.

The group had come to a fork in the road, both figuratively and physically. One path would lead them to the northeast, the other to the northwest. Valfric had been thinking a lot about it and what he was going to do. As the group sat around, a few people began eating lunch and talking to themselves. Valfric noticed a few of the men who had bothered Eira before glaring at him. He didn't think it was so much that they were irritated that he had taken away their toy, but more that he had challenged them—something they weren't used to from someone who could barely walk. Part of him enjoyed it, though. There was something about it. He'd always been intimidating. Even without his Essaeris. He'd always gotten what he wanted, if for no other reason than that people didn't want to fuck with him. But now he was the picture of someone that you could steal from and fuck with. But they couldn't, because Valfric was still an Essaerist, and the men didn't care to have their throats ripped out by wolves. He smiled and nodded at them.

"If I wasn't sweating like a pig, I would love this weather and this place," Osthart mused.

Valfric chuckled in agreement. "The heat has been something, hasn't it?" he said. "I remember on days like this before, I was either on horseback, enjoying it, or lying under the shade of a tree. Just taking it all in," he said.

Osthart grinned. "That's the way to do it. Being on the road is bullshit," he said.

Valfric grinned. "You didn't leave your settlement much, I take it?"

Osthart shook his head. "When I was younger, maybe, but the older I got, no. I was there running my family and running the settlement. I had other things to do. Traveling and raiding, those are a young man's game. Not mine."

He looked over, watching as Eira walked around the field, seeming to smell every flower there was. "She doesn't seem to mind the heat," Osthart said, almost jealously.

Valfric watched her for a moment and sighed. "I don't think she could give a shit about the heat," he said. "She sweats just as much as the rest of us, but it doesn't seem to affect her, or at least she doesn't care."

With Eira was one of Valfric's Essaerites. He had wolves that were nearby standing guard and hunting, but he had kept dogs in the main part of their group. It seemed to be easier for the horses. Thankfully, the mule he got didn't seem to care about Essaerites in the least bit.

At first, Valfric thought it was a good idea to have one of the dogs he created follow Eira around, lest anybody get any bad ideas or she wandered off. Her collar was Essaeris, and he would always be able to know exactly where it was, but he didn't care to deal with her getting hurt. So he thought a dog would be good. His brother had liked dogs as well, and it seemed that she took to it quickly.

What he found odd, though, was the type of dog that seemed to make her the most comfortable. He didn't want to have a puppy or something like that, though he had created one for her at first, and she had seemed fine and content with it, giggling and playing with it, not seeming to understand that it was there for her protection.

So he changed it, making it more like an actual dog. It was smaller and had the personality that Eira expected a dog to have, but it wasn't serving the purpose that it needed. After a while, he had finally settled on one that met his requirements, and oddly, Eira seemed to love. It was large, almost the size of one of his wolves, with a shaggy coat that he kept in a condition that spoke to the dog being well cared for, but the breed and size very much shouted, 'fuck around and find out' for anybody who would want to mess with it.

He would have thought that Eira would have been scared of it, but she wasn't. She seemed to be more attached to the larger dog, and she made it go with her everywhere, no matter how many times he explained that it was an Essaerite. She insisted that it act like a dog.

Osthart watched as Eira found a stick and tossed it. The Essaerite went and chased it down, just like a regular dog, and came back, proffering it to her. She grabbed the stick and threw it again, laughing with delight.

"What did she name it again?" Osthart asked.

Valfric half chuckled and huffed, "Ferngar," he said.

Osthart looked over at him blankly. "Ferngar? That's a man's name," he said.

Valfric shrugged. "I tried to see if she would come up with other ones, standard pet names, but she wouldn't have it. She calls it Ferngar," he said.

Osthart smirked in amusement. "Well, at least someone's happy with the trip," he said, "and she seems to be good for you," he added.

Valfric raised an eyebrow.

Osthart shrugged. "Having something to take care of seems to be good for you. Keeps your mind off of things, and keeps your mood from being sour," he said.

"I don't know about that," Valfric said.

Osthart smiled tightly. "That's fine, you don't need to. I know, and that's all that really matters," he said with a little laugh, and then he went back to watching Eira with the Essaerite.

"Funny thing is," Valfric said, "she knows it."

Osthart raised an eyebrow. "Knows it? What do you mean? It looks the same every day, doesn't it?"

Valfric nodded. "I tried something the other day. I created two versions of it, one that she was used to. But when she went and did something, I swapped it out with another one that was identical in every way," he said.

"And?" Osthart said.

"She knew it wasn't Ferngar," Valfric said. "Never seen anything like that. Nobody can pick out different Essaerites."

Osthart looked at her thoughtfully. "Do you think she has abilities?"

Valfric shook his head. "Not that I'm aware of. I don't think that's how it works; you're either an Essaerist or you're not. But, she just seems to know somehow. Maybe it's the personality of the Essaerites, or maybe it's some minor detail that I'm not catching. I don't know."

Valfric looked at the tee in the road. "What direction are you thinking?" he asked Osthart.

"Northeast," Osthart said confidently. "I know you don't agree with it, but we think it's good to stay in Ulfgarath, and we can get above Ulfgard and skirt around the legions."

Valfric nodded. "I understand. That makes sense," he said.

Osthart smiled tightly. "You're not going to join us, are you?"

Valfric looked over at him and then back at the fork in the road and shook his head softly. "I'm sorry, my friend. No. I have no desire to go back by the legions, especially in this state, and I think they're just going to continue to move north. But I respect your decision."

Osthart smiled warmly. "Thank you, and I yours too. Where are you going to head?"

Valfric shrugged. "Northwest, into Valfarans. I don't think we'll have many problems with just two of us. Plus, if we find someplace decent to live, I'm sure they'll take an Essaerist," he said. "Even if I don't fully recover."

Osthart nodded. "Honestly, you were wasted as a raider," he said.

Valfric raised an eyebrow, and Osthart went on. "Yes, you can kill. I've seen that. You are rather good at it. But in the settlement, there's other work to be done. Unless you're in a settlement that's only concerned with raiding. But I don't think you're going to find that. At least not easily. No, you'll be better spent helping out the people of the settlement," he said honestly.

Valfric smiled. "And here I thought you were like one of our old breed, a raider through and through," he said.

Osthart laughed. "I am, but I'm also a realist. And even though our legends and stories put all the emphasis on warriors, in my experience, you still need farmers to grow the food, carpenters to build the homes and the carts, tanners and weavers, and all of that. It's great if you can steal those things from some-body, but trust me when I say that most settlements—and I can guarantee even your old settlement, even if you didn't see it—produced more of its own food than it stole. And you would provide a great deal of security for a settle-ment," he said. "Any of them would be lucky to have you. I hope to cross paths with you again someday, and if we do, you're always welcome at my fire," Osthart said kindly.

Valfric smiled. "Likewise," he said, and then got serious. "But seriously, Osthart, avoid those legions. I would head just north before you head to the east," he said.

Osthart nodded. "Consider me warned. I do appreciate everything that you've done for us, and I wish you two the best of luck," he said, glancing over at Eira.

He stood and walked over to his cart, talking to some of the people from his settlement.

Valfric sighed, looking at the people. They were different now. Now they were no longer his group. They were their own group, and his old ways clicked in his head. He knew he could trust most of them, but still, there were some that he couldn't trust, and he would no longer have Osthart to back him. He glanced at the men who still had ill wishes against him.

"Fuck it," he said, standing up.

As he stood, he felt the pain in his back, though it lessened as he began to move. He called over to Eira, telling her that it was time to go.

She came walking up to him.

"Valfric, going?" she asked.

He nodded. "We're going. It's just going to be the two of us, though," he said.

She looked confused.

"Valfric, just us?" she said, concerned, looking around.

He nodded. "Just us. Just you and I," he said.

She looked more concerned. She looked over at the mule and then looked down at Ferngar.

He sighed.

"The mule and Ferngar, too. It's just we're the only two people going," he said.

"Valfric, that more than two," she said.

He bit back an irritated retort.

"I'm sorry," he said. "Come on. Let's go."

He began to walk, waving farewell to a few people. They all smiled and waved at him. The nice part about the group was everyone had known they had been temporary, transient in nature. They were all just moving in the same direction, but eventually, they knew those directions would change.

The path they took was narrow and appeared to be more of a game trail than anything else, but he suspected there was enough foot traffic on it that it would eventually lead somewhere. And soon, they were away from the field, and they were surrounded by trees. Behind him, he could hear the gentle clomping of the mule's hooves, and he heard Eira walking next to him, humming and looking around at everything with a bemused smile on her face.

Perhaps Osthart was correct. She might have been good for him. She was keeping his mood from being too sour, and she was enough of a distraction from the pain that he didn't seem to notice it as much.

He still didn't have the foggiest clue about her past, and he very much doubted he would ever learn about it. All he knew for certain was that she was a mix between Lysandrian and Gwenthari and that there was something wrong with her, and she had probably suffered greatly. But she weathered it well.

So they walked along the road, and as they moved, he felt his back loosen up some, and the air cooled down once they were in the shade of the trees, and his nose filled with the scent of dirt, pine, flowers, and other nice things. It relaxed him, and as he relaxed, he felt the pain dull a little bit more. He realized some of it was probably tension.

What did it say about him that the people had saved him, but he still had tension around them, distrust? *That says more about you than it does them,* he thought. Still, there was some validity to it. He knew those men would love to slit his throat, so he kept on pushing himself throughout the day, making sure he opened a wide gap.

He knew he would have Essaerites protecting them, and it was unlikely that they would run into any problems. But still, that little voice in the back of his head, the one that had always encouraged him to do the raiding, do the hurting, reminded him that others had the same thoughts in mind and that he needed to protect himself from them.

So they walked and walked until the sun was going down before they finally made camp. He set up his tent while Eira built a fire. One of his wolves had caught a hare and brought it to them. Eira got to work skinning it and cooking it. It was odd in a way because she seemed to like animals, and she seemed to be very caring, but once something was dead, she didn't have any issues skinning it and cooking it. Once it had died, she saw it differently. He supposed that was good. That was something his brother always struggled with.

As he sat around the fire, he looked at her, noticing her tunic. It was covered in mud and dirt and some blood in places. They hadn't changed or washed since they had left the battle. His own tunic was tattered and covered in blood and dirt and smelled something horrible. Valfric did too. It had been a long time since he had had a bath.

After they ate, he said, "We need to clean up."

"Valfric okay," Eira said, nonplussed.

He walked into the tent and created a basin of warm water with a rag. He would have normally done this with real water, but he didn't care to go fetch it and find a stream. Eira came tottering in and looked at the water.

"Alright, we need to get you cleaned up," he said, wondering how well she would do with this task.

He suspected a lot of it would have to do with how well her old owners had maintained her—something that he suspected was probably lacking. She looked confused, and he said, "We need to get you clean. You need to take off your tunic, okay?"

She nodded tightly and mumbled, "Valfric okay," she said.

He felt bad seeing her uncomfortable, but she eventually obeyed and pulled her tunic off over her head. His eyes widened as she did, not because he thought that Eira was beautiful—though he suspected at one point in time she might have been and maybe in a different life—but his eyes widened at what he saw. Her body was filthy, which he had been expecting, but what he hadn't been expecting, or at least not to this extent, was that she was covered from head to toe in scars of various stages of healing. Some were burns, cuts, all sorts of things. He felt his heart drop at the horrors this woman had faced.

Her timidness began to make more sense to him now. How many times had she been beaten, whipped, and tortured? She looked at him, standing uncomfortable. He reached down into the basin, averting his eyes from her, trying not to show a reaction as he dipped the rag in the water and came up to her slowly. He let her touch the rag, and she smiled, feeling the warmth of the water. He began wiping her down with it.

At first, she seemed tense and timid, but then she seemed to relax some and smiled, almost seeming to enjoy it. For Valfric, it was a surreal experience, taking care of someone else, taking care of a slave. But he did it, and he found it made him feel better in a way. It took him a while, and he had to replace the basin full of water several times, but eventually, Eira was clean. Her skin looked good, and she smelled nice, and he smiled.

"Very nice," he said.

Now it was his turn. Without giving it a second thought, he pulled off his tunic. He instantly saw her collapse in on herself and shake a little bit as she saw him, naked. Her eyes welled up slightly, and her face blushed, and she trembled. Instantly, he was concerned.

"What's wrong?" he said, holding out his hand.

She flinched away from him a little bit and then seemed to stop herself. "Valfric sorry. Valfric, Eira be good," she said. He was confused. Her breath seemed a little ragged, and she muttered, "Valfric, Eira be good," she said.

She came forward, and he was still confused. She began to move down to her knees.

It hit him. "No, no, no," he said, reaching out, putting his hands on her upper arms. "No, I didn't mean," he said.

She looked up at him in horror and concern. "Valfric, Eira be good," she said, terrified. She looked down, looked down at his crotch. "Valfric, Eira be good," she said, reaching out and touching him.

He kneeled down and moved her hand away gently. "No, no, you don't have to," he said. "You don't have to do that again," he found himself saying.

The fear in her eyes was ripping through him, shredding his soul. Quickly, he created a piece of fabric that he wrapped around his waist.

"I'm sorry. I'm so sorry, Eira. I didn't mean it like that. I'm so sorry," he said earnestly.

She looked confused. "Valfric, Eira be good," she said.

He shook his head. "You are good, Eira. You are good. You are the best. You don't have to do that, okay?" he said.

She nodded, seeming relieved. "Valfric, okay," she said.

His heart was pounding in his chest, and his mind reeled. How many times had he seen that same look of fear on people's faces and enjoyed it? He felt guilt inside of him, boiling like acid in his stomach. He had caused that fear in others. He had done that to people. He'd hurt them the way someone had hurt her, the way many people had. He felt his shame building up, and his eyes filled with unbidden tears. Tears that hadn't been there, save for laughter, since he was a small child, since the last time his father had beat them out of him.

"Valfric, okay?" Eira asked.

He nodded. "I'm... I'm fine."

She walked over to the basin and came back with the rag, smiling. She reached out and began running it along his shoulder and arms. "Valfric clean," she said. "Valfric clean. Eira clean Valfric," she said, nodding and smiling.

"You don't—" he started.

"Eira clean Valfric," she said and began wiping him down more earnestly.

He allowed it, though it felt like his heart was ripping in half. While it felt nice to have the grime wiped from his body, as he watched, all he could think of was that he did not deserve this. After a moment, he realized that she was still nude, and he shook himself.

He stopped her. "Eira, you need new clothes," he said. She nodded, reaching for her tunic. He stopped her. "No, those ones are dirty and bad. You need something new," he said, thinking. He almost never created clothing with Essaeris. He could do it, of course. There had been plenty of times during raids that clothes had been destroyed or damaged, but it just wasn't something that he thought of on a daily basis.

That was going to change until they came to someplace more permanent. "What's your favorite color?" he asked her.

She thought. "Green," she said.

He nodded. "Green."

"Pink," she said.

He nodded. "Okay, green or pink?"

She smiled and nodded. "Blue?" she said.

He resisted the urge to sigh. "What's your favorite color, Eira?" he said.

She thought more and got excited. "Purple," she said.

He laughed. "Okay, purple," he said.

She thought again. "Green." She said. "Yellow."

He laughed. "How about green and yellow?"

Her eyes lit up. He reached out with his Essaeris and created a tunic. It was green and yellow. It was probably hideous, but it looked better than the one she'd had before. And the fabric was much softer. Not that he was good at creating fabrics, just that her old one was caked with grime. She oohed and picked it up, looking at it.

"It's yours," he said.

She smiled. "Valfric, mine?"

He felt himself smiling. "Yes, it's yours."

She pulled it on over her head and looked down at it, smiling.

Then she looked at him and grinned. "Thank you," she said. Then she looked down at the basin. "Eira clean Valfric," she said, picking up the rag and going back to her work.

He didn't argue with her. And when he was done being cleaned, he created a new tunic for himself and then beds for them to lay in. He plopped down on his, and Eira laid on hers, looking at him intently.

"What is it?" he asked.

"Valfric, Ferngar," she said.

"Ferngar's outside," he said.

She looked at the front of the tent and then back at him, concerned. "Ferngar needs sleep," she said.

He sighed. "Eira, Ferngar is an Essaerite. He does not need to sleep."

She looked concerned. "Valfric, Ferngar," she said.

He huffed, and with his mind, called the giant dog into the tent. There wasn't room for the two of them and a dog. Eira moved to the center of the tent, pressing up against Valfric, and the dog plopped down next to her. She smiled and petted it.

He felt her against him, and in the heat of the night, he felt himself begin to sweat. He sighed, but didn't make a comment, resigning himself to it.

"Good night, Eira," he said.

"Night," she said. And after a few minutes, "Valfric."

"Yes, Eira," he said, trying not to sound irritated.

"Ferngar not sleeping," she said.

He cracked an eye. "Ferngar's an Essaerite."

"Ferngar not sleeping," she said.

He was confused for a moment. The Essaerite was breathing and even breathing in a way as if it was asleep, and then it clicked with him.

He wanted to groan, but instead, he tested his theory. He made an alteration to the Essaerite, and it started to snore softly. Eira smiled and rolled over, content.

He sighed. *Fantastic,* he thought, *a snoring fake dog in my tent.*

He closed his eyes, but he wasn't able to sleep. For one, it was too hot. Two, the dog was snoring, even if it was soft. And three, his mind wouldn't let him. It was turning over with what he had seen on her, thinking about the horrors she had experienced over her life, and the horrors he had committed.

So he lay awake, staring at the top of the tent, listening to the fake dog snore and feeling Eira's warm form pressed against his side. And he thought about his life. And as he did, he couldn't stop the tears of guilt and shame that filled his eyes.

But he didn't make a sound. He dared not wake her because his faults were not her problem. They were his. He was the monster, not her, and he wasn't going to take a single moment away from her.

CHAPTER 19

ariokos stood with Aresio and the other Essaerists, looking up at the city walls of Ulfgard. Separating them from the walls was a small, murky moat that reflected the gray of the overcast sky. The embankment beyond it rose steeply, rough with jagged stones and patches of scrubby grass, climbing fifty or sixty feet before meeting the weathered stone of the wall. On the other side of the city, a river fed the moat.

The legion would be able to take care of that obstacle relatively easily. All around them, construction was taking place as the legion built counter-fortifications around the city, just as they had done in Hroldenfell. These counter-fortifications, like those, were being built thoroughly with the intention of the legions having to spend months on site.

They hadn't seen much in the way of activity from Ulfgard itself, save for the Essaerite activity they had been experiencing. This was new compared to Hroldenfell, but it hadn't been unexpected. Hroldenfell was significantly smaller and less equipped for what was coming. The people of Ulfgard and all the surrounding settlements had time to build up resources and ensure that they had Essaerists on site. The people inside the walls were not going to make the same mistakes the people of Hroldenfell had. And though they hadn't seen much action from the people of the city, the Essaerists were different.

Over Hroldenfell, they had been able to dominate the skies with their hawks and other birds of prey. There had been a few occasions where the space had been contested, but the single Essaerist that had been inside of Hroldenfell had been young and inexperienced. Mariokos would have never actually thought that there was value in holding the space over a city. Yes, you could see what was going on as far as fortifications went and the placement of men, but by and large, it didn't change the day-to-day activities.

It seemed to be different in Ulfgard. Shortly upon arrival, Mariokos, along with other Essaerists, had sent hawks over the city. They'd almost instantly been engaged by Essaerites who had taken them out. Ever since that point, they'd had a difficult time getting any eyes over the city and spent the bulk of their time defending. This had also been new. In Hroldenfell, there hadn't been any defending that they needed to do, but here it seemed that wouldn't be the case.

The legions were constantly being plagued by birds of prey that would fly out, attacking Mariokos and the other Essaerists, Essaerites, and men. Large eagles would swoop down and attack unsuspecting legionnaires, pecking at them, biting them, and clawing them. It hadn't resulted in any fatalities, and the birds were relatively easy to take care of, even for the men on the ground. But as soon as the Essaerites were destroyed, more would appear. They were a harassing force that Mariokos knew would get under people's skins quickly. They'd also been seen bringing back small game.

This last one could pose a minor problem. Mariokos very much doubted that they had the ability to bring in enough meat to keep the entire city fed, but every little bit they brought in helped the city and was less for the legions. It also meant that Mariokos and the other Essaerists had to keep the air around the camps locked down and try to keep the enemy Essaerites from being able to make it out of the area to either cause harm or hunt. It had been an annoyance, to say the least, but not one that Mariokos was having to deal with heavily. The other Essaerists had been dealing with that.

Mariokos had been helping with construction and planning, and now he and Aresio looked at those formidable walls before them. It was apparent that tunneling was going to be difficult, but perhaps not impossible, and it was certainly worth a shot. At worst, Mariokos's Essaerithon would be unable to make any headway or progress, and the legions would find a different tactic for getting past the walls. At best, the hill would be unexpectedly easy to dig through, and they could be into the city within a few weeks, though Mariokos found that last option relatively unlikely.

Mariokos had his Essaerithon behind him. Along with it was also Kyrillos. Caelwen had a handful of cats with her, and Isolara had a couple of her Essaerites. They were the size of men who had long swords. They were extremely effective. They all looked up at the wall together.

"So what's the plan again?" Xavieno asked.

"I'm going to move my Essaerithon into place and see what it can do on the other side of that moat," Mariokos said. The moat was troublesome for humans but wasn't going to pose a problem for his Essaerithon.

Xavieno nodded. "So we're just here to see how it goes," he said.

Mariokos shrugged. "I think so. And the engineers wanted us to get up close to see the walls. I'm sure all of you will have stuff that you'll have to do," he said with a smirk.

Xavieno grunted. "I have no doubt," he said and smiled. "Alright, let's see how this goes."

With a thought, Mariokos's Essaerithon moved forward, entering the moat. It was quickly submerged but made it across without any issues, its feet digging into the ground. As it came up on the other side of the moat, it began walking up just a little way. It was going to move in between the wall and the moat about halfway the distance. He was expecting to see arrows and spears coming down from the walls, but they didn't. What they did see was large groups of people on those walls looking down, watching what was going on.

The Essaerithon's giant bladed teeth came up and then down into the ground, ripping a chunk out. As the teeth drove in, they were slowed and stopped by large chunks of rock and clay in the hillside, confirming what Mariokos and the other engineers had suspected. This hill was going to be difficult to make it through. Still, it continued to pick and dig, soon creating a small hole.

"This is going to be difficult ground to chew through," Mariokos said to Aresio.

Aresio looked severely at the Essaerithon and nodded, not surprised. But that's when something surprising happened.

From the wall, Mariokos saw something leap off. It looked like an Essaerite. It had to be, because it wasn't likely that a human was going to jump off the wall. It landed and began rolling down the hill towards Mariokos's Essaerithon. As it neared, it leaped into the air, and he got a good look at it. It was shorter than a human, but stockier and thicker, with a jagged, rocky hide that gleamed darkly in the sunlight. Its movements were unnervingly smooth for something so solid, and the long black blades extending from its arms glinted like obsidian. He'd never seen anything quite like it. It landed near Mariokos's Essaerithon, which turned its head, its teeth coming out to take out the Essaerite.

Though the Essaerithon was not designed for combat, it wasn't exactly weak. The enemy Essaerite moved quickly and lashed out at Mariokos's. As the blades made contact, they cut through the tough leathery skin of Mariokos's Essaerithon with ease and then through bone in one of the legs, severing it. It tottered and wobbled as it began to lose its balance.

Mariokos's eyes widened. His Essaerithon twisted again to attack, but the enemy Essaerite was already gone. It was moving up, slashing as it went. Mariokos's Essaerithon registered cuts along its neck and back, and then the rock Essaerite moved both of its blades in unison like they were scissors, and Mariokos lost connection with his Essaerithon as its head was severed. He gaped, as did the others. His Essaerithon was gigantic. It could be taken out, yes, but that it had been so quickly amazed even him.

The enemy Essaerite turned, looking at the gathered Lysandrians. Men began shouting orders in preparation for the attack that they knew was about to come. Kyrillos's Essaerithon moved forward to the head of them, prepping itself, waiting. Next to him, he could see Xavieno in deep concentration as he prepared to create more Essaerites to help. From the walls of Ulfgard, three more of the rock Essaerites came down and landed. They didn't move. They just separated themselves along the base of the wall and seemed to wait, as did the Lysandrian Essaerists.

"What is going on?" Aresio said under his breath.

Mariokos shook his head. "I don't know," he said, his heart beating quickly.

"Be ready for anything," Kyrillos said.

Next to Mariokos, Caelwen was looking at the Essaerites. "Do you recognize them?" he asked.

She shook her head quickly. "No, I have never seen them before," she said.

And that's when the next surprising thing happened.

———

Xavieno watched in detached amazement as Mariokos's Essaerithon was beheaded. He watched wide-eyed, amazed not so much that it could happen— Mariokos's Essaerithon wasn't exactly designed for combat, but it was tough and had a very thick neck to support the head that dug through so many things. Seeing it severed was a surprise and spoke to how sharp the blades were that the other Essaerite was using and just how strong it was. The bigger surprise, however, was that the Essaerite was advanced, something that they hadn't really seen the Gwenthari be able to do yet, aside from Caelwen, though she seemed to be the exception, not the rule.

There was shouting and commotion, everyone waiting for the attack to happen, but the Essaerite stayed on the ground. It looked as though nothing was going to happen, but then Isolara shouted a quick warning, and Xavieno looked up. Over the top of the walls came a group of figures swooping down. They looked like eagles, though much larger than any he'd ever seen, and instead of being normal, their beaks were long, metal, and sharp. Their talons likewise shone in the sun.

Instantly, Xavieno sprang into action, creating as many Essaerites as he could. The air filled with the piercing cries of the birds and the panicked shouts of men as the creatures dove, talons flashing. Wings beat furiously overhead, stirring up dust and chaos as the birds descended upon them. There were dozens of them. They quickly moved down, landing on men, their jaws clamping down, severing limbs and necks with seeming ease, then they would move to another man. Shouting and commotion filled the air all around.

Xavieno dove to the side, avoiding one whose claws narrowly missed his head and back. His Essaerites sprang to action, reaching out, attacking, directly connecting with the birds, ripping them out of the sky and killing them. But there were so many. He saw flashes of Caelwen's cats moving and Kyrillos's

Essaerithon slashing ineffectually at the air as the birds circled around it, distracting it.

Mariokos was out of Essaeris and was just holding up a shield, keeping them at bay. It was Isolara who swooped in and seemed to save the day. Her Essaerites moved quickly. They were in many ways similar to the ones that had attacked Mariokos, though they were thinner, and their blades were not as long or as sharp. But they quickly jumped in the air and moved around, dispatching the other Essaerites. Xavieno recovered as some of his more advanced Essaerites came into existence. They produced bows and arrows and quickly began shooting them out of the sky or otherwise throwing javelins or spears at them.

The whole encounter was only a minute long at the most, but in that minute, several men died, and he looked around, hearing the moans and screams of the injured. Around him, there was a handful of mutilated bodies, men who were missing limbs or their heads, while others writhed on the ground, having been torn up by the talons. Xavieno turned and looked as he heard shouts behind him and saw that some of the birds had made it past them and were moving away from the camp.

"Fuck," he said under his breath, watching them go.

He turned back to his companions. Kyrillos was likewise watching, his expression angry but also somehow excited. The Essaerites were moving in different directions away from the camps. The attack on the Essaerists had been a distraction, just a way of keeping them focused and their Essaerites focused so that some of the Essaerites that the Gwenthari had created could move away.

"Clever fucks," Kyrillos said and smiled.

He looked around, making sure that none of the Essaerists were injured, nor any of the ranking members of the legion; there didn't appear to be. The attack could have been far worse, Xavieno realized, but as a distraction, it had done a wonderful job.

He walked over to Mariokos, who was standing up from the ground. He looked surprised and shaken. Xavieno felt the same.

"Never been attacked from the sky before," Xavieno said.

Mariokos looked over to Caelwen, and she shook her head. "I've never seen Essaerites like that either," she said. "I suppose they make sense in a way," she commented.

"They seem to be pretty effective," Isolara said.

"As a distraction maybe, but on a battlefield?" Kyrillos said.

It was true; the birds, while terrifying, would be ineffective in a regular battle. They could swoop in, yes, but Mariokos had been able to protect himself relatively easily by holding a shield above his head. These were going to be a harassing force, but a very effective one.

Later, Xavieno was in his tent, lying on his belly, while Ilara massaged his shoulders. She poured some oil on his back that he'd created. It was warm and felt nice, and her hands began to move. He felt slightly guilty having her do it, but he'd found that she was bent and determined to try to serve him in some way, shape, or form. Caelwen had told him that she was afraid of being sold.

He had no intention of selling her. He didn't think he could; it just seemed wrong, but he could understand where her concerns were coming from. She'd all but thrown herself at him nearly every night, but after that first time, he couldn't do it. The guilt was too strong, too palpable, so he let her massage him. At least it was nice and comforting, and he didn't feel like such a piece of shit when she was doing it. Even if he wanted to, it was difficult with the movement of her hands. Every time he tensed up, she just worked on that area more, and he told himself that if he just relaxed, she wouldn't have to work as hard. He sighed, reminding himself to relax. As he focused, he tried to let his muscles go limp.

"Do you want to tell me what's under your skin?" she asked as she worked on his shoulder.

"What makes you think there's anything bothering me?" he asked.

He glanced up at her, and she just gave him a flat look. He smiled. She'd finally caved and started treating him the way she said she would treat normal people. There was no more of the formality, which made him feel more comfortable.

"Just the attack today and all of this," he said honestly.

"I didn't think that you would be shaken by an attack," she said, sounding surprised.

"It's not that I'm shaken. It's just..." He tried to think of how to say what he was thinking. "It should be a pleasant surprise, I suppose," he said.

"Having somebody who's worthy of challenging you?" she asked.

"Yes, that's exactly what it should be," he mused.

"But it's not," she said.

This was one of the frustrating things, wasn't it? "I don't know why it's not," he confessed after a moment. "It should be. I've always liked testing myself against others. Even now, I do, but for some reason... I don't know. I think it's going to be more of a pain in the ass than anything else."

"So what exactly happened? I've only heard little bits and pieces of it," she said.

He relayed what had happened that afternoon with the birds. To her credit, her hands never stopped moving, and she just listened to him. When he was done, he said, "So we were sitting there watching the wall to see if those other rock Essaerites were going to attack next, but they didn't. But when we looked up at the people on top of the walls, we saw the group that we think must be the Essaerists," he said.

"What made you think they were the Essaerists?" she asked.

"The way they were watching us," he said. "They weren't watching with the excitement of the other people on the wall. They were looking at it critically, like they were examining their plans to see how they had worked," he said. He remembered looking at them. They hadn't been able to get any birds over the area, but they were able to keep a few birds of prey in the air who had much better eyes than any of the humans did.

He'd looked through the eyes of one of his hawks at the group standing. The hawk's sharp gaze picked out the glint of armor. There was only a handful of them, but in the center of the group was a woman who looked like she was only a few years older than him. Her hair was long and white. He had never seen anything like it before. He described her to Ilara, and finally, her hands stopped moving. He turned, looking up at her.

"Something wrong?" he said.

She shook her head quickly and began rubbing his arm.

"No, it's fine," she said.

"No, tell me," he said, looking at her seriously.

She looked almost embarrassed. "Well, did Caelwen know her or say anything about her?"

He thought back. "She did say something under her breath and looked slightly annoyed and concerned, but I don't know, not much. Why? Is she a famous Gwenthari Essaerist or something?"

Ilara shook her head. "Not if she has white hair, no. She's not Gwenthari at all," she said.

He raised an eyebrow. "She's not?"

Ilara shook her head again. "She's Wyrdrunir."

He thought for a moment. "I don't know that I've heard that name before," he said.

She shrugged. "I'm not surprised. They're far to the north, farther north than the Eirfrosti are. They aren't Gwenthari."

"So what's one doing this far south?" he asked.

She shrugged again. "I couldn't tell you why, but if she's an Essaerist, she's not to be underestimated," Ilara warned.

He wasn't sure if he bought that or not. He laid back down, allowing her to continue to massage him.

"I was more concerned with the man that was next to her. He looked like he was Gwenthari and was older. I know that Gwenthari Essaerists are stronger when they're older since they have more practice," he said. "This woman was only a few years older than me, so maybe she created some of the birds," he mused.

"She didn't create the birds," Ilara said. "If those Essaerites that attacked Mariokos were as powerful as you said, they were hers."

He rolled over on his side, looking up at her. "You sure?"

"You're stronger than most Gwenthari Essaerists who are your age, aren't you?" Ilara said.

"Well, yes, but I've had training," he started.

"Exactly," she said. "And this woman will too. Wyrdrunirs are not Gwenthari. They are very proud people. They're small, from what I understand. I've never met or seen one before, but their Essaerists are supposed to be almost as powerful, if not as powerful, as the Eirfrosti ones."

He thought for a moment. "I have heard that the Eirfrosti Essaerists are better," he said. "Even heard a few people refer to them as witches," he said with a smile.

"That's what a lot of people think they are," Ilara said. "I don't. I know Essaerists, so I just know that they're more trained, but they actually take the time to train their Essaerists. The Eirfrosti are not like other Gwenthari."

He reminded himself that Ilara wasn't a simpleton. She knew and under-stood more than many people did, and she had spent a lot of time around an Essaerist. So, she wasn't taken to the superstitions that some of her people seemed to be led away by.

"So the Eirfrosti Essaerists are difficult then?" he said.

"Very," she said. "They'll be like attacking your own; the Wyrdrunirs will be the same. So I wouldn't take this woman lightly," she said seriously.

He nodded, thinking. He looked at her, reading the expression on her face, seeing slight concern. He cocked his head to the side.

"You almost sound concerned, like you're worried about me," he said.

"I am," she said honestly.

He raised an eyebrow. "Really? Why is that?"

She shrugged. "I like you. You're nice, and you're my owner. I'm supposed to want your best interests," she said with a smirk, "remember?"

He chuckled. "I'm your owner. I would think you'd want bad things for me," he said honestly.

"Well, I guess if you were a horrible person, maybe that would be the case," she said. "But I've seen how other slaves are treated, and I've seen how I'm treated. And let's just say that it's in my best interest to stay your property," she said, though he could hear a slight hint of shame in her voice. Along with it, there was a tint of fear.

He remembered what Caelwen had told him.

"I'm not going to sell you," he said.

She looked surprised. "Caelwen," she said after a moment.

He nodded. "I'm not going to sell you," he said again.

"I appreciate that, but you might change your mind," she said.

He shook his head. "I don't think I will. But even if I were to, or if I were to die or something like that, nothing bad would happen to you," he said.

"You can't promise that," she said.

He nodded, "in a way I can. If I die, then you will be given to Mariokos and Caelwen," he said. "Mariokos would never harm you, and as long as you don't wake up Caelwen, you'll be fine," he laughed.

She looked surprised. "Not your wife?" she said.

"My wife doesn't know you, and you'd have to be shipped down to my homeland. No, that's not how it would go," he said. "But it doesn't matter, because nothing's going to happen to me. And I'm not going to sell you," he said. "Even if you aren't a very good masseuse," he added.

He smiled as she rolled her eyes.

"I'm an excellent masseuse," she said. "Roll back over, and I'll fix that knot on your shoulder."

He chuckled and rolled back, and she began working on a particularly difficult knot on his shoulder. As she worked again, he reminded himself to try and relax.

CHAPTER 20

A cluster of weathered buildings emerged through the haze of the afternoon sun, their rough edges softened by the distance. Valfric and Eira had been traveling for a few days, passing through quiet stretches of countryside where clusters of low stone walls and thatched-roof farmhouses dotted the landscape. The scent of grass mixed with the distant murmur of livestock, and the occasional bark of a dog echoed through the air. The day was warm, and it looked like it might rain later, but he hoped that it would hold out for a while. His back was starting to feel much better, but he was still using a walking stick to help him along. He hoped that within the next week or so, he wouldn't need it. Next to him, the mule trudged along, with Eira and Ferngar wandering along the roadside, looking at plants and otherwise seeming to enjoy themselves. Well, Eira was. Ferngar was an Essaerite and couldn't enjoy himself, but he couldn't not enjoy himself either. It worked out, though, because Eira seemed to inspect nearly everything along the side of the road. She tended to find wild berries and mushrooms for them to eat, which had been a nice addition to their otherwise all-meat diet.

The buildings they were approaching weren't farms but looked to be businesses, likely a small town that supported the farms in the area. From the sky, his hawks noted the number of buildings. They were close together, in a small, open space surrounded by forest. This whole area was mountainous, but it wasn't too steep or rugged. On either side of them, the trees grew high, casting deep shadows that made the warm days much more bearable, but also made it nearly impossible for his hawks to scout.

As they flew over, high above, they made out a handful of people. There didn't appear to be anything wrong with the town. Children darted through the streets, their laughter mingling with the distant barking of dogs. A merchant shouted out his wares from a stall, and the rhythmic sound of a hammer striking iron echoed from a nearby forge. People moved with a relaxed confidence, their conversations drifting through the warm air. There was no reason for them to be concerned. They didn't know about Valfric, nor was he a threat to them, but he always had in the back of his mind that people needed to be on alert. He reminded himself that they had left Ulfgarath and were now firmly in Valfarans territory. The Valfarans, like the Ulfgarath and other Gwenthari, raided and everything of that nature, but they seemed to be more stable than the Ulfgarath people had been.

It wouldn't have been something that he would have been able to pick out until he had left Ulfgarath, but now he could see it. People seemed to feel just a little bit more confident, feel a little bit safer, and were a little bit more open than his people had been. He didn't know if that was good or bad. There would have been a time when he would have said that they were fools, ripe and easy for the taking, but his mind was starting to shift on that. After all, his people had been shrinking for generations. The Valfarans had not. In fact, the Valfarans had been a good part of the reason why the Ulfgarath had shrunk. So part of him had to admit that maybe they had it right.

It didn't matter now, though. All that mattered was heading north, away from Lysandrian and whatever difficulties they would cause. Valfric was sure they would stop at Ulfgard, that the citizens there would finally push back the legions, but maybe they wouldn't. After all, he had thought they had a sure win at the Ilfrun River, but that had been different, hadn't it?

He checked on Eira's Essaeris collar, making sure that it looked like a proper slave's collar. He didn't want her to be uncomfortable, but he also didn't want anyone in the town to think that she wasn't owned. This was as much for her safety as anything else. He also made sure that her clothing didn't look overly nice. This had posed a challenge for him. Valfric had never created garments before, or at least not regularly before their trip, but he was doing it on a daily basis now.

Every day he would ask Eira what her favorite color was, and every day it was different, and he would make her a tunic with that color. The problem was that they were on the road. They should be dirty and slightly tattered. Not unkempt, mind you, but not brand new. It would either make them look too wealthy or would raise suspicions.

Valfric did not want to appear wealthy. He wanted to appear utterly normal, if anything, maybe slightly on the poor side—anything that would make someone decide that they weren't a target worth going after. Not that he was overly concerned about protecting himself, but he thought it was better for them to go unnoticed than to make themselves seen. He also made sure that Ferngar wasn't going to get more than a few feet away from Eira, and would protect her, watching those around for any signs of danger. His wolves were circling the town, not venturing too near, lest livestock or people see them.

That would be bad. Not that the people would assume that the wolves were Essaeris, but rather the opposite.

Few things sent people into panic like a pack of wolves surrounding a town, threatening its people and livestock. The town looked to have a handful of dogs, though they couldn't smell the Essaerites. As they neared the town, he saw two young children playing, one hiding behind a tree trunk, the other trying to find the other one. They laughed and ran around. As they saw Valfric and Eira approach, they stopped and looked up at them, wide-eyed in a way that only children seem to do whenever meeting somebody new.

He smiled as warmly as he could at them. "Hello, my name is Valfric. This is Eira," he said. The kids nodded but didn't say anything. *Children are always so odd,* he thought. Eira smiled at them, and they smiled back at her, seeming to relax some.

"Is there a tanner here?" Valfric asked. One of the kids pointed up the street, and Valfric nodded, continuing along.

He beckoned Eira to follow, and she came up next to him, humming to herself, looking around the town. People were looking at them but didn't seem overly wary, other than giving them appraising looks, trying to figure out what they were doing or where they were from. They found the tanner with relative ease.

During their travels, Valfric had kept the pelts of the hares they had killed, along with some from a handful of deer that they had managed to take down as well when they had been traveling with the larger group. He approached the tanner, who was a large man with blonde hair and a thick beard. The man looked up at him.

"What can I do for you?" he asked.

Valfric led the mule over. "I have some pelts I was wondering if you'd want to buy," he said.

Valfric had money; he just hadn't had a need to use it yet. Before everything had gone so wrong at the Ilfrun River, his friends had given him their coin purses so that they would be traveling lighter when they came across the bridge. That meant that Valfric had not only the money that he'd had on him but all of their money too. And while it felt poisonous in some ways to him, a reminder, he did have a decent amount on him, though he didn't want to be flashy with their money. He reminded himself that at some point in time, if they didn't find a place to stay for the winter, they might need it. But they also needed provisions now as well, so he was hoping that he could at least fetch a decent price for the pelts that he had.

"I might be willing to buy them off you," the man said, seeming more curious.

He came over to the mule and began inspecting the pelts. Eira walked around looking at everything. The tanner glanced over at her but then went back to looking at the pelts, inspecting them curiously.

"You have quite a few," he said.

Valfric shrugged. "We've been carrying them for some time, but I need to buy some supplies. I figured this might be a good place to do it."

The man grunted. "It's as good as any, at least as good as any that you could find for a ways around." He sighed. "I don't have a need for a lot of these, but I suppose I can buy them off you. Could probably use the hare pelts come wintertime," he mused to himself.

"That would be good," Valfric said.

They haggled for a short while before the man gave him a slightly generous price, Valfric had to admit. He suspected it had to do with the fact that Valfric had a walking stick. The man told them to go to a building that was on the northwest corner of the town where they could pick up any other supplies that they might need. He thanked them and walked off.

As they walked through the town, he saw more people wandering around, trading and going about their days, along with dogs and children. No one seemed to pay them much notice. As they got to the edge of town, he noted a couple of men that were readying packs and talking amongst themselves. He tied up the mule outside and went into a building. There he was able to purchase everything that they needed. He bought a few bags of flour for the road, along with potatoes and carrots, a few spices and some onions, along with a handful of loaves of bread, and two jugs of Bryndraught. He got some butter and honey as well and loaded up the mule.

Eira looked at the items with interest, and he smiled as he watched her. "We're going to have an actual dinner tonight," he said to her.

She looked over at him. "Valfric, we not eat dinner every night?" she asked.

"We have, but this one will be a proper one. It just won't be meat. How does that sound?" he said.

She smiled, seeming happy. Though he wasn't sure if she was actually happy about having the prospect of a decent dinner or just happy because he was happy.

They headed out of town, and as they did, the men who were preparing to leave greeted them. He instantly felt himself become wary; it was habit, and he couldn't help it from happening.

"Where you headed?" one of them asked.

"Just north, you?" Valfric asked guardedly.

They shrugged, seeming friendly enough. "Same direction. Maybe we'll see you on the road."

He nodded and smiled. "Maybe you will."

They began moving, and occasionally, Valfric would look back, seeing if the men were following. After a while, one of his hawks noted the men had left and were carrying packs but weren't moving at a hurried pace. He decided they weren't a threat and stopped thinking about them. Instead, he tried to enjoy the summer day as they moved.

Setting up camp was a pretty standard affair at this point, and Valfric worked on the tent while Eira started on dinner. He created a pot for her, and she went and fetched water from a local stream that she set to boil. It didn't take very long before he could smell a stew cooking, and he looked over, seeing her tending it. She'd cut up a lot of vegetables, and with some meat that they had, she had found a few large mushrooms that she was adding. The whole time, she hummed to herself.

He'd been slightly surprised to see that Eira could cook. Not that it was a unique skill to have, but his brother Gaelrik had struggled with tasks like that. Gaelrik did okay enough after enough training, but Valfric had worked with his brother a lot and hadn't thought that it had been the case for Eira. But he decided that she probably had been trained in many things. After all, she was a slave, and her purpose was to do work, wasn't it? So at one point in time, a former owner must have taught her.

As dinner was coming to a close, he created a few stools for them to sit on, and he sat down, feeling his back throb and ache, but it was better than it had been. Eira ladled some stew into bowls, and he broke a loaf of bread in half, giving her a chunk. He dipped his in the broth and ate it, savoring the flavor. After a bite, he remembered that they had Bryndraught as well, and he took the jug, pouring small glasses for both of them.

"It's very good," he told her.

She grinned. "Valfric, thank you," she said, as she continued to eat.

The sun was sinking behind the treetops, casting long shadows across the camp. The fire crackled, releasing the warm, woody scent of burning pine, mingled with the rich aroma of stew bubbling in the pot. The air was cool against his skin, carrying the distant chirp of crickets and the rustle of leaves in the breeze. Soon the night plants would begin to pulse and glow. He finished his bowl and drained the rest of his Bryndraught, feeling his belly full. It was delightful. He hadn't had a proper meal since before the attack at the Ilfrun River, and as he finished his food, he felt himself relax in a way that he hadn't been able to do in some time. For the first time in a long time, he was starting to feel like a person again.

He wondered if it was that way for Eira, too. She seemed more contented than she normally did, but not by a large amount. He'd come to realize that she took the world however it was, didn't think anything of the past, and just lived in the now. He supposed in a way that might have been a peaceful way to live. But she seemed happy, with Ferngar lying at her feet. She scratched behind its ears and down the dog's back, playing with the fur. Valfric had made the Essaerite act like it enjoyed such things, though it didn't feel anything at all near like pleasure. It sensed, and it knew what was supposed to feel good and what was supposed to feel bad. But it didn't care. It gave it as much credence as a rock gave being in a stream or being on a path.

One of his birds caught wind of people approaching. He looked through the bird's eyes, seeing that it was the men. Their packs were missing, and he suspected their camp was a little ways back. They were approaching but were out in the open, not trying to sneak up. Still, Valfric didn't like it.

He felt himself tense as they came into view. Both of them were around his age; one was thin and tall, but the other had more meat on his bones. Both had blonde hair and beards. He stood, as did Eira; she moved to go greet them, and Valfric gently took her arm.

"Stay behind me," he said to her softly.

"Valfric," she said, her voice shaking.

He didn't pay her any attention as he took a few steps forward.

"Good evening," the bigger of the two said.

"Evening," Valfric said, his tone even.

He had his wolves nearby, and he had Ferngar edge closer to Eira. Valfric wanted to think the men before him were friendly, but years of being a killer told him otherwise. *They see a weak man*, he thought.

"What can I do for you?" Valfric asked.

The thin one smirked, but it was the bigger of the two that spoke. "Couldn't help but notice that you bought a lot of supplies in town. That can't be easy to carry bein' hurt."

This was what he'd been worried about when they took on supplies—that others would see not only a weak target but a fat one. He grunted. "That's what the mule is for."

The thin one smiled. "Look... we just want to lighten your load. No reason for violence."

The bigger one eyed Valfric's walking stick. *At least he has sense enough to look for a weapon*, he thought. On the note of a weapon, Valfric only had a knife on him, but he could change that. He was about to create a sword when the big man lunged forward.

The world narrowed the way it only could in battle. Time slowed for him as the man came at him. Valfric couldn't dodge him, and the man slammed into him, sending them sprawling. In the back of his mind, he thought he heard a woman scream, but it was pushed from him as pain exploded in his back. It was white hot and made his vision start to fade. They hit the ground, and instinct took over. Valfric rolled the man off him. His heart hammered in his chest, stoking his rage. As the anger built, the pain in his back faded into oblivion.

Ferngar was barking and growling, keeping between Eira and the scene before her. Blurs behind him flew out of the woods, and the thin man screamed in pain and fear as two of Valfric's wolves latched onto him. Valfric looked down at the man and saw not his enemy but the weight of his failures. It made his rage build, and he slammed his fist into the man's face. He tried to push Valfric off, but the man wasn't a warrior; he was a soft thief who picked the wrong target.

Valfric's fist came down again, breaking the man's nose. And then again, splitting his lip. A tooth dug into Valfric's knuckle with the blow. *You don't need teeth*, Valfric thought as his fist came down again and again, breaking the mans teeth in. Blood filled the man's mouth and flung into the air each time Valfric's fist came up. The man tried to bat him away, but he couldn't. He was too weak. Valfric punched again, feeling the bone around the man's eye break. He was begging and mumbling, Valfric thought, but he wasn't sure. He kept hitting.

Behind him, one of the wolves latched onto the thin man's throat, ripping it open. Blood gushed from the wound, and the other wolf clamped onto his arm, thrashing its head back and forth. The limb ripped and popped, as the joint inside dislocated. The wolf shook the man like a doll, and still, Valfric brought his fists down on the other man.

The man gurgled, and Valfric grinned as his anger poured out of him into the other person. He took the knife at his belt and slashed down the side of the man's throat, cutting deep. He did it to the other side and then did the first side again. He alternated back and forth, cutting deeper each time. The blade was almost to the spine when his anger receded, and Valfric stopped. He looked down at the corpse and spat.

Valfric stood, his back ached, and he felt his hands and arms coated in blood. He panted. His beating heart was like a roar in his ears, but over the roar, he heard the sound of crying. *Eira,* he realized. He turned around, hearing the sound coming from the tent. He burst in, and as he did, she screamed, covering her face and head with her arms and hands. He instantly felt himself grow cold.

"Are you hurt?" he asked, coming down next to her.

She was lying on the ground, curled up in a ball, sobbing. As he touched her, she flinched away, panicked. He looked through Ferngar's memories quickly, but none of the men had touched her. She began freaking out as soon as everything had gone sideways. He tried to calm his breathing, his heart, and his voice.

"It's okay now, it's okay. No one's going to hurt you," he said.

"Valfric, no hurt," she said.

"I'm not hurt," he said.

"Valfric, no hurt, Valfric, no hurt!" she wailed.

He reached out, touching her again. Again, she flinched.

"I'm not hurt," he said, trying to stay calm.

"Valfric, no hurt!" she said urgently.

And then it clicked in his brain. When he had been hurt, she said, 'Valfric, hurt.' But now she was saying, 'Valfric, no hurt.' *She's talking about you,* he thought. *She's telling you not to hurt people.*

He felt a few emotions wash over him quickly. First was irritation and anger that she was telling him what to do, but that quickly evaporated and was replaced by guilt and sadness. Not at what he had done, but that she had seen it. That she had seen him do it. That she had seen *him*. The real him.

He reached out again more gently and touched her again. She trembled and quivered underneath his touch.

"Eira," he said softly, "look at me," he said.

After a few moments, she tentatively moved her hands, her terrified eyes looking up at him.

"I won't hurt you," he said. "I will never, ever hurt you, Eira. Do you understand?" he said.

Her head wobbled a little bit.

"Valfric, no hurt," she said.

"I will never hurt you," he said, his voice aching like his back.

"Valfric people," she said.

He sighed. "I had to do it. They would have killed us," he said.

"Valfric, no hurt," she said.

He felt guilt roiling inside of himself. He knew he had to do what he did, but for the first time in his life, it bothered him. He held her shoulder, and she let him.

"I'm sorry," he said. "I'm so sorry."

To his amazement, his voice cracked, and he felt his eyes fill with tears. What was happening to him? What was he becoming?

Her expression was still afraid but now looked concerned in a different way. She moved.

"Valfric hurt?" she asked.

He shook his head. "I'm fine," he said, his voice oddly quavering.

And then she wrapped her arms around his neck and pulled him close. "Valfric, okay," she said, her voice soft and consoling.

He wrapped his arms around her and pulled her in close. As he did, he felt a shaking in his chest and body.

"Valfric, okay," she said again.

And with her words, he felt a ragged, jagged breath move through him that came up his throat and came with a sound that he hadn't heard from himself in years, a sound so alien, so foreign to come from him that he almost didn't recognize it until it happened a few more times. They were the sounds of sobs. He hadn't made those sounds since he'd been looking down at his dead brother's body, but here they were.

"Valfric, okay," she said again.

He closed his eyes and buried his face in her neck and hair as he felt tears begin to stream out of his eyes. He held on to her tightly as if holding on for dear life. And part of him wondered if he was holding on to her for life. If she let go of him or he let go of her, would he fall apart? Would he be destroyed? He didn't know. He thought maybe he would.

He clung on to Eira until at some point in time he had fallen asleep. He woke to the sound of birds outside. Eira was still in his arms, holding on to him as they lay in the middle of the tent. His back throbbed and ached from his injury and from sleeping in an awkward position. He wasn't sure if she was actually asleep, and after a moment, he realized that she wasn't. Her fingers were gently moving through his hair, and as he stirred, she looked at him.

"Valfric, okay?" she asked.

He nodded. "I'm okay," he said.

He pushed her hair away from her face, looking into her eyes. There were dark circles under them.

"Did you sleep?" he asked.

She shook her head. "Eira, protect," she said.

It made him want to start crying again, made his heartbreak. She'd stayed awake to protect him, to comfort him. *You don't deserve this,* he thought. *You don't deserve anything like this!* And he didn't. But his mind also went out to the previous night's events, and he looked at them the way that he would have in the past; they'd been attacked. By the same number of men that had left the town, men that were not part of the town, but they'd been attacked nonetheless. His mind went to his wolves.

He had them drag away the bodies from outside the tent, lest Eira see them and go into another fit. He also reached out with his mind and created a small Essaerite that was like a person with hands and feet. It climbed on top of one of the wolves that began roving around looking for the men's camp. They'd come without packs, which meant that they had something set up somewhere. It only took the wolves a few minutes to find the camp. There, the Essaerite did what he knew had to be done. He doubted that Eira would have approved, but despite that, Valfric had the Essaerite move and look through their belongings, not looking for items they could sell, not like if he was raiding, but looking for food and for coin. It found both, but the coin outweighed the food by a fairly wide margin.

The Essaerite placed anything that it found into the wolves' mouths for them to swallow, a handy technique for carrying more loot out of an area. He'd learned over the years that a wolf's belly could hold a fair amount of items, and once the wolf was released, everything would come out having been protected.

He stirred in the tent. "We need to get moving," he said.

He didn't want anyone from the town finding the bodies. They would eventually, but he didn't want to be around when they did. He didn't know how they would react. He made sure the wolves dragged the bodies back to the camp and then had them go after the men as if they had been attacked by animals. It would be the smartest way of going. When they were found, hopefully, no one would be any the wiser.

They quickly packed up camp and began moving again. The whole time, Valfric kept the wolves closer to him, watching for danger. *You were a fucking idiot,* he thought to himself. *You thought that you were in some peaceful land. You aren't. You're in the real world, Valfric. Get it through your thick head.*

Though he didn't voice it to Eira. He should have seen what was going to happen before it did. He would have in Ulfgarath, but he let himself be lulled into a false sense of security being in Valfarans. That because there was less raiding there, that somehow there wasn't danger on the road. *Idiocy,* he reminded himself. They could be in the safest place in the world, and there would always be thieves. And those who would see an easy target in a seemingly crippled man and a small slave girl. He should have known better. They'd looked too nice when they'd gone to town, bought too many items, been too friendly. But then also, what else were they to do?

"What's done is done," he said to himself softly.

Eira didn't seem to hear him, which was good. He looked over at her with fondness as she wandered around inspecting everything on the side of the road. *You don't deserve her,* he thought to himself. *And she most certainly does not deserve the life that she's had,* he thought, remembering how much cruelty she'd faced. He felt a small grain of hope inside of himself for the first time in a while. He wasn't a good person, but she was. He was evil; she wasn't. He was strong and violent; she was not. She was prey. But in that moment, he realized he would be her protector. And what better to protect the soft and innocent than a wolf?

CHAPTER 21

Despite being a war camp, it didn't feel like one to Caelwen. Around her, there were fortifications that had been getting more robust with each passing day. There were roads inside the camp along with drainage, buildings for bathing and latrines, and areas for trade and even socialization. It was all extremely orderly. The roads were gravel, leveled, and well-maintained—better, in fact, than the ones in the settlement she'd grown up in.

In many ways, the camps were of a higher quality than the settlement she had grown up in, save for the fact that they were so densely populated. There weren't fields or flowers that she could see when she walked out of her tent in the morning, just seas of tents. Though she suspected that, with time, those would turn into either semi-permanent or permanent structures depending on how long the Legion was going to stay. Some parts of the camp were already turning into this. Wooden structures were being erected, and she knew there were plans to add stone ones. All this, and eventually, the city of Ulfgard would fall, and these fortifications would be destroyed or folded into the larger city. It was fascinating to her in so many ways.

The camp that had been around Hroldenfell was similar. It was always growing, always changing, always becoming more permanent and advanced. As if the legions were like a plant that blew around in the wind, but if it settled for a time, would take up root and spread.

Engagements with Ulfgard had been limited and kept to the space right around its walls and moat. The counter-fortifications around the city were robust, and Caelwen had watched as they had been built up and changed. Her Essaerites, along with everyone else's, were watching those walls. All of the

Essaerists in the area had come together and created Essaerites, combining all of their powers. She'd done this with Mariokos on many occasions, but it had been an odd sort of thing to do with so many others. In many ways, it was personal—an intimate touch, if you will. But it was also incredibly practical. The upshot was that all of the Essaerists were able to see and interact with all of the Essaerites who were watching the city and helping to maintain their presence in the sky. Because that had been turning into one of the most important parts of her day.

Managing the sky, defending the space above the camps, and keeping the Gwenthari Essaerites from venturing out into the countryside to hunt or wreak havoc. Presently, Caelwen was bandaging a man whose shoulder had been slashed by talons from one of the birds. Deep gashes ran from his collarbone to his bicep, the flesh raw and slick with blood. The man hissed and clenched his jaw as she tightened the bandage, his breath ragged and shallow.

On occasion, they would see large groups of the larger birds with bladed teeth come flying out, but that tended to happen at night and was well orchestrated. The bulk of what they had been dealing with were smaller birds that had been coming out and attacking men as either a distraction before others came out or as a dedicated group for harassment. They were larger and more equipped than a regular hawk or eagle, and they'd proven to be difficult. They very rarely killed. Legionnaires had learned to keep an eye on the sky, and the birds could be kept at bay if one was paying attention. But still, they managed to attack some people, maiming them, cutting up shoulders, faces, and heads, and occasionally blinding someone.

The man she was bandaging had been torn up as one had landed on him, its talons digging into his flesh and its beak poking at his face. It had only been on him for a few moments, but in that time, it had caused him a great deal of pain and damage. His tunic was covered in blood.

The men had started to take to her. When she first joined the Legion, they were distrustful of her. Caelwen couldn't quite blame them. She was supposed to be the enemy, wasn't she? Even if her people weren't in direct conflict with Lysandrian, she was Gwenthari. She was also an outsider, but she had proven capable enough when it came to tending to wounds, something that she was getting more and more notoriety for with the birds' constant attacks. Not that she was exceptional compared to the Legion's healers, just that everyone had someone from a squad that had been attacked by the things and had to go get patched up. It meant that she was starting to get to know everybody, and it was hard to be mad and distrust the person who was tending to your wounds.

As she was finishing wrapping the man's shoulder, she paused, her mind reaching out, checking on Essaerites. Checking on everything was a pain in the ass, and she wasn't enjoying it. She wasn't necessarily looking forward to Ulfgard falling and going back on the road, but she was certainly looking forward to being done with this.

They were pretty sure that there were more Essaerists in the Legion than there were in Ulfgard; it only had to be a difference of one or two, and from everything they had seen, there were only a couple of talented Essaerists inside the city. However, the Essaerists of Ulfgard only had to protect the small area above the city and were otherwise free to harass or bother the Legions. The Legions, on the other hand, had a large area that they had to protect. Not only did they have to protect the sky right above the camps, but the surrounding land as men went out scouting and forging.

And it appeared that most of Ulfgard's Essaerists were engaged in activity with the birds. The only one that didn't seem to be that way was the Wyrdrunir Essaerist, who had the rock Essaerites that continued to stay outside of the city, though they never came close to the counter-fortifications. On a few occasions, Caelwen had watched as those Essaerites had been engaged by either Xavieno's or Kyrillos's. Sometimes they won, sometimes they lost. The battles had been more of a test than anything else.

Caelwen had yet to challenge any of the Essaerites with her own, as the Legion still preferred to use Xavieno or Kyrillos for offensive actions, as opposed to Caelwen, Isolara, or even Mariokos, who was better served as support. Something she was finding to have more value than those that were directly involved in battle. She wondered how much of Xavieno and Kyrillos's attempts at the other Essaerites had been just for the Legion's generals to see what would happen.

There hadn't been any of that with Mariokos. There had been no end of work for him to do that seemed vital to their success. But that wasn't to say that a lot of his Essaeris, along with hers and Isolara's, weren't being taken up by dealing with some sort of combat or another. It just was in the form of things in the air, something that none of them were very skilled at.

The current strategy was to have a handful of Essaerites with exceptional eyesight stand along the counter-fortifications, watching the sky for enemy birds. When they saw some, smaller Essaerites, the size of sparrows and swallows that were quick and easy to maneuver, would swoop in on the ones coming from Ulfgard and attach themselves. Sometimes they could take out the bird, but more often than not, they just harried its movements, allowing for Essaerites that were comparable in size to eagles and falcons to come in and take care of the threat.

It was effective, but it also required that a lot of power be invested in a lot of different Essaerites because you also needed the ones that were out patrolling the areas looking for larger ones that made it out of Ulfgard. It was very tiresome, and keeping track of that many had proven to be a headache, to say the least.

She finished bandaging the man and told him to go on his way. There wasn't anyone else for her to care for, so she created a basin of warm water with a cloth and washed the blood off her hands, then walked through the camp, her feet grinding on the gravel roadway as she headed back towards her tent.

Waiting for her there was Ilara, who was tending to the rabbits and otherwise trying to find ways of keeping herself busy. Caelwen felt for her. There wasn't much that Ilara could do. There was hardly anything that Xavieno needed. Well, there were things that he needed, but his Essaerites were more effective than a person. Even the rabbits were like that. After all, their benefit was that they were easy.

Caelwen approached Ilara. "How's your day been?"

Ilara smiled tightly. "It's been exciting," she said.

Caelwen raised an eyebrow. "Really?"

"Yes. Two of the rabbits fought for a few seconds." She sat and sighed. "How was patching up men?"

Caelwen snorted a laugh and then shrugged. "The same as it always is."

"And how was the sky?" Ilara asked.

Caelwen shrugged again, her mood was sour. "Comparatively speaking, the same as it always is." She huffed. "Gods, it's a fucking pain in the ass. I would have never thought that birds would have been difficult before."

Ilara smirked. "If I hadn't seen how many people had been hurt by them, I wouldn't think that they could be. But you're right. They do seem to be a pain in the ass. And the ones that drop fire," she said.

There was that, of course. There had been a handful of birds that had come out holding ropes that were on fire. They would drop them on tents or in fields, trying to set them alight. There had been limited success with it. There had been drizzly rain throughout the month that made catching the fields on fire difficult. And for the tents, men were always on guard, waiting for it. But still, it would make things lively for a while and did a good job of keeping everyone in a slight state of frustration and on edge, which she was pretty sure was the intent behind it.

"I should be thankful that things are boring," Ilara said. "When things are boring, it means that you're probably not dying."

This was a train of thought that Caelwen agreed with. "Yeah, there's that part, isn't there? It doesn't really feel like a war right now, does it?" she said, her eyes scanning over the counter-fortifications. The walls were taller than those of the camps, and she saw men patrolling along their tops in the far distance.

"No, it really doesn't," Ilara said, standing next to her. "I'm sure inside the city, the planners are beginning to feel different as they see their stockpile of food taking a hit. Still, though, Ulfgard has to have months' worth of provisions inside those walls. They can't be feeling too concerned yet."

Caelwen shook her head. "No, I don't think they are, and I agree with you. They'll be prepared for a long siege, but they have to be irritated with how this all played out."

Ilara nodded.

When they'd come into the valley, it was obvious that even though Ulfgard had been preparing, they hadn't expected Lysandrian to move as fast as it had. The people had moved quickly into the city. As a result, they left behind things that she was sure they would have much rather brought inside those walls. For example, crops. Many of them had been left near to the point where they needed to be harvested. Now the time for that harvest was here, and those crops were in the possession of Lysandrian. And Lysandrian was busy harvesting those crops, fortifying themselves for the winter. One could imagine how frustrating that must be for the people watching from the walls, realizing that they fed their enemies.

For the commanders inside, there also had to be the knowledge that at some point in time, Lysandrian was going to begin its process of breaching the walls. And Essaerists or not, Lysandrian would do it. It was just a question of time.

"This battle is already won," Ilara said, her voice holding no emotion.

Caelwen nodded. "It is. Do you think they know?"

Ilara shook her head. "No, I don't think they do. There have to be some leaders inside Ulfgard that know it's inevitable. But there have to be so many that don't think it's possible. That they think that Lysandrian will run out of food or run out of supplies or run out of drive to do it and go away. Or that maybe Gwenthari outside the city will eventually drive them away. But that's not going to be what happens."

"No, it won't be," Caelwen said. "This city will fall now, or during the winter, or maybe in the spring. But it will fall."

"For their sake, I hope it's not like Hroldenfell. But it probably will be," she said.

Caelwen nodded grimly. "Yes, it probably will be, won't it? Though Ulfgard's so much larger than Hroldenfell. I don't see," she said, shaking her head, remembering the Ilfrun River and what happened there. "But I suppose that would be naive for me to think, wouldn't it?" She looked over at Ilara, who was gazing up at the city, stone-faced.

"It would be. We both know how this ends. Everyone in this camp knows how this ends. It's just a question of when."

———

MARIOKOS BENT OVER, TYING OFF A BUNDLE. THE ROUGH FIBERS OF THE TWINE BIT INTO his fingers, and the grain's scent mixed with the faint tang of sweat. Around him, the swish of scythes through dry stalks created a steady rhythm. He stood, feeling the sun warm his back and head. He stretched his arms above his head and breathed in deeply through his nose, loving the scent of the fields around him.

All around, men and Essaerites worked to harvest grain. The scythes swished rhythmically. He turned, seeing a group of his Essaerites that were engaged in the work. They were moving at a steady, even pace, some cutting while others gathered. He had given them large eyes, allowing them to work with just the slightest amount of moonlight. It meant that they could continue to harvest night and day, never stopping for breaks, never stopping to talk or waste time, just engaged in their work.

Something that was important, as there weren't as many people to harvest as there would normally be with so many people in the city, and also because there was the ever-present threat of fire from one of Ulfgard's Essaerites. They focused on harvesting.

Swish, swish, the scythes' sound made.

He saw a group on horseback heading back to the camps. Mariokos recognized some of them and waved. They waved back, and one of the riders separated from the rest.

Wulfgren looked to be in good spirits as he approached. He brought his mount to a stop, and Mariokos looked up at the man. "How was collecting tributes?"

Wulfgren gave a tight smile. "It was fine; no one fought us on it."

That was good, Mariokos thought. "Easier than around Hroldenfell?"

Wulfgren barked a laugh. "Much. These people know what happens if they say no, don't they?"

"I suppose so," he said with a sigh. "Part of me wonders if that's why things went the way they did. But..."

"There's no doubt about it," Wulfgren said, his voice lacking some of its normal lightness. "Hroldenfell was a message plain and clear, and the Ilfrun was wealth and a strategic boon."

Mariokos raised an eyebrow. "I never thought you a tactician."

Wulfgren grinned. "Mariokos, I am a very wise man; you should know that by now."

Mariokos snorted a laugh. "Wise indeed."

Wulfgren looked around the fields. "It's nice."

"The harvest?" Mariokos asked.

Wulfgren nodded, his gaze taking it all in. "Yes, it's how it should be— sowing and reaping. Caelwen tells me you worship a god called Corianthus."

"I do. He's the god of the harvest," he said.

"This must be a good time of year for you then," Wulfgren said.

"It is," Mariokos said, and it was. He loved this time of year. He wondered something. "I know Caelwen worships Caelith. Which one do you? Ulfgara?"

Wulfgren shook his head and gave a dry laugh. "No, I don't. I used to, I suppose, but now I think my heart lies with Hrodic."

"Craftsmanship and industry?" Mariokos confirmed.

Wulfgren grinned. "Look at you, learning barbarian culture!"

Mariokos laughed. "I'm a wise man," he said with a smile. "But why Hrodic? If you don't mind me asking."

Wulfgren looked thoughtful. "I guess in the hereafter, I want to build something. Ulfgara's halls will be loud with drinking and song, but the floors will be slick with blood and the fields scattered with the slain." He shook his head. "Not sure why any of us want an eternity of that." He sighed. "I should be off. Tell my sister I expect a report on the rabbits?"

Mariokos laughed. "Not a chance. I like my head on my shoulders, thank you."

Wulfgren began to ride and grinned. "Maybe you are a wise man after all."

CHAPTER 22

Valfric's hands and arms were coated in blood, something that wasn't necessarily new for him. The coppery scent mixed with the crisp air, and the sticky warmth clung to his skin, seeping into the creases of his knuckles. What *was* different was that the blood belonged to a cow, not a person. The cow had been older and unable to produce calves or milk anymore. Valfric knew the farmer had been loath to slaughter it, but it was inevitable. So here he was.

Valfric's knife separated bone, sinew, and muscle as it glided through the meat. He gripped the knife tightly, slicing expertly as he moved through the animal. One of the things he had mastered, besides killing people, was butchering animals. It was necessary if you were going to be on the road a lot or if you tended to steal livestock.

He didn't mind the work. He'd found it distasteful when he was younger. Not that he'd been squeamish around blood or anything of that nature, just that it was time-consuming and much harder than he ever would have thought it would be. But there was something to it that he could get lost in.

The farmer had an injured wrist, so Valfric was doing him a service. He also helped him with various tasks around his field, while Eira was helping his wife around their home. All in all, it had been a very useful arrangement.

In exchange, Valfric and Eira were able to sleep in a small barn, with their blankets on soft hay that kept them warm and comfortable at night. He was thankful for this, as the days had grown shorter and the nights had taken on a chill. Winter was fast approaching, and he was slightly irritated that they hadn't found a permanent place to stay.

They'd been moving deeper into Valfaran territory, past any areas where there was fear of Lysandrian or the war going on to the southeast. The only thing people here were concerned about was the harvest. But wasn't that the story of time? In the summertime, there was raiding and killing and talk of war, but this time of year, everyone's mind turned to more practical matters. Fields needed harvesting, and animals needed slaughtering. Supplies had to be stored to last through the winter. Repairs to roofs and homes needed to be completed, lest they be too drafty and cold. And, of course, firewood piles needed to be cut and built.

He'd never cared for this time of year. There were a few festivals he enjoyed, but by and large, it represented a time when he would be done for the year. When he'd be relegated to his home over the long winter, with only the occasional company of his friends, or perhaps Ilara's warmth, to keep him going throughout the winter. He didn't have to worry about harvesting any fields because he wasn't a farmer. He didn't worry about taking care of livestock because he had none. Even that which he stole, he sold as soon as he got back home. He didn't worry about firewood either, as he had Essaerites who could cut it for him.

No, winter had always been a time when he had to stay in, suffering through the long nights with only his thoughts for company. It was a reminder that he could be out raiding—if not for the snow. That had been his whole life: a season of raiding, of taking, of doing, and then having to wait until the next season could start. He knew that life was gone. His back was almost completely healed, though it still ached and throbbed at night after a hard day's work, and he couldn't push it nearly as much as he used to. He wasn't sure if that was going to change or if that was just going to be his life now.

Even if that wasn't the case, he wasn't sure that he'd go back to a life of raiding. How could he? He didn't have a settlement to raid for. He didn't have friends to do it with, and he had to take care of Eira. He couldn't leave her anywhere, and he very much doubted it would be a good idea to take her on the road while he went out raping and pillaging his way around the countryside.

So what was he to do now? Was he to be a farmer, a carpenter, a tanner, or a smith? Some of those were laughable. He couldn't be a smith. He had never learned the skills, and he very much doubted anyone would ever teach him the trade. Smiths were very secretive about their ways. He didn't blame them. Warriors could be the same. You didn't want to give a competitor an edge. The same could be said for tanners. So he thought that left carpenter or farmer. But he was shit at carpentry. And he certainly didn't have the temperament for it. Beating things with a hammer? Yes, he had the temperament for that. Beating things constructively with a hammer? Well, that was a little different.

He didn't really like the idea of sowing and harvesting fields either, but that would probably be the way of it for him. And he reminded himself that it could be far worse. After all, it likely wouldn't be him who would be sowing and planting those crops, it would be Essaerites. Of that, he had no doubt. So what was he going to do with his time? How was he going to pass it? These were the things he thought of as he cut through the cow. Until finally, the light began to fade from the sun, and he looked over his day's work, happy with what he had accomplished. Next to him, the farmer had been working silently as well, both of them lost in thought. Perhaps this would be a good life for him.

He went to a bucket of water and washed the blood off his hands and arms, as did the farmer, and they made their way to the cottage that the farmer shared with his wife and two children. Inside, he was hit by the scent of food and bread cooking, along with the smell of Bryndraught being brewed. He saw Eira tending to some bread, and she looked at him and smiled happily. The farmer's wife shot her a look but didn't comment. The people of this small settlement didn't seem to care for Eira. They didn't care for Valfric either, for that matter, and he wasn't surprised. Most people didn't like outsiders, but Eira seemed to set them off in a way. He wondered if it was because she was very obviously both Lysandrian and Gwenthari, and because there was something wrong with her. People were always wary of individuals like that.

"Valfric, Valfric, how day?" Eira asked brightly.

He smiled, walking up to her. "My day was good. How was your day?"

She smiled back, happy. "Made Bryndraught and bread," she said, holding up a loaf of bread. It smelled wonderful.

Then he smiled again. "Well done, thank you," he said, and then turned to the farmer's wife, looking at her. "Thank you for letting us eat with you."

She smiled tightly, in a way that told him she knew she had to be polite because her husband had told her to, but that she didn't really want to be. She didn't trust Valfric. He doubted that she considered Eira to be a threat—perhaps a nuisance or a bad omen—but she was no threat, of that it was obvious. Valfric, on the other hand, was. Everything about him screamed, 'I'm a threat.' He knew what he looked like. He looked like a man who had spent his life fighting and killing. And here he had come into town with a slave and nothing to his name, asking for work and for a place to sleep, though he was just passing through. No, she was right to suspect that there wasn't something on the complete up and up with him. He had been guarded about his past, directing questions away, and Eira didn't seem to be very forthcoming either, though he knew that wasn't because she was a secretive person, but just because her mind didn't seem to care much about the past. So, he had to be a threat, hadn't he? If he had made it all this way, unmolested, with money and food, a healthy slave, and a seemingly healthy dog.

Though he had been cryptic and secretive, he knew the thing that she was really concerned about, even if her mind didn't know it; she sensed there was something just off about him. And he knew that it had nothing to do with the fact that he was a killer—the farmer nor his wife would be able to place it—but they knew he was hiding something. They probably thought he was a murder or a thief, and he was those things. But the thing that would have bothered them most would have been the fact that he was an Essaerist, something he had yet to reveal and wasn't planning on doing. A rogue Essaerist in the area from Ulfgarath could be seen as an opportunity or as a threat. If he was an opportunity, that could prove beneficial for some settlements; they could try to get him on their side. But if it appeared that he wasn't going to do it, then he would move to threat, and he didn't care to deal with any of that.

When he found a place where they wanted to settle, he would reveal what he was. But until that time, he wasn't going to bother with it.

He ate dinner with the family, who seemed to be slightly perturbed that a slave was going to be eating with them, but they didn't push it too much. The dinner was good, as he had been hoping, and the Bryndraught was also good.

When they were done, he bade the farmer, his wife, and children good night, and he and Eira went out to the barn. The air was chilly and cold, biting through him, both physically and mentally. They went inside the barn, which was slightly warmer and safe from the wind, and Valfric laid out blankets for them on top of some hay to sleep on. They lay down, and Valfric pulled a blanket over them, Eira nuzzling up against him as she had taken to doing.

What had started as a slight annoyance was now a comfort for him. As soon as she nuzzled into his side, he would wrap his arm around her, pulling her in close and safe. Her warmth was a reminder that she was there, who she was, and that she was safe. He depended on that now, and it was something he was sure he would need if he wanted to sleep. He didn't know if he could sleep without her next to him now. As soon as she was near, his nerves would calm, and his mind would smooth and slow down. Its negative edges would start to fade away, and instead, he would feel more content.

And as soon as she was asleep, her chest slowly rising and falling, her breath against his chest and neck, he felt like he could drift off himself. As she dozed off, he absentmindedly ran his fingers up and down her back and arm, something she seemed to enjoy. She didn't like being touched. He'd noticed that most people couldn't touch her. But after a while, she let him touch her, even seemed to seek it out, much as she had with Ferngar.

Valfric tried not to laugh at the thought when he wondered if she saw him as more of a dog than a man. That would be amusing. He thought of his old friends, the ones that were now dead and gone because of him. They would have rather enjoyed this sight. They would have given him no end of grief about being Valfric, the dog; Valfric, the pet; Valfric, the meek. Ilara would have particularly enjoyed seeing how he was with Eira.

"Ilara," he said softly, trying not to wake Eira.

He felt a hollowness in his chest as he saw her in his mind's eye, as she had always been for him—confident, beautiful, deadly, clever. But as his mind gazed upon her, she changed. She looked more and more timid and haggard, the way she had near the end.

You knew, he thought. *You knew what was going to happen. You tried to warn me*, he thought to himself.

And she had. She'd begun questioning their life shortly after the fall of Hroldenfell. And then, everything had gone so wrong. She'd only gotten her confidence back for a little while before everything had gone to shit. He should have encouraged them to go north, encouraged them to move away from Lysandrian. On that first day when they had seen the legions north of them along the Ilfrun River, he should have encouraged them to flee. Some had done just that. People they had assumed to be cowards and commented as such. But those people had been smart, hadn't they?

After all, had the people that fled with him been cowards? No, they hadn't. He would have been dead if it wasn't for them. No, the true cowardice was not accepting reality and thinking they could change it. They'd been on horseback. The legions were in no rush and no hurry, and Valfric was an Essaerist; they could have gotten clear. They could have run away.

That's what they should have done as soon as Hroldenfell fell. They should have moved north into Valfarans or Wulfharboria territory where they could have found a comfortable life and lived far away from death and destruction.

It's what a smart man would have done. It's probably what Ilara would have done if he'd brought it up to her. He could have convinced Thraindel and Aelric to go with it. He could have convinced them that they could go north to find allies. They could have found others to help take on Lysandrian, or they could have waited for the legions to move through the region and then raid the fresh supply lines. Of that, he was sure he could have convinced them. But he didn't do that, did he? No, because that would have required looking down the road, thinking, and using his brain for something other than death and destruction.

Eira shifted in his arms, and as she did, his mood lightened some. She rolled onto her side, and her arm went over his chest. He pulled her close, and she sighed contentedly next to him.

I can't change that, he thought. *All I can do is try to manage the future.*

The next morning, Eira awoke him, and he opened his eyes, looking at the ceiling above him. The air in the barn was thick with dust and the scent of hay. It was somehow relaxing. He stretched, and next to him, she yawned, squirming in his arms slightly.

"How did you sleep, little one?" he asked.

She smiled. "Eira, good. Valfric sleep?" she asked.

He nodded. "Valfric, sleep," he said.

His arm gave her a quick squeeze, and they got up. He rolled up the blankets and opened the barn door, feeling the chill air outside. The sun was coming up over the horizon and would soon warm them. Still, all around them, the morning dew had turned to frost, covering all the shoots of grass and plants in the area. His breath puffed out in front of him like a great cloud, and the cold air against his skin made it prickle and made him feel awake and alive.

He found the farmer and his wife and family inside their home. They were already up, thanks to having small children, something that the farmer pointed out to Valfric was the best way to ensure that you didn't have to worry about getting a good night's sleep again in your life. They had a breakfast of boiled oats and then got along with the business of the day.

Valfric finished up his work on the cow and washed off his hands around mid-afternoon when a cart came rolling up outside. He eyed it critically, wondering who the newcomer was. It almost felt laughable that he thought of somebody as a newcomer when he was the interloper in this settlement. But the farmer smiled, seeming to know the man.

"Durnhart, how are you?" the farmer called out. He turned to Valfric. "Come," he said.

Valfric followed the farmer out to meet the man and clasped his hand.

"The name's Durnhart," he said.

Valfric smiled. "My name is Valfric."

Durnhart nodded. "You new to these parts?"

Valfric shook his head. "Just moving through the area, looking for a place to settle," he said.

The farmer spoke up. "This one might know a place for you," he said. "Durnhart hits all the settlements in the area. He's a damn good merchant, but be careful. He'll swindle you," he said good-naturedly.

Durnhart grinned and laughed. "You're not still sour about that Duskwood oil from last year, are you?"

The farmer chuckled. "No, never," he said sarcastically.

Durnhart turned to Valfric. "So, you're looking for a place to settle," he said. "What's wrong with this one?"

Valfric paused for a moment. He glanced around. How did he say it? "I don't think this would be a good place for me," he said.

Durnhart raised an eyebrow, and the farmer spoke. "People here don't trust him," he said. "You know how we are. We don't like outsiders. This settlement is small. Plus, he's got an idiot with him for a slave, and she's mixed with Lysandrian blood," the farmer said.

Valfric resisted the urge to be irritated with the farmer. He was trying to help them, even if he was being an asshole about Eira.

Durnhart looked thoughtful. "You have an idiot slave?"

Valfric huffed slightly. "She's not an idiot. She's just different," he said.

Durnhart looked at him pensively and nodded. "Alright. Well, what are you good at?"

Valfric chuckled. "I don't know that I'm good at many things," he said honestly. "I used to be a warrior," he finally said after a moment.

Durnhart nodded. "But not anymore?"

Valfric shook his head. "Not anymore."

Durnhart looked thoughtful. Eira came out of the house with the kids. They were laughing and running around her, and she was laughing with them. She seemed to be good with them.

Durnhart looked over at her. "Hmm. Very mixed breed," he said.

"Yeah. Yeah, she's got some Lysandrian in her," Valfric said.

Durnhart nodded thoughtfully. "I can see where that might cause some problems around these parts. Even if she's a slave." He was thoughtful for a few moments. "I do think there's a place that might welcome you, though," he said.

Valfric raised an eyebrow. "I'm listening."

Durnhart smiled. "You're going to head almost due north from here. Should only take you a couple of days. There's a settlement, smaller than this one. The head of the settlement is a man named Bergthral. His wife is Hildrana. They're both Essaerists. I'll warn you. And she is Eirfrosti."

Hearing that there were two Essaerists gave him pause. Hearing that one of them was Eirfrosti gave him even more.

"She's Eirfrosti, and she's here in a permanent settlement and an Essaerist?" Valfric asked.

Durnhart nodded. "Yep. So I think some oddballs like you might fit in just fine up there. Tell them I told you to come and see them. Bergthral is a wonderful man. He's fair and thoughtful. But I would warn you, don't mess with them," he said.

Valfric nodded. He knew that Eirfrosti Essaerists were supposed to be incredibly talented. Most people called them witches. He knew better. He knew they didn't hold some special powers; they were just very good. Not unlike the Lysandrians.

"Thank you," he said. "I appreciate it."

He looked over at Eira and nodded to himself, making his decision in that moment.

"You don't think they'll have any problems with her?" he asked.

Durnhart shook his head. "Nah, I don't think so. I don't actually even think there's any slaves in the settlement. She'll be a first," he said.

Valfric was surprised by that. "Really? There isn't?" he said.

Durnhart shrugged. "There are two Essaerists in a small settlement. What use have they for extra labor?"

He clapped Valfric's shoulder and started walking away. "I have some rounds to make, but hopefully, I'll see you up there at some point," he said.

"Hopefully," Valfric said.

The farmer was next to him. "That went well," he said.

Valfric smiled tightly. He turned back to him. "We'll be out of your hair today," he said after a moment, realizing that they might have overstayed their welcome. Not with the farmer, necessarily, but maybe with some of the others in the settlement.

The farmer nodded. "That might be a good idea. You don't want people to start thinking that you're permanent, would you?"

Valfric smiled. "No, we wouldn't want that."

The man chuckled. "We'll send you on your way with some meat and some Bryndraught," he said.

"That would be much appreciated," Valfric said.

This, too, was an odd sort of feeling. Leaving a settlement on good terms with somebody, bringing something with him that he had earned through work, not through killing. This was a strange new world that he was walking into, and he wasn't sure what to make of it.

CHAPTER 23

A cold breeze rustled the leaves, sending a chill through Valfric. A few trees still had leaves on their branches, golds, purples, and reds rustling softly in the crisp air. The small road they were on spoke to how out of the way the settlement they were going to was. It wasn't that it wasn't well-maintained. If anything, Valfric thought the road was rather nice; it just showed no signs of travel. This lined up with what Durnhart had told them about the settlement—that it was small, tucked away, and isolated. He knew there were other settlements nearby, but he suspected that for whatever reason, Bergthal's was not one that was often contacted.

A knot tightened in his chest as they walked, his breath shallow and his hands clenching involuntarily at his sides. He had been irritable all morning, something Eira had been all too happy to point out. *She wasn't happy to point it out,* he thought to himself. She just pointed out what she saw. She didn't seem to be bothered at all and was humming to herself as she walked. Next to her, Ferngar stayed by her, and occasionally she would scratch its ears or pat its head, content and happy as could be. He had wolves in the area as well, but he kept them close. He questioned the wisdom of doing what they were going to do.

Two Essaerists, one of them Eirfrosti. You're going to get yourself killed, and her too, a voice in his head said. But Durnhart had said that they would be welcoming, or at least could be. Durnhart also hadn't known that Valfric was an Essaerist.

"Valfric happy?" Eira said next to him. He glanced over at her. He must have had a sour look on his face. He tried to look happier.

"I'm fine. How are you?" he asked.

She smiled. "Eira happy." She scrunched up her face, looking at him. "Valfric grumpy?" she asked.

He sighed. "I'm not grumpy. I just have a lot on my mind. Today's a big day for us. It could go poorly."

"Valfric, why?" she asked.

He shrugged. "Because I'm an Essaerist, and we're going to be meeting two other Essaerists. They may not like that."

Eira looked thoughtful for a moment. "Valfric, no hurt," she said.

He groaned a little bit. "I don't want to hurt anybody."

"Valfric, nice," she said.

He rolled his eyes. "I will be nice. I can handle myself, believe it or not."

She was thoughtful for a moment, then smiled. "Valfric grumpy."

He resisted, growling. "Fine. Valfric grumpy," he echoed.

She nodded. "Eira knows," she said and went back to humming to herself as she walked.

He shook his head. He remembered a time when most people would be afraid of Valfric being grumpy. Though it didn't seem to bother Eira at all. *You've gotten soft,* he thought to himself. Though the thought didn't necessarily bother him. In a way, it was almost a comfort. Still, he may not want the softness today.

He rolled over in his mind what he was going to do and then made his decision.

"Eira," he said.

She turned to him and smiled.

"When we meet the people today, I need you to stay close to me, okay? And stay close to Ferngar," he said.

She nodded and smiled. "Eira will. Valfric, nice," she said.

He rolled his eyes. "I'm going to be nice, but that doesn't mean that they'll be nice to us, okay?"

He saw a small bit of concern cross her expression, and she nodded. "Okay," she said.

He knew she was all too familiar with other people not being nice, and that seemed to strike home with her. He didn't want to make her nervous, but he didn't exactly want her to do something that might get her hurt, either.

He also decided that he was going to be open about being an Essaerist. Not only did he think it would be unwise to hide it from them and then tell them later, but it was also something that he may not be able to hide. He wasn't sure just how talented Eirfrosti Essaerists could be. He had heard rumors, of course, but those rumors could have just been fiction. They could have been tales made up to scare children at night. But some of those same rumors had existed for Lysandrian, and he was all too well aware of how talented Lysandrian Essaerists were.

Still, the rumors and stories of the Eirfrosti were far scarier than those of Lysandrian. What was true and what wasn't? It was best not to start things out poorly. While it could be uncomfortable with them knowing that he was an Essaerist, at the very least, he could avoid something in the future, he hoped.

They were coming to a clearing in the trees, and around him, he could see a couple of small farms. There was a man standing outside of one, and Valfric came to a stop, Eira coming up next to him.

"Valfric," she said.

"Let's just wait here for a moment," he said.

The man looked at them curiously, and Valfric waved him over. As the man approached him, he could see curiosity and concern in his expression.

"Something I can do for you?" the man asked, guarded, staying a few feet away.

Valfric forced a smile, his voice measured and calm as he said, "Yes. My name is Valfric. My companion here is Eira. Can you please tell the heads of the settlement that I am here to see them, and that I am an Essaerist?"

The man looked a little skeptical, and Valfric produced a hawk on his shoulder, and then it vanished. The man took a small step back, but not one of amazement, just one of apprehension.

"Stay here?" he asked.

Valfric nodded. "Yes. We aren't here to cause problems. I'm just telling you that I'm an Essaerist, so that way I'm being open about everything."

The man nodded. "That's probably a good call. I'll go get Bergthral and Hildrana. Wait here," he said and walked off.

Valfric felt his heart beat a little bit faster. *Well, there's no hiding it now,* he thought.

The reality of it was, with two Essaerists in the area, they already knew he was here. There was no doubt in his mind that they had hawks or something else that was watching, and as soon as Valfric and Eira had walked in the area, they'd known. They'd probably also seen his wolves and maybe had wondered if they were tracking or following Valfric. But no one had come out to save them, so maybe not.

Still, his wolves walked out of the trees and came and sat behind Valfric and Eira. The mule didn't seem to give a shit, which was nice. There were three wolves that he had right now, all big and strong.

As they'd been around for a while, it took less Essaeris for him to keep them around, giving him more of a reserve should they need it. His mind thought of what he might need should things go poorly. He suspected it would be very unwise to fight whoever this Bergthral and Hildrana were. Two-on-one weren't exactly the odds he liked, not to mention that as soon as things went to shit, Eira would probably freak out. Ferngar could probably keep her safe, and maybe the wolves could too. The mule would be a lost cause, and Valfric doubted that they would be able to scramble on it and ride away in time, though it was something that he was considering.

Instead, he tried to think of Essaerites that he could create that could spirit them out of the area. He felt sweat run down the back of his neck as his mind went through the possibilities. He wouldn't be able to create something big enough to carry both him and Eira. He would have to depend almost whole-heartedly on this going well.

Valfric nice, her words echoed in his head. *You can do this, just do what she told you, be nice,* he thought to himself. It was amusing. He was going to be taking negotiation advice from Eira. Any slight levity he felt vanished as some figures came into sight. Two people, one was male; he was a tall, muscular man with a long beard and blonde hair. He looked formidable. Next to him was a lean woman with hair as black as coal and pale skin. This is what made his heart thump—the woman, the Eirfrosti woman.

What also made his hands begin to feel clammy and made him feel like there might be slight bits of ice water trickling through his veins were the two Essaerites that were with them. Next to the man was a bear that was very obvi-ously an Essaerite, as its hide appeared to be a type of black scale. The top of its head was metal, and it walked purposefully next to the man. Next to her was an Essaerite that he couldn't quite place. It looked like a stag, but the antlers looked like blades, and off of the animal's shoulders were arms that, like the antlers, had long, shining blades coming off of them. It had the same hide as the bear. He had never seen anything like either of them. He had seen Essaerites that were built for form, to be pretty or intimidating, and he had seen ones that were functional, but he suspected these were a cross between both of those things, and he suspected they were done in a way that was expert and far more advanced than he ever had been or ever would be.

He resisted the urge to take a step back as the group approached them. He glanced over at Eira, worried that she would be panicked by the terrifying-looking Essaerites, but she didn't seem to be. She was standing stock-still next to him, almost like she was on her tiptoes looking at the newcomers. Curiosity was on her face.

"Remember to stay near me," he said softly.

She nodded quickly. "Okay," she said.

His mind reached out, and he made sure that Ferngar would be ready at a moment's notice to defend her if need be, but he kept the dog next to her, keeping it appearing calm and placid. The group was almost to them now.

————

BERGTHRAL TOOK IN THE NEWCOMERS, HIS GAZE MOVING OVER THEM. NEXT TO HIM, Hildrana was silent. They had spotted the pair coming long before they had made it anywhere near the settlement. They had also spotted the wolves that had been behind them. At first, they had wondered if the wolves were hunting them. If they were going to go for the mule or the dog or all of them, but it became apparent after watching for just a few minutes that the wolves were not normal. They didn't move the way regular wolves did. They weren't hunt-ing. They were too close to the group, and they were circling around them. Not in a way that said they were going to pounce and kill, but in a way that said they were on patrol, that they were guarding. Bergthral found it very unlikely that anybody had managed to train a pack of wolves to work in perfect unison as guard dogs. It left only one possibility: that one of the duo was an Essaerist.

From one of his hawks' perspectives, he had assumed it to be the female. She had a dog that was next to her that was far too behaved to be a dog, but now he thought it might be the male. He took them both in. The woman was short, with long, curly, auburn hair. She had green eyes, but her skin was pale like a Gwenthari. She was a cross; that much was obvious. She also had a slave collar around her neck that was an exceedingly nice one. As Bergthral looked at it from the sky, he hadn't let the hawks get too close, and he thought it might have been jewelry, but now he could see otherwise. She was looking at them, curiosity on her face as she looked at both his and Hildrana's Essaerithons.

The man was tall and muscular, though not muscular like Bergthral was— muscular like a man who spent a lot of time on the road and spent a lot of time fighting. He had blonde hair and a long goatee and piercing blue eyes. He looked very concerned and tense. Yes, this was the Essaerist.

Three wolves sat behind them. On closer inspection, they were larger than regular wolves would be, and he could see slight glints of metal from their mouths. Definitely Essaerites. But nothing that he or his wife couldn't handle with ease and a mere flick of their minds. He wondered if there were other Essaerites in the area but reminded himself that he was dealing with a Gwenthari man. Probably someone from Valfarans or Ulfgarath. And he was young. He wouldn't be as trained as Bergthral or Hildrana were. These were probably the extent of his Essaerites, though Bergthral suspected that the man could create others in a hurry if he needed to.

But he wasn't sure if they were a threat or not. After all, they'd approached at a respectful distance and said what they were. So they decided to give him a chance.

Bergthral stepped forward. "My name is Bergthral. This is my wife, Hildrana," he said.

The man nodded respectfully. "My name is Valfric. This is Eira," he said.

"Hello," Eira said, her voice bright.

Valfric tensed for just a moment and whispered something to her. She looked confused for a second and then nodded. "Valfric, okay," she said.

"What can we do for you?" Hildrana asked.

Valfric still looked uncomfortable, but he took a step forward, trying to appear open, and Bergthral could tell it was a difficult feat for the man.

"We are looking for a place to settle," he said.

Bergthral raised an eyebrow and spoke, "A place to settle?"

Valfric nodded. "Yes. A place to settle. I am from Ulfgarath. I don't know where Eira is from," he admitted. "But a man, Durnhart, said that we might be able to find a place here."

"Durnhart sent us an Essaerist," Hildrana said.

Valfric looked a little chagrined. "He didn't know I was an Essaerist."

"Why not?" Bergthral asked.

"Because I thought that would be wise to keep to myself on the road," he said.

Interesting, Bergthral thought. Most Essaerists were pretty open about what they were.

"Why did you leave your old settlement?" Hildrana asked.

He saw pain cross Valfric's face. He looked down and was quiet for a moment, like he was controlling his thoughts or emotions.

"My settlement's gone," he said.

"Gone?" Hildrana asked.

He nodded. "Did you hear of Hroldenfell?" he asked.

Bergthral felt his heart drop. He had heard of Hroldenfell.

"Your settlement was there?" he asked.

"Yes," Valfric said. "We were headed there, and unfortunately, by the time we got there, Lysandrian was already there." His voice was thick. "We watched it happen. We tried to help, but..."

"There's no stopping an army," Hildrana said.

Valfric nodded. "There's no stopping an army."

"Then why didn't you go to Ulfgard?" Bergthral asked, curious.

"We were going to," Valfric said, "but my friends and I—we were along the Ilfrun River. Did you hear about that?"

Bergthral had. They had heard whispers of a massacre, but he hadn't heard of it firsthand.

"A little. Tell me about it," he asked.

Valfric shook his head. "I'd never seen anything like it," he said. "I thought for sure we were going to win. There were so many more of us than there were Lysandrians."

He shook his head again slowly. "I got injured the first day. I was able to be taken across the other side of the river, but I was controlling my Essaerites during the next day of the battle," he said, his voice thick. "They all died. Everyone. The last of the people I knew, I watched them die. As I was being carted away, unable to even walk," he said, his voice filled with regret.

The slave girl moved and placed her hand on Valfric's shoulder. "Valfric, okay," she said. "Valfric, okay." Her voice was soothing.

He nodded. "Thank you, Eira. I'm okay now."

"Eira, take care of Valfric," she said.

He smiled softly. "You did take care of me. Thank you, Eira. I'm just telling Bergthral and Hildrana," he said, his voice patient.

As he spoke, Bergthral and Hildrana shared a glance. They'd never seen anyone treat a slave this way. *There's more here,* Bergthral thought.

Valfric turned back to them. "I'm done with fighting," he said. "There's no point in fighting Lysandrian. So here we are."

Bergthral nodded. "Here you are."

"Eira nice, Valfric nice," Eira said.

"I'm sure you are," Hildrana said, and Bergthral could hear a softness to her voice.

"Well, we would like to talk to you more," Bergthral said.

He took a few steps forward. As he did, he and Hildrana's Essaerithons stayed next to them. Valfric looked concerned, but he didn't run away or attack. Bergthral could feel the tension. *This is a man who has seen a lot of battle, who has seen a lot of death. He's wary,* Bergthral thought. He didn't necessarily disagree with him. It was a smart way of being, but it could make this difficult.

As they got closer, Bergthral's bear neared them. And to all their surprise, Eira walked forward. She reached out and touched the bear's nose. Valfric flinched, his face blanching, reaching out for her. But it was too late. Her hand was already on the Essaerithon's nose. She smiled.

"Durnhart," she said and ran her fingers along the Essaerite's face and neck. It didn't react. Bergthral made sure of that. But he looked at it, and her, his head cocked.

"Durnhart is the merchant you met," Bergthral said.

She smiled as she patted the head of the Essaerithon bear. "Durnhart," she said. "This Durnhart."

Bergthral saw Valfric pinch his nose. "Just go with it," Valfric said a little exasperated. "Eira, it's not nice to touch other people's Essaerites."

Eira looked confused. "Why?" she asked.

"It's fine," Bergthral said.

Eira smiled. "Eira, fine," she said, and went back to petting the bear.

He was letting her do it just because he'd never seen anything like it. People in the settlement interacted with the bear, but only passingly, and he'd never seen a newcomer approach it before. She looked over at the dog that was with them.

"Ferngar, Durnhart," she said. "Ferngar, Durnhart," she said again. Then she looked at Valfric. "Valfric, Ferngar," she said.

Valfric sighed, and Bergthral felt some tension leave the encounter.

"What, Eira?" he said.

"Durnhart, Ferngar," she said, "friends."

He sighed again. "Eira, they're not."

"Durnhart, Ferngar, friends," she said again a bit more insistently.

Valfric sighed and looked over at Bergthral. "Can I have my Essaerite approach yours?" he asked.

Bergthral was curious. "Sure," he said.

This whole encounter was so bizarre to him. His Essaerithon could rip Eira in half without a moment's thought, and it could do the same thing to the dog, but the dog approached it and wagged its tail, something that was very uncommon for an Essaerite.

She scratched behind the bear's ear. "Durnhart," she said.

Next to him, he heard a slight chuckle from his wife, and he looked at her. She smiled, bemused.

"Make the bear friendly," she said. Bergthral scowled for a second, wondering what she was talking about. "Do it," she said.

He sighed and made the bear sniff the dog. Eira clapped, happy.

"Durnhart, Ferngar, friends," she said.

Hildrana was smiling more openly now.

She had her Essaerite approach. Eira looked at it and oohed, running her finger up the nose and head and along the antlers. "Are you going to name this one too?" Hildrana asked.

Eira shook her head. "Girls' name," she said.

Bergthral was confused, and Hildrana's bemused smile grew. "You're right, Eira. Girls do pick the names, but why don't you pick the name for mine?" she said.

Eira grinned and thought for a moment. "Kaelia," she said. "Durnhart, Ferngar, Kaelia, friends," she said.

Hildrana smiled. "Yes, they are."

Bergthral looked over to Valfric, who just shook his head. "I'm sorry," he said.

Hildrana chuckled—something that he didn't hear very often from his wife. "No, I don't think there's anything to be sorry about. I think she just made this whole first encounter much easier for all of us," she said. She looked up at the sky. "It'll be dark soon, and I think it might rain. You can stay with us this evening; we would like to hear more about you," she said.

Valfric nodded. "Thank you, I appreciate it," he said and walked over to them.

Eira was busy with the Essaerites, trying to get them to play together. "Ferngar, play," she said. The dog began to bark playfully, and she looked over at Hildrana and Bergthral.

Hildrana smirked. "Bergthral? I think they're supposed to play together," she said.

Bergthral couldn't believe this, but he sighed and chuckled. "Very well." His Essaerithon began to prance around, playing with the dog, and then soon, Hildrana's Essaerithon joined in.

"This is something I never thought I would ever see," she said.

"Yes, I've never had an Essaerite play before. Not an Essaerithon, anyway," he said.

Next to them, Valfric sighed. "Yeah, she has that effect."

Bergthral turned to him. "And I've never seen someone show so much concern for a slave," he said, his voice a little cooler.

Valfric looked chagrined. "It's safer this way," he said. "I bought her after the river. People were—," he looked down. "Well, she's mine now. She's a slave, but she's not."

"Is she like your wife?" Hildrana asked.

Valfric shook his head quickly. "No, no, she's not. She's my companion, but," he scratched his head. "It's hard to describe. She panics if you take the collar off her. And I figured by keeping it on," he said with a shrug, "I suppose if it keeps her calm and makes people not do anything to her."

Bergthral said, "It's a wise call. Does she panic easily?"

"Thank you, and yes, she does. She doesn't like loud shouting or any kind of violence," Valfric said.

That explained the calm manner he'd seen with Valfric. "Come on, let's head back to our place," Bergthral said.

They began trudging up the road. Behind them, Eira led the group of ridiculously acting Essaerites. Bergthral couldn't help but smile. As they got home, Fernwen came out to join them. She peered at the newcomers and then looked at the Essaerites as they moved around. "It's easier not to ask," Hildrana said, her voice amused.

"I like it," Fernwen said. She walked up to Valfric and Eira. Eira smiled, and Fernwen smiled back up at her.

"Eira," she said.

"I'm Fernwen," Fernwen said.

Eira beamed, and Bergthral noticed Valfric watching, apprehensive for a moment. *He's so protective of her,* Bergthral thought.

"Eira nice," Eira said.

Fernwen smiled. "I can tell. You seem very nice. Do you want to come in and have something to drink?"

Eira nodded. "Thank you," she said, and walked past them. Bergthral noticed Valfric seemed to relax.

"You're going to see different things here," Bergthral said after a moment, and Valfric eyed him. "We're a different type of community."

"Yeah, Durnhart. I guess the real Durnhart said that," Valfric said.

Bergthral couldn't help but smile. "If you do stay here, I'll enjoy seeing the look on Durnhart's face when he finds out that she named an Essaerithon after him," he said.

Valfric looked confused. "An Essaerithon?"

Bergthral nodded, understanding. "It's what we call larger Essaerites, the ones that are more powerful. I take it you do not have one of those."

Valfric's face reddened a little, looking slightly ashamed. Before he could speak, Hildrana said not to worry. "Most Gwenthari don't have them. They tend to be areas of expertise for the Eirfrosti, Wyrdrunir, and Lysandrians," she said.

Valfric nodded. "I've heard things about Eirfrosti Essaerists," he said honestly, "and I've experienced the Lysandrian ones, and I've seen some big ones that they have."

Hildrana nodded curiously. "I look forward to hearing more about that," she said.

After dinner, Valfric and Eira slept by the fire in the front room, and Bergthral held Hildrana in his arms in their bed, talking softly.

"What do you think?" she said.

"I think they've been through some things," Bergthral said.

"Yes, that part is obvious. I don't think he means us harm, though," she said.

Bergthral nodded. "I agree. I think he's looking to get away from it, and I think his biggest concern is her," he said.

"It's very curious, isn't it?" she said.

"Extremely," he said.

"So what do you want to do?" she asked.

He sighed and ran his fingers up and down her arm as he lay there. "I think we should offer them a place here. There are other settlements in the area that would take them, maybe a little begrudgingly, but they would love to have an Essaerist, and even though he doesn't want to fight, I think he could be useful here," he said.

"He doesn't seem to be a very powerful or skilled Essaerist, but I agree with you. He could be problematic somewhere else. The man's looking for a peaceful life, and I think she's just looking for a life. Fernwen seems to like them," she said.

Bergthral sighed after a moment, thinking. "Alright, we'll give them a place here. They'll need to build a home; I suppose they could stay here for a little while while they build it," he said.

Hildrana curled up in his arms. "You're a good man, Bergthral."

"Thank you," he said, then kissed the top of his wife's head. "And I'm not sure that man out there is a good man, but I think he's trying to be."

She nodded. "I agree; he may not be one now, but he's certainly trying, and I think she has a lot to do with that."

CHAPTER 24

Cold Bryndraught slid down Valfric's throat, the sharp chill biting at the back of his mouth before settling heavily in his stomach. The wooden cup hit the table with a dull thud. The thick, bittersweet taste lingered on his tongue, mingling with the scent of bread and smoke from the nearby hearth. He took another bite of breakfast: boiled oats with some bread and cheese. Next to him, Eira was happily finishing her own meal. Across from them sat Bergthral, Hildrana, and Fernwen.

It had been a comfortable evening, and he thought he would have been more concerned being near other Essaerists, but Bergthral and Hildrana had been open with them, and he with them. As he finished his meal, Bergthral looked thoughtful and finally spoke.

"Hildrana and I have discussed it, and we would like you to stay in this settlement with us," Bergthral said.

Valfric felt a small weight lift off his chest at the words. He nodded and smiled. "Thank you," he said.

Bergthral smiled warmly. "I'm not sure what your role as an Essaerist was in your last settlement," he continued.

Valfric thought for a moment. "I wasn't there a lot, but I was there for a few months out of the year. During that time, I usually helped protect the people. I had scouts, and I had my wolves," he said, "though I would also occasionally use Essaerites to assist with cutting wood, things of that nature, but that was about all of it. Why? Are you going to expect me to raid here?" he asked, worried. He had zero desire to go out raiding, and he had made that clear, but still, that might be the price that Bergthral and Hildrana had.

Bergthral shook his head. "We don't raid here," he said. "Well, I should say

Hildrana and I don't raid. We don't require it of anybody. We had some men who went a while back to raid in Ulfgarath lands. They perished," he said.

"I'm sorry to hear that," Valfric said.

Hildrana looked down and sighed. "Nothing you could have done about it. Bergthral warned them."

Her husband went on. "No, we don't expect you to raid, but we do expect that you help out around the community. We are a community here. Both Hildrana and I have used our Essaerites extensively to help. And someday Fernwen will, too," he said.

Valfric's eyes widened a little, and he looked over at Fernwen. In many ways, she looked like a younger version of her mother. Though where Hildrana's eyes were a vibrant, pale blue, Fernwen's were a blue, like deep water or the sky right before dusk.

"Your daughter's an Essaerist?" he said, surprised.

Fernwen gave the hint of a smile. "I'm an Essaerist," she said.

Valfric looked over at Hildrana and Bergthral. Bergthral grinned, and Hildrana smiled.

"It is very rare for Essaerists to have other Essaerist children," she said.

"I've never heard of it before," Valfric said honestly.

Hildrana smiled warmly. "We didn't think we'd actually be able to have a child. It's so difficult for Essaerists to reproduce, you see. So when there are two of them together, it's even harder." She looked over at her daughter fondly. "But then we had Fernwen. You can imagine our surprise when it turned out that she could use Essaeris."

"Surprise was a bit of an understatement," Bergthral said.

"Fernwen like Valfric," Eira said.

Fernwen looked over at Eira and smiled.

"Yes, I'm like Valfric, and so are my mother and father," she said.

Eira smiled and looked over at Hildrana and Bergthral as if that seemed to make sense to her. Maybe it did.

Bergthral returned to the subject they were on before.

"So, you're willing to help out around the settlement?" he asked.

Valfric shrugged. "I'm happy to do whatever you need," he said. "Do you need help with protection?" he asked. "I may not be interested in raiding, but I understand the importance of protecting a settlement."

Bergthral smiled tightly. "That would be welcome, yes. It's relatively easy between Hildrana and I, but having a third person can't hurt."

Valfric smiled. "Very well." He felt a little chagrined. "I have to admit, I'm not as talented as I suspect you're hoping for."

Bergthral raised an eyebrow, and Valfric went on.

"If you want somebody dead, I'm your man," he said.

Next to him, Eira stiffened a little. "Valfric, no hurt," she said.

He placed his hand gently on top of her arm. "I'm not going to hurt anybody. I'm just telling them what I used to do," he said.

She looked at him, her eyes a little tight with fear. "Valfric, no hurt," she said again.

He sighed, feeling guilty. "I'm sorry, Eira. You're right. I won't hurt anybody," he said, meaning it.

He looked back to Hildrana and Bergthral, who were watching him curiously.

"But I'm not as skilled with other types of Essaerites," he said.

"It's fine," Hildrana said. "You can learn, and so long as you can create basic Essaerites, I don't think you're going to have anything to worry about."

She looked at him curiously. "Odd, though. I haven't met many Essaerists your age that aren't, well, overly confident. Especially the male ones," she said with a sly glance at her husband, who just smirked.

"I wasn't that bad," Bergthral said with a laugh.

"Mmmhmm," Hildrana hummed and looked at Valfric.

He couldn't help but smile. "If you had talked to me before Lysandrian invaded, I would have fit exactly what you were talking about," he said with a laugh.

"But that's different now," she said.

"That's different now," he echoed soberly. "Before, I just thought that it was the older Essaerists who were incredibly powerful. I'd obviously heard rumors of the Eirfrosti, but I always just chalked them up to be rumors. Same with Lysandrian, but now, after having seen it," he shrugged. "Well, let's just say that I'm more convinced than I ever have been that I may not be as good as I've always thought I was."

Hildrana's expression softened. "I think that's a good lesson for all of us," she said.

"Agreed," Bergthral said. "Well, I can show you a plot of land that is yours. You're welcome to stay in our home until you build one of your own," he said. "I will be happy to help you if you'd like. If nothing else, to help you create the Essaerites and to teach them how to build. It should be relatively quick work if we create enough of them."

Valfric smiled. "That'd be most welcome, thank you. We can live in a tent, though. I don't want to impose," he said. "But the help with the Essaerites would be much appreciated."

They stood from their meal, and Bergthral led Valfric and Eira out of the house. Fernwen joined them, and they walked through the cool morning together, making their way through the small settlement that surrounded them.

"Do you have common buildings?" Valfric asked.

Bergthral shook his head. "No, we have a common area, but nothing like a hall or inn or anything of that nature. It's too small here, and everyone just spends time in each other's homes anyway," he said with a smile.

Valfric nodded. "It's a beautiful area," he said.

"It is," Bergthral said. He pointed to the north. "If you go through those trees, it's about a ten or fifteen-minute walk, and you'll make it to the beach."

Valfric raised an eyebrow. "Oh, is there a lake here?"

Bergthral shook his head. "No, it's the ocean. It's just the channel, and then Eirfrosti."

Valfric nodded. "I knew we were close to the sea, but I didn't realize how close."

"Very close," Bergthral said. "We eat a lot of fish here," he commented.

"Good to know. I'll have to learn how to fish," he said with a chuckle.

Bergthral laughed. "We have a couple of Essaerites that might be useful. I've seen your hawks, so it's just some alterations to create birds that are good at fishing."

"I've done a little bit of that," Valfric said, "eagles going after river trout and fishing lakes."

"It's a lot like that," Bergthral said. "However, there are bigger fish that are out in the sea, if you want. There's also some hunting in the area, and people have livestock. You can kind of do what you like," he said.

They made it to an area that was on the northeast part of the settlement. At the edge, there were fields all around them that ended in a thick tree line. Valfric looked around, and Eira went looking and smelling at the few flowers that were left, with Fernwen next to her. He watched the two of them.

"Your daughter seems very kind," Valfric said.

Bergthral traced his gaze, seeing the two women together. Bergthral smiled warmly. "She can be, unless you're asking her to do a chore she doesn't like," he said with a bit of a chuckle, "but yes, she's a good person. She's an exceptionally good judge of character as well."

He raised an eyebrow. "I'm surprised you let me in then," he said.

Bergthral smiled. "Well, she seemed to like you well enough, and she certainly likes Eira. We all have pasts, but that doesn't mean that's our present or our future."

"Thank you for that," Valfric said, "and I'm glad that your daughter is being nice to Eira."

Bergthral looked concerned. "I imagine she hasn't had the easiest of lives."

Valfric shook his head. "I don't think so," he said. "When I met her, the people were horrible to her; everyone was so cruel."

He remembered the first time he had seen her undressed. "When I bought her. One night, when we needed to bathe," he said, shaking his head. "The scars on her body," he commented.

Bergthral seemed bothered. "The cruelty of people seems to know no ends," he said. "I'm sorry she went through that, but I'm happy she found someone to take her away from it."

"Thank you," Valfric said and then sighed, "but she should have never needed someone to take her away from it." He turned his attention to the field.

"Thank you for this plot of land. I will make sure that I help out the settlement a lot."

Bergthral didn't seem to fight the change of subject and nodded. "You are welcome to it. There are some stones in the area that you can use to build with if you'd like, and you're welcome to harvest anything from the forest that you need. How good are you at making Essaerites other than your wolves?"

"It depends on what you need," Valfric responded. "I have some that look kind of like people, that are just as effective as them."

Bergthral nodded. "That's all you need. As long as they can learn basic things and you can make them."

Valfric nodded. He let his Essaeris well up, and it came out of him. Next to him, an Essaerite came into the world. It had two legs and two arms with five-digit hands and a head, but it didn't look like a person after the form. It was all simple shapes and rough textures.

"They can see as well as a man, as well as hear," he said. "I can make them look a little bit more like people."

Bergthral nodded. "I've met Essaerists that can create Essaerites that are indistinguishable from people," he said.

"Have you really?" Valfric said.

Bergthral nodded. "Yes, the Eirfrosti. I know the Lysandrians can as well, as well as the Wyrdrunirs, but these are perfect. They're everything that you need. They're simple, they use nowhere near as much Essaeris as something more complicated, and they can work. Shall we get started?"

————

MATERIALS MOVED IN A STEADY LINE PAST MARIOKOS, GOING INTO A COVERED BUILDING that could move. The buildings were like little screens to protect the men and Essaerites from anything coming in from the city. Mariokos looked at them. They had pitched roofs that were covered in animal hides or wood. They were light and could be picked up and moved around, which was useful as they were moving regularly. The men were bringing in dirt, timber, rock, and gravel. He was standing at the base of a very long ramp that was moving up towards Ulfgard. It had been under construction for over a week now.

The Gwenthari didn't seem to see it coming, but Mariokos thought they should have. After all, once the legions were able to take care of the moat, it had only been a matter of time. The moat had predominantly been filled by the river that ran on the other side of the city. The legion had stopped up the inlet for it and then the outlet and was able to drain the water, making the moat just a ditch that they would have to move past, albeit a wide and deep one. Then they'd begun construction of the ramp.

The construction began far back from the wall, as the slope that the legions would travel up would be gradual and easy for them to walk and defend. The base of the ramp was wide and tapered up as it went further up, allowing them to use fewer materials. It also had the benefit of being made out of timber, dirt, and rock, making it very hard-wearing and difficult for the defenders to deal with.

Mariokos had several Essaerites that were helping in the effort. He had pulled all of his Essaeris away from the defense of the skies and put it on construction. Near the front of the ramp, he had several Essaerites that were working tirelessly on adding new layers, building it up layer by layer. Smaller versions of his Essaerithon were likewise working to break up some rock and carry some of the larger stones.

They moved in at a regular pace, moving stones, putting down the larger ones that other Essaerites or men would pack in with dirt and clay, while others were working on the internal wooden frame that generally held the whole thing together. It was a slow process, but it was inevitable.

The tops of the little buildings that the Legion were using were constantly being peppered by arrows and spears, some on fire, but most weren't. Mariokos had created other Essaerites that scuttled along the top, pulling the flaming arrows and spears from the roof and throwing them down. He'd encased the outside of them in metal and ceramics, making them immune to the fire, and with the distance that the defenders were having to fire from, the Essaerites had little in the way of issues dealing with impacts.

The Gwenthari were also throwing stones, but that didn't have any impact on the structures at all. He knew the closer they got to the city, the more that would change, but not by a wide margin. After all, the defenders had other things that they had to deal with as well, namely the legions.

When they had first moved into the area, they hadn't attacked the city at all. They'd almost left it completely alone and just focused on building up their counterfortifications. The Gwenthari had seemed all too happy to let this happen. Other than the attacks from the Essaerists, there hadn't been a real concerted effort from the Gwenthari of the city to do anything about the Lysandrian legions as they built those counterfortifications. They should have been harassing them, but they hadn't. And now the city would pay for it.

All manner of siege engines had been constructed, erected, or set up, and were now actively engaged with the city. Bolts fired from all around, sailing over the walls. Some would hit people on the walls, but most, he knew, would fly over to cause havoc inside. There were also catapults sending a steady stream of rocks towards the city. Some of them were on fire, but the vast majority were not. From other siege engines, there were large wooden towers that likewise had ballistae or catapults atop them being used and fired.

All in all, it was making for a difficult time for Ulfgard, and he suspected the defenders were starting to get tired and worn down. They also would be running low on supplies. They were able to use the bolts that were shot at them, in some cases, and fire them back at the legions. But it wasn't always the case, and he suspected that their internal resources were beginning to feel the pinch. Soon, they would have to start conserving what munitions they had and pull people back from the walls lest they be maimed or killed.

Mariokos walked with a group of men underneath the covers and made his way down the ramp. All around him were the sounds of people working. The inside of the little mobile buildings was hot and stifling. The air was filled with dust and the scent of sweat. The inside was a mix of both legionaries and slaves as they worked. Mariokos moved around people, making his way near the front. As he got there, he heard the occasional thump or tap on the roof above him as it was hit by an arrow or a rock. Those sounds became more consistent as he neared the front.

The front was predominantly filled with his Essaerites. He had gone with smaller versions, not like the legionaries, but instead ones that were similar to what he used for throwing darts and javelins. They didn't look like people; instead, they resembled a poor clay statue from a student who was learning how to sculpt. They were mostly formless and featureless, just having arms, legs, and hands, but they were strong enough and were working diligently and quickly.

Near the front, he could hear the sound of things banging and clanging much more distinctly. He reminded himself that both Kyrillos and Xavieno were actively engaged on the other side of the walls. He inspected the work of the Essaerites quickly, not wanting to be there in case Kyrillos or Xavieno's Essaerites were pushed back. It was one of the few times that he felt nervous being in the legion. He had been in combat, and that had been frightening, but there was a sense of control that you had then. You were standing shoulder to shoulder with men or Essaerites, and you were fighting. When it came to standing in these little buildings, that wasn't quite the case.

Upon completion of his inspection, he walked back down, finally exiting the row of buildings. He felt the breeze instantly begin to wick away sweat and heat from his body, and he took in a deep breath, enjoying being out of the stifling heat. His tunic was coated in sweat, and he was thankful to not have to deal with it anymore. He felt for the men that were having to go to work. Mariokos had just wandered in and then wandered back out, and it made him feel drained and exhausted. He could only imagine what it would be like working an entire day or night inside that place.

He walked over to a tent where Aresio and the other engineers were. Aresio looked at him. "So," he said.

Mariokos nodded. "The progress is going well. I don't see any issues, and all the roofs seem to be holding out well, too," he said with a smile.

Aresio chuckled. "I always hate being under those things when they're under attack," he said, looking back at a large piece of paper on a table. It was the plan for the ramp and the city of Ulfgard.

"How much time do you think we have left?" Mariokos asked.

"A few weeks, maybe less. It's inevitable."

And it was. Mariokos knew that. As soon as the ramp was completed, the legions would spill over the walls of Ulfgard. There was no stopping it. Just as the leaves would finish falling and the snow would begin to come, the city of Ulfgard would fall, and it would fall soon.

CHAPTER 25

Valfric felt his Essaeris pulsing and racing inside him. It came ripping out as five Essaerites came into existence. They all resembled men and were holding various digging tools. As he created them, he felt the power wash out of him. It felt good, in a way, to be using it. Not that he hadn't been using it, but to be pushing it. Around them was a field comprised of brown, dying grass, weeds, and flowers. The air was cold and held a wet chill that he suspected came from the ocean.

Bergthral and Valfric had laid out an area for the cottage. There would be a few other small structures as well, but the cottage was the one that Valfric most concerned with right now. It needed to be done before winter set in. Like all Gwenthari homes, it would be partially dug into the ground. That's where the Essaerites were going to come into play.

Eira was standing next to him, watching with excitement.

"Valfric," she said.

"Yes," he replied.

"Valfric, dig?" she asked.

"My Essaerites are," he said with a smile. "Do you want to help?"

She looked at the ground. "Eira, need shovel," she said.

He chuckled. "I'm just kidding. I don't need you to help dig," he said.

His mind reached out, and the Essaerites began to move. Shovels and pickaxes dug into the turf. They heard the sound of ripping roots and ground as they began making a perimeter around where the home was going to be.

Big chunks of sod came up and the Essaerites piled them to the side while others dug into the dirt. This was going to go much faster, he thought. He had seen homes built when he was younger. It was always a long affair, taking several weeks, but that was with men and women who were human, who couldn't do what the Essaerites could do—humans who needed breaks and weren't as strong. These would be different. He realized it wouldn't take them long to dig down as far as they needed to, nor would it take them long to erect the rest of the structure. They would work day and night until it was done, never complaining, never slowing, never getting tired. It was damn handy.

He turned his attention to the area that he would be working on. Bergthral had given him a handful of tasks, namely in the form of cutting up and working some timbers that would be used in the rest of the cottage. *Alright, now you just need to not fuck this up,* Valfric thought. Fucking it up was very likely. Valfric could do all sorts of things. He was very skilled. He could precisely drive a dagger through somebody in just the spot he wanted to. He could lift most things. He could deal with pain. He could deal with fear. But the frustration that came with doing something and not doing it well? That was going to be interesting, wasn't it?

He could hear the rhythmic thuds of the Essaerites as they dug into the dirt, the sound of metal striking ground mixing with the tearing of roots and the gritty scrape of soil. He looked over, and they were making quite a lot of progress already. He smiled.

"I don't think we're going to be in the tent very long," he said to Eira.

She grinned and bounced on her feet, watching. He couldn't help but smile. She seemed so excited to see the Essaerites work. Next to her, Ferngar sat. She would occasionally reach down and pat its head or scratch behind its ear. In a way, it had become his favorite Essaerite. Not because it did anything for him —it didn't. The Essaerite never did anything for him, but it was busy tending to Eira, and she loved it. And it was the most pure form of love there was. In a way, he realized it was like she loved him because the power that made Ferngar was his.

He heard the sound of something being dragged, and he looked over to see Bergthral approaching. With him was his massive bear, which had a harness around it, dragging several large logs behind it. Bergthral smiled as he came up to him.

"Good morning," he said.

"Morning," Valfric replied, coming up and clapping Bergthral's hand.

"Bergthral, morning," Eira said.

He smiled at Eira. "Good morning, Eira. You look lovely today," he said.

Eira beamed, looking down at her tunic. Today, her favorite colors were red and brown. The fabrics were a deep rich brown and crimson. He'd also taken to making different shoes for her every day. He found the challenge to actually be kind of amusing. Today, he had gone with one shoe that was the color of mud and the other one the same crimson as the tunic.

It had made her happy, and he had found that he was starting to have an easier time creating some of the items. Not just the tunics themselves, but the fabric, the leather of the shoes, the buckles of any belts. They now fit her perfectly, as did the shoes. The boots wrapped perfectly around her feet and calves. His did likewise.

He'd never really appreciated that this would have been a possibility. His whole life, he had just worn regular tunics, regular boots. He'd always thought that Essaeris clothes were frivolous, or not something that a warrior would do. His Essaeris was better spent elsewhere. But with each passing day, and with each outfit that he created for both of them, he found that it was useful. The clothes were comfortable, they were dry, and they made him feel better. The shoes kept his feet from aching, and the items were taking far less power than they had before.

I've been stupid, he thought. There were things that he could have been doing for his whole life that would have made this easier. He thought back to his old teacher, the old man who wasn't an Essaerist but seemed to know the ways of the world. He'd always made Valfric make little trinkets and little things, wanting him to focus on the simplistic. Valfric had hated it. It wasn't what he wanted to do. He wanted to create things that killed and maimed, and all the other stuff. But here, he realized the old man might have been onto something.

————

BERGTHRAL TURNED TO THE WORK AT HAND. HIS ESSAERITHON HAD BROUGHT SEVERAL large tree-sized logs with him, enough to make the frame for Valfric and Eira's new home. He got to work on it, creating Essaerites. He lost himself in the work, enjoying the feel of it. Despite the cold air, he felt himself warm. So many Essaerists didn't like doing work with their own hands. That wasn't Bergthral's way. He thought it was important to take part in it.

Next to him, he heard Valfric swear. He turned to see the other man holding his finger, blood trickling out of it.

"You alright?" he asked.

Valfric looked up at him, his face red. He kicked the piece of wood he was working on. "Fucking blade jumped," he said.

"Valfric grumpy," Eira said.

Valfric's head snapped to the side. "Yes, I'm mad," he said, his voice dangerous.

"Valfric grumpy," she said again. "Valfric no grumpy."

He saw Valfric turn red with anger. It looked like he was about to say or do something. Bergthral wasn't sure what he should do. After all, Eira was his slave. *Is he going to hit her?* he wondered. Eira didn't seem to be aware of the danger, and he could see Valfric's shoulders moving up and down with each breath, and then he stopped. He saw his skin go back to a normal color, and he huffed out.

"Yeah, I was grumpy. I won't be anymore," he said, almost in defeat.

Eira smiled. "Valfric happy," she said.

"I'll try," he huffed.

Bergthral walked over to him. "I honestly didn't see that going that way."

Valfric looked at him and chuckled in embarrassment. "Yeah, I guess there would have been a time that it wouldn't have gone well."

Bergthral smiled. "I don't think it has anything to do with time and everything to do with the person. You telling me if I told you not to be grumpy, you wouldn't have just taken a swing at me?"

Valfric grinned but looked a little chagrined. "Yeah, you might have a point," he said. He looked over at what he'd been working on. "I'm sorry, I'm shit at this," he said. "I guess I'm going to have to get better at it."

Bergthral laughed. "We all do. Look, we've been at it for a while; why don't we have some lunch? I see Fernwen coming," he said.

And indeed, his daughter was on her way. She looked to be carrying something in her arms, probably bread, Bergthral thought. As she neared, she smiled up at Eira, who grinned back at her.

"Fernwen," Eira said.

"Eira," Fernwen said with a smile.

Eira walked over to her, and seeming happy, Fernwen turned back to her father. "I brought bread."

He smiled. "Such a good daughter."

"Mom made me do it," Fernwen admitted.

He laughed. "I figured."

Fernwen handed them each a small loaf of bread. Bergthral tore his in half and dug into it. "Did you bring any Bryndraught?" he asked.

"No, I couldn't carry it," she said.

He sighed and then sent an Essaerite to go back to the house to fetch a jug.

Fernwen and Eira finished their bread first, and Bergthral watched as the two of them ran around the field. He smiled. "They're getting on well."

Valfric nodded. "Yeah, it's nice to see Eira have a friend. Thank you for all this, by the way."

"Of course," Bergthral said. Then he paused. "May I make a suggestion?"

"Sure. Though, I'll warn you, if it's about carpentry, I'll listen, but it doesn't mean that I'll actually be able to do it," he said.

Bergthral chuckled. "No, it's not about that. It's about your anger," he said.

Valfric looked down. "Sorry about that."

"Why? We all get angry," Bergthral said. "I just think you might need an outlet for it."

Valfric sighed. "Yeah, I guess one of those would be nice."

"Well, you can't have always been an angry person, have you?" he said.

Valfric had a cocky smile. "Yeah, maybe a little bit, but no, I used to have outlets."

"What were they?" Bergthral asked.

Valfric shrugged. "Fighting and fucking, the same as every other man."

Bergthral laughed. "And those aren't options anymore?"

"No," Valfric said.

"Really?" Bergthral said. "You don't want to fight anymore? And Eira seems to like you."

Valfric shook his head. "Eira likes me the same way she likes Fernwen and Ferngar and you. I don't think that other is an option. Honestly, I don't even think I could do that with her."

Bergthral raised an eyebrow. "Why is that?"

Valfric looked over at him and then back at the ground. "Just some of the things that have happened to her."

He nodded, deciding not to push the subject. "Well, I don't think there are any women here who you'll find, but alright, if that's not an option, what about fighting?"

Valfric shook his head. "Eira doesn't like violence, and I'm worried that if I do, I'll go back to what I was."

Bergthral nodded, understanding. Here was a man who was keeping everything in his life under control. There was value to that, to an extent, but there was danger in it, too.

"You don't have to fight to hurt or kill. You could spar," he said.

"I don't know," Valfric said. "With who? I don't want to be the new guy who just comes here and starts beating on people," he said, shaking his head. "Plus, I don't know."

Bergthral put his hand on Valfric's shoulder. "You want to be able to protect her and all of us, don't you?" he said.

"Of course I do," Valfric said.

"That means you have to continue to train. Look, you can train with me if you'd like," he said.

Valfric glanced at him and smiled. "Yeah?"

"Come on," Bergthral said. "The Essaerites are doing work."

"I can't," he said and glanced in Eira's direction.

Bergthral called over Fernwen and Eira. "Fernwen, why don't you show Eira the sea?"

Eira's eyes widened. "Sea?"

"Fernwen, why don't you go show her?" Bergthral said.

Fernwen beamed up at him. "Come on, Eira. You'll love it. There's so much water. It's so pretty, and you can see forever," she said, taking Eira's hand and leading her away.

Bergthral turned to Valfric. "She's not here now."

Valfric looked thoughtful and then sighed, getting up. "Alright. How do you want to do this?"

"Well, I'm assuming you know how to make a training sword, don't you?" Bergthral said, standing up.

Valfric nodded. "I do."

"Okay, we each make one and we give it to the other person," he said.

Valfric raised an eyebrow. "Why?"

Bergthral shrugged. "Well, I figure if you hit me as hard as you can with one of my own Essaerites, I'm going to release it without thinking about it and not get hurt. I figure you'll do the same."

Valfric looked thoughtful for a moment. "I never thought of that before. Never had the opportunity," he said.

"Well, you do now, don't you?"

They created weapons and squared off against each other. As soon as there was a weapon in Valfric's hand, Bergthral could see the change in him, could see him come alive. *He's a killer,* he thought. He could see why Valfric was afraid. This was his nature. *I wonder, are you a good man who's been living a bad person's life, or are you an evil man trying to live a good man's life?* He thought as they circled each other.

Bergthral was far from being a pushover, but he thought it might be useful to keep Valfric's confidence up. *Push him, but let him win,* he thought.

Valfric came at him quickly. Bergthral caught the blow, twisted, and lashed out on his own, but Valfric wasn't there.

What the? Bergthral thought. He felt a sting across his back and felt his Essaerite release. He turned and looked at Valfric.

"How did—" Bergthral said.

Valfric grinned. "I might be shit at carpentry, but I'm good at killing. And I never left it solely to my Essaerites."

There was a fire in Valfric's eyes that Bergthral could see, but the fire felt cold to him. Cruel.

"I see," Bergthral said, creating another training sword and giving it to Valfric. "Most Essaerists aren't like that."

They began sparring again, though this time Bergthral did not hold back. It didn't matter. Time and time again, Valfric scored hits. Even when it seemed like he was pulling his punches and blows, Bergthral struggled to win.

He panted after a while and held up his hand, calling a stop to it. "Honestly, I'm impressed," he said. "Most people can't best me."

Valfric was covered in sweat and was moving in a way that told him that his injury was probably hurting. He sat down on the ground. "Don't take it personally. Your job has been being a good person and taking care of your family and settlement. Mine hasn't."

Bergthral sat next to him and took a long drink of Bryndraught. "So I take it you trained a lot," he said.

Valfric nodded. "Almost every day, my friends and I would, or more often than not, I would train with an Essaerite," he said.

Bergthral raised an eyebrow. "Really?"

Valfric nodded. "Really? They have the same skills that we do, don't they? So? It always made sense to me. Plus, my friends would get tired and wouldn't want to do it anymore, and I kept on training. I'd do it until I dropped," he admitted.

"Interesting. That's the same thing the Eirfrosti and the Lysandrians do," he said.

Valfric looked at him. "Training until they drop?"

Bergthral shook his head. "No. Using their Essaerites. Have you ever controlled one Essaerite while the other one fights?" he said.

Valfric nodded. "A couple of times. Useful for technique, but leaves something to be desired," he said.

"I could see where someone like you would say that, but it's something that the Lysandrians and Eirfrosti do. The Wyrdrunirs as well, I suspect," he said with a shrug. "On that note, how was it fighting them? Not the whole legion, just the individual soldiers?" he asked, curious.

Valfric looked thoughtful. "Not like what I expected," he said honestly. "They were so much better than us."

Bergthral raised an eyebrow.

"Not that the average legionnaire was better than all of us, just better than most of us," Valfric explained with a shrug. "Most people don't train. These men do. They do every day. And while they may not be the best swordsmen or fighters that I've ever fought, they're all better than most, and they're disciplined, and they all fight the same," he said, shaking his head.

"We came at them like a horde," he said, his eyes far off as if he were looking to the past. "It's no wonder they beat us," he said after a moment.

"They're professional soldiers," Bergthral said.

Valfric nodded. "And we were farmers and robbers who fancied ourselves more powerful," he said. They took a drink of Bryndraught. "And it cost us everything."

––––––

CAELWEN'S BIRD ESSAERITE TWISTED AND TURNED IN THE AIR, LATCHING ONTO THE Essaerite of one of the defenders of Ulfgard. Its beak and talons bit into the other one, likewise receiving wounds of its own. The creatures fell from the sky, heading towards the ground, and broke apart at the last moment, swooping away. She pumped more Essaeris into her bird, healing it. She'd altered it since the start of this campaign; the bird now had a long, wicked beak that was metal with metal talons. Otherwise, it was simplified. Gone were the days of the Gwenthari in Ulfgard trying to harass the countryside. Everything was so focused on the wall now, as it should be.

She could see smoke. It had been over the city for days. She didn't know if it was from the Lysandrian artillery or if there had been an accident inside the walls. Both were possible. They hadn't been able to get any hawks over the city to see.

Her attention was brought back to the battle overhead. Her bird swooped around again, meeting up with the others. She felt sweat drip down her brow and back. The strain was unbelievable. She'd only experienced it a few times in her life—when she'd been forced to push her Essaeris as far as it would go and then hold it there.

Eventually, the sun started to go down below the horizon, and she felt relief wash over her. No one was pushing at night. There was no purpose in it. Below her bird, she could see both Xavieno and Kyrillos's Essaerites fighting some of the other ones. The Wyrdrunir woman's Essaerites, made of stone, slashed and fought. Xavieno and Kyrillos were holding up well against her, in many cases winning, but she wasn't alone. Some of the city's other Essaerists had Essaerites that were similar to the legionnaires that Mariokos made, though they were not as defined.

As they broke for the evening, Caelwen trudged back to camp and into her tent. All around, men were talking and working. She wasn't the only one who had been pushing hard. The ramp's construction was nearly complete, and once it was, she suspected the real fighting would begin, or at least would begin for the Legionnaires.

As she got back to her tent, she saw Ilara working around a fire. Her tent was next to Caelwen's, and she looked up as she approached.

"You look like shit," Ilara said.

Caelwen smiled half-heartedly.

"I feel like shit," she said, plopping down on a stool next to the fire.

She breathed in deeply, catching the scents of an evening stew. She didn't think anything had ever smelled so good to her before in her life. Not that Ilara was a good cook. In fact, she might have been on the poorer side when it came to cooking, but after the day that Caelwen had had, anything would smell amazing.

"What are we having?" she asked.

"One of your rabbits," Ilara said. "But seriously, you look like shit. How's it going?" she asked, concerned.

Caelwen sighed. "It's going. It's a stalemate over the city."

"I'm surprised," Ilara said.

Caelwen shrugged. "We're evenly matched, or at least there are enough Essaerists that are making it seem that way. It's hard to tell. On the ground, it's much the same, but this is how it'll go, won't it? It'll just be a stalemate until all of a sudden it's not."

Ilara nodded. "I suppose you're right."

Eventually, the ramp would be completed, and all the fighting of the Essaerists would be just a little thing in the grand scheme of it all. There were so many in the legions and so many in the city.

Mariokos came into view with Xavieno. Both of them looked haggard and tired, though for different reasons. Mariokos had been spending a lot of his time inside the covered structures, helping supervise the construction of the ramp. He'd also been pushing his Essaeris to its limits. Xavieno, on the other hand, had been engaged in fights on the ground with his Essaerites. He looked tired and haggard, and his mood had been sour for days.

Both men came and sat down. Mariokos's expression was blank and numb.

"How was your day?" he asked, looking over at her.

"I think you know. How was yours?" she replied.

"I was in the buildings covering that ramp most of the day." he said.

"How goes the ramp?" she asked.

"Well," he said, "it will be done soon. Xavieno, how was it for you?" he asked.

Xavieno grunted. That seemed about right.

———

As Xavieno finished his dinner, he felt his body and mind begin to come back alive. With it, he felt a slight throbbing behind his forehead, along with a deep irritability. As he finished, he stood, intent on going to bed, and walked into his tent. What little Essaeris he had left reached out, creating a basin of warm water. The tent flaps flapped behind him, and he saw Ilara come in as he disrobed.

She walked up and dipped a rag in the water.

"You don't have to," he said.

"You're tired," she said, and began wiping him down.

He sighed, not in the mood to argue with her. If she wanted to clean him off, that was her business, not his, he decided. It felt nice feeling the warm, wet rag move over his body, taking with it sweat and grime.

"You seem tense," she said.

He cracked an eye, looking at her. "We are sieging a city," he said shortly.

"More tense than usual," she said.

He sighed. "I'm fine."

"Mmhmm," she said as she continued to wipe him down.

He opened his eyes and looked at her, irritated. "What the fuck do you want from me?" he asked.

She looked at him. "Just saying that you're tense. You might need to take care of it, or you can keep being tense. It's up to you," she said, dipping the rag back in the water.

She went to touch him, and he grabbed her wrist. "What would you have me do?"

To her credit, she didn't flinch away from his touch. She shrugged. "Well, you seem to be getting enough fighting in. Maybe there's something else that you need," she said.

He rolled his eyes. "What?"

"You act like you're the first man I've been around. I've been around plenty of men and soldiers," she said. "I know what you need, and I know it's been a while since you've gone to one of those brothels. I don't know why you go to them," she said.

He sighed. He didn't want to have this conversation with her. "Why wouldn't I go to them?"

She looked at him. "Why pay for something you own?"

He sighed. "Why do you want me to?"

"Because you need it," she said, "and that's what I'm here for."

He looked over at her. "I..." he started.

She pulled away from him, and in a quick move, her dress was lying on the ground. She stood before him, nude. His eyes widened a bit.

"Do you not like me?" she asked insistently.

"It's not," he said.

"What?" she said, walking up to him. "I've seen you with other people. You can't tell me you don't desire it, or that you're bothered by doing something without your wife," she accused.

He looked at her, feeling flinty. "I can't do it with you," he said.

"Why not?" she asked.

He looked down, feeling shame inside himself. "Because... because of what I did."

He turned and sat on the bed. She sat next to him.

"What did you do?" she asked.

"You know what I did. At the Ilfrun River," he said.

"You did your job," she said.

He looked at her. "How can you not hate me for what I did? I killed so many of your people."

She didn't back down. "So did I," she said.

This took him off guard. It always did when she was bluntly honest about her past.

Her expression softened. "Look, I don't hate you," she said. "I wanted to..."

"You did?" he said.

"Of course, you own me," she said flatly. "Even if I know I'm a fucking horrible person, that doesn't mean that I exactly wanted to be a slave. But—"

"But what?" he said.

She sighed and looked at him, her expression soft. "But you're an exceptionally good man. So is Mariokos, for that matter. And I like Caelwen. But you're kind. You're gentle."

"I'm a killer," he said.

"Everyone's killers," she said, "some people just don't know it yet."

"But," she said, looking down, her cheeks flushing a little bit, "I'm ashamed to admit it, but you're a far better man than any that I've met," she said with a sigh.

"Even your dead friends?" he said, shocked.

She flinched a little. "Especially them."

This gave him pause. "I've never heard you speak poorly of them," he said.

"They were what we were brought up to be," she said, "but it doesn't mean that they were good."

Look, I get that you feel guilt about what might happen to me. But think about all the horrible things that I've done. I'm not exactly some innocent."

"But I don't think you're a bad person," he said.

She smiled softly. "I said you were kind and good, not smart."

He couldn't help but chuckle. "I just... I don't know. I can't force you," he said.

"You wouldn't be, and so many of those other women in those brothels, they're slaves. Do you mind forcing them?" she asked.

This made him flinch. He'd never really thought of it that way. He knew that's what it was, but he didn't like to think of himself in that light.

"They don't," he said.

"They do," she said. "What do you think? If they don't agree to spread their legs for patrons, that nothing bad will happen to them?" she said. "Lysandrian law or not."

It was true. Rape was illegal, even for a slave. You couldn't technically force them to do it, but they all did. He sighed. "Great, now I feel bad about doing that."

She shrugged. "Why? You can't change the past. Look, Xavieno, I think you're a good person. I think you're lonely," she said. "I'm lonely, too."

He looked at her.

"Because all of your people are dead," he said.

"That. And even now I realize I don't know why I was with them," she said.

He raised an eyebrow. "What do you mean?"

"After Hroldenfell, after I realized the things that we had done," she shook her head. "Well, I was with them in person, but not with them," she said. "I wasn't myself anymore."

"Are you yourself with me?" he asked.

She shrugged. "No, I don't know who I am, but I know that we're both lonely. And I know that it's my job to take care of you. And it's your job to let me do that," she said.

He snorted. "Still trying?"

"Not trying so much as... I don't know what," she said.

He sighed. "I just feel..."

She stopped him. "Look, how about this? You don't want to use me. You'd feel bad about that," she said.

He nodded. "Yeah."

She shrugged. "Then don't," she said.

"I'm sorry, you're confusing me," he said.

"I keep on hearing about what wonderful lovers the Lysandrians are," she said. She smirked. "Prove them right. Not tonight. You're tired tonight. But prove them right," she said. "Unless I've heard wrong," she added.

He snorted. "Nice try," he paused. "But you didn't. The rumors are true."

She rolled her eyes. "Bullshit, all men say that, and they're rarely right." She sucked her lip, something he would have found sexy even if she hadn't been naked. "Maybe there's an Essaerite or something..." she trailed off.

He stood, and she looked at him. "Okay, that's enough."

"Is it?" she asked, her tone petulant.

Erosino, how is she able to do that? He thought. The tone of her voice and the look on her face had him bursting.

"Yes, it is," he released his tunic. "I won't have the reputation of my people questioned."

She stood with a lopsided smile on her face. "Are you going to punish me, Dominaro?"

He almost lost it then, but his irritation was gone. He ran his hand up her arm. "In a manner of speaking," he said as his eyes traced her body, "but not with a whip or belt." He turned his gaze to hers. "But that's not to say you aren't going to struggle to walk tomorrow."

CHAPTER 26

ariokos's gaze followed the rise of the covered ramp toward Ulfgard. Lines of men moved in and out, some bringing in new materials, others coming out to grab more. Its wide base tapered gradually until it came to a much narrower top. The Legionnaires had been packing it down to give it a steady surface. *Almost there*, Mariokos thought. It would only be a few days until they came to a critical juncture.

His eyes traced up the ramp to where it neared the walls of Ulfgard. Above those walls, there was the ever-present flight of birds, and in front of them, the melee of Essaerites as they clashed with each other. The sky was likewise filled with bolts and rocks as they came from siege weapons on both sides of the conflict. The sky hung heavy with gray clouds, and the cold air bit at Mariokos's skin. There had already been a handful of light snowfalls, and Mariokos was looking forward to the ramp being completed. It would have to be soon anyway, before the ground froze up and made things too difficult, but it would be done before that happened. Again, it was inevitable. In the next few days, it would reach that critical point where it would become increasingly difficult for both the Gwenthari and the Legions. When the ramp made it up near the height of the wall and came close to it, the Gwenthari would be able to easily attack those working on it, but the same could go for the Legionnaires, as they could likewise attack them. It would be a quick juncture, Mariokos knew.

The Legion had created a wooden bridge that would be moved up in the last minutes to cross the gap between the wall and the ramp, and then the Legionnaires would pour over. But there was also a chance, albeit a small one, that the Gwenthari could do this first, that they could put down planks and wood and stream onto the ramp, attacking the builders and his Essaerites. It would be fine if this happened, really. Either way, this is where the fight would take place, and whether it was the Gwenthari or the Lysandrians that initiated it, the end result would be the same. It would mean the fall of Ulfgard.

He didn't know how long it would take the city to fall once the ramp was constructed. It could be hours, days, or weeks, depending on how layered the defenses were inside the city and how well those defenders held out. After Hroldenfell, he suspected that the Gwenthari's determination would be extremely high.

He caught a glimpse of fire-red hair out of the corner of his eye, the strands lifting slightly in the breeze. He turned to find Caelwen slowly walking toward him, her gaze fixed on the ramp. As she walked, her eyes remained on the ramp. When she got near him, Treftune came out from under her hair and leapt onto his shoulder.

"Why, hello there, Dominaro," he said, smiling.

The little Valfglidea climbed down his tunic to his belt to pull out the small bit of cheese that he had waiting for lunch, Treftune came back up and sat on Mariokos's shoulder, eating it. He stroked his soft back and tail.

Mariokos put his arm around Caelwen's waist. "It will be done soon, won't it?" she asked.

He nodded grimly. "Yes, within a few days. Then it'll be inside the city," he said.

"Do you think they're going to have me help?" she asked, her voice calm and curious.

"I don't know," he said honestly. The Legions had been slow to use the female Essaerists, but in taking a city, that might have been different. "Maybe they will, maybe they won't, but either way, I think it'll be up to you," he said.

"They should. The people of Ulfgard will use their female Essaerists," she said. "It's silly that Lysandrian doesn't."

He didn't disagree with her, but it was still odd to hear someone say it. It was so rare to hear someone speak out about this aspect of Lysandrian life. There really didn't seem to be a difference between men and women for the Gwenthari. And that showed in their fighting. They had fought almost as many women as they had men, and he knew that would be no different once they got past the city walls and the Essaerists that they'd been dealing with, particularly the Wyrdrunir.

"Do you want to fight?" he asked.

She shook her head and looked at him. "Not particularly, but that doesn't mean that I won't and that it isn't a good idea. It should be Essaerites going after Essaerites, not men trying to take them down," she said.

He nodded, her practicality making sense to him. He admired it in so many ways. She could do something that she didn't want to do but thought was necessary. Likewise, if things weren't necessary and she didn't feel like doing them, she just didn't and had no guilt or reservations about it.

"Do you think it'll be like Hroldenfell when we go in?" she asked.

"No, I don't," he said, genuinely meaning it. "Ulfgard is far too large, and it'd be a waste."

She raised an eyebrow. "Were the lives in Hroldenfell so few that they weren't a waste?"

He felt his face redden a little bit in embarrassment. "I didn't mean," he started.

"You're fine, it's a genuine question," she said.

He sighed. "No, they were a waste. You know I feel that way," he said.

"I do, but I'm not asking a question about my husband's thoughts or views. I'm asking him why the Legion would do what it does," she said, with just the hint of a smile touching the corners of her lips.

Bellisara, she's beautiful, he thought. He cleared his mind. "Well, I think Hroldenfell was a statement."

"A statement," she confirmed.

He nodded. "A statement. I don't think the same thing will happen to Ulfgard. I don't think whatever does happen here is going to be good, but I don't think we'll see the wholesale destruction and slaughter that we did in Hroldenfell. But I could be wrong."

She nodded. "I could see that. But I'm curious why this city would hold more value. Couldn't you take out more Gwenthari in one swoop? We certainly did at the Ilfrun River."

His mood darkened a little. He didn't like what had happened at the river. "There's a lot of land here," he said. "Hroldenfell didn't have that. There was no agriculture. It was there because it used to be of strategic value to the Ulfgarath. A strategic value that was no longer there once it was absorbed into the empire. I think Ulfgard will be different. But that also might just be my hopes and dreams," he said.

She leaned into him. "I hope that those hopes and dreams come true," she said warmly.

———

XAVIENO'S ESSAERITES DUCKED AND DODGED AROUND THE BLADED ARMS OF THE ROCK Essaerite that the Wyrdrunir Essaerist was using. One of his Essaerites lashed out with a sword, and the rock Essaerite raised its forearm, blocking the blow with ease. His Essaerite tried pushing against the rock one with its shield, but they were incredibly sturdy. Xavieno's got hit but was able to recover. Another one came in for an attack.

Around him, Kyrillos was likewise engaged with his Essaerithon. There was fighting all around. The rock Essaerites had been joined by other man-like ones. Xavieno had been surprised by this. After all, most Gwenthari preferred animals for their fighting Essaerites—creatures that were relatively ineffective against both Xavieno and Kyrillos's Essaerite types. But the rock one had been effective. However, that was just one Essaerist. The other Essaerists were using

Essaerites that were much like people and were armed. They weren't as effective in individual fights, but as they had all grouped together, Xavieno found them to be tiresome. He was annoyed when he had to deal with them, and he knew Kyrillos felt the same.

He didn't feel that way about the Wyrdrunir Essaerist. Hers were something else. They were wonderful in a way, and they pushed him in a way that he'd never been pushed before. He knew Kyrillos felt the same.

It's a pity, Xavieno thought. *She's going to die. It's such a waste.*

Speaking of, he thought, as he saw a smaller Essaerite coming down the hill.

He could tell it was from the Wyrdrunir because it appeared to be well-crafted. It was humanoid-looking but wasn't brawny or tough. It was slim and small and very non-threatening.

It was holding a scroll in its hand. It came and stopped, waiting. As soon as it stopped moving, the other Essaerites backed away. Xavieno paused.

The smaller Essaerite spoke. "We have a message for your command," it said, its voice monotone.

Xavieno looked over at Kyrillos next to him, who shrugged.

Xavieno closed his eyes and spoke through his Essaerite. "Very well, I'm going to come and get the message."

He knew his voice would sound monotone as well. The Essaerite he was using wasn't designed for communication. They could speak. He found that it was always useful, even in fighting Essaerites. You might need to say something to another soldier, or you might need to say something to an enemy. But the voice rarely needed to be expressive.

His Essaerite walked forward and took the parchment from the other Essaerite and retreated back. The others did not engage. This was something of an understanding. Each side would wait until there was another message that came back.

The rest of the battle was waging on, with things coming over the walls in both directions all around him. But for the moment, the Essaerites waited.

Xavieno's Essaerite came down and handed the scroll off to a messenger, who in turn took it to command. He waited for them to respond. He moved back and forth on the balls of his feet. He popped his neck and rolled his shoulders.

"Fuck, in some ways this is harder than regular fighting," he mused.

Next to him, Kyrillos chuckled. "It really can be."

Controlling Essaerites wasn't as physically strenuous as being in a fight, obviously, but it strained you mentally. And it also meant that you spent a lot of time either sitting or standing still as you focused.

Xavieno was increasingly finding at the end of the day that his muscles were stiff and sore from playing statue all day long. Thankfully, Ilara was pretty good at taking care of those knots, but still, he was looking forward to the fighting around Ulfgard to be done, if for no other reason than so he could move.

A soldier came back with a scroll in his hand. He handed it to Xavieno, who in turn handed it to his Essaerite, who went to deliver the scroll. As it did, Xavieno saw one of the officers approach them.

"As soon as that scroll is delivered, you aren't to engage with those Essaerites anymore," he said.

Xavieno nodded, and Kyrillos spoke. "A meeting?"

The man nodded. "Yes, in a couple of hours. On that note, we need all of the Essaerists in the camps available for this. Bring your Essaerites with you. Tell Mariokos that he needs something that's a little bit more combat-ready. And tell that Gwenthari woman that she'll need those cats of hers," he said and walked off.

Xavieno exchanged a glance with Kyrillos and nodded.

———

It had been a nice day thus far for Caelwen. The birds above the city had not been pushing the way they had been before, and as the fighting had grown on the ground, there were fewer and fewer of them to deal with. She still couldn't get any of her own over the city, but it was a nice change. She was standing next to her cart, tending to the rabbits with Ilara, when a soldier came tramping up to them.

"Dominara," he said, giving her a nod.

She raised an eyebrow. "What's going on? Is Mariokos okay?" she asked, instantly feeling concerned.

"Sorry, Dominara. Didn't mean to concern you. Your husband is fine. Your presence has been requested, along with every other Essaerist," he said.

"Why?" she asked.

"I don't know, Dominara."

He gave her directions on where to go and moved off. She looked over at Ilara. "I wonder what it is," she said.

"I don't know," Caelwen said. "But if I had to guess, I would say it has to do with the fact that the Essaerites aren't fighting anymore," she said as she checked in on one of her hawks.

"Really?" Ilara said.

"Really," Caelwen said. "Well, I guess I better go to this meeting."

She could see concern in Ilara's eyes. "Would you like to join me?"

"No, it's... would you mind?" she asked.

Caelwen smiled softly. "Not at all."

They trudged off and found where the meeting was taking place. Mariokos, Xavieno, Isolara, and Kyrillos were all there. She walked up to her husband. His forehead was creased with effort.

"Are you creating Essaerites?" she asked.

He nodded. "Yes. You need to as well. The cats," he said.

"Why?" she asked, though she began to let her Essaeris build inside of her.

"There's going to be a meeting with the Gwenthari," he said.

Caelwen raised an eyebrow. "I take it all their Essaerists will be present?" she said.

"Supposedly," Mariokos said.

He looked over at Ilara, and then back to Caelwen. "I told her she could be here. Do you want me to send her away?"

He looked back at her.

"I can go if you need me to," Ilara said.

"No, it's fine," Mariokos said. "Xavieno has you assisting Caelwen during the day, and that's an excuse we can give. But if things go bad..."

"If things go bad, no one's touching your wife," Ilara said with flint in her voice.

Caelwen felt herself smile; she'd never heard that tone from Ilara. "That's sweet of you, but I think we know if things go bad it'll be me protecting you."

Ilara gave a slight snort. "We'll see about that."

Caelwen chuckled. "I like her."

Mariokos laughed. "Oh, I know."

Caelwen felt inside of herself, and her Essaeris came bubbling out. Her large cats began to take shape next to her. As they did, she released some of her birds. She made some slight alterations to the cats.

"I won't have enough Essaeris for my Essaerithon," she said.

"I don't think you'll need it," he said. "You and Isolara and Ilara will be staying back. Xavieno, Kyrillos, and I will be slightly too, but we need to be there to be a presence," he said.

"You need to have Isolara and me next to you," Caelwen said.

"Why is that?" a voice said.

They turned to see Damianello approaching, the Legion's general. She gave him a respectful bow, as did Ilara after a moment.

"Who is this?" Ilara asked under her breath.

"The general," Caelwen hissed.

"You need to have us there because the Gwenthari Essaerists will all be there as well. One of them is a Wyrdrunir woman. She's the one that's been giving us the most problems," she said.

Next to Damianello, Caelwen saw Alessandros roll his eyes. He began to speak, but Damianello held up his hand. "Explain."

"To Gwenthari, when it comes to Essaerists, women and men are the same. We are largely equal in society anyways, but doubly so when it comes to Essaeris. If you have Isolara and I standing in the back and the other Gwenthari Essaerists are not, it'll make it look like we're either weak or you do not trust us. It's better that we all look strong," she said.

Damianello considered this for a few moments, then nodded.

"Very well. The Essaerists will be back from the main meeting anyway, but perhaps by showing a unified front. Especially since you're Gwenthari," he said, and then glanced over to Ilara, "as is this slave. Who is she? Is she yours?"

"She's Xavieno's, but she assists me during the day. She's also a very capable warrior," Caelwen said.

"I can vouch for that," Mariokos said.

Damianello looked at him, and then glanced over at Xavieno, who was coming up. He seemed surprised to see Ilara there.

"You fine with her being here?" he asked.

Xavieno shrugged, "Yes, I trust her, and like they said, she's very capable."

Damianello nodded, "Lose the slave collar during the meeting."

"Yes, sir," Xavieno said.

Caelwen saw the collar around Ilara's neck vanish.

"You're not going to go running off now, are you?" Caelwen said.

Ilara smirked, "No, I wouldn't make it very far. And then, I'd have to go buy my own rabbits," she said.

Caelwen snorted, "I'm glad to see it's the rabbits that keep you around."

Leadership from the other legions gathered, a tent set up near the edge of the counter-fortifications. Caelwen watched as, all of a sudden, everything from the Lysandrian side of the camp stopped firing into the city. A few moments later, the same was true of anything coming out of Ulfgard, and then the gates to the city opened and figures came out. They started moving down the hill towards where the tent was.

Caelwen felt her heartbeat pick up a little bit. As they moved, all of the Essaerist's Essaerites moved as well. Caelwen created the last of her cats. They stood before her. Next to her, her husband had created some Legionnaires that were likewise standing off to the side. Xavieno had his, and there was Kyrillos's Essaerithon and then all of Isolara's smaller, menacing ones. It was a force to be reckoned with, to say the least. She would have liked to have Fioralba with them, if for no other reason than to have made their numbers larger.

The group came up near them, and next to her, Ilara tensed. Caelwen followed her gaze to a woman with bright white hair and cold gray eyes. Her hair was long and straight. The woman was thin and strikingly beautiful. She was probably in her early or mid-twenties, and she was wearing a tunic and boots that looked pristine and perfect. Other Essaerists stood around her. All of their Essaerites gathered. Caelwen noted that it was the Wyrdrunirs who were the most advanced. Up close, she could appreciate just how powerful-looking her stone Essaerites were.

With them was an assortment of men and women who were older. These must have been the leaders of Ulfgard. They walked forward and met with the leaders from the Legion, and then the group walked into the tent, leaving the Essaerists outside, looking at each other. It was an odd sort of feeling. There was a tension in the air as they stood and waited for whatever the discussions would be from inside the tent.

"What happens if this goes south?" Ilara whispered under her breath.

"I don't know," Caelwen said.

Xavieno answered, "They'll go back to the city. There won't be a fight here. It'd be too risky for both sides' leadership."

"And do you think the Legion would keep their word on that?" Ilara asked.

Xavieno gave a slight nod, "Yes. That's the only reason why they'd be willing to meet with us. They know the Legion keeps its word."

Caelwen felt her muscles bunch and tense, like she was waiting for the attack to come. Across from them, the gathered Essaerists looked the same, all save for the Wyrdrunir woman. Her expression was calm and controlled. It sent a slight chill through her. She'd never seen a Wyrdrunir before. She'd heard of them, but never seen one. She knew their Essaerists were comparable to that of Lysandrian's or Eirfrosti's—something she suspected the white-haired woman was all too aware of.

Time droned on, and then more, and on, and on, and on. The sun was beginning to fade in the sky when the groups finally came out of the tent. Everyone looked grim but relaxed.

"Is that a good sign?" Caelwen said to Mariokos.

He shrugged, seeming unsure.

The Gwenthari walked up to their Essaerists and walked away. Then the leadership stood before the Legion's Essaerists. They looked at them all in turn. Damianello's eyes rested on Xavieno.

"The collar," he said.

Xavieno nodded, and Caelwen saw the collar come back into existence around Ilara's neck. She saw the other woman's shoulders sink just a little bit. She felt for her, but now wasn't the time to be concerned with that.

Damianello began to speak. "Orders are being given down to the rest of the legions. Ulfgard and all of the leaders inside of it have surrendered," he said. "That smoke we've been seeing the last few days was from fighting inside the city. Apparently, there was a disagreement about holding out and fighting us or surrendering. The side that was in favor of surrendering won," he said, his voice cool.

This was a bit of a shock to Caelwen.

"So our orders are to prepare to go into the city. No one in the city is to be harmed or maimed," he said.

This seemed to surprise all of them. Damianello went on, "The leaders have not only agreed to surrender, but they've also agreed to terms to join the Empire. The terms of these agreements are not important, but suffice it to say that this is an agreement that works very well for the Empire. And you are all to be commended, and you will receive bonuses commensurate with your work. The tributes being paid now and for years to come will be a great support, but that also means that as of this moment, the territory that these leaders are over is now part of Lysandrian," he said.

She could see tension rolling off the shoulders of everyone around them, and she saw Xavieno and Mariokos smile slightly.

"Orders will be coming down, but please go back to your camps. You should not see any more engagement from the Essaerists. Also, we can halt construction on the ramp," he said. "I daresay we're going to be having to take it apart anyway."

They all walked back into the camps, Isolara and Kyrillos smiling, enjoying it. Mariokos and Xavieno likewise looked happy. Ilara looked confused, as did Caelwen.

"I suppose this is good, right?" Caelwen said.

Mariokos grinned. "This is fantastic. This is the best outcome there could be," he said.

"It really is," Xavieno said. "No one has to die now, and we've gained Ulfgard," he said with a grin.

Ilara's look of confusion deepened. "Aren't we going to either way?"

"Yes, but now they're coming along willingly. They're joining the Empire. That's far more cost-effective, easier, and better than had it been us conquering them," he said.

She looked confused. "I don't see how they're different."

"They are," Mariokos said. "We're not subjugating them. Well, I suppose we are, but we're not subjugating them by torture or burning their lands or killing their people. They're agreeing to do it. And while people may not be happy about it, they're alive and they can go back to their lives. And for us, it means we don't have to fight across this whole place," he said.

Caelwen thought she understood, but Ilara still seemed confused.

"They aren't like us," Caelwen said to the other woman.

"What do you mean?" Xavieno asked, his voice a little tight.

"I don't mean that in a bad way," she said, smiling. "But Gwenthari, when we take something, it's a possession. It's not something that we are making a part of us," she said, "if that makes sense."

Ilara nodded. "This is a completely foreign concept to me. Sacking a city, I understand, but keeping it? I guess enslaving it?" she said.

"Not slaves," Mariokos said. "These people will all be citizens of Lysandrian," he said.

"Really?" Ilara said.

"Really," Mariokos said. "My guess is that the tribute that was offered was not people, but monetary. Could be fields, could be allegiances. I don't know, but these people will be citizens of the Empire. Some of them will even be Citizanos, and I dare say that there will even be a small few that'll be Aristolios. The Essaerists certainly will be," he said.

This got Caelwen's attention.

"Really? That high up in society?" she said.

Mariokos shrugged. "I wouldn't be surprised. The Empire wants everything to work well. The inside doesn't work well if the outside doesn't. That means you need Aristolios, and Citizanos, and Subalteros. Just how it goes," he said.

She nodded, thoughtful. "Well, I suppose this is good news, then, and cause for celebration."

"It could be," Xavieno said. "I'm sure there'll still be some difficulties when we get inside the city. There will be holdouts or people who disagree with it. We'll also probably have some soldiers do dumb things that young men do who are stupid, but all in all, this'll be good, and we'll make the winter much better," he said.

"Because we'll have homes to live in?"

"No, we'll still live in the camp," Xavieno said.

"Why not take over the homes of the people in the city?" Ilara asked.

Xavieno chuckled. "Because that's their home, not ours. We'll live in the camps, I'm sure, or we'll move the camps inside the city walls. But, again, this isn't a raid. These people, they're still the same people. They own the same lands, all that. They're just now part of the Empire." He barked a laugh, "And in time, they will have a representative in the Senate."

Ilara looked over at Caelwen. "You're right, I don't understand it."

PART THREE

CHAPTER 27

Cold air bit at Mariokos's face and cheeks as he stood outside his tent, the gray sky above him spitting snow that stung his skin. He wore a thick woolen cloak over his regular tunic and uniform, with leather boots wrapped around his feet and calves. He looked up at the sky, which appeared angry and dark. The breeze was teetering on the edge of becoming wind, and the little snowflakes whipped and whirled all around the camp, moving between the tents and coating everything in icy coldness.

Caelwen came to stand next to him. Today, she looked the perfect mix of Gwenthari and Lysandrian. Her beautiful red hair was braided and adorned the way that other Aristolios women wore it. Over her dress, she had on a thick fur cloak made of what he presumed was bear. Though he knew it wasn't actually bear, as she had made it using Essaeris. Still, the effect was there. She looked like quite the contrast—beautiful, delicate, graceful, and terrifying all at the same time.

They were going into the city for the first time. It had been several days since Ulfgard had surrendered—eventful days. He was thankful that the whole ordeal was over, as the weather was turning nasty, and he didn't care for the idea of being in battle in it. If he was being fair, though, he rarely cared for the idea of being in battle regardless of the weather.

They were to meet with two of the Essaerists who had been inside the city. The others who had been there had left when their settlements had. That had been the way of the last few days—people pouring out of Ulfgard, heading back to their homelands to reclaim farms, settlements, and towns. The legions had been going into the city, making sure that everything was safe, and likewise had been sending out messengers to those towns and settlements that were now in the fold. He suspected that there would be little problems along the way, but nothing so much that the legion couldn't handle.

The real questions were what territory could be salvaged to the west. As the Ulfgarath had moved out of the area to head to Ulfgard, he knew that Valfarans raiders had taken advantage of the situation, and he wondered what many of these people would be coming home to. Many had left their belongings in their homes, only able to take what they could carry with them. Those items would likely be gone now. Also, crops would have gone bad and spoiled, as they didn't have time to be harvested. He knew it would be a difficult winter for most.

The empire was going to ship grain from the south to help support the region. This had been a surprise to both Caelwen and Ilara when they had heard about it. He reminded them that Ulfgarath was now part of Lysandrian, and while subject to her laws, was also subject to her help. They began walking, the gravel under their feet crunching and grinding as they moved. Close to her, Caelwen had two of her large Essaerites in the form of cats.

They were the same deep, chocolaty brown as her cloak, though the fur of her cloak was long and shaggy. Their teeth and claws were made of a flat black metal. They were giant and extremely intimidating.

They flanked either side of Mariokos and Caelwen as they walked. They made it to the edge of the camp, and as they passed the wall, he felt the wind whip around them more, away from the tents and temporary structures of the camp. With it carried the scent of burning flesh. To their right, he could see large pyres where the dead were being burned. The city hadn't been full of them, but they'd been slowly accumulating casualties during the siege, either from the Lysandrian attacks, natural ailments, crime, and, of course, the small infighting that had occurred at the end. Something had to happen with those bodies, along with any rotten meat from animals that had been trapped under buildings or things of that nature. So, the pyres were built and burned. As they neared them, he felt wafts of heat coming from them, and he tried not to breathe through his nose. To her credit, Caelwen didn't seem to pay them any mind.

As they made their way, the small path led up to the gates of Ulfgard. People were mostly leaving the city, though some were still coming in—many of them legionnaires, others merchants, or others conducting business for the day.

It was surprising to him in so many ways how quickly the city had gotten back to being a city. He had assumed that it would take them a while to get back on their feet, but winter was coming, and the Gwenthari were practical people, if nothing else. There wasn't time to think about that they were now part of the Empire. There were things that needed to be done, preparations that needed to be made, and the people were busy with that work.

Caelwen and Mariokos walked up the path to the gates and then walked inside. As he entered, they were assaulted by the smells of the city, along with the rich scent of mud and manure. There were the sounds of a city in full swing. He looked around, pausing for a moment.

"What do you think?" she asked next to him.

He shrugged. "It's certainly not a Lysandrian city," he said with a smirk.

"Oh," she replied.

"Do you think how our camps are laid out is different from everything else that we do?" he asked with a smile.

She seemed to roll her eyes. "I should have suspected that cities were planned out as well," she said, but smiled.

"I know deep down you like that," he said.

Her smile deepened. "I might like that part about Lysandrian."

They began to walk and saw two figures standing off to the side of the road. Mariokos walked up to them. One of them was a tall man with broad, thick shoulders, short blonde hair, and blue eyes. He had a firm jawline and a shaved face. He was wrapped in a cloak much like Caelwen's. He looked to be in his early or mid-thirties, if Mariokos had to wager a guess.

Next to the man stood a woman with white hair and gray eyes. She was of average height, her hair straight and her gray eyes piercing. Her face was beautiful, and she had a cloak that looked to be of some sort of black fur. The fur had a slight shine to it, and she wore a fur hat over her head. Both eyed them with curiosity.

Mariokos approached. "Hello, my name is Mariokos, and this is my wife, Caelwen."

The man glanced over at Caelwen and muttered, "I see the Wulfharboria have managed to weasel their way deeper into Lysandrian than I thought."

Mariokos felt a flash of irritation, but before he could speak, the woman spoke, her voice holding an accent he had never heard before. "My dear, Lysandrian Essaerists only marry Essaerists, you see, and since this man is an Essaerist, that means that his wife, likewise, is one," she said, her voice flat and calm. "Likewise, Lysandrian, like us Wyrdrunir, don't tend to use animals as our Essaerites. That is a Gwenthari thing, not a Lysandrian or Wyrdrunir thing, which means that these two giant, powerful cats that could rip each of us in half without any effort also belong to that same Wulfharboria woman," she said, her voice a little cooler.

She looked at the man. "Perhaps speaking with respect would be wise." She turned her attention back to Mariokos and Caelwen. "My name is Lorna, and this is Gundor," she said, referring to the man. "Please forgive him any slights. It has been a long siege, and we are all tired," she said, glancing at Gundor, who, to his credit, looked a little abashed.

He nodded at both Mariokos and Caelwen. "Sorry. That was out of line," he said.

Mariokos felt irritation rising, but Caelwen solved the problem for him. She chuckled. "I like her; she seems wise," Caelwen said.

Mariokos didn't roll his eyes, but he wanted to. "Oh, I'm sure you do," he said. "Well, it is a pleasure to make your acquaintance. I am under the impression that all the other Essaerists have left the city. May I ask why you haven't?"

The man spoke this time. "Yes. Those are people from other settlements, towns, and villages. They went back to where they came from. We are the Essaerists for this city."

"Are you assigned here?" Caelwen asked, curious.

The man shook his head. "No, I am from Ulfgard. When I came back, I brought Lorna with me, and she agreed to help the city."

Lorna spoke. "We've been told that we are under your purview," she said to Mariokos. "May I ask what you have planned for us and where the other Essaerists in your legion are?"

"They are out in the field," Mariokos said. "And yes, from my understanding, you will be working with me and Caelwen. I would like to get to know more about you and the city. Could you show us around?"

"Of course," the man said. "Please come with me."

Gundor motioned for them to start walking. Caelwen and Mariokos joined them, walking up a muddy street. On either side of them were buildings where people were going in and out, and animals moved along the street. It wasn't hard to walk, but it wasn't easy, and his feet squished and slid around. As he moved, his eyes scanned the architecture, noting damaged buildings and roofs and areas where water was pooling and running along the street. He didn't tisk, but he made a mental note of all the issues.

"You'll find that the city is mostly open," Gundor was saying. "The curtain wall is larger than was strictly needed. The city's old planners always assumed that it would continue to grow," he said.

"It didn't," Mariokos said.

Gundor shook his head. "No, this city is very old and hails back from a time when Gwenthari lived in fortress cities. The city planners assumed it would always be that way," he said with a shrug. "Obviously, it wasn't sustainable."

"It worked well for the siege, though," the woman said. "There was a lot of open space where people could set tents and bring livestock and provisions," she said.

Mariokos nodded. "Very interesting. Also, I must commend you; your Essaerites were something else," he said.

She looked at him and gave an approving smile. "Thank you."

Mariokos looked over at the man. "Were yours the birds with the metal beaks?" he asked.

Gundor chuckled and shook his head. "No, I can make those, but didn't. You didn't face any of mine," he said.

Before Mariokos could ask a question, a boy came out of a building, walking up to them. He looked young, with shaggy blonde hair and shocking blue eyes. As he approached, Mariokos heard Caelwen take a slight breath in, and a moment later, Mariokos felt it. The boy came up to Gundor, and Gundor knelt down, letting him whisper something in his ear.

"He's an Essaerite," Caelwen said softly.

Mariokos could feel it too. You couldn't always sense Essaeris. Sometimes, if something was small or innocuous, you couldn't detect it unless it was very close to you. But an Essaerite as advanced as a child—well, you couldn't mask that. Not to another Essaerist.

The boy scampered off, and Gundor looked back at them.

"That's quite an impressive Essaerite," Mariokos said.

The woman smirked. "Yes, those are his expertise and why you did not experience any of them," she said.

Caelwen raised an eyebrow.

For the first time, the man looked happy. He smiled in a proud way. "Others focus their Essaeris on creating weapons that slash and kill. Some of us put our focus on other types," he said, and began to walk.

"So you create Essaerites that are indistinguishable from people," Caelwen said.

He nodded. "Yes, that is my specialty. Obviously, they wouldn't be able to trick an Essaerist, but a normal human can't tell."

"I've seen them before," Mariokos said.

"I'm sure you have," Lorna said. "But I doubt your wife has unless she grew up in the Empire."

Caelwen looked a little abashed. "No, I have not seen them," she said.

"They aren't common in the Empire," Mariokos said, "though I had some trainers that had them. Usually, it tends to be older Essaerists that put a focus on them."

The handful that he'd seen usually resembled their creator and were able to act as a proxy for that person, or like a puppet that a person could control if they wanted to avoid a potentially dangerous situation. Mariokos had seen the appeal in it. The Essaerites could never be as intelligent as their users were, but they were passable and could be more clever than the average person.

"They are not common in Wyrdrunir, either," the woman said, "but they have their places."

Mariokos could see that.

"I'm a spymaster and assassin," the man said honestly. "These Essaerites," he said, pointing to where the boy went, "were fairly crucial in securing this city for you."

Surprise hit Mariokos. "You were part of the disagreement, I take it?"

"Yes, the people who I answered to were, and I agreed with them. I didn't care to be killed or have those that I grew up with die, either," he said matter-of-factly.

The woman spoke. "Nor did I care to die in this place. This isn't even my country."

"But my Essaerites were very useful," Gundor said. "They are able to get information that regular Essaerites cannot, and they can also be useful in other ways."

"I'm sure you could send an assassin anywhere. It could be anybody," Mariokos said, thinking of it. Now, when he was considering it, it made more sense how close Isolara and Kyrillos stayed to the emperor. It wasn't just to defend him when they were out in combat; he realized it was to be able to see something like what Gundor could produce coming before it could cause any harm.

In this way, he felt over his head. Mariokos and his Essaeris had always been for practical purposes. Not that this wasn't practical, but a different type of practicality. He could see where Gundor would be formidable. In some ways, the man could almost be more dangerous than Lorna. Her Essaerites were advanced and powerful, and in combat, he suspected that she was far stronger than Gundor. But in a city like this, he could see where Gundor would be very terrifying indeed, even if he didn't pose a threat to Essaerists.

They were coming to one of the open areas that Gundor had talked about. There was trampled grass where people had been staying for months as the siege had gone on. As they got higher in the city, he felt the wind chill him more, especially in the open areas. They stopped and looked around. The two Essaerists looked at them.

"You don't seem like other Gwenthari Essaerists that we've encountered," Mariokos said.

Gundor smiled. "I'm not. I'm much more like the Wyrdrunir ones, or admittedly, like the Lysandrians," he said.

"Lysandrian and Wyrdrunir Essaerists have a lot in common," Lorna said. "Gundor came to my lands when he was in his twenties without a clue of how to use his powers. We took him under our wing," she said. Then she turned her attention back to Mariokos. "So, what is it that we'll be doing?"

"I have one more question first," Mariokos said. "What was the boy telling you? And why did he come up to you to begin with?"

Gundor nodded. "Wise of you to ask. He was telling me about a plot to kill some of your soldiers," he said.

Mariokos's eyes widened. "What?" he said, concerned.

Gundor held up his hands. "Don't worry. The boy went and tipped off some of your guards. It is being dealt with," he said, his eyes going out of focus. "You shouldn't have any problems. And your legionnaires are just fine. He made it look like he told me so anyone watching would think I have children acting as spies for me. It is very useful," he explained.

Mariokos wasn't sure how that would be useful, but he heard Caelwen hum in thought. "I can see where that would make people wary of unknown children, but how is that effective? Couldn't they just conduct business elsewhere?"

Gundor smiled. "Fear of being caught will deter most and make those who wish to deal in dark corners seek those dark secluded places."

She laughed dryly. "The kinds of places that are known and where no one would notice hidden Essaerites."

He grinned. "Not bad for a Wulfharboria."

Caelwen snorted.

Mariokos was unsure if he felt uneasy or not. "So you're fully on our side then?" he asked.

Gundor shrugged. "We had a choice. We could have either fought and lost, or we could join the empire. It seemed like living and joining the empire was the wiser way to go. And I'm not about to bite the hand that just spared me," he said. "So yes, we are loyal."

That would have to be good enough for now.

Mariokos nodded, getting down to business. "Alright, well, this shouldn't be too difficult," he said. "Well, I shouldn't say that. There's a lot of work that needs to be done. But with Essaerites, it shouldn't be difficult for us personally," he said.

"And what work is that?" Lorna asked.

"Well, you might have noticed that the streets are mud. We need to get them repaved with gravel, or preferably cobble," he said, thinking to himself. "I'm going to be working with a lot of our engineers, and you will be assisting me. We have other Essaerists that will deal with security issues. Though Gundor, I do think it could be useful if you have a network that can keep the city safe," he mused.

"So we're going to be doing road duty?" Lorna asked.

"Oh, I'm sure we'll be doing more than that," Caelwen said. "In my experience, the Legion spends just as much time building things as it does destroying them," she said, and he couldn't tell if it was irritation or not that he heard in her tone. She looked at her husband. "Am I wrong?"

He smiled. "No, you're not. So, there will be a lot that needs to be done. I saw a lot of repairs that need to be made to the city as well as upgrades. The legions will be doing the vast majority of the work, but Essaerites are effective, and we happen to have a large amount of resources sitting right outside the city."

"Do we now?" Gundor asked.

Mariokos nodded. "Yes, that ramp is mostly stone, dirt, and timber. We will be able to dismantle it and use much of those materials throughout the city. Also, when we were first in the area, I noticed that there was a lot of work that needed to be done on roads, drainage, and things of that nature. It will take us a few months, but we should be able to get everything fixed up," he said with a smile.

The woman cocked her head to the side. "You are serious, aren't you?"

He was confused. "Yes, why wouldn't the legions build this area up?"

"I guess I didn't think there was anything wrong with it," she said, though she didn't seem upset—more bemused than anything else. "And it's expected that Essaerists assist with this?"

He nodded. "Yes, it is. I assume that's not the Wyrdrunir way."

She shrugged. "We do some, yes, but not as much as most. It's very curious," she said.

"How so?" Caelwen asked.

Lorna shrugged. "The similarities and the differences between groups. For example, Wyrdrunir and Lysandrian Essaerists are very similar in a lot of ways. They're very practical. They're advanced. And they tend not to follow natural body shapes in the sense that we do have human-like anatomy in our Essaerites, but they're usually stone or metal. Gwenthari tend to use actual animals, like the cats," she said.

Lorna went on, "but Gwenthari, like Wyrdrunir, tend to put more emphasis on combat and battle prowess." She said, "though I think this is different for the Eirfrosti; they, in that regard, seem to have more in common with the Lysandrians when it comes to the role of Essaerists. Because in Eirfrosti, Essaerists spend just as much time, if not more time, helping the regular people plow and tend their fields as they do with anything else. Wyrdrunir Essaerists tend to stay in an area, and we are there for defense, for power. It's just different seeing the mix and differences between them."

That was interesting to Mariokos. He didn't know much about the Eirfrosti Essaerists other than they were advanced.

"Have you encountered many Eirfrosti Essaerists before?" he asked her.

She nodded. "A few, yes. We are much closer to Eirfrosti than we are to the rest of the continent," she admitted. "So I've had interactions with them. For your next question, yes, they are as advanced as your rumors have probably told you. They are on par with both Wyrdrunir and Lysandrian," she said. "Unfortunately for the rest of the Gwenthari, Valfarans, Ulfgarath, and Wulfharboria don't seem to put the same effort into their Essaerists as Eirfrosti, Wyrdrunir, and Lysandrian do," she said.

He felt Caelwen tense next to him. It was something that she was always self-conscious about. Gundor, for his part, looked somber and nodded. "Yes, this is true," he said. "We've let so much of ourselves go." He shook his head, looking around the city. "That was also part of the reason why I agreed with this whole idea of surrendering to you."

"How so?" Caelwen asked.

He looked at her. "While I may have made a comment about Wulfharboria before, I know you are no different than the Ulfgarath or the Valfarans." He sighed. "Perhaps you have stayed more true to your roots than we ever did, but our people used to be great. Look at this city," he said. "Can you imagine when it was first built, when it was in its heyday?"

Mariokos could imagine that. He could see it around them. It would have been beautiful. It wouldn't have been as dilapidated as it was now.

"I can see it," Mariokos said.

Caelwen nodded.

"But we forgot who we were, and we let it fade," Gundor said, his voice dark.

"You mean you forgot about raiding," Caelwen said.

Gundor shook his head. "No. No, that is what we focused on," he said, sounding disappointed. "Our people think that they are supposed to be warriors," he scoffed. "We used to be merchants. We used to be artisans and craftsmen. We used to be so many things.

"Do you know why we beat Lysandrian hundreds of years ago?" he asked.

"Because you were better than us," Mariokos said honestly.

"Yes, we were," he said, "but we weren't better than you because we were warriors," he said, almost scoffingly. "We were more advanced. We had better swords, armor, technology, training—everything. You were just behind us, that's all. And now," he said, looking around again, "not only have you passed us, but we have gone down.

"Do you know why so many Gwenthari warriors swear by the old blades that their forefathers used? It's because that's when we were actually good smiths. What we make now is shit," he said, his voice holding contempt.

"I've heard that before too," Caelwen said, "though I know my people weren't as advanced as the Ulfgarath or Valfarans."

"No, you weren't. You were always more connected to the land. You traveled. You moved around. You were merchants. You weren't what my people think of as now. Now they see you moving into our lands and they think you are encroaching," Gundor said. "But you've always moved around. It was your way. No, our people used to be strong. The Eirfrosti didn't lose their way," he said, "and that is why they are so much more advanced than us and why so many Gwenthari dislike them. The Wyrdrunir, they did not lose their way either." He said, looking over at Lorna, "You should see their cities. You should see their lands. They're in a frosty, cold wasteland, and yet they thrive. And Lysandrian, if it is anything like what I've been told, is nothing like this land. You continue to push forward, and that is why I supported us becoming part of the empire," he said.

He looked at Mariokos. "Tell me, will this land just be used? Will our people just be drained, or will we be built up?"

Mariokos was taken aback by the question. "Of course, we will build it up," he said. Caelwen looked at him, and he went on, "I know I've said this war is about money, and it is. And Ulfgard and all of the Ulfgarath lands—the wealth that's going to come out of them is unimaginable. Not just in tributes and spoils and looting," he said, "but the real wealth, the real wealth will occur over time."

Gundor nodded. "Yes, as they build us up, we will be able to produce more to pay higher tributes. In exchange, we will have a better life as well," he said, "hence why I helped the city fall." He held out his hands, gesturing around. "For these people, there was no reason for them to die. Now they can live," he said.

"And we will help you," Lorna said. "So, tell us what we need to do."

CHAPTER 28

All around Valfric were loose clumps of trees. He could smell the strong scent of a campfire burning and the sour tang of excrement mixed with the metallic smell of blood. He breathed in and opened his eyes. *This is a memory*, he thought, *I must be dreaming.*

He looked around. He knew this memory. It had happened years ago, one of the first times that the men of the settlement had taken him raiding. They had found a couple traveling along, unaware of how dangerous it was to be alone in those parts. They were Lysandrian, and arrogant, as was their assumption that they were safe to move about in a country that wasn't theirs and that they had no business in.

The group had taken them easily enough but had been disappointed to find that they didn't have anything of value save for themselves. Yet the leader had said that they were too far away to reliably bring back slaves, so instead they were to have some fun.

Valfric was not yet so advanced as to be able to create the wolves that he would be able to when he was older. The tools that he created were rudimentary and basic, brutal and effective in so many ways.

He looked down. A Lysandrian woman was lying on the ground. Oh, how he remembered her, how she had been the gateway for him. She had allowed him to understand how much pleasure there could be in cruelty, how much freedom there was in the fear and pain of others. She had been such a good experience for him.

She lay on the ground, coated in blood and dirt and everything else filthy and vile in this world. Her wrists were nailed to the ground. Valfric had created long spikes with flat ends at the top. Her first screams had sent a thrill through him as the men had held her arms down and driven the spikes through her wrists into the dirt, pinning her to the ground. Her screams had been even louder and more acute as they'd driven similar ones through her feet. Then, she couldn't move, stuck there like the toy she was born to be.

They'd tied her husband to a tree so he could watch as they nailed his wife to the ground. And then all of the men in the raiding party took turns ravaging and tormenting the woman. The man had begged them to stop. The woman had too. Valfric and the others hadn't. They had laughed. They had joked. They had enjoyed it. It had been so sweet, so wonderful. Valfric had felt a thrill, an almost uneasy feeling in his gut, before it had all begun. And then that feeling was gone and the thrill had changed to excitement, to exhilaration, to legitimate freedom for the first time in his life. He was the one doing the hurting, not the one being hurt. It's how it was supposed to be. It's what the strong did and what the weak had to endure.

Then they had made the Lysandrian woman watch as they took apart her husband. Oh, his screams had been different. They beat him, yes, lashed him, yes. But the real screams had come when they had taken his teeth, his fingers, his toes, and then began to slowly remove his skin.

Eventually, he had died. Valfric didn't know if he had bled to death or if his heart had just given out. Both were equally possible. Now he stood over the woman. Her face and body bruised, covered in cuts and abrasions. He looked over to where the fire was being built, larger and larger. He smiled.

"We're going to shovel some coals onto you," he said, "and place some of those burning logs by you and let it cook you."

She looked up at him, not with fear, to his surprise, but with—was it anger? No. It was a new look. One that he'd felt, but one that he had never seen anyone give him. Hate.

Her voice was surprisingly strong. "Someday this will be visited upon you," she said. "I curse you to know the pain that you have caused. You are the reason they all die, why your loved ones will perish, and why your world will turn to ash," she said bitterly.

He looked at her for a moment and then laughed hard. The men around him had laughed as well, surprised at what she had said. "Is that so?" Valfric said.

"It is," she said.

"Oh, I see," he said.

He walked over to the fire and created some metal tongs. He grabbed a log and walked over to her. Her feet had been nailed to the ground, with the soles of her feet flat, her knees bent. He placed the burning log under one of her legs. She instantly began to scream.

"Odd, I think it's you that's gonna be turning to ash," he said with a laugh.

He went and grabbed a few other logs with the prongs and laid them at her side. She screamed and wailed, and he saw the flesh on the side of her body begin to bubble and blister. It smoked, filling his nose with the noxious scent of burning flesh. The men laughed, and a few of them shoveled some coals onto her arms and belly. Then they splashed them over her face. She twisted her face quickly, but he still saw the burns on it, and her hair began to smoke and burn.

They laughed.

She got quiet quicker than she should have, and he heard a scream behind him, but not from one of the men. He turned, confused, and there, where the husband had been, Yrthorn hung.

"Yrthorn?" Valfric said.

Valfric's voice was no longer that of his youth. He looked down at himself. His hands, his arms, were that of a man. *This is a dream,* he reminded himself, but Yrthorn screamed again, and he looked up. Standing before him was a Lysandrian woman. She turned. Her face, that had once been beautiful, had scars on it. She smiled. It was Nefeli, the woman that Yrthorn had taken. She was running a knife along Yrthorn's arm, slicing into the flesh. He screamed and wailed and begged. She grinned.

Valfric moved to stop them, but he tripped. He looked down, feeling something on his ankle. There were chains around his ankles. He looked up to Nefeli. She grinned, the knife moving down. Yrthorn screamed as her arm moved, and she turned around, holding Yrthorn's cock in her blood soaked hand. She'd cut it free.

She held it up, inspecting it. Blood ran down her forearm, and she looked at Valfric. "That's much better, isn't it?" she said with a smile.

She walked up to him, her smile growing with each step.

"It's good to see you, Valfric," she said. "I've missed you so much. I already got acquainted with your friends," she said.

Valfric turned his head in the direction of her gaze and looked, seeing all of his friends' corpses on the ground, their bodies mutilated, their faces all held in a mask of pain and agony.

"What's going on?" he panted. He turned back to her.

"Well, this, this is what's going on. The seeds that you've sown have fully grown, and it's time for harvest," she said, with a shrug.

"Nefeli," he said, his teeth gritted, his voice hollow.

He heard another scream.

"Valfric, Valfric," he heard Eira scream, her voice filled with terror.

His head snapped to the sound. "No!" he yelled.

There were Lysandrian men, legionnaires. They had Eira. They were pulling her by her hair, throwing her down to the ground. She screamed and panicked. The men laughed, some of them grabbing her wrists, pinning them to the ground. And then he saw it. He saw a set of spikes like the ones that he had pinned the Lysandrian to the ground with.

Eira thrashed and cried, begging.

"No!" Valfric yelled, feeling angry tears fill his eyes.

"No, this is not going to stop," Nefeli said, "this is your doing. This is what has to be done. I think the legionnaires are going to enjoy it though, don't you?" She said, "You are going to watch them like you made that Lysandrian man watch as his wife was ravaged and tortured. You're going to watch that happen to her. Then they're going to kill her just like you killed that woman." She looked into his eyes. "Don't worry, Valfric, you and I will have lots of fun together," Nefeli said.

"No," he screamed in agony.

Eira screamed. It sounded like her throat was ripping with the force of it. The men laughed, and a hammer came down to the top of the spike. Eira screamed again, and he saw the spike burying itself in her wrist. She thrashed, blood pouring from her. Again, the hammer came down, and again she cried out.

"No! Get away from her!" Valfric yelled, pulling against chains that were holding him ever tighter.

Then they were driving a spike through her other wrist. He sobbed. "Please no! Please stop!"

"I remember saying that to you. I remember begging for it to stop," Nefeli sat next to him. She grinned a madwoman's grin. "Did you stop? Did you make them stop?"

He looked at her. "No! I'm sorry. I should have. I'm so sorry!"

"Did you stop when you were doing that to the Lysandrian woman? The one from when you were young?" Nefeli asked.

He collapsed to his knees as Eira screamed again. They were driving the spikes through her feet. He could hear bones crack as it went through. He begged the gods, "please!" He begged. But the men didn't stop.

Nefeli knelt in front of him and twisted his face to look at her, gripping his chin hard. "There's no stopping this, Valfric. I'm coming for you!"

His eyes snapped open in fear and panic. He was covered in cold sweat, and he threw the blankets off of himself, his heart hammering and pounding in his chest. He shook with fear, and his back throbbed with pain.

"Eira," he said desperately, looking around. Their new home was empty. Just a few coals in the fireplace were crackling and spitting.

"Eira," he said, getting up, feeling his panic rise even more.

He ran to the door, flinging it open, crashing outside into the cold morning air. Snow crunched under his bare feet, but he ignored the sensation. His eyes looked wildly around.

"Eira, Eira!" he called.

"Valfric Firewood," she said.

His head snapped, seeing Eira coming around the side of the cottage. She had on a cloak. In her arms was a large stack of firewood. She beamed at him.

"Valfric Firewood," she said.

She stopped, looking at him. He came running at her.

"Valfric hurt?" she asked, concerned.

She dropped the firewood and closed a few steps to him. He scooped her up in his arms. He felt her tense for a moment. He held her tight, feeling waves of relief wash over him.

"I was so worried," he said, "so, so worried."

He felt her arms around him, then he collapsed down to the ground, his knees digging into the frozen soil.

She knelt in front of him, "Valfric okay," she said.

He began to sob and shake, holding her. "Valfric okay," she said again. He gripped her again, holding her tightly to him. He cried under her hair and her neck, like a little kid.

"Valfric okay," she said, her voice softer. She began to caress the back of his head.

He couldn't control himself. He shuddered and sobbed, clinging on to Eira for dear life.

She's okay, he thought, *she's alive, they haven't hurt her, she's okay, she's okay. She's okay,*

———

HILDRANA'S HOME WAS FILLED WITH THE RICH SCENT OF COOKING PORK AND BREAD FROM the fire behind her. She breathed in, enjoying it. Outside she could hear the whirr and whistle of wind as the storm set in, though she didn't think it would be a bad one. It would mostly, if she was correct, blow around and coat the ground with a few inches of snow, but it would make for a bitterly cold night.

Behind her, the fire popped and crackled, filling the space with its warmth and flickering light. In the corner of the room sat Fernwen, Eira, and the Essaerite Ferngar. It had taken some convincing, but eventually, Hildrana, Fernwen, and Valfric had been able to convince Eira that it wouldn't have been appropriate for the other Essaerites to come into the house because they didn't like being inside. It hadn't been as easy with Ferngar, and so they had all given in. Hildrana smiled warmly, watching her daughter play some sort of dice game with Eira. Sitting next to them was Ferngar. He sat close to Eira, who would occasionally pet his head or back, Fernwen playing along for Eira's sake.

Hildrana sat at the table, and she looked at Valfric across from her. His face looked more haggard than normal, more like what it had been when they had arrived at the settlement. He was looking down at his mug. She took a sip of her own, tasting the Bryndraught. It was darker than most Gwenthari preferred on the continent, but she liked it. It reminded her of home. It had a thick, rich, heavy flavor, with hints of herbs in it. She took a few sips.

"You look rough," she said to Valfric.

He glanced up at her. "Thanks," he said. He sat back in his chair.

"Do you want to tell me why?" she asked.

He glanced over at Eira and then back to his Bryndraught. "Is there something going on between the two of you?" she asked, feeling a slight bit of concern.

He shook his head. "No. There's nothing going on between Eira and I. How could there be?" he said. "She's... look at her?" He shrugged. "She's Eira."

Hildrana smiled softly, "She is Eira. So what is it, then? Spit it out."

He sighed. "I just didn't sleep."

"Nightmare?" she asked.

He looked at her for a moment. "Are the rumors about your people being witches true?" he asked.

She grinned. "Maybe. Let's just say they are. So there's no point in fighting me on it? Nightmare?" she repeated.

"Yes," he said. He glanced back over at Eira and shook his head. "Just my past is all."

"What about it?" Hildrana asked.

"That I was shit. That I got everybody I know killed." he said.

She raised an eyebrow. "I didn't know you led the legions to Hroldenfell. Even through the walls?" she said.

He looked up at her, his eyes narrowing in anger for just a moment. "I didn't lead them to Hroldenfell."

"Then how did you kill everyone you ever knew?" Hildrana asked.

He continued to glare and then his expression softened, turning to shame. "It's just my fault. That's all. You wouldn't understand."

"Of course not. You're speaking nonsense," Hildrana said. Before he could get angry, she reached out and placed her hand on top of his. "I'm not trying to make you mad. It's just, maybe not everything in the world is your fault," she said, trying to soften her voice.

He looked at her and sighed. "It feels like it is."

"I can't imagine what it must have been like, having to watch Hroldenfell fall. And then, your friends," she said. His expression darkened in sorrow.

"It's nothing worse than I ever did to others," he said after a moment.

She nodded. "I see what this is then," she said.

"What is it?" he asked flatly.

"You're guilty that you're alive, and they're not," she said.

"No," he said, then after a moment, "that'd be stupid. I am stupid, though," he mused.

She smiled. "Most men are. Bergthral's not, because he's had me training him his whole life."

He chuckled. "So what if I am, guilty for living," he said.

"It's natural," she said.

"Yeah, well, how do you know I'm not the monster that I say that I am?" he said.

She shrugged. "You might be. You might not be. You could be the worst man that there is alive, but I wouldn't know. And because I don't know, and Bergthral doesn't know, and we likely never will, that gives you the opportunity to be a new person. To be whatever Valfric you want to be. Whatever Valfric best serves her," she said, glancing at Eira.

"I'm trying," he said.

"I know you are," Hildrana said, and she could see it. She saw all the times when there were little flashes of anger in Valfric's eyes that he instantly reined in and controlled. He had been putting in so much effort, but that was tiring and wearing, especially when the effort was put into being somebody who you didn't think you were.

"Valfric, you are the man that you want to be. Remember that, and maybe it'll get easier," she said.

He looked thoughtful for a moment and was about to speak when the door opened. With it came a blast of cold air and a few snowflakes. Bergthral came walking in. He had a thick, heavy cloak around his shoulders that he released standing in the doorway. Snow fell to the ground, and he stepped in, closing the door. Fernwen got up, and he scooped her up in his arms, making her laugh. He sat her down and came up and kissed Hildrana and then smiled at Eira and Valfric.

"Thank you for coming over for dinner," he said.

Valfric smiled. "Thank you for having us."

"Bergthral, Hildrana, Fernwen, thank you," Eira said brightly.

"You're most welcome," Hildrana said. "And thank you for catching the hog," Hildrana said to Valfric.

He nodded. "Thank you for cooking it. Eira is fairly good at cooking, but to be fair, I'm shit at it. I'm fine if you need to camp," he shrugged.

Bergthral smiled. "I understand that. If it wasn't for Hildrana here, I'd be half the size I am now," he said.

She rolled her eyes. Her husband was all muscle and no fat, but she appreciated the compliment anyway. Bergthral's expression darkened.

"I have news," he said.

Hildrana could see tension in his eyes, and she tensed up. Valfric seemed to do the same. Bergthral sat down next to them and nodded at his daughter, who led Eira away a little bit further and started their game again. Bergthral spoke softly.

"Ulfgard fell," he said.

That was fast, she thought. Valfric's eyes widened a bit.

"So fast," he said, and she could hear fear in his voice.

Bergthral went on, "they surrendered, from my understanding. The Lysandrians hadn't breached the city yet, but I don't know much more," he said.

Valfric seemed relieved at this, but still on edge. "I guess that means that the people of the city aren't dead then," he said to himself. "That's a comfort."

Bergthral shared a glance with Hildrana. "Do you think they would really kill off a whole city?" she asked.

Valfric shrugged. "They mostly did at the Ilfrun River and at Hroldenfell."

Bergthral was looking thoughtful. "I suppose you're right. So I wonder why Ulfgard surrendered then, if they just knew they were going to die," he said.

Hildrana thought, "Perhaps they made a deal. Perhaps what happened at Hroldenfell and at the Ilfrun River was on purpose," she said.

Valfric scoffed. "How could it not be on purpose?"

"No, not for the reasons you think," she said. "When Hroldenfell fell, it was brutal and quick, wasn't it?"

Valfric shrugged. "Yeah. Once the wall came down," he shook his head, "the legionaries just streamed in and killed and burned and destroyed everything. It was like watching a wave crash over the city."

"And at the Ilfrun?" she asked.

Another shrug. "It took a couple of days, but yes, I didn't watch the very end of it. We were moving and were over a hill, but I know what happened. Anybody who they might have spared would have been enslaved," he said.

She nodded. "Exactly. I think they were sending a message."

Bergthral looked at her.

"The message being, surrender or we'll kill and enslave all of you," she said.

Bergthral's expression was darkening. "That could work," he said.

"Are you sure?" Valfric said. "They could have lied to get into the city and wiped them all out."

"To what ends?" Hildrana said. "To have empty, open land where the legions could walk around in?"

"Perhaps Lysandrian settlers," he said.

She shook her head. "Lysandrian's not so densely populated that it needs that. They aren't going to spread themselves thin. All that would happen by killing off everybody in Ulfgarath would be to make it so that the Wulfharborias and the Valfarans could move into the area. Lysandrian would be at it again in a few years."

"Perhaps they're just taking everything of value," Bergthral said.

"Oh, I'm sure they will do plenty of that," Hildrana said. "I think there's more here, perhaps."

"They aren't going to stop," Valfric said.

The conviction and sorrow in his voice gave Hildrana pause. *Do you think he's right*, she thought. *Would Lysandrian stop? No, they wouldn't.*

"You're probably right, but..." Bergthral said.

"But what?" Valfric said. "They aren't stoppable."

"They can be stopped," Bergthral said. "They just haven't been yet. And they can overreach, too," he said.

That would be their only saving grace, Hildrana thought, that Lysandrian would overreach and could be conquered. But she found that unlikely. "No, it's more likely that they will wait, that they will reinforce, that they will make themselves solid. And then they will move. The question would be, where would they go next? Would they move to the northeast or to the northwest?"

Both were plausible. To the northwest were the Wulfharborias. They were largely a loose collection of settlements and peoples, but they were fierce and ferocious. To the northeast were the Valfarans. Valfarans that were so much weaker in so many ways than Wulfharboria. And the Wulfharborias had been mercenaries for Lysandrian for decades now, hadn't they?

"Valfarans will be next," Hildrana said softly.

"You can't know that," Bergthral said.

"Yes, I can. How many mercenaries did they get from Wulfharboria?" she asked.

"I don't," Bergthral started.

"A lot," Valfric said. "We saw them all the time. The legions themselves are mostly infantry, but all their cavalry, it's all Wulfharborias."

"Exactly," Hildrana said. "Do you think those mercenaries are going to slaughter their own?"

"No," Valfric said. "They won't. You're right. Valfarans will be next. It's just a question of when."

She sat back in her chair and looked over at her daughter and Eira playing in the corner. She wanted to be worried, wanted to be afraid, but she pushed those thoughts from her mind. They weren't productive.

"It won't be anytime soon," she said.

Bergthral grunted next to her. "No. They have a city in all of its territory to deal with," he said. "But still..." he trailed off.

"But still..." she echoed.

CHAPTER 29

Caelwen felt the damp, cold air brush against her face, seeping into her skin and making her shiver. The scent of wet soil mingled with the faint tang of wood smoke, curling through the chill. Thankfully, her bear-skin cloak kept her warm, the heavy fur brushing against her skin and holding the chill at bay. Underneath the cloak, Treftune would occasionally poke his head out and then settle back inside, keeping just his nose out as he sniffed around. Today, his fur was the same brown as her cloak. She walked down a cobbled street, glancing around her.

All around, Ulfgard had recovered rather nicely, something she hadn't expected. The winter hadn't been pleasant as far as the weather had gone, but for her, it had been fine. The Legions had built temporary housing inside their camps that had been comfortable enough, and then she, Mariokos, Xavieno, and Ilara had moved into the city as Essaerists were working there. They had taken up residence in an inn that was near an open patch that the Legion was turning into space for the garrison troops that would eventually be there. They were building offices and constructing a fortress in the space as well. She'd been amazed watching the Legions work. She'd always known them to be part construction worker, part soldier, but she still found it amazing. Her husband, most of all.

Around her, the muddy streets were gone. They were wet, icy, and cold, but they were either covered in gravel or, in many cases, had been cobbled. He'd likewise taken care of many of the drainage issues inside the city. Though she amended that thought, it wasn't just Mariokos. The Legions had done it too, but they'd done it with her husband's help, and with her help, and the help of both Lorna and Gundor, though the latter had spent far less time helping with construction. That wasn't to say that he hadn't been up to useful tasks, because

he had been. In many ways, Caelwen wasn't sure how the city could function
without him.

Gundor knew everything about Ulfgard's inner workings. His little network
of Essaerite spies had proven to be indispensable time and time again. It had
kept groups from being able to form that could cause unrest and had managed
to thwart a few legionnaires who had also been planning untoward things. He
was rather useful. And he had proven that his loyalty was with the city, with
the people that he had grown up with, though she didn't entirely trust him.
Lorna, for her part, had also been useful and had helped Mariokos quite a bit.

Caelwen was nearing the gates of the city. The heavy iron-bound doors
loomed above her, the scent of cold metal mingling with the musty tang of
damp stone. The muted sound of distant voices and the rhythmic stomp of
people and animals blended with the occasional creak of wooden cart wheels
on cobblestone. She walked out, nodding at some of the legionnaires who were
standing guard. She was well known now by everyone, even the other legions.
She had had a bit of a reputation, she realized, if for no other reason than she
was an Essaerist and an Essaerist who had helped in both Hroldenfell and in
Ulfgard. But now they all knew her, and most people were grateful for her
efforts in keeping the skies above the camps clear. Everyone knew people who
had been attacked by some of the Essaerite birds at the beginning of the
campaign, and so she had earned a level of respect from all of the men.

She continued walking toward where the people of her old settlement
were. She found them in a camp outside of one of the legion's camps. Her cart
was there, next to her brother's tent. He had been tending to the rabbits, or
more appropriately, he was supposed to be tending to them, but Ilara had been
going out and doing it, or Caelwen had an Essaerite that did it. She found her
brother sitting at a campfire, warming his feet and hands. He grinned at her
and stood up.

She smiled as she approached him. He wrapped his arms around her in a
big hug. She squeezed him back. As they hugged, Treftune shot out of her cloak
and crawled around on his shoulders.

"Hey there, little fella," he said, smiling, petting the little Valfglidea. He
looked down at Caelwen. "How's the city?"

"It's good," she said. "How is our investment?" she asked, glancing at the
cart.

"I think they're doing pretty well." He looked at the cart and scratched his
head. "I think. I don't know. How are they doing?"

She rolled her eyes. "They're doing fine. You would know that if you
checked in on them more often."

He waved his hand. "No, my business partner does that. So what news do
you bring?"

She decided to let him change the topic. "Nothing major, though I did get
some word about the settlement. Is our uncle around?" she asked, feeling a
slight distaste in her mouth.

He grunted. "A few tents down. We can go talk to him if you'd like."

"Well, I don't think I'd like to, but yes, we should," she said. He chuckled and got up. They walked down a few tents until they found her uncle. He was sitting next to a fire, scowling at it. A woolen cloak was over his shoulders, and he glared up at Caelwen and Wulfgren.

"Ah, look who's come down from her palace to meet with the common folk," he said gruffly.

She chose not to comment. "Good morning, uncle. How are you?" she asked.

He looked at the fire, then around them. "I'm in a city of tents. How do you think I'm doing?"

"Good, I'm glad you're enjoying your surroundings," she said thoughtfully. He muttered something under his breath, and she resisted the urge to smirk. "I have news for you."

He grunted. "What's that? Are we gonna be moving to some new field?"

"In a manner of speaking," she said.

He looked up at her, mouth agape. "They're going to march in the wintertime?"

She scoffed. "No, the Legion isn't going anywhere." She said, "But the part about the new fields, though..."

He said, "What about them?"

"The Legion has found land for our settlement to settle on."

He perked up at this. "Did they?"

She nodded. "Yes. There's a lot of open farms and steadings around here, around the city, that don't have occupants anymore. People from our settlement are being given the land. Your contract is up now that both Hroldenfell and Ulfgard have fallen," she said with a shrug. "Though people are welcome to continue to fight and be paid."

Wulfgren whistled. "Very nice being given lands," he said and then looked at her. "Are you Mariokos going to join us?"

She shook her head. "No, he's not done with his time in the Legion yet. And our lands are back in his home province," she said.

He nodded. "I guess that answers whether I'm staying here or not," he said.

She couldn't help but smile. Ilfthandor was standing. "So what? You're going to plant us here and then leave?"

She shrugged. "I'm not really planting you here, but I'll go wherever the Legion goes because my husband is with it. You had something to do with that. Remember?"

He snorted. "It worked out well for you."

She smiled. "Yes, it did. It worked out very well," she said, thinking fondly of Mariokos. She hated it, but she had to give Ilfthandor credit, even though he hadn't been trying to make her life easier or better.

Ilfthandor turned to Wulfgren and said, "You're going to stay with the legions? You're going to abandon your people?"

"I'm not abandoning anybody," Wulfgren replied. "I'm staying with my sister. As for the rest of the settlement, they'll be fine here, and I suspect I won't be the only one that goes with the legions. It's still good money to be made."

"And after?" Ilfthandor questioned.

Wulfgren shrugged. "And after what? Yes, if she'll have me, I'll continue following Caelwen. Why wouldn't I? Do you really want me around?"

Ilfthandor grumbled. He didn't want either of them around, but he saw them as a source of power. Power that he no longer had. Not only was his settlement gone, but no one from it respected him anymore. They had respected Caelwen and Wulfgren, but people were moving on. Now they would have lands of their own to go back to, that they could farm, that they could build a life on, and they would be around a large city. No, Ilfthandor's days of being able to control people were over.

This was made even more apparent by the fact that in Lysandrian society, Ilfthandor was not high-ranking. None of the people of the settlement were, save for Wulfgren and Caelwen. He was a Citizano as a result, but everyone else was Subalteros. A few that had proven distinction in battle might have the opportunity to be Citizanos, but she knew that it would be few and far between. The people didn't care. It was all the same to them, but it did make Ilfthandor see himself differently, and she thought that it probably made the people of their settlement see him differently as well. After all, Wulfgren had been made a Citizano, and Caelwen was an Aristolios. They were people in society, but Ilfthandor wasn't, and they had realized that he never really had been.

"I will get the details on the lands that you'll be given," she said. "For those staying with the legions, I'm sure there's a provision allowing you to transfer the value of the land you'd be given to stay with you until after you leave."

"So am I to be a farmer now?" Ilfthandor huffed.

She shrugged. "If you'd like. Or you could be a merchant. You could be a carpenter, a smith, anything you want, Uncle," she said with a smirk.

He grunted. "I'm old. What am I supposed to be? You're just going to be abandoning me here?"

She shrugged. "I'm not abandoning you, Uncle. But I am giving you the opportunity at a nice life. Take the land and sell it. Use the money to do whatever you'd like. You've been profitable before, and it wasn't as a farmer," she pointed out.

"I'm not the leader anymore. No one around here cares or respects me!"

"Then try something different," Wulfgren said. "Or maybe try being the type of man that people would follow and respect. Either way, this is better than we could have ever hoped for."

Ilfthandor was about to say something when Wulfgren added, "You might remember that. Do you remember when you alienated every settlement around us and made them hate us?"

"Yes, and then they attacked us. We're lucky to be alive and not be dead or enslaved," Caelwen said.

Ilfthandor's face flushed for just a moment, his jaw tightening as his eyes narrowed. His hands curled into fists before he abruptly stood and walked away, grumbling under his breath.

"That went better than I thought it would," Caelwen said.

Wulfgren nodded. "Old fuck. I'll be happy to be done with him."

"He is a cunt," Caelwen agreed. "So you're going to follow me, huh?"

"If you let me," he said with a shrug.

She smiled. "I'll let you. This wouldn't have anything to do with Ilara, would it?" she asked.

He snorted. "No. Why would it be anything to do with her? I'm just watching my investment."

They began to walk.

"Mm, I see."

"Besides, she's a slave anyway," he pointed out, though she noted that his voice sounded a little sullen. "She belongs to your friend."

Caelwen sighed. "She does. But she may not always, and that doesn't mean that you can't," she began.

He waved her off. "I'm not interested," he said. "But I am looking forward to what our new homeland will be like, and all the profits we'll be able to make off these rabbits."

She snorted. "Assuming they'll sell in the empire."

He looked concerned for a moment. "Do you think they won't?"

"I don't know," she said. "I've never been in the empire before."

"Haven't you and your husband talked about it?" he said. "Or do you spend all your time romping around in bed? I'd have thought that phase would be over by now, and you'd get onto the serious matter of talking about our futures."

She laughed. "Spending all of our time romping in bed, seriously?"

He shrugged. "What? What else is a new couple to do? But you need to start thinking about our future," he said.

She rolled her eyes. "I'm not having this conversation with you. We have our rabbits. If they make us money, fantastic. If they don't, we will find something else. Mariokos and I have lands in the empire, and I'm sure we can find something for you to do," she said, as if closing the subject.

"Well, there's going to be stuff for me to do," he said flatly. "I'm not just going to sit around all day listening to you two romp in bed."

She glared at him.

"Ouch," he said, and then clapped his hand to his ear. Treftune jumped onto her shoulder. "Little shit bit my ear. I wouldn't have thought he'd want to listen to you two all day long either." He grumbled.

She scratched under Treftune's chin. "Good boy," she said.

CHAPTER 30

Caelwen breathed in deeply, the morning air carrying the delicate scent of blooming flowers. Signs of spring were creeping in every-where around them. Patches of grass were beginning to shift from brittle brown to vibrant green, the blades softening under the warming sun. Shoots of plants were coming up, and the air and weather had turned mild. The days were getting warmer and longer. Next to her, Ilara also looked happy. Caelwen smiled softly, looking forward to the day and the new season. Treftune sat on her shoulder, content as well.

Caelwen looked up, seeing Lorna approach them, her white hair drifting in the breeze. With Lorna were two Essaerites. They were the size of men, though their arms were longer, ending in long fingers that had black claws at the tips. Their backs were slightly humped, and their heads were large. Their skin was made of rock, with sharp bits jutting out from random places along their bodies. Everyone gave them a wide berth.

Lorna was wearing a deep blood-red dress with black embroidery weaving a pattern of flames along her arms and body, a style unmistakably Wyrdrunir. Her white hair hung around her shoulders, with a few braids that had black and red bits in them that Caelwen couldn't quite place. Perhaps rubies?

Next to Caelwen, she had one of her cats, though it was one of the larger ones. Lorna approached and greeted them. "Good morning," she said, her accent thick.

"Good morning," Caelwen replied.

Ilara nodded her greeting.

Lorna looked down at Caelwen's cat and cocked her head to the side.

"Is something wrong?" Caelwen asked, feeling instantly self-conscious.

The other Essaerist hadn't been unpleasant to her in the least bit. If anything, she found Lorna to be a bit of a kindred spirit. The woman was practical and straightforward in everything she did, but Caelwen couldn't help but feel inferior around her. Lorna was so much more advanced than Caelwen, something she'd gotten used to being around Mariokos, Xavieno, and Fioralba. They had had a lifetime's worth of training. It was the Lysandrian way, but apparently, it was the Wyrdrunir way as well, and Caelwen felt once again like she was behind.

When Lorna spoke, her voice didn't sound concerned, just curious. "Why does it look like that? I've always wondered; they're so powerful."

Caelwen was taken aback. "What do you mean? It's a cat. I know some of the shapes are off, but that's more functional than anything else," she said, referring to the elongated jaw and altered paws that could grip better than regular animals.

Lorna nodded. "Yes, all useful, but I mean it has fur. Why not give it something else?"

Caelwen raised an eyebrow. "What? Like scales?" she said. "You're starting to sound like Xavieno."

Xavieno had been harping on her to change the way her Essaerites looked for some time, putting more weight behind the aesthetic side of them, like he did his own. Ilara had generally backed her up, not seeing the point in it. Caelwen saw it sometimes. Her Essaerithon, for example, had many features that were more meant to intimidate and inspire awe.

Lorna looked thoughtful, as if she were trying to figure out exactly how she wanted to make her next statement.

"Yes, they are practical, straightforward, and brutally efficient. Delightfully so, even," she said with her thick accent. "But there is more to Essaerites than just function. Surely you've seen that with the Lysandrian ones. And had you seen those from Eirfrosti, well, you would see that as well—that there can be so much more to an Essaerite than just what it does on a rudimentary level."

She waved over her own. "These, for example."

Caelwen looked at them. "They are intimidating. They make you think, I suppose," she said, trying not to be defensive. *This woman has a lot more experience than you do,* she thought to herself. *You should listen to her. Indulge her this once,* she reminded herself.

Lorna nodded. "Yes, they do, and in that is their power. You see, you cannot change aesthetics at the sacrifice of function. But on top, I think you'll find that it can have function of its own."

"This, I think, is a problem for Gwenthari on the Continent. Because the Eirfrosti don't do this," Caelwen said.

Lorna nodded. "Yes. And what do your people think of Eirfrosti Essaerists?"

Caelwen chuckled. "That they are witches, that they have mystical powers, that they are to be feared and respected..." she stopped mid-sentence.

She saw the corners of Lorna's lips twitch up in a smile. "Yes, all of those things." Lorna pointed at one of her Essaerites again. "Do you think the people of the city say the same thing about Wyrdrunirs, now that they've seen one?"

Caelwen thought and nodded. "Yes, I've heard them make comments about some of the Lysandrian Essaerites, but yours? It's like they're talking about the Eirfrosti."

"Yes, and when they see your husband's Essaerithon, or Xavieno's more advanced ones, or that bladed monstrosity of an Essaerithon that the man from the Aeterna legion has, people give pause," she said in reference to Kyrillos Essaerithon. "They do with your cats, of course, but it's not the same. I do not mean this as an insult."

Caelwen sighed. "I'm not taking it as an insult, just listening. Xavieno has been telling me this for a while, but I don't want my Essaerites to look like they're made out of ceramics like his, or rocks like yours, sorry," she said.

Lorna smiled. "There's no need to apologize, and I don't think yours should look like that either; that would be wrong," she said, her expression showing it. "I am from a cold land of cold people; that is the rocks. The Lysandrians are from an industrious land; Xavieno's Essaerites look like sculptures; they fit. But you, my dear," Lorna said, walking up and looking into Caelwen's eyes, "you are Wulfharboria. Your people are connected to the land; they are connected to plants and the things that grow, to the moss and trees and the flowers."

As she spoke the words, Caelwen felt the truth of them inside her. Lorna went on, "You are a healer, are you not?"

Caelwen nodded. "Yes, I am. That's what I prefer to do."

Lorna smiled. "Exactly. You are things that grow and live," she pointed at Caelwen's cats. "These should reflect that. Indulge me, will you, for just a little while before we go and get on with the tediums of the day?"

Caelwen glanced over at Ilara, who smiled and nodded. "It can't hurt."

She sighed softly. "Very well. What should we change, then?" she said, looking at the cat.

Lorna was thoughtful. "Can you make it its full size?"

"Sure," Caelwen said. The cat grew larger. She felt a toll on her Essaeris, but it would replenish.

Lorna walked around it. "This should be a representation of you, but perhaps we can guide you," she said, sucking on her lip. "Your Essaerithon. It looks like it's made of vines and trees. What if you did that with the outside of this Essaerite? Not the inside, mind you. They're so effective. But the outside."

Caelwen thought about it. It hadn't occurred to her before.

"She's got a point," Ilara said next to her. "Your other Essaerites all look like they're made of wood. Think of the stump that you have that takes care of things around your camp. And even the other ones that you make look more like vines than men, but these don't."

It was true. This had always been what Caelwen connected her Essaeris with. She closed her eyes and thought, then reached out with her mind. The fur on the cat vanished, replaced by bark. But that wasn't right. She altered it some more, making the outside of the bark twist, almost looking like vines, though of wood. It was dark brown, and little bits came out, like mini twigs and branches. Leaves came into existence along them.

Lorna oohed in satisfaction. "Yes, that's it!"

Caelwen looked at it, liking what she had done.

"But there needs to be more," Lorna said.

Caelwen found herself agreeing, but what to do?

"The eyes," Lorna said, "they blink. Surround them in glass, maybe, like dark glass. Here," Lorna said, and in the palm of her hand, a dark, shiny rock came into existence. "It's obsidian. Read it."

Caelwen reached out, placing her hand on the Essaeris obsidian. It was cold and smooth, with a faint, almost glassy chill that seemed to sink into her skin. She instantly was able to get a read on it. She recreated one just like it in her own hand.

"This is the glass that I use on some of my blades," Lorna said. "It's extraordinarily sharp, sharper than any steel could ever be, but brittle. Still, it could be good for the eyes."

Caelwen smiled. She changed the outside of the eyes to the same shiny, dark black. They no longer blinked. She made them glow a deep green. "Perfect," Lorna said, smiling.

"What else?" Ilara walked up. "Oh, you could change the ears," she said, animated. "Make them longer, more pointy."

Caelwen cocked her head to the side but did it. She elongated the ears, making them larger and sweeping back. She liked it. It was looking much less like a cat now.

Caelwen smiled. "Hmm," she said.

Lorna was by the tail. "Does the tail serve a purpose other than balance?" she asked.

"That's it," Caelwen said.

She saw Lorna smile. "You have on your Essaerithon those vines," she started.

Caelwen nodded. "Yes, the ones that can shoot spikes," she said.

Lorna shook her head. "Yes, those. Perhaps the tail?"

Caelwen altered the tail. It wasn't the same thickness as the vines on her Essaerithon, but it was smaller. She looked at it, the tail now a vine that ended in a blade and spike. She thought, then split it in three. Xavieno and Mariokos had helped her with these on her Essaerithon, giving them little eyes that allowed them to target on their own. It made it easier. She did that with these as well. She liked it more and more.

Caelwen walked up to the front of the Essaerite, looking down at it. She changed the forehead to look like solid wood or bone, and then an idea came to her.

The front canines jutted out from the upper jaw, and she changed them to be obsidian. Lorna looked at it, thoughtful. "They will break?"

Caelwen nodded. "Yes. I have the regular teeth underneath it, the metal ones."

Lorna nodded in approval. "Very good. What else? Can it see in all directions?" she asked after a moment.

"No," Caelwen said. "I never thought of that before." She put a couple of black beaded eyes behind the ears. It disoriented the Essaerite, but she made a few corrections to it, and it seemed to do better. "I'll have to work on getting those exactly perfect," she said.

Lorna smirked. "Every Essaerite should always be a work in progress," she said.

Caelwen smiled.

"I like it," Ilara said. "It's terrifying. And also, so very you," she said.

"It is," Caelwen said. She cocked her head to the side.

"What is it?" Lorna asked. "What is it missing? What's it saying to you?"

What was it saying to her? There was something here. This felt like her, but not at the same time. She snapped her fingers. "That," she said.

Up and down the spine, three rows of spikes made of the same obsidian came into existence. They were curved like rose thorns. Along the top, little flowers blossomed at the end of some of the twigs. They were pretty—something that she liked. "Much better," she said.

Ilara looked at it. "Odd. It makes it seem more mystical," she said to herself.

"Yes, like your people," Lorna said.

Even Caelwen could feel the rightness of it. "One last thing," she said. She created small deer antlers that came out of the head, adorned with more flowers and little leaves, like the ones that she had on her Essaerithon. "They'll be shed as soon as it gets into a fight," she said.

"That's fine," Lorna said. "This is perfect. Look at this," she said, walking around it. "It's beautiful. It's nature incarnate," she said, and it was.

"It needs an attitude," Ilara said.

Lorna grinned. "She's right!"

Caelwen was surprised at how much fun she was having. She made the Essaerite give a deep, guttural growl that was barely audible, but she could almost feel resonate in her chest. Caelwen grinned even more than she had before. Yes.

"Can you make the tails do something? They should always be watching everyone around," Ilara said.

That was a good idea, Caelwen thought. She made the tails look around, almost as if they were creatures of their own.

Off in the distance, she saw a few legionnaires staring at them, looking very uncomfortable. Caelwen beamed.

"I think it looks perfect," she said.

Ilara and Lorna stood next to her, both nodding.

"Yes, it looks like you," Lorna said.

Caelwen nodded, then looked at herself through her Essaerite's eyes.

"But I don't," she said.

Ilara raised an eyebrow.

"I look like a Wulfharboria woman trying to be Lysandrian."

"You are someone of both worlds," Ilara said.

"Yes, but I shouldn't look like I belong to just one or am trying to," she thought.

She changed her dress, transforming it from the white fabric and bright colors that it was to a combination of deep green and brown. She changed her boots to be dark leather that wrapped around her calves and feet, and she created little twigs and vines that wound through her hair, with little blossoms at their ends. She gave herself jewelry that looked more Wulfharboria.

The dress had a Lysandrian cut, and there were elements of both. She looked at herself through the eyes of the Essaerite, and then she created a pigment of deep red and smeared it on her lips. It almost looked like blood. The crimson of it contrasted against her pale skin. She smiled.

"This is me," she said.

Next to her, Ilara looked her over. "It is you."

Lorna grinned. "It is good to meet you, Caelwen."

Caelwen smiled. "Thank you. I'm glad you're on our side," she said.

Lorna nodded. "As am I. So shall you create another of these, and then we can go on with the day's tedium?"

Caelwen nodded. "That we shall."

As they left the city, people parted for them, seeing both Lorna's and Caelwen's Essaerites. She was surprised at how much she enjoyed it. Not the attention, but the confidence that she felt. People had always parted for her. After all, giant cats had that ability. But now, something about it was different. As they left the city, the air was warming, and Caelwen found herself enjoying it more.

"I have been surprised," Lorna said.

"With what?" Caelwen asked.

She looked around at all the legionnaires who were working. They had spent much of the winter toiling away, adding on to the city, working on roads, and now they were finishing up work on irrigation in the area. "All of this. I know they said what they were going to do, and I know what our Essaerites have been helping with, but it still surprises me. You can't say it's not a surprise to you," she said.

Caelwen nodded. "I suppose in a way it is, or I should say the extent of it."

"And all the ponds," Ilara said.

Yes, there were those too. Mariokos's Essaerithon had been instrumental in those, but there were ponds that were being dug throughout the area, places where excess water could go, and dry times that could be taken out to water fields. They walked along a road that was graveled and leveled, something that she suspected was rare for the countryside. The legions had also been hard at work building culverts and ditches along the roads, keeping drainage in front of mind.

They were coming up to a group of them working. Alongside them was Mariokos's Essaerithon, which was trenching a new ditch. Caelwen looked at it.

"It is truly impressive, perhaps more so than any of the others," Lorna said.

"Kyrillos said the same thing," Caelwen said. "He's the one with the monstrosity of an Essaerite."

Lorna smiled. "I enjoyed fighting that. But what did he say?"

"That Mariokos's Essaerithon is so much more useful than all the combative ones. I've seen it dig ditches for camps, dig here for irrigation, pull lumber around, break up rock. Do so many things," she said. "In so many ways, it is more powerful," she added.

Lorna nodded. "Yes, I do think so. And the work the legions are doing here, building up this area, it'll not only increase profits for the empire, but it is also going to make the lives of the people here easier and make them more loyal," she said. "And in that way, this Essaerithon is doing more for Lysandrian than any army ever could."

They were nearly to the men now. Some of them were Essaerites that were working. She saw Mariokos. He was wearing a pair of linen pants, his shirt off. His skin glistened in the sun with sweat. He looked up at Caelwen coming and smiled, running his hands through his hair. He put down the shovel he was digging with, the metal scraping against the gravel with a dull, hollow clang.

Mariokos walked up to Caelwen and gave her a hug. He kissed her and then looked over at her Essaerites. His eyes widened.

"Do you like them?" she asked.

After a moment, he smiled. "Yes. They look like they fit," he said, looking down at her with pride.

She heard a whistle and looked over, seeing Xavieno approach. Like Mariokos, he wasn't wearing a shirt. She could see defined muscles underneath his skin, which glistened in the sun.

"Now that is what I am talking about!" he exclaimed, walking up to one of the cats. He walked around it, inspecting it. "Oh, it's delightfully wonderful. It's so uneasy to look at with the flowers and all the scary things about it," he said. He got to the tail. "Very nice. Smaller versions of the ones from your Essaerithon," he said approvingly.

"Lorna was able to convince her to change them," Ilara said.

"Lorna, well done. Are the tails the same as the one on the Essaerithon?" he asked for clarification.

Caelwen had one of the tails turn, a spike shooting out of it, sticking into a tree. Xavieno nodded approvingly. "Very nice. If you hit someone in the right spot, it would kill them. Smaller than the ones from your Essaerithon, but effective."

"Oh, they have venom on them," Caelwen said.

Everyone looked at her. Mariokos's eyes widened, Ilara looked a little shocked, Xavieno looked confused, and Lorna's expression might have been the best of all.

"They have what?" Lorna asked.

"Venom," Caelwen said. "Obviously not that one, but if it was in a fight, they'll have venom. Really, if it hits anywhere on somebody, it should kill them pretty quick," she said conversationally.

Lorna's expression had a smile plastered on it, but it looked stiff. She nodded.

Xavieno looked at the spike that was stuck in the wood, back to the Essaerite, then to Caelwen. "These might be the most dangerous Essaerites I've ever seen," he said.

"The venom would only be effective against living targets. I don't think most Essaerites would struggle with it," she mused.

"How quickly would it kill?" Mariokos asked.

Caelwen shrugged. "I don't know, pretty fast, within a few seconds or minutes. Why?"

"That's impressive," Xavieno said.

Ilara looked over at Lorna. "Now, I bet you're very glad that you're on our side," she said. Then she walked up to Caelwen and hooked her arm in hers. "Caelwen, we're friends," she said.

Caelwen was confused. "Yes, we're friends."

"I want you to remember that," Ilara said. "Also, I want you to remember what we do with things that can kill," she said.

"What do you mean?" Caelwen asked.

Mariokos took over, standing in front of his wife. "My love. We only hurt," he started.

Caelwen rolled her eyes. "I'm not going to kill the cunts that blow the horn that wakes us up," she said, then instantly regretted that she had made that statement. *Damn it,* she thought. *Now that I've said that, I've given my word!*

Ilara nodded next to her. "Good, now that we've got that cleared up," she said.

"I hate all of you," Caelwen said. She stared daggers at Mariokos. "And you're supposed to support me," she said, though she couldn't quite keep the accusation from her tone.

"I am supporting you," he said, coming up to her. "And keeping somebody alive."

Lorna looked confused. "I am not following this," she said.

Xavieno spoke. "When we're on the march, we're woken up at the same time every day by men blowing horns. Let's just say that somebody doesn't like it."

Ilara spoke. "The men who do it are terrified of Caelwen. And now," she said, looking over at the Essaerites.

Caelwen felt a wicked smile tug at her lips. "They're not going to like these changes, are they?"

"Caelwen," Mariokos said.

She shushed him. "I told you I'm not going to kill them. But there's nothing wrong with these Essaerites watching." She said, her tone darkening.

Mariokos sighed but seemed to give in, his shoulders lowering. "I suppose... well... whatever."

CHAPTER 31

Bergthral looked through the eyes of one of his Essaerites, seeing three men on horseback approaching the edge of his settlement. They wore the same colored tunics. Two of the men had shields, mail, spears, and swords. The man in the center appeared to be older than the other two. *Messengers*, Bergthral thought. He was in one of the fields near the edge of the settlement. Behind him, some small Essaerites were working on plowing fields, readying them for planting. His mind flicked out to the bear he had, and the two of them ambled over to the road, near where the men would be coming.

Bergthral wondered what the news would be, though a nagging feeling in the back of his mind told him it involved Ulfgarath and whatever trouble was stirring there. He hoped it would be news. He was desperate for it. There had been scant information that had come out. All they had heard were rumors that Ulfgarath was completely subdued save for a few patches and that Lysandrian was looking west to Valfarans. Bergthral stood at the edge of the settlement, watching the men approach. The horses tossed their heads and stamped nervously, their ears flicking back at the sight of the bear. The men leaned forward in their saddles, murmuring sharp commands and tugging the reins to keep them moving. He couldn't help but smile a little. There was something satisfying about newcomers seeing his Essaerithon for the first time. He was sure this encounter wouldn't prove to be disappointing.

As they neared, he could also see apprehension crossing the faces of the two guards, though the messenger didn't seem quite as bothered. *He's probably seen Essaerists before,* Bergthral thought. As they drew closer, he was able to see how fine their clothes were. This was not a missive for news. This was something deeper, he realized. The two men came to a stop. Bergthral walked forward.

"Greetings," he said.

The man in the center nodded. "Greetings to you. Based on that," he said, glancing at Bergthral's bear, "I assume that you are Bergthral, the head of this settlement?"

"I am," Bergthral said. "Why have you come?"

The man sat up a little straighter in his saddle. "To deliver a message and a request."

Bergthral raised an eyebrow at that. "Go on," he said.

"Lysandrian is preparing to move into Valfarans," the man said. "Of this, there is no doubt. You have been requested to come to Ilfglen to speak with the other heads of settlements to decide our course of action."

Bergthral felt a pit in his gut. "I understand," he said. "When is this gathering to take place?"

"In a week," the man said.

So soon, Bergthral thought, though he reminded himself that he was likely at the end of the path that this man had been taking.

"Very well, thank you. Would you like to rest?" Bergthral asked.

The man shook his head. "I would love to, but unfortunately, we have more settlements to talk to. Best of luck to you," he said, turning the horses and moving away.

As he watched the men's retreating forms, he felt his mood darken. Next to him, his bear seemed tense, sensing his mood. He sighed, turning and walking back down the road toward his house. He didn't go back to the fields. His Essaerites were able to plant without his attention, but his mind worked the entire time. *War,* he thought. He'd suspected that it would come once Ulfgarath fell and Lysandrian was able to enjoy the spoils, the profits, and the lands. He'd wondered if they might turn their attention to the west, but he'd thought it would have been years from now, after a long and bloody campaign subduing the Ulfgarath territory. But that had changed, hadn't it? Ulfgard had surrendered, and if the news they had heard was any indication, surrendered in a way that made it very easy for Lysandrian.

No, there would not be a bloody campaign in Ulfgarath to finish the work that they had started. They had completed that work in Hroldenfell, and then at the Ilfrun River, as Valfric had witnessed. He came to his home, pausing outside the door before walking inside. He saw Hildrana and Fernwen working. They were sitting in the center of the room, both of them facing each other, their eyes closed, deep in thought. In front of them was a bowl that looked to be made of pearl and wood.

He smiled, watching his daughter focus, trying to hone her abilities. Hildrana opened her eyes and looked over at Bergthral.

"Sorry to interrupt," he said. As she glanced at him, he saw her read his expression.

She turned to Fernwen. "Why don't you go practice outside?" she said.

Fernwen looked concerned but nodded and got up, leaving.

He smiled at his daughter. She walked out the door and then turned back to his wife. Her expression was hard.

"What is it?" Hildrana said.

"There's a gathering in Ilfglen. It's about Lysandrian," he said.

She gave the slightest of nods and stood up gracefully. He went on.

"They believe that Lysandrian is preparing to attack. They didn't receive much in the way of resistance in Ulfgard, and the rest of the lands have fallen," he said.

"This was in the message?"

"It was implied," she said.

She nodded. "So this gathering then, it will decide if we go to war or not?"

"I suspect so," he said.

Hildrana looked thoughtful. He could see the weight on her shoulders, an invisible but nonetheless real burden. He felt that same weight on his.

She looked at him. "What do you think we should do?"

He looked down at the ground, thinking. "I don't know. I think we will have to fight," he said. "After the easy victory they had in Ulfgarath, I don't think that Lysandrian is going to give up."

"No, you're right," Hildrana said. "If they had had to pay for it in blood and effort and money? Maybe not. But as is, they were able to traipse across Ulfgarath without much in the way of resistance," she mused.

"But if we fight them, if we can hold them," he said.

She looked at him and nodded. "They might decide better of it, or they might at least decide to wait a few years or generations before continuing their campaign," she looked thoughtful.

"What are you thinking?" he asked.

"That this is happening so much faster than it should have. We should have had time to prepare, to be ready." She shook her head. "But hoping for things to be different is a fool's hope. And I do not want to be a fool."

He couldn't help but smile. "Nobody could ever consider you to be a fool." And he meant it. He couldn't think of anybody he respected more than his wife.

She smiled softly at him. "That's just because you're in love with me. I have you wrapped around my finger," she said with a smirk.

He chuckled. He came up to her and wrapped his arms around her waist.

"This is true. You do," he said. Her hands were on his chest and shoulders. She kissed him softly and then looked into his eyes.

"You must go to this thing, and you must convince them to fight," she said, though her voice sounded hollow.

His expression hardened. "I will."

"I mean it, Bergthral," she said. "This can't be like last time. I think we were right to say that we shouldn't be raiding in the Ulfgarath territory during all this. Perhaps Lysandrian would have ignored us that way, but they know we're a threat. We've irritated them the same way the Ulfgarath did, and we saw how well that worked out for Ulfgarath.

"We have to be unified on this. If we are able to gather an army, actually fight," she said.

He nodded. "We stand a chance, even if it's a small one."

Her smile was tight, not small. "We can do this. Remember, for Lysandrian, as soon as this becomes too costly, they'll stop."

"Do you think they'd be willing to run away in shame like that?" he said.

She shook her head. "No, of course not. They'll go back to Ulfgarath, tell the people that they pacified, the barbarians, to the West, whatever they need to. But if you make it so it's not profitable for them, they will leave."

"Will you be fine here on your own?" he asked, his eyes searching hers.

"I am more than capable," she said, "but we also have Valfric here with us, if you are worried about Fernwen and I's safety."

He was. It wasn't that his wife wasn't deadly and capable, but he knew that they weren't liked. Hildrana was not trusted. She was an Eirfrosti Essaerist, which made her a witch, and also made him a pariah as well. And though their settlement seemed peaceful and calm, all around them were dangers.

It had always been this way. It's why the people of the settlement tended to be the outsiders, the ones that had nowhere else to go. They could find sanctuary with Bergthral and Hildrana; they could find a family, but they knew that outside the borders of their settlement, there was no guarantee of safety.

He did feel better that Valfric was there, though the man did not want violence. He was violent. Bergthral had been sparring with him for several months now. Over time, Valfric had gotten stronger, his injury continuing to heal, and his confidence had come back, along with a sense of control and calmness.

Now, if there was anybody he would trust to protect his wife and daughter, it would be Valfric. "I'll speak to Valfric," he said. Hildrana nodded. She didn't look disappointed. If anything, her expression was bemused.

"Overprotective fool," she muttered and walked away.

He smiled and turned, walking out the door, heading toward Valfric's.

———

VALFRIC RAN HIS FINGERS THROUGH HIS SWEAT-SOAKED HAIR. HIS BREATH WAS RAGGED, the heat of the sun pressing down on his shoulders and the distant hum of insects making the air feel heavier. He breathed deeply. He looked out over the field. Most of it looked just as it had when he'd first seen it.

"Fuck," he said.

"Valfric Grumpy," Eira said.

He looked over at her and glowered. "I'm not grumpy."

"Valfric Grumpy," she said.

He huffed and walked over to a bucket filled with water. He dipped in a ladle and pulled it up to his lips, taking a deep drink, feeling the cold, icy water cool his mouth and throat. He panted a few more times and looked out over the field.

Not grumpy, he thought.

One of his Essaerites noted the approach of Bergthral. He looked over at the other man as he walked up. Bergthral smiled and greeted Eira.

"Good afternoon, Eira," he said.

"Bergthral," she said and smiled.

"You look beautiful today," Bergthral said.

Eira grinned. "Bergthral nice."

Valfric couldn't help but smile at this. The people of the settlement seemed to go out of their way to make Eira feel welcomed and cared for. He could see it in her. She had been changing. She was happier, less timid. And the thing that he noticed the most, and maybe the thing that bothered him the most, was that she was getting more advanced. She was saying more things than she had before. Her speech had always seemed kind of broken to him, very rudimentary. That it changed at all made him wonder how much fear and terror she'd endured over her life.

Valfric approached Bergthral and reached out to clasp his forearm.

"To what do I owe the visit?" he asked.

"How are you doing?" Bergthral asked.

"Valfric Grumpy," Eira said.

Valfric grimaced, and Bergthral raised an eyebrow.

Valfric spoke softly. "I'm not grumpy."

"Valfric Grumpy," she said, walking over to pet Bergthral's Essaerithon.

Bergthral gave him a look, and Valfric sighed. "I might be a little grumpy," he said, looking out at the field.

"Farming not going the way you thought it would?" Bergthral asked.

Valfric chuckled dryly. "Fuck, no, it's not. This is a goddamn pain in the ass. If I would have known it was this difficult, I'd have let somebody kill me on the road."

Bergthral laughed. "That bad?"

Valfric looked over at Bergthral, who he was starting to count as a friend. "We've spent our time digging up rocks in the field and plowing it so we can plant shit and what, wait and watch for it to grow?"

"You'll have to tend to it some, yes, and deal with pests, and then harvest it."

"Oh, yes, harvesting, that was fun," Valfric said, and sighed.

"How did you think food happened before?" Bergthral said good-naturedly. "How did you get it? Did it just grow itself?"

Valfric laughed. "Fuck, no, it didn't. The way you got food before was by stealing it from some poor cunt," he said, putting his hands on his hips. "I'm sure there's satisfaction to it, just, I don't know. It doesn't matter," he said after a moment. "What brings you by?"

"How do you know it's not just a social call?" Bergthral said.

Valfric smiled. "Oh, that's easy, because you're walking like you're trying to seem calm, happy, and in control. There's something up."

Bergthral smiled darkly. "You catch on quick."

Valfric shrugged. "You have to. In my old line of work, reading people was important."

And it had been. You needed to be able to tell if someone was about to attack you, if they were trying to cheat you, or what they might do next. Valfric was as good as he was, not because of his skill with a blade, but because of his skill in reading his opponent.

"So what is it?" Valfric asked.

"There's a meeting in Ilfglen. All of the heads of settlements, towns, cities, you name it. Everyone's going there to discuss Lysandrian," he said.

Valfric instantly felt his mood sour more.

"And you're telling me why?" he asked flatly.

"Because I'm going, and I need you to watch the settlement with Hildrana," he said.

"Is Hildrana not up for the task?" Valfric asked.

"She is," Bergthral said. "But you know we're not popular in this area."

This was something that Valfric did know. He'd known it before they'd come here, but he'd learned it even more over the winter. He didn't understand it, and frankly, it didn't matter to him. The people here were good to him, and more importantly, they were good to Eira, and Bergthral and Hildrana had taken them in.

"So what do you need me to do?" he asked.

"Just watch over the settlement," Bergthral said, "an extra pair of eyes and ears. And if we're being fair, if anybody causes any trouble, they're a whole lot less likely to do it with you around."

Valfric nodded. "I suppose they may not want to deal with someone who they think is a witch," he said, shaking his head. "Dumb fucks."

Bergthral smiled. "They are dumb fucks. But you're willing to?"

Valfric nodded. "Of course. This is my home too. I'll protect it, don't worry."

Bergthral placed his hand on Valfric's shoulder. "Thank you. I know you're trying to be a peaceful man, and I understand."

Valfric shook his head. "There's a difference between seeking peace and protecting it," he said.

He looked out over the field for a few more minutes.

"When are you leaving?" Valfric asked.

"The day after tomorrow. We were at the end of the messenger's route, so I need to get moving," Bergthral said.

"Is there anything I need to keep an eye out for?" he asked.

"Just anything that's coming along. You can use your hawks if you like, or perhaps some mice. I find those to be effective as well," Bergthral said.

Valfric had learned that as well. Bergthral and Hildrana had taught him a few things in his short time there. One of them was a better way of surveilling an area. They created small Essaerites that were simple. They didn't move around much, but if they noticed something, then they got more advanced, or they alerted the Essaerist. It wasn't a step up from Valfric's hawks, so much as a step down, but he could create many more of them than the hawks. They took less Essaeris, and between the three Essaerists, they could be spread out everywhere, giving them more than enough notice. It was handy.

"Alright, I'll check in on them from time to time," he said.

"Is there anything that you need from Ilfglen?" Bergthral asked.

Valfric thought, dumbfounded for a moment. "It's been so long since I've thought about trade," he said. He thought for a while. He watched Eira playing with Ferngar and Bergthral's bear. "Perhaps you might be able to find something that she might like."

Bergthral smiled tightly. "I think I might be able to do that. Do you have anything in mind?"

Valfric shrugged. "I honestly haven't a clue what she likes, but she's doing better here."

Bergthral nodded. "She seems to be. She gets on well with Fernwen."

Valfric grinned. "Yes, they do well together. Thank you for that, by the way."

"Nothing to thank. Eira's a good person, and I think you are too. I'm glad you're here," Bergthral said.

"Thank you," was all Valfric said. He agreed about the part about Eira. She was good. She was all that was good in the world. But Valfric, he was the opposite.

That's what makes you so well-suited for protecting this settlement, he thought. *What better to keep away the evil than evil itself?*

———

CAELWEN AND MARIOKOS HAD MOVED BACK INTO THE CAMP FOR THE LEGION IN preparation for its movements to the Northwest. She was presently doing an inventory of all the herbs that she had managed to gather in the surrounding countryside in preparation for leaving. She cataloged them in her mind and packed them, wrapping them up securely to keep them dry and safe on their journey.

Next to her, Ilara was doing an inventory of her own items that she and Xavieno had, also in preparation for the trip. The other woman had seemed tense about the whole thing, and Caelwen could understand why. She had been hoping that they would have stayed in Ulfgard for longer than they had. Spring was well underway. The thaw was over, as was the runoff. Fields were being planted, and soon summer would be upon them. But for some reason, she had assumed that they would stay in the area, that perhaps the Legion would send out platoons or squads to make sure the surrounding countryside was secured and built up, or perhaps that they would spend a year or two in the area. But instead, that appeared not to be the case.

Ilara was looking around the camp.

"What are you thinking?" Caelwen asked.

Ilara shrugged. "Just a little surprised is all, that we're moving again, or that we're going to be moving again, I should say."

"Yeah, it's been on my mind as well. Does Xavieno seem surprised by it?" Caelwen asked.

Ilara shook her head. "No, not even a little bit. In a way, he almost seems to be restless, like he's been waiting for this for some time," she said. "How about Mariokos?"

"The same," Caelwen said.

Caelwen stopped what she was doing and sat down on a log that she created. She took out a water skin and took a drink, feeling the cool liquid move down her throat into her belly. "I suppose I shouldn't be surprised. Since I've been with the Legion, all they've done is move," she mused.

"Yes, from what we saw, they moved a lot," Ilara said, sitting next to her. She took out her own water skin, taking a drink. "But this has started to feel more permanent," she said. "But at the same time, I suppose it didn't, too." She ran her fingers through her long, blonde hair. "I suppose in a way, it does feel right that we're moving now that I think about it. Feels more like how my life used to be," she said.

"Really? How's that?"

Ilara shrugged. "As soon as spring came, it was time to go out and raid," Ilara said. "We started moving before the thaw was even fully underway."

Caelwen nodded. "Yes, things did start to get lively around then, didn't it?" she said, thoughtful. "Did you enjoy the winters?"

"Parts of them, yes. I enjoyed the solitude of them. There was relaxation to it. I don't really care for the cold, though. And I could get bored," Ilara said. "There were always things to do, but not as much," she said. "How about you?"

"Winters could be busy for me," Caelwen said. "If people were sick, I had more that I had to do. But otherwise, I agree. They were a calmer time, a time when you were just on your own. It made for a lot of time around fires and hearths, talking, singing, and laughing. But it also meant a lot of time at home.

"For me, spring started to get busy. There was everything to do around the home, but I was able to start looking for herbs again to replenish supplies. There was repair work to be done, I suppose. People getting hurt as they started moving around again and futzing with things on their farms. But I also always enjoyed it, too. Everything waking up, flowers coming to life, trees starting to grow leaves." She shrugged. "It was nice."

"Which is your favorite of the seasons?" Caelwen asked.

Ilara was thoughtful. "Probably summer. It can be damned hot, but it meant warm nights where you weren't shivering next to a fire. It meant that there was lots of daylight, lots to do." She said. "You?"

"I think I preferred autumn," Caelwen said. "Autumn has so many niceties to it. Everything is starting to relax and cool down. The colors are beautiful.

And it's just those last preparations for winter that you're worrying about. I enjoy summer, too, and spring, but I think autumn might be my favorite," she said.

Ilara smiled.

Caelwen looked up, seeing a familiar figure approaching. As Wulfgren got closer, Treftune chitted in Caelwen's ear. She smiled, scratching the Valfglidea's chin. He always enjoyed it whenever Wulfgren came by. Or she thought Treftune enjoyed stealing from Wulfgren and occasionally biting him. So maybe it wasn't that Treftune enjoyed Wulfgren so much as Caelwen enjoyed seeing Treftune torment Wulfgren. That was probably more likely the case.

"Ladies," he said, smiling broadly. "Are you all ready to start our trek?"

"You're going with us?" Ilara asked.

He nodded. "Of course. There's good money to be made in the Legion, and I have to watch my investment. I can't have somebody eating all of my product," he said, giving Ilara a slight glare.

She narrowed her eyes. "I don't eat your product."

"I've seen you eat plenty of rabbit," he said.

Ilara rolled her eyes. "Rabbit that I got from your sister."

Wulfgren barked a laugh. "I didn't say that she was any better."

Caelwen shook her head. "So what brings you by, brother?" she asked. "Would you like to learn how to take care of our investment?"

He waved her off. "No, no. I have people for that. But I did want to check on you," he said.

Caelwen rolled her eyes. *Don't let him get a rise out of you,* she thought.

He paused, waiting for a moment, looking at her eagerly. He sighed a little.

"Ass," Caelwen said.

Ilara smirked. Wulfgren turned to her. "What are you smiling about? I got what I wanted from you," he said.

Ilara laughed, her tone turning to seduction. "Oh dear. I don't think you've gotten what you've wanted from me. Not what you truly want," she said and gave him a wink. Caelwen enjoyed seeing his cheeks flush. Ilara laughed. "Look, now we both got what we wanted."

He snorted. "Fair enough. But on a serious note, how are you two holding up with this? I know you probably got used to being around here. Heck, you were in the city," he said.

Caelwen could see how this might be perceived differently for Wulfgren than for her and Ilara. Xavieno had also been stationed in the city for much of the winter. Their accommodations had been far more comfortable as a result. For Wulfgren, he, like most of the Legionnaires, were still in the camps. The camps were more robust than they obviously had been the day that they had arrived, but still were not like being inside permanent buildings in the city. Caelwen was sure that for them, the winter was a little bit long, tiresome, and tedious, and she could see where he was looking forward to being on the move again.

"Do you know much about where we're going?" Caelwen asked.

He shook his head. "Just to the northwest, towards Valfarans, I suspect. I know there's been problems out that way," he said.

"Has there?" Ilara asked. "Like what?"

"The normal. Raiding. A few settlements that aren't quite coming in line, but also there's been some push from Valfarans into former Ulfgarath territory," he said. "All things to be expected. But I think after the win that they had here, Lysandrian wants more."

"That doesn't seem to bother you, brother," Caelwen said.

"It doesn't bother me or not bother me," he said. "I've been doing mercenary work for enough time now that I don't question it. Countries go to war, and people get paid to do it. Still, someday it'll be nice not to be on the road and not to be on the warpath."

"That it will," Caelwen said.

He turned to Ilara and nodded. "Though don't worry. I'm sure you'll be very safe in the camp," he said, his tone just a little sarcastic.

Ilara raised an eyebrow. "I wasn't worried about it," she said.

He's trying to get you going, Caelwen thought, but chose not to say anything. She rather enjoyed watching Ilara and Wulfgren banter. There was something fun about it. It was light-hearted, flirty, and carefree.

"Well, that's good, because don't worry, Caelwen, Mariokos, myself, and Xavieno will always protect you," he said.

She snorted, "I don't need protecting."

He held up his hands, "I'm just saying."

Ilara glared at him, "you know I'm twice the warrior that you are, right?"

Caelwen turned back to what she was doing, in an attempt to hide her smile.

He won, she thought, and Wulfgren had won. He was getting a wonderful rise out of Ilara now.

CHAPTER 32

The air was thick with smoke in the meeting hall. Bergthral sat on a creaking chair at a table on the outskirts, the rough wood pressing into his back as the low hum of conversation mixed with the clink of mugs and the scrape of boots on stone. His shoulders ached from the long ride, and the heavy scent of smoke and sweat settled into his chest like a weight. All around him was the loud commotion of men and women speaking, drinking, bickering, and laughing. His gaze swept around, looking for those he knew. He didn't know everybody in the room by a long shot, but he recognized a few faces. Some were friendly; some were not.

In the corner, he saw Tirwalden, the head of a settlement that neighbored Bergthral's. The two had never gotten along, and Tirwalden hated Bergthral and Hildrana something fierce. If there was a bright side to seeing the man, it was that he was at least at the meeting and not back in his settlement, where he could cause problems for Hildrana and Valfric. But perhaps Tirwalden would be an asset to him today. It was hard to tell. Tirwalden wasn't stupid. He was cunning, cruel, clever, but he was also very concerned with his own self-interest, and Bergthral couldn't think of anything that would serve that more than ensuring that there weren't Lysandrian legions traipsing through their settlements. But he could be wrong.

The little conversation he had overheard upon arrival seemed mixed. Some were in favor of defending all of Valfarans against the legions. Others didn't think it would come to that. Still, others didn't care at all. It was fend for yourselves. Valfarans was no longer a nation. It hadn't been in generations. Many wondered why they should bother putting their own people at risk for something that might never happen.

Bergthral took a pull on his Bryndraught, swishing the liquid around in his mouth a few times before swallowing it. His bear, Essaerite, was outside, but standing next to him was one that looked like a person. Or more appropriately, it was shaped and proportioned like a person, though it didn't have any distinguishing features. The outside of it was black and blue. It almost looked like it was made out of ceramics. The surface was smooth. He didn't need it. He didn't particularly want it, but being an Essaerist was important. Otherwise, Bergthral was just a leader of an extraordinarily small settlement that probably didn't even deserve the title of settlement. But being an Essaerist gave him authority. That made him powerful. And most Essaerists in Valfarans had a reputation.

Bergthral was no different. He had forged his reputation when he was younger. It was a reputation not unlike Valfric's, though his had never been because of raiding prowess. Bergthral's battlefield conquests had been just that: battlefields. Usually in defense of his people. He hadn't always hailed from a small settlement. He'd once been from a normal one on the western coast. Those days were behind him now. But in those early times, he had seen battle on several occasions. On each of those occasions, he'd come out looking good. That reputation might help him today. He hoped.

As he tried to read the faces of those around him, he thought, *Some of these are undecided, but many have already made their minds up. What they're planning on doing is all but set in stone.* He wondered if there was even a point to the meeting. He pushed away the thought, deciding that it was better to be open-minded than negative. For all he knew, the yeas in favor of going to war with Lysandrian would outnumber the nays. Not that it would necessarily matter in the end. If a settlement wasn't planning on going, no one would force them.

A woman sounded a horn from near the center of the room and yelled for everyone to "shut the fuck up." Bergthral looked at her. She motioned over to a man who looked to be ten or fifteen years older than Bergthral. Though he was older, Bergthral could see that he was still strong. The man looked around, waiting to make sure that everyone was silent, that everyone was listening.

"You've all come for one reason," the man said, his voice strong. "I'm not going to bore you with pleasantries or waste any of our time. I will say a few words, though, before we begin. My name is Mirthgar, and this is my city. This is my territory. I know that many of you in this room count each other as enemies," he said, looking around at a few select individuals. "Let me make this clear. In this city, you will not cause problems. If you do, you will die," he said, not as a challenge, just as a flat statement. Bergthral noticed a few people shift in their seats.

I suppose that tells us who was planning on doing something stupid, he thought.

Mirthgar's gaze hardened. "All of you have heard the news by now—Ulfgard surrendered." When they surrendered, the leaders there decided to join the Lysandrian Empire," he said, his voice holding cold contempt. There were shouts from the gathered group of leaders. After a moment, they settled down. "That means their settlements, their towns and villages, came into the fold as well. There is not going to be bloody conquest in Ulfgarath because of this," he said. "Not all are satisfied, but enough are," he said, shaking his head.

"Pathetic. The Ulfgarath used to be something worth talking about. At least the raiding was good!" a man shouted, and there was a roar of agreement from the gathered leaders.

Mirthgar gave a grim smile. "Yes, they have become weak. Their former conquests made them fat and lazy; they reaped what they sowed, but Lysandrian will not stop, at least not so easily," he said as he walked around the center of the room. "We have been able to gather that their legions are prepping to leave Ulfgard. I doubt it will be all of them, and I do not know where they are going to go, but I think it's safe to assume that they will push their conquest to the northwest."

There were grumbles from the crowd. "I have spies, but they do not know Lysandrian's aim," the man said. "They may look to just secure the countryside around Ulfgard, perhaps expand a little. Or they could be coming for all of us," he said with a bit of a scoff.

There were a few chuckles and groans from the crowd. Another leader spoke. "They'll continue to move along the Ilfrun, take the rest of the territory in the mountains to where it starts, and push out to the western coast," he said confidently.

Mirthgar nodded. "Yes, that is what I think they will do, too. I think they will look to expand their borders, but I do not think they will push into all of Valfarans."

Bergthral resisted the urge to say something. This was a foolish statement. You couldn't know what an enemy was going to do. Why would Lysandrian stop?

"But be that as it may," the man said, "we need to decide what we are to do. For me, the path is clear. Ilfglen will go to war. I am not willing to risk my borders and my people on the hope that Lysandrian will settle with just expanding to the coast, and that they won't decide in a few years to push up through the rest of the land."

There were some shouts of agreement, and for the first time, Bergthral felt comforted by what he was hearing. However, there were those who seemed to disagree.

Bergthral was surprised when he saw Tirwalden stand and walk forward. Mirthgar looked at him, and Tirwalden spoke. "So what is it you're asking us, old man? You have dragged all of us, from our homes, from our crops, down to this city. Is it just to tell us that you're going to war, or is there something that you want?"

"I'm asking for others to join me," Mirthgar said.

"You want us to just stop what we're doing and join you?" Tirwalden spat.

"No, you will need to gather your men, need to gather your settlements, but yes, I want you to join," he said, holding Tirwalden's gaze.

There was a silence in the crowd, and Bergthral wondered if Mirthgar had thought that he'd be challenged or not. Tirwalden shook his head. "No, I think this is about expanding your power. I think it's your hope that we will send our warriors to go die, weakening ourselves so that you can expand your reach!"

Bergthral furrowed his brows in frustration. He heard agreement among the groups.

This is ridiculous, he thought.

He stood before Mirthgar spoke. "This is foolishness, Tirwalden. If we provide a unified front to Lysandrian, they will not push into our territory," Bergthral said.

Everyone in the room turned to look at him, some confused at who he was, but others noticed the Essaerite that was standing behind him. As they did, they seemed to give Bergthral's words more credence.

He took a few steps forward. "We all have heard what happened along the Ilfrun River; we all know what happened to Hroldenfell. If we remain divided, Lysandrian will merely march through. With each easy win, their confidence will be strengthened, and we shall be weakened."

There were some grumbles of assent. Mirthgar nodded. "This is wisdom that this man speaks," he said, pointing at Bergthral. "Because for every easy win that Lysandrian has, they will be emboldened. If they face actual resistance or are beaten, they will be done. They will go back to Ulfgarath to count their winnings."

Tirwalden barked a sharp laugh, his mouth curling into a sneer as his eyes glinted with cold amusement. "No, they won't! None of this is going to happen. I'm not surprised to hear this, though. Of course, Bergthral, you would want settlements like mine to be weakened so that you and your witch can take over!"

Bergthral shook his head. "My wife and I have never attacked any settlement around us, Tirwalden. You of all people should know that. But I don't think that you can claim the same, can you?" he asked, an edge to his voice. Tirwalden glowered.

Mirthgar raised his hands. "Enough. We are not here to discuss the rivalry between settlements. We are here to decide who is going and who is not." He looked around the room. "And for those who are not going, who will vow to stay within their borders and not take advantage?"

Bergthral noticed how many people were brought up short by this. He was amazed to see how many there were. Tirwalden's eyes narrowed, and he saw the hint of a smirk at his lips. Bergthral knew what was going to happen. Tirwalden was not going to commit his settlement. And as the others went off, his settlement would raid. *Pathetic,* Bergthral thought.

As soon as the old man stopped talking, a murmur built among the group that turned into heated conversations and then yelling. Bergthral watched as sections of the room moved into two camps: those going and those not. He sighed, seeing that there were so many in the would-not camp. Tirwalden seemed to be stirring them up, convincing them that there was a ploy to take over land. "Fucking ass," Bergthral whispered under his breath. He caught Tirwalden's eye and saw the other man smile. It wasn't a kind gesture.

As leaders made their pronouncements, they left the room and turned to other business. Bergthral sat at his table and finished his Bryndraught, asking the server for another one. He ate dinner, and after a while, he saw a figure standing before him. He looked up and glared.

"Tirwalden," Bergthral said.

Tirwalden grinned down at him. "Your tactic didn't work."

Bergthral shook his head and sighed. "Yes, now maybe we can all be killed by the Lysandrians."

Tirwalden glared down at him. "You're a fool for going to war, but I'm sure it'll go well for you. Don't worry, I'll make sure your wife, daughter, and settlement are safe," Tirwalden said, in a veiled threat trying to get a rise out of Bergthral.

He laughed and shook his head. "You really are an idiot, aren't you, Tirwalden?" he said, looking up at him, seeing the other man's face redden. "Tell me, between my wife and me, which one are you truly more afraid of?" he asked, looking into the other man's eyes.

Bergthral knew the answer to this. Hildrana was seen as an Eirfrosti witch. Their Essaerists were almost mystified, and while Hildrana and Bergthral knew this to be ridiculous, that was still what it was. But he would have been lying if he said that his wife was anything less than lethal.

With Bergthral, you knew what would be coming for you: a head-on attack. Hildrana? Not so much. He could see Tirwalden's expression change, and Bergthral grinned. "Ah, I see now. It is she that you're more afraid of? So thank you for being willing to take care of them while I'm gone," he said and laughed. "Fucking idiot."

Tirwalden's hand moved to his belt, to a knife there, and Bergthral raised an eyebrow. "Do you think that's wise to do in Ilfglen?" he asked. "It doesn't bother me, but for you," he said, glancing around. All around inside the hall were soldiers from Ilfglen, there to keep the peace.

Tirwalden grimaced. Bergthral wondered if he would attack him on the road, on the way back home, but he thought not. Tirwalden didn't have very many warriors with him, and Bergthral was an Essaerist. The reality of it was, if Tirwalden wanted to kill Bergthral, this was probably going to be his best chance to do it, with a single Essaerite that was more form than function standing behind him—not when he was with his giant bear that could rip men into pieces without any effort whatsoever.

Bergthral gave Tirwalden a slow, mocking smile, letting the silence stretch until the tension coiled tight between them. "I didn't think so. Enjoy your Bryndraught, and enjoy waiting for Lysandrian to come to your doorstep," he said darkly.

CHAPTER 33

Caelwen looked up at the cloudy sky. The clouds above her were a light gray with a few dark patches that hinted at rain later in the afternoon. The air carried a faint chill, and the damp scent of soil rose as the breeze stirred the camp. She wasn't sure if that was a good omen or not. More likely than anything, it wasn't an omen at all, because rain happened, and rain was generally a good thing, especially in the spring when plants were starting to bud.

All around her was the controlled chaos of the camp preparing to leave. Her cart, along with Ilara and Xavieno's, was packed and ready to go. She had one of her Essaerites that was still in existence. It sat next to the cart, its head looking around at all those around her, and its tails doing likewise. People found it unsettling, but she noticed that the people who were around them the most seemed to have gotten used to it.

She'd also created an Essaerite to pull the cart. She could have created more cats or other types of Essaerites, but she decided against it. She wasn't going to waste her power, even if there was some value in showing some of it.

She was wearing a light and breathable dress. As the breeze blew, she felt it caress her skin and exposed neck as she'd piled her hair atop her head. She decided that maybe the clouds were a good omen. It was still warm, but the sun wasn't burning down on her. Yes, the clouds were a good omen.

She opened her eyes, seeing two people approach her, Lorna and Gundor. With Lorna was her usual contingent of Essaerites. They stood, imposing and intimidating, glaring—if an Essaerite could glare—at those around them. Gundor, on the other hand, looked completely ordinary. He blended into the surroundings like any normal person would, though Caelwen had come to learn that he was anything but that. This was a man who was more deadly than most she'd ever met. He could kill without you knowing who killed you. He could start a riot or end one without anyone being any the wiser of how things had transpired.

He'd infiltrated groups inside the city for the Legion's benefit, and though she knew he said that he was supportive of the Legion, she wondered how much of his abilities were spent on fringe projects—things that, should things go poorly with the Legion, would give him and Lorna options. He would be stupid not to have those contingencies in place. And Caelwen very much doubted that somebody like Gundor could ever stop doing what he did. He loved the shadows. He had turned them into his home, into his plaything. That wasn't something that people left behind.

Caelwen smiled at the newcomers. "Good morning. Are you joining us?" she asked, her tone light and teasing.

Lorna looked around. "I think I would rather be flogged," she said. And Caelwen laughed.

Gundor watched the people move about. "The efficiency of the Legions, it truly is awe-inspiring," he said.

Lorna echoed his thoughts. "Yes, it is this efficiency that they seem to have that's made them so powerful," she mused. "I wonder what would happen if they ever met a force as efficient and practical as they are."

Caelwen had wondered that as well. What if Lysandrian did meet some-body just like them? When she thought about it, she imagined the two groups would probably just combine into one giant bureaucratic blob. After all, they had so completely absorbed the people of Ulfgarath that part of her wondered if there was even a desire for war, or if war was just the means to the end of building a bigger, more productive empire.

"Do you know where you're going?" Lorna asked.

Caelwen shook her head. "About twenty miles away, I know that much," she said with a laugh. "That's how much we move every day when we're on the march. But where we're going, I couldn't say. I don't think Mariokos knows either. He thinks there we'll probably have to deal with towns and settlements that haven't come in line."

Lorna shrugged. "I'm sure there are some that you will encounter, but nothing that should prove to be too difficult, I think." Her gaze swept around the camp again. "And all this goes," she said. "It seems like such a waste."

Caelwen looked around, too. There had been many structures that had been built, most of them made of wood, and they all looked permanent to her. But they were coming down. Some of the lumber was being sold off, but some small things would stay, but she knew by and large, by the end of the day, this camp would have disappeared.

"It is the way they work," Caelwen said.

Gundor smirked. "You mean the way *you* work," he corrected.

She resisted the urge to roll her eyes. "Very well, the way I work and my people work," she said, "but it is something that has confused me, though I suppose there's no way that any enemy could ever take a camp and turn it into a fort."

"It is odd," Lorna said. "They do not fight offensively so much as defensively," she mused.

Ilara raised an eyebrow. "Can you come again? I've seen them be pretty offensive," she said.

Lorna shook her head. "I do not mean to oversimplify," she said, her accent thick. It sounded like she was considering how to say what she was thinking. "I mean to say that when the Legions go someplace, they stop and build a fort. In a way, even when they are attacking, it's almost like they are forcing their opponent to be the attacker, allowing them to defend from a position of strength. It's remarkable," she said, and it was. Caelwen couldn't deny that.

Next to her, Ilara seemed to tense just a little bit. "You have no idea how true that statement is."

Caelwen could see a far-off look in her eyes. "Even at the Ilfrun River, they built a camp. Each Legion did, the day that there was fighting. They started building it while the fighting was going on. And then the next day, you're right. It's like they were defenders in a way, not the other way around. People had set up some carts and obstacles for them, but..." Ilara shrugged.

A horn sounded, indicating that the supply train was about to begin moving. Ilara shook herself, as did Caelwen. She walked up to Lorna and reached out her hand.

Lorna took it. "I hope to see you again, Caelwen," she said.

Caelwen nodded, "And I you." She turned to Gundor, also taking his hand. "Keep safe," she said.

He smiled, his expression warm. "You too. It would be a shame to have gone through so much work securing the city for the Legions just to have them wander off on me," he said with a wink.

She snorted a laugh. "Oh, I don't think they're going anywhere any time soon. I'd say you're going to be dealing with Lysandrian in Ulfgard for some time."

He smiled, and it appeared to be genuine. "I truly hope so," he said. "I know that this is a hard time for many, but I do believe that in the long run it will benefit my people."

She knew his views were not necessarily shared by most of the people of Ulfgard. They had accepted Lysandrian control and were seemingly fine with it, but it was hard to think of your conqueror as good, and Caelwen knew that it would be generations before there would be full trust between the Lysandrians and the people of Ulfgarath, if there ever were truly full trust at all. But she also reminded herself that the Ulfgarath territory had been going back and forth with control from one war leader to another for generations now, so maybe to the people of Ulfgard, this was just the next warlord that came in. It wasn't anything to pay attention to.

She climbed onto her wagon with Ilara and waited as those around them began to move. The creak of wood and the steady crunch of gravel beneath the wheels filled the air, mingling with the low murmur of voices and the distant clang of metal. When it was her turn, her Essaerite began to move, bringing them in line with the rest of the supply wagon. She waved at Lorna and Gundor, who waved back, and then turned, heading back towards the city.

————

MARIOKOS MARCHED IN FORMATION WITH THE REST OF HIS SQUAD AND PLATOON, feeling his feet chew up the distance as they moved. Behind them, Ulfgard was shrinking on the horizon, and before them was a valley that ended in mountains. Those mountains were growing larger. The gravel of the road crunched beneath his feet. It felt good to be moving. The sun was warm on his face and head, and his pack rested as comfortably as a pack could on his shoulders. The soft rustling of leaves mingled with the distant chirping of birds, and the faint scent of wildflowers drifted through the air. He pulled his water skin from his belt and took a long drink, then secured it back again without missing a stride, keeping in step with the men next to him and ahead of him.

The Legion moved on, *left, right, left, right, left, right*. It created a rhythm in his mind that allowed him to relax in some way. As he did, he was able to see through the hawks and other birds that he had circling the area. He would glance through them and then pay back attention to what was in front of him. If he needed to pay more attention, he could tell the man on either side of him, and they would hold on to his elbows, keeping him from weaving about as he looked through the Essaerites' eyes. But there was nothing for them to see. All his hawks could see was the long line that was the Legion's as they moved.

It stretched around for miles as three full legions moved west. They snaked their way through the bright green farmland as fields were fully coming to life. Everything was alive around them. Flowers bloomed along the sides of the roads, and trees had thick canopies that were coming into existence. Other trees were covered in flowers, and around them, they could hear the sound of birds chirping and hear them fluttering around.

There was so much work that needed to be done—nests that needed to be built, eggs that needed to be laid, worms that needed to be pulled from the ground. But it was happy work, Mariokos thought. How could it not be? The world was coming alive. It was awake and ready for the year ahead. They continued to march onward.

He could hear conversation amongst the men around him. "What do you think we're heading into?" Helioz asked.

Luciakos answered, "More of what we had before we got to Ulfgard, I suspect."

"Yeah, probably," Helioz said, "but it feels different this time. They aren't going to be surprised."

"They may not, but they may not resist either. After all, look at what happened to Ulfgard. That was Hroldenfell, and that massacre at the river," Luciakos said, "make no mistake about it."

It was true. Mariokos knew this. He could see it now. Hroldenfell had been a statement. The Ilfrun River had also been one, but he thought it more had to do with the emperor taking an opportunity to keep the Gwenthari in the area from joining other armies, and it was a wealth grab. While so many had perished there, the wealth that the empire had gained was significant. All of the people's belongings, livestock, and then the living people themselves. There hadn't been a single free Gwenthari that had been in the group. They were either dead or they had become slaves, save for a handful who had gotten across the river.

At the time, he'd almost been a little surprised that the order hadn't come to pursue, but later he realized why it hadn't. Aside from the fact that it could have been wasteful, it would have slowed the Legion's progress towards Ulfgard, and more importantly, those people were able to bring word to Ulfgard to let their leaders know what was coming.

It gave them a choice. They could resist and be killed or enslaved, or they could join the Empire. Mariokos suspected that the Emperor would not have done to Ulfgard what he did to Hroldenfell, but the people and leaders inside the city couldn't guarantee that, could they? No, they had taken the option that gave them the best chances. He thought they were wise for doing it.

"I think we're headed to Valfarans," Mariokos said.

"Really?" Helioz said.

"Think about it," Mariokos said. "Valfarans makes sense. Yeah, there's going to be some that need to be pacified around here, but the Valfarans started moving into Ulfgarath territory as soon as everyone went to Ulfgard."

"From what I heard, they were starting that before," Helioz said.

"I heard that, too," Luciakos said.

"So it makes sense," Mariokos said. "We'll have to push the Valfarans back out of Ulfgarath, and then why wouldn't we continue on? This hasn't exactly been a bad war for the Empire, has it?"

"No, it hasn't," Helioz said.

"Well, I suppose we know what we have to look forward to, then," Luciakos said.

"Yeah," Mariokos said. "At least it's nice out."

He wasn't really looking forward to any more war, though. He hadn't hated his time in Gwenthari territory. After all, he was married to Caelwen, and there was no way that he could ever suspect in a thousand lifetimes that he could have gotten lucky enough to find her. But he didn't want to deal with the killing. He didn't want to besiege anything, and he most certainly didn't want to live in one camp after another. He longed for his homeland. He longed for sowing seeds and watching them grow, for harvesting crops, and making wine.

He thought of helping and working out at the mills, using Essaerites to grind grain down into flour and then smelling that flour turn into bread. He thought of the festivals they used to have in the spring, summer, autumn, and winter. Of the dancing, of the food, of the laughing. At the time, he hadn't thought that he'd cared for any of that stuff—that it was more of a waste than anything else. But now he remembered those times fondly. Remembered how relaxed and easy life was. He thought Caelwen might enjoy it. He definitely thought she would enjoy the estate that he had once he was done with his time in the Legion. It wasn't in a secluded area, but it was rural and nice, next door to Xavieno's. There they could plant whatever they wanted and do whatever they wanted. Two Essaerists had an easy life ahead of them.

He tried not to daydream too much, though, as they marched. Because unless he told his companions that he was looking through his Essaerites. And if he was looking through Essaerites, why would he have a bemused look on his face? He couldn't and they'd know he was full of shit. So instead, he pushed those thoughts from his mind and focused on the back of the head of man in front of him and continued to march. Left, right, left, right, left, right.

Bergthral felt his Essaerithon moving beneath him. He snorted, just about to fall asleep, as the bear moved and it jostled him. He opened his eyes, the sun blinding him momentarily. He sat up in the saddle. He'd been leaning back in a way that he could lay across the bear's back. It wasn't terribly comfortable; nothing about traveling on the Essaerithon was, but leaning back was better than sitting upright. The morning had been so delightfully warm and nice, and the air filled with the scent of wildflowers as they bloomed. It had been a struggle, to say the least, to keep his eyes open as he traveled.

He was alone, only with his thoughts, and with that warm sun on him. He tried to sit more upright and tilted his head to the side, hearing it crack resoundingly. He stretched his arms. *I need to come up with a better Essaerite to travel with,* he thought, but it was so difficult. The bear was his primary Essaerite that he used for so many things. It was combat effective, it was strong, he could technically ride on it, but it wasn't fast, and it wasn't as comfortable as a horse. He could have taken a horse, of course, but practicality got the best of him, and he always forgot how uncomfortable the bear was over long trips.

Soon, though, it wasn't going to matter. He recognized the area that he was in and knew that he was close to home. Thinking about home made more way on his mind. Two things, really. First, the excitement at seeing Hildrana and Fernwen, and second, the concern about the meeting. He'd committed himself to the fight. That commitment came with its own challenges and problems, but those were more for the future than anything else.

The real concern was that so few had said that they were going to commit to the fight. Bergthral didn't know if it would be enough to make a difference, or if they did make a difference, how many of those would be left. He was coming to a clearing in the trees. He could see the fields of farms from some of the people from his settlement just beyond the clearing. Despite the concern that he felt, he smiled. There was something about coming home, even though the trip hadn't been long. It always felt wonderful when he came back.

His bear entered the clearing, and he waved at a handful of people who were out in their fields. It continued lumbering along towards his house. As it did, he felt his mood lighten, and he smiled as he took in his home. It had a steep, thatched roof, and smoke was curling out from the chimney. It was partially dug into the ground, like all Gwenthari homes were. And there was a small paddock where livestock could be kept, though he rarely found use for them unless it was to store them for a short period of time before slaughter.

As he gazed around, he looked to see who was there. He saw Hildrana's stag Essaerite standing out front, and he thought he caught a glimpse of Fernwen out by the woodpile. As he neared his house, he slipped off the saddle of the bear and continued walking on his own two feet. And as he got closer, he saw Fernwen looking at him from the woodpile. She caught his eyes and grinned, running up to him. "Papa," she shouted happily.

He smiled and scooped her up. "Oh, I missed you," he groaned as he picked her up and squeezed her tight.

She laughed and hugged him back. "I missed you, too. How was Ilfglen?" she asked.

"It was fine," he said.

"Really? Just fine?" she asked, looking up at him with twinkling eyes.

He smirked. "Yeah, just fine," he said. He knew what she wanted. She was curious if he got her anything, and he had, but it wasn't like he wasn't going to make her work for it.

"So did you do any shopping while you were there?" she asked as they started walking towards the house.

"I did, as a matter of fact," he said. "I got Eira something from Valfric," he commented.

"Oh, that's nice," she said, a little disappointed.

He grinned. "Yes, it was. I think she'll enjoy it. How have you been?" he asked.

She looked up at him, giving him a playful glare. "Papa," she said.

He tried to look confused. "What?"

She stopped, placing her hands on her hips. "Papa," she said, taking on the tone that his wife had whenever he was about to be in trouble.

He shook his head and laughed. "Did your mother teach you that?"

"Teach me what?" she asked.

"That expression, that tone, that way of standing," he asked.

From the door, he heard his wife's voice. "No, it's something that comes naturally to us. But it's something that we get better at the more time we spend training the men in our lives," she said with a smile.

She walked up to him, and he wrapped his arm around her waist, pulling her in close, kissing her deeply.

"Training the men in your lives," he grumbled. "I did get you something," he said, smiling at Fernwen.

He walked over to the bear and opened up his pack. He pulled out a paper-wrapped package and handed it to her. She opened it up.

"Ooh, what are these?" she asked.

"There's some sort of candy. Pretty good. I tried some at the stand," he said.

Fernwen picked up one of the pieces. It was red and shiny. She popped it in her mouth. Her eyes widened.

"Ooh, this is good," she said. "Thank you."

She gave Bergthral a hug, and he squeezed her back. "You're very welcome," he said.

He reached into his bag and gave a similar one to his wife.

"Ooh, I get treats, too," Hildrana said.

"Yes, but you have to earn them," he commented.

She snorted and hit his arm. "Later. I'll earn them later."

Fernwen made a gagging sound, and that made them both smile.

He always tried to bring his wife and daughter back something whenever he went anywhere, but it wasn't necessarily easy to do. Most of the towns that were in the area didn't have anything that was all that unique or good when it came to treats. He could have bought them trinkets or baubles, but that just wasn't very effective for Essaerists. After all, Hildrana could create whatever she wanted, and she didn't really care for gifts. Bergthral was the same, and being an Essaerist, Fernwen turned into that as well. When she was younger, she enjoyed trinkets, but now that she was growing in her powers, they didn't hold the same appeal.

Treats, on the other hand, were different, and all three of them rather enjoyed getting them.

He pulled out another package from his bag. It was a little glass disc made of different colors of glass that hung on a chain.

"I did get this for Eira. Valfric asked if I would get her something that she might think was pretty." He held it up. Sunlight shone through it, sending different colors and patterns on the ground.

"It's very pretty," Hildrana said.

"It is," Fernwen said, looking at it. "She'll like it."

Bergthral smiled. "I think she will, too." He wrapped it back up, handing it to his daughter. "Will you take it over to Valfric's farm and ask him to come over?"

Fernwen nodded, and then looked thoughtful.

"Should I say that I'll spend time with Eira, so the three of you can speak?" she asked.

He nodded grimly. "Yes, that would be good. Thank you for doing that," he said.

Fernwen nodded. "Will you tell me what you talked about later?"

This had been something that he and Hildrana had struggled with—how much of the world to share with their daughter. Both of them were firmly in the camp that they didn't want Fernwen to be soft, and that they didn't want her to be ignorant of the ways of the world. But they also didn't want her to be jaded. It had been a difficult line to draw.

Hildrana's training and mentorship that she had had growing up as an Essaerist was a bit of a guide for them. It provided ages at which young Essaerists would learn more about the world. When he had first heard of it, when he had met Hildrana, the whole concept of it had sounded silly and stupid to him, but now he appreciated it. The thought-out training of the Eirfrosti had proven to be rather effective in so many ways.

He nodded to her, and Fernwen went off to go fetch Valfric and spend time with Eira, and he turned to his wife.

"That bad?" she asked.

He shrugged. "Not that good. Some are fighting, but, well," he said, letting it hang out there.

She saw her expression darken. "I suppose I'm about to hear all about it."

———

VALFRIC SAT LISTENING TO BERGTHRAL TELL THE STORY OF THE MEETING. HE FELT HIS gut twisting and turning with a whole set of emotions. The first was fear. Fear that Lysandrian was coming. He was surprised that he felt it. He'd never been afraid of battle. He'd been hesitant about it. He'd been concerned by it, but he'd never felt afraid. *I wonder if I'm getting weak,* he thought. The other emotion that he felt that seemed to be dominant was that of anger. These people were being fucking idiots for not wanting to stand against the Lysandrians. He'd seen what happened when you stood against them. He'd watched Hroldenfell burn, and he had watched his friends and so many others be slaughtered, but he didn't exactly think you could just roll over and take it either. But maybe you could. Hearing about Ulfgard made him question that. Perhaps there was a value in just surrendering, just becoming part of the Empire, paying whatever tribute was required and going along your way. Another part of him railed against that. The old part of him. The part that sought to fight and kill and take what the strong deserved. But wasn't Lysandrian strong? Didn't they deserve this under that same thought process? He tried to push these thoughts from his mind and listened.

A name popped out to him. "What the fuck is up with this Tirwalden idiot?" Valfric asked, stopping a side conversation that Bergthral and Hildrana had started.

"He's the leader of another settlement around here," Hildrana said.

"I know, but why does he hate you so much, both of you?" he asked. He saw Bergthral's expression tighten a little bit and Hildrana's darkened. Valfric held up his hands. "Look, I don't care what you did. This is my home, and these are my people now, just as much as yours. I'm just curious why he hates you, because it might affect me."

"It might," Bergthral said.

"It probably will," Hildrana said.

Bergthral sighed. "I'm sorry," he said to Valfric.

Valfric shook his head. "It's fine. There's always rivalry between settlements, but I'm curious about this one. I understand that he thinks you're a witch," he said to Hildrana. "Dumb as that is, it's probably actually a good thing."

She smiled tightly. "Yes, there is power in fear, isn't there?"

"There is. But it seems like there's more to it than that," he said.

"There is," she said.

"What is it?" he asked.

"Years back, right around the time when we were first founding the settlement," she said, "there was an issue with Tirwalden. He tried to raid the settlement."

"It didn't go well for him," Bergthral said, and Valfric could hear a slight edge of amusement in his voice.

Valfric couldn't help but smile. "Two Essaerites, as powerful as the two of you are? No, I'm sure that raid didn't go well for him."

"No, but be that as it may. His brother was injured. Not killed, mind you, but injured. He would later die, though I don't think it was from his wounds," Hildrana said.

Valfric shrugged. "Even if it was, they were the idiots dumb enough to attack Essaerists. Is that why he hates you?"

"That. And he doesn't like some of the people of our settlement. If you haven't noticed, we're a bit of a place for outcasts. For me, he thinks I'm a traitor for being with an Eirfrosti Essaerist, and obviously he has his issues with Hildrana," Bergthral said.

"Also, he's from an area that has been raided before by my people," Hildrana said. "It's not common that we do it."

"Apparently, when Tirwalden was younger, a boat that some of his family was on was attacked and sunk by an Eirfrosti Essaerist," Bergthral said, with a shrug that said he didn't quite believe it.

"Were there witnesses?" Valfric asked.

"I don't think so," Hildrana said.

Valfric snorted, "But I'm sure that's what the townspeople decided to think, that it was some witch that did it," he said, trying not to roll his eyes. He reached down, grabbing his cup, taking a drink of Bryndraught. "Fucking idiots."

"We're glad you feel that way," Hildrana said flatly.

Valfric shrugged, "People give Essaerists too much credit," he said. "I should know that better than anyone. The people who were with me, they thought that they were indestructible because of me. Not my friends, mind you, but those people of my settlement. And certainly those poor bastards at the Ilfrun," he said, his mood darkening. "So when do you head off to war?" he asked Bergthral.

"Soon, but I don't know," he shook his head.

"You don't know what?" Valfric asked.

"I don't know with how few of us are going if it's going to make a difference. Others may rally, but I don't know," he said.

"And there's my people to think about," Hildrana said.

"What do your people have to do with it?" Valfric asked, curious.

"The Eirfrosti could pose a problem for us," Bergthral said.

"Do you think they would align with Lysandrian?" Valfric asked.

"No," Hildrana said, "they won't align with Lysandrian, but take an opportunity? My people aren't known for raiding, but it's not exactly like they won't take something that's being offered up to them. As people in Valfarans get weak, well, you know the temptation."

He sighed, "I do know the temptation."

"I could go to them," Hildrana said to her husband.

Bergthral glanced over at her and sighed, "That crossed my mind."

"Do you think your people would listen to you?" Valfric asked.

"She's an Essaerist," Bergthral said as if that answered the question.

Hildrana explained, "We're power brokers in Eirfrosti. Essaerists. We hold a lot of sway, though I probably don't as much as I would have at one time."

Bergthral looked over at Valfric, "Yeah, they weren't exactly happy when she married some idiot Valfarans and moved to the continent," he said.

Valfric couldn't help but smile a little bit, "Ah, I can see that. But if it wasn't for women's poor judgment, none of us would ever settle down," Valfric said, nodding his cup towards Bergthral.

Bergthral chuckled and held his cup up.

Hildrana shook her head, "Idiots," she said, but he could tell that she was amused by it. She got serious, "We can wait and find out, but if things get bad, I might need to travel there."

Bergthral nodded, "I think there's something to that. Do you think you could convince them not to raid or not to help Lysandrian?"

She shrugged, "Maybe. My people are much more rational and reasonable than those here. I think they could see that if there's an easy win for Lysandrian on the continent, that it won't be long before they're dealing with them as well. Though, Lysandrian might be hesitant to do that," she said.

"Why is that?" Valfric asked.

Bergthral answered this time, "About ten or fifteen years ago, Lysandrian tried to invade Eirfrosti. It was only one legion, but it went badly," he said.

Valfric was surprised, "I hadn't heard that."

"Yes, they did try. I think they wanted to hold the channel or have influence over it. They landed, after taking a lot of losses at sea, but then they were pushed back," she said with a shrug. "We are not the rest of the Gwenthari."

Valfric took another drink, "Yeah, I'm starting to see that."

Hildrana looked at her husband, "We will watch and wait, but if I need to, I will go."

Bergthral looked resigned and nodded, "If you think you need to, do it."

CHAPTER 34

Mariokos marched in formation with his squad, letting the rhythmic sound of footsteps lull his mind into calm. It had been a couple of months since they'd left Ulfgard behind them—months spent bringing a handful of territories in line and otherwise securing the former Ulfgarath lands. They were in the dead of summer now, and the hot sun bore down on him and everyone else. Little clouds of dust swirled in the air as the legions marched, the rhythmic thud of boots mixing with the low murmur of men's voices. The dust scratched at his throat and filled his nose, making him want to sneeze and cough.

This was life in the Legion. You'd walk in the dust and the heat, which was preferable to the cold and snow or a torrential downpour. Though the weather had been cooler than it had been in his homeland, it was still warm. In Ulfgarath, the mountains had been tall and sharp, with steep faces covered in dense trees. The forest had remained dense in the new areas they'd moved into, and they were approaching the Aelindale mountain range. Unlike its counterpart to the east, it had rolling mountains that weren't so steep and jagged, but were more like waves on the ocean. It was a pretty area, and he enjoyed it.

As they moved along, he could hear the sound of birds in the trees, and his Essaerites could sense other life around them. It all moved far away from the columns of marching soldiers, but Mariokos could see it and appreciate it. The land was lush and vibrant. The people here had been sparse as well when they had still been moving through Ulfgarath. So many had fled the area when the legions had moved in, but they had also been moving away from the Valfarans as they encroached on Ulfgarath territory. That was different now. Now the legions had entered Valfarans territory, and what they encountered confirmed what Mariokos had assumed the Gwenthari would be like before the whole campaign had begun.

In Ulfgarath, they had encountered minor resistance, taking down Hroldenfell and Ulfgard. There had also been the massacre, but by and large, it had been easygoing for the legions. The Valfarans seemed to be different. They were Gwenthari, and they looked just like the Ulfgarath did, but they appeared to have a different attitude. Mariokos found that they were resourceful and adaptive. Towns, settlements, and villages would be abandoned by the time the legions arrived. All of the homes were cleared of valuables, livestock missing—everything. They would move through the area, and then they'd be attacked from behind, or supply lines would be hit.

It had been tiresome, to say the least, and it also slowed how quickly the legions could move, forcing them into a pattern of moving into an area, securing it as best they could, and then slowly moving on to secure the next area while having to go back and re-secure much of the ground behind them. It meant that the legions would need to spread themselves out, and Mariokos wondered how the Emperor was planning on taking care of it. Would this stop him from moving north? Would they just move west and secure along the Empire's borders?

This had caused much speculation among the men, but for Mariokos, his gut feeling was that what they were doing now was more expeditionary than anything else. He suspected that after a season of this, there would be more than enough wealth flowing into the Empire from the Ulfgarath territory that Senators in the Empire would dedicate forces to the North. Then the campaign would change.

The legion was entering a large valley, and he could see in the distance that the other legions were stopping to create camps for the night. As he saw this, he tried to bring his mind fully back awake; there was work that needed to be done. Work that would be a nice break from the marching of the day.

As their legion came to its campsite, orders began to be issued, and Mariokos joined the other legionnaires in the work of building the camp. As per his usual, Mariokos created his Essaerithon to work on trenching for the outer perimeter. He got to work with the large Essaerite, turning and digging its way through the soil of the Aelindale Valley. Mariokos lost himself in the work, feeling the roughness of the dirt under his fingers and the weight of the shovel in his hands. The rhythmic scrape of metal against dirt and the strain in his muscles were almost meditative, grounding him in the present moment. By the time the camp was built, he was covered in sweat and dust. He ran his hand through his hair, feeling little clumps of dirt in it. He wiped them away and smiled. Around him was the completed wall, with a ditch in front of it. He asked his commander if there was anything else needed of his Essaerithon. There wasn't, so he released it and went to his designated spot in camp to clean up and have dinner.

He found Caelwen there with Ilara. Caelwen looked up at him and smiled, her bright blue eyes seeming to twinkle, her skin glowing, her hair shining in the sun. He came up to her and planted a kiss on her lips.

"How was your day?" he asked.

"Fine," she said. "You taste like salt and dirt," she added with a smile.

He laughed. "Yeah, I know. When we were digging the trench, I slipped and fell in it," he admitted.

She snorted. "Are you okay?" she asked.

He shrugged. "Physically, yes. But my dignity...?"

She laughed. "Go wash up."

He entered their tent and created a basin full of water. He released his clothes and grabbed a rag, beginning to wash himself off. After a while, he decided better of it, put on some pants, and created another pail of water. He walked out of the tent, stood off to the side, and poured it over his head, getting all the dirt and debris out from when he had fallen in the trench. After he was sure everything was out, he released the water, and his hair dried. He ran his fingers through it and walked back into the tent. He finished cleaning himself off and then created clothes for himself. It was a tunic that looked to be military issue, though the fabric was softer and nicer. He also created new shoes for himself that hugged his feet. He walked out and saw Xavieno approaching.

Xavieno smirked. "I heard building the wall went well."

Mariokos rolled his eyes. "I wondered if you'd hear about that or not."

Xavieno grinned. "Oh, I have my sources," he said.

Mariokos saw Xavieno glance over at Ilara. He gave her a small glare, and she shrugged. "I am his property. I'm supposed to give him what he wants," she said flatly.

Mariokos coughed a laugh. "Traitor," he accused.

Ilara smiled.

He could smell a fire burning as Caelwen and one of her stump Essaerites worked on dinner. As he smelled it, he felt his hunger grow and heard his belly rumble. The food they had been eating had been changing as of late. Caelwen knew all of the herbs and fruits that grew naturally in the area, and their meals had been changing accordingly. Before, Caelwen had cooked meals that had a Lysandrian feel to them, but they were meals that were common for the legions. That appeared to have changed now, and she was cooking more food from her homeland. Mariokos wasn't sure about it. Some of it was good, but a lot of it was bland, though they seemed to use a lot of herbs, which he enjoyed.

The breads were wonderful. She had also taken full advantage of the lessons that Mariokos, Xavieno, and especially Fioralba had taught her about using Essaeris to create ingredients to add flavor. It was something that Caelwen did quite a bit now. At first, she had seemed hesitant, worried that if she did something wrong, someone would get sick, but she had grown more confident with it. Mariokos thought that had a lot to do with spending a winter in Ulfgard having real food—something she hadn't had much of before she had found the Legion, as her settlement had been on the move.

A thick stew was bubbling in a pot, its rich aroma of simmering meat and herbs filling the air. The surface rippled with slow, oily bubbles, and the scent of rosemary and garlic mixed with the smoky undertone of the fire beneath it. Mariokos created a chair for himself and sat down, inhaling deeply the scent of the stew as it cooked.

He looked over, seeing Treftune raiding somebody's pack, and he smiled, not calling any attention to it. Treftune's stealing was what the Legion was accustomed to now. In fact, if a man didn't have something stolen from him on a regular enough basis, there'd become a slight superstition about it, as if the little Valfglidea somehow had prescient abilities, and if he avoided you, something bad would happen.

Another figure approached, with the same fire-red hair as Caelwen, but with rippling muscles.

"Wulfgren," Mariokos said in greeting.

"Mariokos," Wulfgren replied. He glanced over at Ilara. "Slave," he said.

She rolled her eyes. "Moron," she said, her tone respectful.

Wulfgren laughed.

Mariokos watched them talk. Their relationship had been growing over the winter, and Mariokos wasn't sure what would happen with it. There was nothing against a Citizano being with a slave, so long as the slave's owner was alright with it, and Mariokos very much doubted that Xavieno cared at all about the relationships that Ilara had. He knew his friend was still on the fence about having an attendant, but he wasn't going to get rid of Ilara and put her in a tough spot in life.

Xavieno came out of his tent in clean clothes and sat next to Mariokos, breathing in the scent of the stew. "That smells wonderful."

"What do they have you doing?" Mariokos asked.

Xavieno shrugged. "Scouting, mostly, and some sentry duty."

That was the way of it. Mariokos was the construction worker, Xavieno the warrior. It suited both of them, though Mariokos wasn't sure if it completely suited Xavieno anymore.

"Did you hear any news?" Mariokos asked.

Xavieno nodded. "I did, actually." This got everyone's attention. Wulfgren and Ilara stopped their flirtatious banter and paid attention. Caelwen came and sat next to Mariokos. Xavieno waited until everyone was seated. "So it sounds like the legions are going to be splitting up."

"Yeah, I suppose that's not a surprise," Wulfgren said.

Xavieno shrugged. "No, it's not. We've been on the move for a few days, but we're in Valfarans territory now," he said.

Wulfgren nodded. "That will complicate things. I think we'll have to start moving slower, would be my guess."

"We might," Mariokos said. "So, do you know anything about the split-up and what's going to happen?"

Xavieno shook his head. "No, I don't. Just what I overheard some officers saying. But part of the legion will stay here." He looked around. "This valley seems like it could be a good spot for a winter fort."

Mariokos nodded in agreement. "That crossed my mind. There's a river in here. Plenty of access to roads. Lots of space," he said.

"It's the middle of summer, and you're already thinking about winter," Ilara asked.

"Yes," Wulfgren said. "You have to be able to supply an army, and you have to be able to take care of it. Having small forts? It's the way Lysandrian works."

Xavieno tipped his head to Wulfgren. "That it is. We have several of these all throughout Ulfgarath as well, but this is as good a place as any for one of them. So, my guess is the rumors are correct. We'll build something here. It'll keep the legions in the area supplied, and for winter, it'll give us a good fallback position and place to stay."

———

XAVIENO STOOD LISTENING TO THE RUMORS FROM THE DAY BEFORE BEING CONFIRMED AS Alessandros told them that the Legion was going to be splitting up. Xavieno and his squad were going to be some of the people staying back to build and maintain a fort that would act as a hub for supplies, men, and a fallback position for the rest of the Legion. He also found that Wulfgren and the other Gwenthari from Caelwen's settlement who had remained with the Legion would be joining Xavieno's group as well. He couldn't help but feel a small twang of apprehension about it—not so much about being on their own, but about being separated from Mariokos and Caelwen for a few months. They'd all turned into a family. Mariokos had always been family, but Caelwen had turned into it as well. At least he would still have Wulfgren and Ilara around. Though part of him found it amusing that some of the closest people he would have with him outside of those who were members of his squad were going to be the barbarians they were here to conquer.

As the meeting adjourned, Xavieno went back to his tent. He found Ilara there, and she looked up at him.

"You're done with your day sooner than I thought," she said. "Is everything alright?"

He nodded. "It's fine. We were just right about the Legion splitting up."

She nodded. "So do we move out in the morning?"

He shook his head. "No. Mariokos and Caelwen will be, but we won't be."

"Oh, we're staying behind?"

"Yes, so is Wulfgren and his people, but we're to build a fort and maintain the area and keep it defended," he said. He was surprised that she seemed not only okay with it but almost a little relieved.

"Are you done with marching?" he asked with a smile.

She smiled softly. "You could say that, but I like the idea of being someplace more permanent. That feels more comfortable, honestly."

"Even after years of raiding, you like the idea of staying put for a while?" he asked.

She shrugged. "There's something to be said for not having to move around all the time," she said. "I'll miss Caelwen and Mariokos, but it will be nice to be here for a while. And marching when it's hot out has been less than enjoyable."

He smirked. "You don't march; you sit on a cart with Caelwen."

"Yes, behind every other cart that's kicking up dust and has animals that are shitting everywhere. It's delightful," she said flatly.

He laughed deeply. "I never thought about that before."

She smirked. "Why would you? You're up at the front of the legions, aren't you? They want the Essaerists up front, so you don't deal with being at the end of a group of thousands," she said.

"I could see where that might be a little tiresome," he said.

"It's great in the rain, too," she said. "If the legion hasn't been in the area to build up the road, well, after that many people marched on it and the carts before us and all that. Let's just say I'm thankful that Caelwen's Essaerites are good at pulling us out of anything."

He grinned. "That's true. You're going to have to do more attendant-type things now, aren't you?"

She raised an eyebrow. "I suppose. But what?"

"I don't know, cooking, taking care of the camp," he said.

"I already do a lot of that," she said. "Caelwen's stump cooks, but that's just because it's a better cook than her or I. But otherwise, I already do a lot of that. I need something to do during the day."

"So you're telling me I'm about to take a hit on my meals?" he asked. "I'm not sure how I feel about that."

She chuckled. "Well, you can beat me, whip me, punish me whatever way you want, but either way, you're taking a hit on your meals. Without that stump, we're just out of luck."

He walked up to her and placed his hand on her hips. "I do suppose you have other things that you're good at, though. Things the stump wouldn't be so good at."

She looked up at him, her eyes twinkling, a little smirk tugging at the corner of her lips. "Do I? And have you tried the stump?"

"Yes, you do," he said, deciding not to comment about the stump.

She placed a finger on his chest and ran it down. "Well, that's good. After all, I do want to make sure that I am serving my owner properly," she said, her voice getting a little husky.

She looked up at him, and he felt his heart thump. There was something about this woman that he couldn't quite place. She seemed to have a power that was, in so many ways, something he'd seen before, yet so completely unique.

She glanced around. "It won't be time for dinner for a while. Perhaps you could make use of me?" she said, her voice almost innocent and sweet.

He couldn't help but grumble. "How are you able to do that?"

She smiled. "Do what, Dominaro?" she said in that same innocent voice.

"That," he accused.

She smiled softly and took his hand. "We all have talents."

"Yes, I am well aware of some of your talents," he said.

She looked up at him and bit her lip. "Yes. Is there a particular one of my talents that you would like now?"

He felt his heart thrumming in his chest, and he wondered why he had fought this for so long. He was thankful those times were behind him.

"You have a very wicked mouth. You know that," he said.

"I have been told that, Dominaro," she said, her voice soft and silky, and she slowly began to move to her knees.

She looked up at him, her hands expertly removing his belt from around his tunic and then lifting it. *A wicked mouth indeed,* he thought, and then he moaned softly as he felt soft lips and her tongue running up him. She took him into her mouth, and the world began to vanish as Ilara's head moved up and down.

———

THE NEXT DAY, XAVIENO WATCHED AS THE OTHER LEGIONS LEFT THE AREA, AND THEN, eventually, as the other half of his own legion left. Mariokos was already marching in formation when Caelwen came up to Xavieno and Ilara.

"You two watch out for yourselves," she said.

"You too," he said, giving her a hug.

She hugged Ilara and then turned to her brother.

"Aren't you going to ask me to watch out for myself?" he said.

Caelwen thought for a moment and shrugged. "Eh, it's fine," she said, then smiled and hugged him. "Be careful," she said.

"You too, little sister," he said, and Xavieno could see the seriousness in both their eyes.

In a way, it had to be so odd for them. He had been gone, being a mercenary for Lysandrian, then come home, and they had nearly died, found a new home in the legions, and were separating again. He could only imagine what that would be like.

After they were gone, he joined his squad and began the work for the day, which was going to be building up the fort. Mariokos had trenched around the original camp, which would be the basis for the fort. Now they would be building up more permanent walls. That would mean harvesting timber from the surrounding areas, as well as rock and anything else they could find.

They would need more drainage and space for permanent buildings. Xavieno knew that he'd be spending a great deal of time doing construction. They'd also need to set up patrol routes to the areas they had already taken and brought to heel. They'd be needing supplies from those areas and would need to make sure that nothing went poorly for them. They didn't want their new subjects to be killed or, conversely, for their new subjects to change their minds. He suspected that Wulfgren and his lot would have a lot to do with that, as the Legion didn't have much in the way of cavalry, except for those mercenaries they had hired. But he knew that it would be Legionnaires guarding the main routes to and from Ulfgard. He hoped he wasn't going to be part of that group, or at least not one that stretched too far away from the fort.

CHAPTER 35

There was a loud clang of metal on metal as Bergthral's Essaerite brought a hammer down, welding a small metal ring into place. The heat of the forge pressed against his skin, the acrid scent of burning metal mixing with the thick, smoky air. The rhythmic pounding of the hammer created a steady pulse, underscoring the tension in the room. Fernwen was working on making a shield or repairing one; it looked like. She had a small Essaerite that she was using to try and hold things together as she worked. He smiled watching his daughter. She was advancing quickly, so much more quickly than he had as a young Essaerist. He knew this was due to their mother's teaching, but he was still happy and proud of her to see it.

Next to her, working on a spear, was Eira. The woman didn't like violence, though for some reason, she didn't mind working on the tools of it. *I suspect she spent a lot of time doing things like this,* he thought. Eira was simple, but once you taught her how to do something, she was effective at it and could work for hours without complaining or slowing down. He suspected that's why she had lived as long as she had—because she was useful.

Valfric was busy sharpening a sword on a grinding wheel. He had a small pile of them next to him. There were only a handful of people from the neighboring settlements who were going. Bergthral had offered to help them prep weapons and armor as they got their farms and settlements in order. They were almost done prepping everything for their departure. There wasn't anyone from his settlement who would be joining them, something he was grateful for. They'd already lost people to the Lysandrian's and they didn't need to lose anymore.

Valfric turned the wheel and then checked the edge. Satisfied, he placed the blade down. "You seem to be rather good at this," Bergthral said.

Valfric grunted. "Well, I had to make a lot of repairs in the field, didn't I? If you don't know how to fix your equipment, well..."

"You didn't make your armor and sword with Essaeris?" Fernwen asked.

Valfric stopped what he was doing and grabbed a cup full of Bryndraught. He drank some. "Yes, I did, but the people who were on my team with me didn't, so we had to maintain everything that they had—shields, weapons, armor, saddles, you name it. Anything that was out with us, we had to be able to keep in good working order."

Fernwen looked thoughtful. "Why didn't you make Essaeris armor and weapons for them?"

"Simple," Valfric said, "because if I died, that equipment would go away," he said honestly.

"But not for a few hours or days," Fernwen said.

It was true. When an Essaerist died, their Essaerites or anything they made with Essaeris stuck around for a time. It depended on how long the Essaerite had been around, how much energy had been put into it, and how complex it was. But for something simple, you could expect a few hours, days, or even up to a week if it had been around for a long time.

Valfric spoke. "Maybe, yes, but it would go away eventually, maybe even in battle. Then all of a sudden, my friends would be there, standing with no weapons, no armor, no nothing, ready to be killed," he shook his head. "I wasn't going to put them in that position, and honestly, no warrior will ever put themselves in it either. It's fine for me. After all, if my Essaeris were to fail me, that would mean I was dead. I wouldn't have much need for a sword or a shield at that point anyway," he said with a chuckle.

"Valfric no hurt," Eira said.

Valfric sighed. "I'm not going to hurt anyone. I'm just explaining." He looked at the sword he had just sharpened, a scowl on his face.

"What is it?" Bergthral asked.

Valfric shook his head. "It's nothing."

"Obviously something's on your mind," Fernwen said. "Spit it out."

Valfric glanced at her. "Aren't children supposed to be quiet and let adults do their own things?" he asked. She just stared at him, and he grunted. "I think this is a bad idea," he said simply.

Bergthral spoke this time. "You think it's a bad idea for me to go and fight?"

Valfric shook his head. "Not you. The people who are going to be using these swords," he said. "All of this equipment. We're making it for them, repairing it for them. How long has it been since any of these people have ever had to swing a blade?" he asked, looking intently at Bergthral.

Bergthral ran his hand through his hair. "I don't know. Some of them have fought, but many haven't," he admitted.

"And they're going to die," Valfric said. "I'm sorry, Bergthral, but they have no business going against Lysandrian. I get that they want to, and I wouldn't ever tell someone that they couldn't. But they aren't going to be going after a group of bandits or vandals that are running amok in the area. They're going to be going after professional soldiers. And they're going to shit themselves the moment they hit Lysandrian's shield wall."

Bergthral saw Fernwen flinch just a little bit, but he wasn't going to pull her away from this conversation. He thought it would be good for her. She needed to learn, needed to grow. For her part, Eira didn't seem all that bothered by it for some reason. Perhaps it was because the violence wasn't happening now but was something that was being talked about.

Bergthral was thoughtful. "That might be the case," he said after a moment. "Tell me about it. Not about particular battles, but tell me about the legions, how they fight. You spoke about it before, but I'm about to face it," he said, trailing off.

Valfric re-situated himself in the seat that he was in and took another drink of Bryndraught. "I think that's a good idea," he looked over at Fernwen, "and I think it's good that you learned this too. Someday you might have to face them as well."

Valfric thought for a moment. "We fought them a lot, but we watched them even more, around Hroldenfell. There are a few things that you need to learn. For one, they dig in wherever they go. They create walls and forts; I've told you about them, but you'll need to watch for them. It makes it very difficult to fight them. You're not going to ever come up on them in a camp like we have, where there's just a bunch of tents and maybe some sentries. No, you'll have to get over a wall, through it, or through one of the entrances."

"How about in battle? How are they like on the field?" Bergthral asked, paying more attention to the words this time than he had when Valfric had first come into the settlement. He was going to need this advice.

"There's groups," Valfric started. "As we watched, we started to realize that they're separated by how good the men are in the legions. You see, when you first engage them, there's a group that's in front. I don't know if they have a name or what they are, but it's a bunch of men, just like us. Never any women, though—not like us," Valfric said. "But they're just a loose group. They come at you, just like we fight. There doesn't seem to be a lot of organization to it. You'll see a lot of different weapons, but most of them will also have javelins or large darts that they'll throw at you first. They tend to be more of a harassing force. You'll see them if their lines of the main legionaries ever break," Valfric explained.

"But once the fighting starts, they push back. And then, then you reach the real Lysandrian," Valfric said, looking down, his mind lost in memory.

Bergthral took a seat, and he saw Fernwen watching intently. For her part, Eira was just busy doing what she had been doing before, as if nothing had changed. But it did. Bergthral could feel it in the room, could feel the air shift.

Valfric continued to speak. "This first group, they look like the other ones at first, but when you get up close, you see they're different. They're all young, but they're good," Valfric said, looking up at Bergthral. "We watched them drill every day, train all the time. Their shields are large and rectangular. They cover a lot of them. When we first saw them, we thought it was silly, that it'd be difficult for them to truly fight. But then you see them fight as a unit. There's a wall of them. And they move slowly, one step at a time. They don't charge or rush you."

"Well, I suppose that will make some of it easier," Bergthral said, "with spears and arrows and the likes," he commented.

Valfric shook his head. "Spears and arrows don't do shit," he said. "The men behind the front line hold their shields over the heads of everyone. They completely encase themselves in them. You'll be throwing shit at them, shooting shit at them, and it does absolutely nothing. They just continue to walk slowly forward," Valfric said, a cool edge to his voice.

"They don't make a sound. You hear them shouting commands. You hear them giving marching orders, but they don't scream, they don't yell, nothing. It's almost more intimidating in a way, because it's just another day for these men. They're professionals, and war is their trade.

"You clash with them, and they work together. Many of the men in this first line are just as capable of fighters as any Gwenthari that I've ever met, but even though there's chaos along the lines, each of the units seems to work on their own, but they all work the same, you see. Whereas our groups," Valfric shook his head, "we didn't. We all have different weapons, different shields, different ways of fighting, different commanders. Not Lysandrian. Each unit is just like the other one. They all think and work the same, to the same end goal," Valfric said.

"But then eventually, you stop dealing with this first line. They retreat back, or they get tired, and then you deal with the next group," Valfric said. "These men are older, they're far better, their equipment is nicer and in better repair, and they," Valfric shook his head, "they are better than most Gwenthari that I've ever met. When it comes to battle," he said, "they won't rush you; they have no fear. They hold their discipline far better than the first group. You'll fight for a while, the battle will pulse, and you'll take a step back, and they take a step forward—always forward, never back. They progress on and on, and behind them are the fucks that you dealt with at the beginning. The loose men, waiting for a break in the line, the whole while they throw shit at you over the line of the legionaries in front of them.

"And then there's the last line," Valfric said.

Bergthral couldn't help but feel trepidation. He wasn't afraid of battle; he'd seen it many times, he'd experienced it. It was always terrifying in the moment, but never before, never the thought of it. Now, listening to Valfric, he could feel that slight fear creeping into him. Here was a man who had spent his entire life in violence. He had bathed in blood, and yet here he was, speaking of how terrifying and awe-inspiring this army was.

Valfric went on, "the last line, their equipment is far nicer than anything I've ever seen. Their armor gleaming. The men there are older still, and all of them are experts," Valfric said. "Many of them, most of them, are some of the best fighters that I've ever seen. They've been drilling for years, you see, training for years, longer than most Gwenthari have. When you reach that line, or if that line engages you, they don't lose, and they're fresh while what's left of your forces are tired and bloody." Valfric said. "That's what you're going against. That's what these farmers and tanners and smiths who've never swung a blade in their life are going to be going against. It's not going to go well. For you, well, you're an excellent fighter, and you're an Essaerist. You're going to do alright. They won't," Valfric finished.

Bergthral glanced over, seeing Fernwen looking down. He could see concern and worry on her face. His first instinct was to tell her to go away, to take Eira and go play, but he resisted that urge. *She needs this. She needs to know what the world is,* he thought.

"Tell me about the Essaerists," Bergthral said. "Tell me anything you know about them."

"They're good," Valfric said, "they're like you and your wife; they aren't like me. There's a few that we encountered," Valfric said, thinking, "There's a Gwenthari woman." He shook his head, "Fuck, I'm probably the reason why she joined the goddamn legion." He said, his voice bitter. "She's Wulfharboria; we were stalking her settlement; they were leaving the area. I don't know why, but we made to attack them. She was talking with some Lysandrian soldiers. I didn't know that they were Essaerists. One of the Lysandrian soldiers, that is. Anyway, I attacked them. She has large cats that she uses; they ripped through my wolves. She also created a type of armor, almost like vines and branches." Valfric shook his head, "Not like anything I've ever seen before, but with the Lysandrians, there was an Essaerist with them. He created Essaerites that were like legionaries."

This caught Bergthral's attention. "How did you know they were Essaerites?" he asked.

"Their faces," Valfric said. "They're in the shape of people, but not perfect. You could tell that it was an Essaerite. They fight just as effectively as any legionnaire does, if not more so, because they all work in unison."

Bergthral thought about that. "That's interesting."

"Yeah, that's exactly what went through my mind when I was getting my ass kicked," Valfric said, but he smirked. "Anyway, I don't think that man usually does a lot of combat."

"Why is that?" Bergthral asked.

"We watched him at Hroldenfell; well, we watched all of them, but he has a much bigger Essaerite. The thing's a giant monstrosity, but it doesn't fight. I watched it dig under the walls of Hroldenfell and bring them down," Valfric said.

"So he has an Essaerithon," Bergthral confirmed.

"Every Lysandrian Essaerist does," Valfric said. "One of the other ones that we fought creates these Essaerites that are slightly bigger than a person. They look almost like they're marble statues. They have four arms and can create blades, spears, bows and arrows, and shields." He said, "They're very quick, they're very powerful, and they're very deadly." He said, "I fought them on a few occasions and didn't do any damage to them. I watched them at Hrolden-fell, too, and obviously at the Ilfrun. You don't want to deal with them, but that bear of yours could probably take them down." Valfric said, "and then there's this other one." Valfric thought for a moment, and Bergthral could see him lost in some memory that was probably horrifying.

"It's giant, like the one that does the digging and the tunneling, but unlike that one, this one has four arms on the front of it. There are blades, like the ones that Hildrana uses on her Essaerite, but they're much longer. The arms can twist around, and the body also looks like it's made out of stone or ceram-ics." Valfric said, "I watched men throw spears at it, hit it with swords. It didn't do anything. I don't think I ever saw it take a single bit of damage at all." He said, "and those arms and those blades are sharp and powerful. I watched it cut a horse clean in two in Hroldenfell."

Bergthral shook his head. "It sounds terrifying."

"It is terrifying, and I hate to say this, but your bear isn't gonna stand a chance against it," Valfric said. "Believe me on it. It's got a bunch of legs. At the Ilfrun, I just watched it chew through groups of people. Nothing seems to stop the thing. It's not particularly fast. A horse can outrun it, but it can most certainly outrun a man. If you deal with it, you get the fuck out of there as fast as you can."

Bergthral nodded. "I will. Thank you," he said, trying to think of what an Essaerite like that would be. Anything that he could think of that would be able to take out his bear. Bergthral spoke. "On that note, how do you think my bear will fare against the legions?"

"Good," Valfric said. "It's big. It's tough. It can bull through their shield walls with ease. Just watch out. Those legionnaires don't back down from anything. I'm not sure they think of fear at all. Or if they do, it's been drilled out of them."

Bergthral nodded. "Thank you," he said. He looked. "It's starting to get dark. We should go in and have supper."

Fernwen looked a little pale. Her head bobbed, and then she seemed to get some life back to her. "Okay, Papa, we'll go in," she said.

As she walked by him, he placed his hand on her shoulder. "I'll be fine," he said.

She looked up at him and nodded. "Okay, Papa." She walked off.

As she left them, Bergthral turned to Valfric. And Valfric spoke. "I'm sorry."

Bergthral shook his head. "No, I wanted her here for this. She needs to know."

"That doesn't mean that I'm not sorry," Valfric said.

———

HILDRANA LAY IN HER HUSBAND'S ARMS, COVERED IN SWEAT FROM THEIR LOVEMAKING. IT had been so passionate, so desperate. It had to be. He was leaving, and they needed a memory in case things didn't go well. She felt her heart slowing down as her breathing did as well. She kissed his neck, tasting salt and sweat. She rolled on her back and thought. A breeze from the window came in, cooling her skin.

"What are you thinking?" he asked.

"You know what I'm thinking," she said.

He rolled on his side, his arm draping over her belly. He pulled her close. "I'm coming back to you," he said.

She tried to smile. She turned and kissed him. "You don't know that; I don't know that."

He ran a finger along her cheek and jawline, looking into her eyes. "I will try," he said.

"I know you will." She rolled on her side, facing him. Fernwen was also worried about him. She had seen it during dinner, and he had told her about the conversation they had had in the forge. She thought it was right that Fernwen had heard it. She needed to know what the world was, what her father was going into, and what possibly awaited her.

But what was on her mind was everything that Valfric had told them. When he had first come to the settlement and told them about everything that he had seen, it seemed like something far away in the distance. They'd listened, and they'd cared, but they hadn't really listened, and they hadn't really cared because it was something that they were potentially going to have to deal with years from then, not months. Now, that was different, and she was thinking of it differently as well. Her mind was racing, reeling with possibilities of what needed to happen and what could happen.

Her mind finally settled on something. "I'm going home," she said.

She saw Bergthral's expression darken for only a moment, and then he sighed. "I think that's probably a good idea. Valfric can protect the settlement," he said. That was one of the reasons why she was willing to do it. She wouldn't leave otherwise. She was loath to do it now, but Valfric could keep their people safe. Or at least the threat of an Essaerist could.

"I'll leave soon," she said. "I'll bring Fernwen with me."

"That's a good idea," Bergthral said. "It's good for her to see her homeland anyway, I suppose."

"It's only half her homeland," Hildrana reminded. "But I'll see what I can do. See if maybe I can get my people to at least abstain from what's coming."

Because she knew it was coming now; they couldn't afford to think otherwise. There weren't enough settlements that were going to be joining them. She was confident that her husband and the other people from Valfarans would be able to hold the Legion at bay. But the question was going to be for how long. Maybe forever. But probably not.

She didn't say this to her husband. She didn't need him to think that he was running on a fool's errand. That he was going to go fight in a war that wouldn't matter. Because it did; the battles that would soon come for her husband would give time for the rest of the people. It would give them time to figure out a way out. A way to make it so that they could live and so that they could be safe. Or, perhaps, if they were lucky, give them enough time that the Lysandrian Emperor went back to his capital and waited for years before returning.

She slept fitfully that night, and when the morning's rays came in the window and woke her, it was easy for them to do. She rose and had breakfast. Bergthral was quiet, and Fernwen was quieter still. Afterward, she helped him pack, and he and the other men from the settlement were gathered together at the edge of the settlement. Valfric stood next to her.

Valfric clasped Bergthral's hand and said, "I'll keep everyone safe."

Bergthral nodded, "I know you will." He walked up to Hildrana. Her heart was breaking and screaming, telling her to beg him to stay. He would. If she begged, if she asked him to do it, he wouldn't leave. But she wouldn't let her heart win. Instead, she kissed him deeply, wondering if it was going to be for the last time. He held her close, and then he looked down at Fernwen.

She looked up at him, her eyes red and ringed, dark from a night probably spent crying. He held her close for a moment and then stood and turned. She watched as he walked away, feeling as if part of her heart and part of her life was going with him. She sighed and turned to Valfric.

"Thank you," she said, her voice a little broken and hoarse.

He nodded solemnly. "Of course, he'll come home," he said.

"Do you really think so?" Hildrana said. "I do not believe in false hope."

Valfric looked at Bergthrals retreating form for a moment, then nodded. "Yes, yes, actually I do. I think he'll make it home."

"I hope you're right," she said.

CHAPTER 36

The legions had been splitting into smaller groups as they entered a "Secure the Countryside" phase of the campaign. Mariokos and his platoon, along with two others, were heading north. They were in a secluded area, or at least it appeared to be. Around them were short mountains that were more like forest-covered hills, their slopes draped in moss and thick undergrowth. The scent of damp soil and pine hung in the air, and the distant rustling of leaves hinted at unseen movement deeper in the forest. In between them were green patches with ditches and small streams that ran alongside. The road they were on was narrowish, and the legion moved along. Mariokos had hawks in the area that were keeping close to the trees, but with how dense the forest was, it was difficult to spot anything.

When he looked off to the side of the road into the trees, the forest floor was kept in perpetual twilight, the canopies so dense and thick that you could see only a little ways before it turned dark until night came and some of the plants began to glow. He knew for anything inside those trees, seeing out wouldn't be as much of a problem. Occasionally, he would have a bird try to weave through them, but the Essaerites spent more time avoiding tree trunks and branches than they did looking at the ground for threats, so they'd been relying heavily on soldiers to scout. It wasn't ideal, but it was unavoidable. The trees did provide one benefit, though: it would be difficult for armies large enough to pose a significant threat to their group to move around unseen.

As one of his hawks went high, he could see in the distance where they would be camping for the night. It was a small field, but it was the perfect size for their group. He was looking forward to being done with marching for the day. The road had gone up and down several of the smaller hill-type mountains, and his calves and legs were burning with the effort. Likewise, the heat wasn't helping either. He reached down to his belt and pulled out his water skin. He unstoppered it and took a long pull from it. The water wasn't cold, but instead was lukewarm, matching the temperature of the day and air around him. But still, it was nice. He had used Essaeris to flavor it, making it taste like a sweet juice. He put the stopper back in and continued his march forward.

Around him, there was only a little conversation. It was always like that at the end of the day—people trying to push through until the end. Then there would be the inevitable building of the camp. Then men could talk and relax while dinner cooked around the fire. One of his hawks landed on a branch. It gazed out over the formation of men as they marched along and then turned its attention to the deep, dark forest. Mariokos was about to turn it away when he noticed something. He had the hawk look back, and he caught the slightest bit of what looked like white fabric. The hawk looked more intently at the fabric, trying to make it out. Then it shifted and moved a little bit. It caught the movement of other things on the forest floor. Mariokos felt his heart jump in his chest.

Instinctively, his Essaeris rippled out of him, creating a horn. He brought it to his lips and blew hard, sounding the warning. As soon as he sounded the horn, his hawk noticed the forest floor explode as men and women in full armor came out.

Mariokos blasted the horn again, in a series of patterns telling everyone where he had seen the threat. Instantly, commanders began shouting orders, and legionnaires dropped their packs, quickly grabbing swords and shields. There wasn't time to don armor. Mariokos's Essaeris built and flooded through him, rippling out creating legionnaires in front of him. They quickly ran forward, creating a small shield wall. From the forest, he could see men and women running. They screamed at the top of their lungs in a battle cry.

The men of the legion hastily began forming up. And not a moment too soon, as soon the Gwenthari were on them. Mariokos joined, holding his shield up, moving alongside his Essaerites just in time to feel the attackers slam into him. He grunted, being pushed back, but he held his ground. He pushed against his shield and lashed out with a spear, batting another person's weapon away. There were more commotions as the battle began.

He heard orders being issued, and his panic and fear eased as his mind calmed and moved into the steady rhythm that was combat. His shield was hit by a sword, and he grunted, pushing the person away. He thrust with his spear, feeling it clack against the other person's shield, but it knocked them off balance, and as it did, one of his Essaerites next to him stabbed a man in the gut. The man groaned and collapsed, his hand trying to stop blood as it gushed from him, and the next moment, Mariokos's Essaerites all moved in unison, similar attacks lashing out all along the line. People fell and pushed back.

Though they were surprised and unarmored, the legion was gaining its footing. There was a shout of orders, and the men slowly moved forward. The Gwenthari crashed against them, and he heard the sound of some of his comrades' screams as they were cut and killed, but he kept his focus on the fight before him and on his Essaerites as they worked in unison. Pushing ahead, but not pushing too far, Mariokos didn't want to create an opening in the line.

Then, a ways down from him, he heard a crashing sound of wood splintering and saw a group of men falling to the ground. Behind them, something rolled. An Essaerite that was smaller than a man unrolled itself. It had the body of a lizard, its spine covered in some sort of armor. It had wide jaws and sharp teeth. Claws were on its feet, but the thing that was worrisome was the tail. It had a long tail with a blade running along it. It lashed its tail around, almost like a whip, cutting men's feet out from under them, literally.

More Essaerites crashed through the lines of men, and Mariokos's sergeant, Erastos, shouted to him, telling him to deal with the Essaerites. He pulled his own legionnaires back and had them run over, engaging the enemy Essaerites as they approached. Yet more were hitting. *Fuck, there's so many,* he thought. They weren't large, and they were rudimentary, so he suspected that the other Essaerist could create a decent number of them. They lashed out at Mariokos's Essaerites, and then rolled themselves up, coiling in on themselves and rolling away to go start the mayhem somewhere else. Mariokos gritted his teeth. "Fuck."

He saw one barreling through the underbrush rolling towards a group of men. It launched itself into the air, and then was hit by a brown blur that had colors on it. The Essaerite went down, and he saw one of Caelwen's giant cats rip its throat open. As it did this, its triple tails whipped around, looking for Gwenthari. He saw spikes shoot from them, hitting men and women. They gasped and screamed, then fell dead, falling victim to the deadly venom on the ends of the spikes. The Essaerite finished ripping the other Essaerite to pieces and then turned its attention to a group of people. Mariokos watched in awe and horror as it ripped a man's ribcage in two while its tails killed others. The other Essaerites were converging on it now, but Caelwen's other cats were there. He saw all four of them.

———

CAELWEN SAT IN HER CART, FEELING THE THING BUMP AND ROCK AROUND. THAT'S ALL the fucking thing had been doing—bumping and rocking around. She grunted as it hit a particularly big bump and jumped up, then came back down. Her back throbbed with a dull ache, despite having done nothing but sit in the damned cart all day. That's all she'd been doing. She would sit in the cart, make camp, sleep, be woken by a cunt with a horn, and do the same thing all over again. Without Ilara or Fïoralba around to keep her company, Caelwen had decided that she definitely did not enjoy life in the legions. It was something that Treftune seemed to feel as well. He was lying in what little shade he could find on the cart, on his back, his legs stretched out, his belly up in the air.

Whenever the cart would jostle around, he would move and occasionally twitch and grumble. "I feel you," she said to him.

They were next to a small stream, if it could even be called that. It was more of a ditch that had trickling water in it, but with the heat and the dust of the road, Caelwen looked at it longingly. *I could just go out and take a dip for a while,* she thought. It wouldn't matter that people would see her. Why would it matter at all? The water would be cold and cool and feel wonderful on her, wouldn't it? *No, I can't do that,* she thought, though the water did look so nice.

She squinted, looking closer, seeing moss and grime along its banks. She sat back. Maybe it didn't look nice after all. Perhaps the cart was better. It hit another bump. This time, it sent her slightly off her seat, and she came back down with a wince. Now, the ditch was winning again; it was so difficult to decide where she wanted to be miserable—in a filthy ditch or on her cart.

From up ahead, she heard the blast of a horn. She perked up instantly. That was the warning horn. Then there was another series of blasts. Next to her, Treftune scrambled up her back to curl around her neck. "Fuck," she said, feeling her heart instantly pick up.

Thoughts of the road and the ditch vanished. The entire column was stopping, and she heard men shouting. She turned her attention to the tree line, seeing figures moving. "Fuck," she shouted. She closed her eyes, and her Essaeris surged inside of her. It ripped out of her, creating one of her large cats.

She began building up Essaeris again. The cat that she'd created prowled around, anxious and eager to fight. She created another one. In the distance, there were shouts and screams. She opened her eyes, looking, feeling her blood run cold. There was another Essaerist. She closed her eyes again, focusing, pulling up the dregs of her power. The last cat came into existence. She created a little bag for Treftune to hide in, and she jumped off her cart. As she did, she felt her Essaeris ripple out, changing her attire. The last trick that Lorna had taught her before she left Ulfgard. She didn't have enough Essaeris to create her Essaerithon, but she didn't need that. She'd learned there were more effective things that she could create and do. Her boots shifted into vines that rooted into the ground, raising her taller than a man on horseback. Her dress extended down to her legs, just as if she had always been this tall, but it changed, turning into heavy leather. Her arms were covered in sleeves of the same leather, and along her chest and abdomen, bone armor came into existence.

Along her back, other armor came in, and from her waist, four vines that were like the tails on her cats came into being. Lastly, her deer skull helm came into existence and came down over her eyes. She created a staff of gnarled wood, with a roughly hewn giant emerald on the top, completing the ensemble. She knew she looked terrifying. She ran up the line towards the commotion, but stayed away from the front. Her cats bolted, moving up to the front ahead of the men, trying to head off any Essaerites that came around. She focused on one of them. It leapt into the air, crashing into one of the other Essaerist's Essaerites. It was some kind of lizard, she realized, but it didn't matter. Her cat was significantly larger than it, more advanced and more powerful. It ripped it into pieces, its tails whipping around, shooting venomous darts into the oncoming attackers. They gasped and screamed, dropping to the ground. Whether the dart hit them in the chest, arm, or leg, it didn't matter. All died to their deadly poison.

She was around back of the commanders now, and she came running up, seeing several of the officers on horses, including Theoliano and Alessandros. The latter turned, looking at her, his eyes going wide in shock. Her vined arms from her back lashed out, moving, shooting darts of their own over the heads of the legionnaires, killing more. She came to a stop next to them and focused on her Essaerites, guiding the cats in their work of death. The vines on her back automatically found Gwenthari to attack and took them out. It may not have been the most tactical way of fighting, but it was effective. She looked around, trying to find the enemy Essaerist. Caelwen was obvious and easy to find, and that was the hope—that perhaps the other Essaerist would focus on her.

Caelwen's eyes frantically scanned the group as the battle continued, and then they rested on somebody, and she felt a cold smile creep across her face. There ahead of her was a woman who was not engaging in the fight. She was middle-aged and wore nice armor. She locked eyes with Caelwen. Caelwen's vines came out and launched a dart at her. The woman's eyes widened, and she moved out of the way, but not fast enough. She screamed as the dart dug into her hip. Caelwen felt satisfaction as soon as the dart hit; she felt Essaeris pushing against her own. The woman's Essaeris instinctively kept the foreign object from spreading inside her body. In so doing, it stopped the venom that was on Caelwen's dart. She didn't know if you could push past it or not, but it didn't matter. The resistance on her dart meant that Caelwen had found her prey.

As the woman howled in pain, she saw her Essaerites flinch, unable to focus. Caelwen fired more darts at her. The woman was trying to stumble away, crawling, the dart deep in her hip. Caelwen's darts buried themselves in the trees and dirt around her. Finally, one found purchase in the woman's neck. She gave a gurgled, bloody scream, clasping at her neck. She choked on her own blood. This time when the third dart found her, the woman's Essaeris was not there to protect her, and she quickly died, succumbing to the venom. As she did, her Essaerites seemed to become confused, and it only took a few moments for Mariokos and Caelwen to dispatch them. As soon as they were gone, the other Gwenthari turned and began to retreat. Caelwen chased a few of them down with her cats, taking men and women down, hamstringing them, claws going into their backs, ripping spines out and ribcages open, and then it was over.

Her helm came up, her face wet with sweat, and she looked over, seeing both Theoliano and Alessandros looking at her. Alessandros's face looked pale —well, as pale as a Lysandrian face could. She found that amusing. The man was an ass. Theoliano likewise looked surprised, but she saw that shock and surprise fade, and she saw him smile. It was a grim smile. She returned it.

———

MARIOKOS STOOD BY A COMMAND TENT THAT WAS BEING ERECTED AS THE REST OF THE platoons worked on building the camp. Next to him stood Caelwen. Her dress was back to the one that he'd seen her in that morning. It was a light fabric, and the dress was sleeveless. He thought she looked lovely in it, and he suspected it was much cooler than the tunic he was wearing. She had been like something out of a nightmare during the fight. She had changed so much since they had been in Ulfgard. She was an altogether different Essaerist when it came to fighting. He was proud of her and, if he was being honest, a little bit scared of her as well.

With them were Theoliano, Alessandros, and Erastos, along with a few other commanders. Alessandros looked furious. "How did you not see that coming before it happened?" he demanded of Mariokos.

"I can't scout very far with the trees being this dense. Honestly, I think we're lucky we got what we did," he said.

Alessandros sneered. "Lucky we got what we did? Do you have any idea how many people died today?" he spat. "I should have you whipped!"

Next to him, Mariokos noticed Caelwen tense. Theoliano stepped forward. "He's right. You know how dense these woods are. That he found anything at all is a miracle. We looked where the Gwenthari had been hiding. They were in the underbrush and camouflaged. They've probably been there since last night," he said.

Alessandros looked over at Theoliano and seemed to deflate a little bit. This usually was how it worked. Alessandros was all hot air, but Theoliano actually knew what he was doing. "Why do you think they'd be so confident we'd be coming by then?" Alessandros asked.

Mariokos could see the effort it took Theoliano not to make a rude retort. "This is the only road in the area, sir, or at least the only one that a legion would travel on. I'm sure there are some goat paths around here," he said.

Alessandros's eyes narrowed ever so slightly. Then he huffed. "So how do we keep this from happening again? We aren't moving slower."

"We need to find a better way of scouting," Theoliano said. "Other legions have to do this with men. We're going to have to do it more now, too." Theoliano turned his attention to Mariokos and Caelwen. "Unless you two have any suggestions."

Mariokos thought for a few moments, then shrugged. "Dogs," he said. "I could create some small dogs. They'd move faster than the legion and could spread out farther than what our normal scouts would," he said.

"And they'd help?" Alessandros said.

"Dogs smell things," Caelwen said flatly. "It's useful."

Mariokos resisted the urge to smile. Alessandros could make Mariokos's life hell, but he would struggle to do so with Caelwen. He glared at her for just a moment, and then seemed to remember what she was like earlier in the day. His expression softened. "Alright, what's the catch?" he asked.

"I won't be able to create as many of them as I can hawks, and I won't be able to do as much in a fight," he said. "And it will pull a lot of my focus."

"That could be problematic," Theoliano said.

Alessandros was looking down and nodded. "Yes, but not as problematic as being caught off guard," he said. It was true. It was a balance. Mariokos was useful in combat. He could create more legionnaires, but the legionnaires they had could be far more effective if they had more warning.

Alessandros looked up. "And we do have you," he said, looking at Caelwen.

"You have me," she said, nodding.

"Though, it's not proper to use a woman in combat," Alessandros said with a sigh.

Caelwen snorted. "Fine. Think of me more like one of the barbarian mercenaries," she said, her tone a little acidic. Before Alessandros could glare, she said, "If you lose, I die just the same as the rest of you. And today, I didn't feel like dying. Should I have?"

Alessandros was taken aback. "No. No, you shouldn't have. You're right," he said. He looked over to Theoliano to save him.

Theoliano glanced over at Caelwen, and Mariokos noticed the corner of his mouth twitch in a smile. "I think if you had more of those Essaerites ready, it would be useful."

"I can do that," Caelwen said.

"Alright, then it's decided," Alessandros said. "Mariokos, I'm going to put you on one of the carts near the front, around command. If you have to put all your focus onto your Essaerites, I don't want you tripping and falling on these fucking roads," he said. "And you," he said, looking at Caelwen, "You're going to be on a horse, up with us as well."

"If you insist," Caelwen said. And Mariokos could hear the amusement in her voice. She hated being in the support caravan.

"Very well, then," Alessandros said. Theoliano looked over at Alessandros, and then back to Caelwen. Alessandros sighed. "Right. You did well today. I suppose there's a little compensation in order," he said.

Caelwen was thoughtful.

Theoliano spoke. "Perhaps I could handle this, sir. One hour."

Caelwen looked at him. "For four days."

Theoliano shook his head. "For two days."

"Four," she said.

He sighed. "Half an hour for five days."

She thought for a moment and nodded. "Very well."

Mariokos was resisting the urge to laugh or show any emotions at all as he was in front of command, but Alessandros looked confused. "A half-hour for five days? What is this, Theoliano?"

Theoliano barked a laugh. "The cheapest bonus we ever gave. The Legion will wake up a half hour late for the next five days," he said.

Caelwen nodded, satisfied.

Alessandros still looked confused, and Theoliano spoke. "She hates hearing the horns in the morning."

Mariokos knew that if Alessandros had bothered to learn about those around him, he'd know Caelwen hated the horns. But Theoliano knew because he actually gave a shit.

Alessandros looked a little dumbfounded. "So instead of taking money, you're choosing to sleep in?"

"Yes," Caelwen said. "For an extra thirty minutes for the next week," she beamed. "It's been a pleasure doing business with you, gentlemen," she said, and turned and walked away.

Theoliano chuckled and looked to Mariokos. "You're dismissed."

Mariokos nodded and turned, catching up to his wife. "Someone seems proud of herself."

She smiled. "I am."

"And taking out another Essaerist," he said.

This darkened her mood a little. "It was necessary."

He stopped her, taking her hand gently. She looked at him. "It was necessary. You saved a lot of lives," he said.

Her expression softened. "Of course."

Erastos was next to them. He looked down at Caelwen. "You did good today, but things need to start changing," he said.

She raised an eyebrow. "Excuse me?"

"You," he said. "Look around you."

She did, and Mariokos noticed it. All the men were looking at her, not in fear, but with respect. Erastos went on. "You're used to being underestimated. You need to stop that now. These men respect you. You're an icon for them. You've proven yourself all the way from Hroldenfell," he said. "I'm proud of you. Let them be proud of you, too," he said and walked off.

Caelwen didn't look like she knew what to say.

"He's right," Mariokos said.

She looked at him. "About what?"

"About being respected," he said.

"I don't know about that," she said as they began to walk. But within a few steps, they heard a handful of muttered 'Dominara' as she passed by, and men dipped their heads in respect.

"Just from today," she said under her breath, and he could tell she was uncomfortable with the attention.

He shook his head. "No. You helped us at Hroldenfell. You helped before. You've patched up the wounded. You kept those birds off people's heads in

Ulfgard. And you've fought alongside them. You've helped them. You've taken care of them. And now, you've also proven that you're willing to be brutal to protect them. These people respect you, Caelwen. You may not have been Lysandrian before, but you might be the deadliest person in the whole of the empire," he said with a smile.

She snorted, but he could tell that she kind of liked it. He gave her hand a squeeze. "Well, I guess there's a worse thing than being adored by a large group of men who keep themselves physically fit," she mused.

He laughed. "Do I need to be worried?" he asked.

She smirked. "No, but I can still like the idea of it," she said.

He laughed again. "I suppose there's nothing wrong with that."

CHAPTER 37

Before Hildrana was a large leather sack. The inside of it was divided into compartments with other pieces of leather. It was time for her to go. With her was Fernwen, and the two of them worked silently as they packed, the soft rustle of fabric and the faint creak of leather straps the only sounds in the quiet room. There wasn't a lot that they needed to bring. On the table rested three rectangular Essaerites. They were called Essaerums, and to her knowledge, the Eirfrosti were the only Essaerists that regularly employed them. Gwenthari did not write, strictly speaking. There were some runes that were used for religious purposes and ceremonies, and she knew that the Wyrdrunirs wrote, but the Gwenthari didn't. This was part of what Hildrana thought held them back. They weren't able to pass knowledge on from one generation to another as easily. Lysandrian did not have that problem. From what she had been able to gather, they had more paper with writing on it than they did grains of wheat. The Eirfrosti had Essaerums, but only the Essaerists. She looked over at Fernwen, seeing them sitting on the table. Hildrana reached out, touching them, letting her mind read through their contents.

"You're doing very well with it," Hildrana said.

Fernwen nodded. "Thank you," she said.

Fernwen hadn't fought learning Essaerums like Hildrana had when she was younger. They were something that she hadn't seen the value in. Now she could see how wrong she'd been, especially with how heavily Eirfrosti Essaerists leaned on poisons, tonics, and other things of that nature.

"Mama, why do we have three of them?" Fernwen asked. "Plus that little one that you keep on you."

Hildrana smiled. "For redundancy," she explained. "You see, even though they're very tough, if they're broken or destroyed, you have to recreate them. And the little one is so I can keep notes for my day."

Fernwen looked thoughtful. "So, couldn't you just copy them from another Essaerist?"

"Yes, but that would require that you find another Essaerist, and all of your own personal notes would be lost," Hildrana explained. Fernwen nodded.

Essaerums were different in their level of complexity. The materials they were made out of were exceedingly simple, and they took almost no Essaeris to make. Essentially, each of the rectangles was a little box. Inside the box were sheets of material that had differences in them—slight differences. It created writing and words, though very compressed.

Copying them was likewise easy. You could copy your own Essaerites with little to no effort, and if another Essaerist allowed you to inspect their creations, you could do likewise. In this way, messages were passed between Eirfrosti Essaerists, and they could be small enough for a bird to carry. It gave the Eirfrosti an incredible edge over other Gwenthari.

Most Essaerists also had an Essaerum that contained their personal notes —all of their teachings, everything they'd ever thought worth recording. Hildrana kept three of them: one near her or on her person at all times, and the others hidden, just in case something went wrong. Even if she wasn't right next to one, she could copy it just by feeling it.

She also kept a small one on her where she could put thoughts or tasks for the day. To others, it made it seem as though she was incredibly knowledgeable and good at everything that she did. But Hildrana knew it was just that she had a very large repository of information, information she had copied from her mentor, who had copied it from his, and so on and so forth. All of the knowledge of the Eirfrosti Essaerists could fit in her pocket.

But they were difficult to learn. One had to master reading materials and also making materials with very fine control. She had never taught it to Bergthral. It was one of the things that was a secret for her people. They were also difficult to create from scratch—not the object itself, but all of the knowledge in it.

She saw Fernwen holding a small doll Eira had made for her, out of some scraps of fabric and twigs. It wasn't anything to look at, but Fernwen loved it.

"What's wrong?" Hildrana asked.

Fernwen looked at the doll and then placed it in the bag. "I'm going to miss everyone here," she said, "and I'm worried about Papa," she admitted.

Hildrana stopped what she was doing. "I worry about him too," she said honestly.

Fernwen looked up at her, and Hildrana sat down, taking her daughter's hand. "But he's doing what he needs to do, and we're going to do what we need to do."

"And Eira and everyone else will be okay," Fernwen said. "They have Valfric to protect them."

Fernwen looked thoughtful, and Hildrana smiled softly. "He may not be the best craftsman," she said.

"No, I know. He's good at the other stuff," Fernwen said.

Hildrana raised an eyebrow. "How do you know that?"

"I've watched him and Papa training and sparring."

Hildrana hadn't known about that, and she doubted Bergthral had either. She nodded. "Did you have an Essaerite watching them?"

Fernwen's cheeks flushed. "Yes. Sorry."

Hildrana shook her head. "Don't be sorry. I'm happy that your Essaerites have progressed that far. I didn't know that they had."

Fernwen shrugged. "It's really basic, but it is able to see stuff. I watched them. I'm sorry," she said.

"Watching and listening is what our people do," Hildrana said. "Always remember that. Think of how much time we spend learning to sense with our abilities. There's no difference when it comes to our eyes and our ears and our noses. We are always watching, always looking," she said.

Fernwen nodded.

"So does seeing that make you feel worse or better? Having seen Valfric spar," Hildrana asked.

Fernwen was thoughtful for a few moments. "Better. Valfric seems nice, grumpy, but nice. I know his back hurts him. But he's very good with a sword. He's a different person," she said, her eyes far off.

Hildrana nodded. She had watched, too. Valfric was indeed a different person. Hildrana suspected that it wasn't the real Valfric, but it was the Valfric that he thought was the real him. The brute, the warrior, the raider. But she wasn't sure that was actually who he was, or who he was ever meant to be. It was just what he learned to be, and he'd lost himself to it. *Maybe someday he'll find his way back,* she thought. But she thought it unlikely. Valfric's hands were too drenched and stained in blood—not the blood of defense, not of honor or love, but of greed, lust, and vengeance.

It had poisoned him and turned him into whatever he'd been before he met Eira. Hildrana knew that it was only Eira who kept Valfric's learned nature at bay. Eira made him better. Hildrana turned her attention back to the conversation.

"I've watched, too. He's a different person when he fights. That's why I think our settlement will be safe," Hildrana said.

"Even though his Essaerites aren't as powerful as yours or Papa's?" Fernwen asked.

Hildrana nodded. "Yes, they aren't as powerful, but he has more of them, and Valfric thinks differently than we do. I think people would be unwise to test him," she said, and she wholeheartedly agreed with that. She knew Valfric would struggle with some of the people of the settlement, but she didn't think it would be for reasons other than the normal disputes between neighbors.

No, if anybody tried to do anything to their settlement, Hildrana knew that those people would regret it. And unless they came with a large force, Valfric would easily be able to push them away. "Besides, if Valfric sees something he thinks is too difficult, he'll get everyone out," she continued.

Fernwen nodded. "He's good on the road and hiding, isn't he?" she asked.

Hildrana nodded. "Yes, and there aren't many people who live here. I dare say that he would be able to get them someplace safe," she said. She patted Fernwen's hand. "We need to finish packing. Speaking of Valfric and Eira, they should be here before too long."

Fernwen turned and then paused. "What will it be like in Eirfrosti?" she asked, but she continued packing.

Hildrana started packing again. "I don't think you will find it so different. We'll be in a larger settlement, but your father and I run this settlement like the Eirfrosti, so I'm not sure you will see much of a difference."

And this was true. In many ways, Bergthral and Hildrana led their settlement like it was an Eirfrosti one. There were no slaves. There was not the same power dynamics that there were in other settlements. For Fernwen, she'd just be seeing something larger.

Not long after, there was a knock on her door, and she opened it, finding Valfric and Eira.

"Good afternoon," Hildrana said warmly.

"Afternoon," Valfric said, walking in.

"Hildrana," Eira said, and then greeted Fernwen.

Fernwen walked up to Eira and smiled, "How are you today?"

Fernwen led Eira outside. Hildrana saw Valfric watching.

"She's going to miss her a lot," Valfric said.

"Who's going to miss who, Fernwen or Eira?" Hildrana asked with a wry smile.

"Both," Valfric replied. He looked over at her bag and sighed. "When are you leaving?"

"Tomorrow," Hildrana said.

Valfric nodded. "Very well, what do I need to keep in mind?"

Hildrana sat down. "There are a few relationships with people around here that you might want to know about, but nothing too drastic."

He looked thoughtful. "Have you talked to everyone about leaving?"

She nodded. "Yes, I have. Everyone's on edge, but they understand," she said.

He looked thoughtful. "How do they feel about me being their protection?"

Hildrana chuckled dryly. "They actually feel pretty good about that, I think. They know you were a warrior, and that you're not someone to be messed with, so I think that's good. It's just with both Bergthral and I leaving..."

He nodded. "No, it's a lot. I'd be lying if I said I wasn't uneasy about it."

She couldn't help but smile. "You're worried you won't have me to protect you?" she teased.

He snorted. "Worried I won't have you to make decisions. I know I'm not leading this settlement, but," he said, letting it trail off.

She nodded. "I understand. We felt the same way when we first started this settlement. People look to us for wisdom and protections, and it just naturally led to leading them. You're a natural leader, Valfric, so the people will look to you."

He sighed. "Yeah, that seems to happen to me a lot."

"So why are you worried about it?" she asked.

He shrugged. "I know how to lead raiding parties. I know how to teach people how to hide. I know how to teach them how to fight. Everything. I don't know how to run a settlement," he said honestly.

"Well, thankfully there aren't very many people, and they'll always tell you when you're wrong," she said lightheartedly.

He chuckled. "I have no doubt that people will have no issues telling me that I'm wrong." He ran a hand through his hair. "Will you be okay over there?"

"I'll be fine. It's my family," she said.

"I know, but it sounds like you didn't leave on good terms," he said.

"I didn't leave on bad terms with my family," Hildrana said, "but, well, we'll see how it goes. We're not going to be in any danger over there. Truth be told, the people over here are in far more danger if Lysandrian is moving as fast as we've heard," she said.

He seemed to think about that for a bit. "Yeah. Yeah, that's crossed my mind, too. And if things get bad here," he asked.

Hildrana was thoughtful. "The settlement has enough fishing boats for you to make it across the channel to Eirfrosti," she said.

"Would we be welcome there?" he asked.

"I can make it so that you are," she said.

"Right," he said. "I'm not in a rush to do that either. Still, it's good to know that it might be an option."

———

CAELWEN WAS STANDING ON THE SMALL SLOPED HILL THAT THE CAMP WAS BUILT ON. SHE looked out over the walls, seeing the town that was in front of them. It was much larger than most of the towns they had seen thus far, and it was creeping up the side of a small mountain. The mountain was rocky and craggy and surprisingly well-placed as far as tactical things went, or at least that's what Mariokos had told her. With the rocks and the hill, it was difficult, if not impossible, for his Essaerithon to tunnel underneath the walls like it had in so many other places. And those walls were different from so many of the small villages and towns. They were made of both soil and timber. Atop them were covered walkways where men and women shot down at the legions the few times they'd approached them. They had been here for a couple of days. The platoons that they had been traveling with were the first to arrive, and a few others had trickled in. The idea was to wait until there were enough legionnaires here to take the town without too much issue. They had tracked the people that had attacked them to this place, and she wondered if they had any other Essaerists inside, though part of her doubted it as she hadn't seen any activity that would indicate it. And after all, if they had more than one Essaerist, why just send the one out into the field? She had all four of her cat Essaerites standing guard, and she was making her way to the command tent.

It had been an odd change. She'd always been ignored, by and large, by command. The general, Damianello, would give her credence, but Alessandros didn't, and while she liked Theoliano, he didn't have many reasons to talk to her. That had changed as she had been moving with command. As she walked towards the tent, Mariokos joined her. He reached down and interlaced his fingers in hers.

"How was your day?" he asked.

She smiled.

"Fine. Yours?" she asked.

"Fine. My Essaerithon has just been helping some of the other platoons with drainage and things of that nature," he said. "But I need to work on it more," he commented.

"Why?" she said.

"To just make some alterations for when we have to attack the town. I assume, anyway," he said.

They were to the command tent now. There was an assortment of men inside. Some she knew, others she didn't. Alessandros and Theoliano glanced up at them, Theoliano giving her the slightest of nods. He spoke to Mariokos.

"Are all the other camps good to go?" he asked.

Mariokos nodded. "Yes. They are finishing up some drainage, but nothing that should be any consequence," he said.

"Good," Theoliano said.

Alessandros spoke. "So, can it make it through the wall of this town?"

Mariokos shrugged. "Eventually, yes. But I think we're going to need to use regular siege engines, unfortunately. The walls are just high enough that they're able to get rocks and other things to come down with enough force to actually do damage to my Essaerithon. Plus, it'll take a little while to chew through it," he said.

Alessandros looked thoughtful. He looked over at Caelwen. "Do you have any ideas?"

She thought for a moment. She did have ideas, and it was strange that they were asking her about them. *Perhaps they've decided to look past the fact that I'm a barbarian woman because I'm an Essaerist,* she mused.

"I can attack the walls," she said, "but my Essaerites can't make it through them. They could climb over them, harass, I suppose," she said. "Has the town offered to surrender?"

Alessandros shook his head. "No, they haven't, and I don't see any reason why they would," he said.

She looked thoughtful.

"What is it?" Mariokos asked.

"Well, I don't know," she said.

"Spit it out," Theoliano said.

"Maybe they just aren't scared enough," she said.

Alessandros gave her a flat stare. "You don't think the legions are frightening?"

"Of course they're frightening," she said. "But the people are behind tall walls, aren't they?"

"So how would you plan on making us more frightening?" Mariokos asked.

"You and I," she said.

He raised an eyebrow and then nodded. "Oh, right, I see. We're Essaerists. We killed their Essaerist," he mused.

"That makes us frightening," she said.

"They haven't been worried about you so far," Alessandros said, his voice sounding irritated.

"We haven't really been that spooky, though, have we?" Mariokos said. She could see him getting animated. "What if I," he thought, "I need to make changes to my Essaerithon anyway before I can start really going after that wall. I could make some of the changes more on the appearance," he said, "like you did with your Essaerites. That's had an effect."

She nodded, and Theoliano spoke. "Yes, your new Essaerites have definitely had an effect," he said, thinking.

Alessandros didn't say anything.

This wasn't surprising. Alessandros, at his core, was an idiot and coward. He always stepped back and let the others hash things over before coming to a decision.

"So we make yours look more intimidating," she said.

"And then flanked by your four cats," he said. "But that might not be enough. But with the legionnaires in armor and in formations behind them," he said.

Caelwen nodded. "That would be terrifying."

Alessandros looked thoughtful. "So what? They're going to be scared of us, so they're going to open their gates and let us kill them," he said.

"We haven't offered them a deal yet," Theoliano said, and Alessandros looked over at him.

Mariokos perked up. "We haven't?"

Alessandros shook his head. "No, we've been waiting for reinforcements," he said. Alessandros seemed to like this idea. "So, we intimidate them, ask them if they want to surrender," he said.

Theoliano shrugged. "It could work. We could give them the same deal we've given everybody else who hasn't resisted," he said. "If they turn it down, we still attack. It could save time and resources."

"But they did lock up their city," Alessandros said.

"Because there was an army sitting outside of it. I'd lock the gates too," Caelwen said.

Alessandros was thoughtful. "It's worth a try. But if not, how do we get through those walls?" he said.

She could understand this line of thinking more than most people did. You had to be practical about things.

Mariokos was thoughtful. "It'll take me a few days to make the needed changes to my Essaerithon, but I have a few changes that I think I could make that would make it so it could get through the wall a little bit quicker. Plus, with the extra things to make it look more intimidating," he mused.

That seemed to satisfy Alessandros. He turned to Theoliano. "Drill the men over the next few days. Make sure the Gwenthari can see it," he said.

Theoliano nodded. "Yes, sir. We can do that."

Alessandros dismissed them, and they walked out of the tent.

Theoliano came out a minute later. He patted Mariokos on the shoulder. "Good job. You impressed him, I think."

"Thanks," Mariokos said.

Theoliano looked over at Caelwen. "And he's fucking terrified of you." He smirked and walked off.

Mariokos couldn't help but smile, seeing Caelwen grin—the way her eyes sparkled with a blend of mischief and pride.

"I think you're enjoying your new role," Mariokos said.

"I am," she said. "I like being scary."

CHAPTER 38

Hildrana felt the small fishing boat that she and Fernwen were on rock and roll on the water. She had two Essaerites attached to the belly of the boat. They had large tails that swished back and forth in the water, pushing them along. It was mid-morning, and the fog had almost burned off the water when she could make out the dark form of Eirfrosti before her.

She had sent a bird ahead to warn her family that she was coming. It was not only the polite thing to do but also a tradition for any Essaerist returning to a settlement or town after being away. The boat rocked and rolled more and crested over waves as they drew closer. As they did, the dark shape before them transformed into land, shifting from dark to green, and she could hear the sound of water lapping against the shore.

Soon enough, new shapes began to emerge from the fog. First, the pier came into view, then fishing boats pulled up along the beach. She could hear the sounds of gulls and the murmur of people. The Essaerites underneath the boat pushed forward, continuing onward. She was looking forward to this portion of the trip being done with. She didn't enjoy being on the sea, though she had done it plenty as a girl.

As they traveled closer to the shoreline, she had thrown one of her Essaerums over the edge. It was the perfect hiding spot for one. The water was deep, and she made the outside of it look like any other rock. This was a trick she had learned long ago: *The water hides all.* The pier came into focus, and soon she could make out the texture of the old, worn wood as it emerged from the water, with figures standing atop it.

She couldn't help but feel a mixture of happiness and unease as she saw her family waiting for her.

"We're here," she said to Fernwen.

Fernwen had been quiet during the entire trip, and Hildrana knew it had been hard for her to leave her home, but this was her home too, and it was time that Hildrana showed her that. The boat pulled up to the pier, and she threw a line over the edge.

An old man with long graying hair and a bald spot caught the rope and tied it to the pier. He held out his hand, and Hildrana took it, feeling her father's grip as firm as it had ever been. He pulled her up onto the pier, and then he looked down with his watery blue eyes and grinned, "Is that my granddaughter?" Alaricth asked in a deep, booming voice.

Hildrana smiled. "Yes, it is. Come, meet your family, Fernwen," she said.

She pulled Fernwen onto the pier, who looked at her family quizzically. "It's good to meet you," Fernwen said.

Alaricth grinned and, without warning, moved down and scooped Fernwen up into his arms, holding her tight. "Well met, little one. I have waited a long time to meet you," he said, and Hildrana caught the sound of true joy in his voice. It was a rare tone to hear in her father's voice, and she savored the moment.

He set a surprised Fernwen down, and then Hildrana's mother, Aelis, approached. Her hair, too, was gray like her father's, something that hadn't been the case when she'd last been home so many years ago. Aelis knelt down, holding Fernwen's shoulders and looking into her eyes. She smiled.

"It is good to have you home," she said. Aelis stood and looked at her daughter. "It is good to have you home, too," she said.

"Thank you, Mother," Hildrana said. She looked over at her father, who nodded, his expression of joy gone, replaced by the stoic grimness she had been accustomed to her entire life. The next figure shuffled forward: her brother, Branrik.

He was a little younger than Hildrana. His hair was coal black and shaggy, and his eyes a vibrant blue. He looked sickly and thin, and he walked with a limp. Next to him was the hulking form of a Wolxaran. Its black fur was shaggy, and it regarded all of them with cold eyes. It had always looked that way at everyone.

She felt Fernwen move just a little bit closer to her. Branrik smiled and stepped forward, reaching out his hand. Hildrana ignored the gesture and walked forward, wrapping her arms around him. He hugged her back.

"It is so good to see you," Branrik said, and his voice sounded earnest. He looked down. "It is so good to meet you," he said to Fernwen, pulling a little flower out of a pocket. "This is for you," he said.

The flower was white, and Fernwen took it and smiled. "Thank you," she said. The Wolxaran stepped forward, gave Hildrana a noncommittal sniff, and stared at Fernwen for a moment before sitting down.

"I think that's the warmest reception I've ever gotten," Hildrana said.

Branrik looked down at the beast. "I think that is the most excited I've ever seen Eilfrik to see you, but I think it's Fernwen that he likes," he said.

Eilfrik stood up and walked towards Fernwen, sniffing her. She held out a shaky hand. The Wolxaran in Eirfrosti were much larger than those on the continent. Hildrana had almost forgotten how much so. Eilfrik was a beast that inspired fear and awe, but he was good luck and bonded to her brother Branrik. This made Branrik something of a special person, which she thought was probably good considering that he had always been frail and weak.

Eilfrik sniffed Fernwen's hand, gave it a lick, and then walked off the pier. Hildrana was shocked. Fernwen stood next to her, trembling a little bit. Alaricth grunted.

"That monster growls at me every day, though I give it food and shelter. And here, it licks your hand," he said, inspecting his granddaughter. "Well, I guess that confirms she's special."

"That she is," Aelis said. She turned to her daughter. "Please, come in; you must be hungry."

Hildrana smiled and nodded. "Yes, that would be most welcome."

They walked along the pier, hearing the wood creak beneath their feet, to a gravel path that led up into the main part of the settlement. All around were houses that were dug into the ground more than those on the continent. Many of them had grass and plants growing right over the roofs.

She noticed Fernwen looking around, wide-eyed, as people worked and went about their day. "It's so much bigger than our home," Fernwen said softly.

Hildrana nodded. "Yes, Branthorn is much larger than our home. It's a proper town."

And it was. Her father had been the head of it for as long as Hildrana could remember, and they wound their way through the town with people greeting them, waving, smiling, and nodding at her parents in respect. The same was said for Eilfrik, though he growled at a few people. They came to a house that was mostly stone and had a high thatch roof, its weathered walls stained by years of coastal wind and brine. The gravel path beneath their feet crunched softly with each step, and the distant call of gulls mixed with the hush of waves meeting the shore. A salty breeze tugged at their cloaks, carrying with it the scent of hearth smoke and the faint tang of the sea. She looked up fondly at her childhood home, feeling herself smile.

"It always feels good to come home, doesn't it?" her father said.

She nodded. "Even if it's not really your home anymore, it always is," she said.

He nodded. "I felt that way every time I came to my parents' house."

He pushed open the door, and they entered, met with the smell of cooking bread and a fire burning in the fireplace. Aelis went and gathered cups, pouring Bryndraught into them and handing them to Fernwen and Hildrana. She took a grateful sip and sat around the table, hearing the fire crackle in the fireplace.

She noticed her brother limping along. He winced and stopped for a while, before he heavily sat down next to her, Alaricth and Aelis joined him.

"So, what brings you home?" Alaricth asked.

He wasn't going to stretch out the pleasantries. That wasn't the way her father was. It wasn't their relationship.

"There's problems on the continent. Lysandrian is attacking Valfarans," she said.

Alaricth grunted. "We heard a few things about that. I take it your husband is off fighting them like a fool?"

"Papa's not a fool," Fernwen said, glaring at Alaricth.

He glared right back at her, and Hildrana spoke. "He and I both thought about it, and yes, he's gone to fight, to hold Lysandrian as long as possible, or to dissuade them from moving further north," Hildrana said. "I think this is the wisest course of action." Her tone was formal, cool, and collected.

Her father glanced at her, then nodded. "Fine. So why are you here? Are you worried that he's going to fail?" he asked.

She shook her head. "No, I'm here to make sure that Eirfrosti doesn't help Lysandrian."

Her father barked a laugh. "Why would we side with the Lysandrians?"

"You wouldn't, but if given the opportunity with a weak Valfarans..." she said.

He sighed, and it was Branrik who spoke. "We would take advantage of it," he said.

Branrik may have been weak of body, but he was sharp of mind, and Hildrana didn't know anyone who could think down the road more than he could. It was something their father must have trusted, because he seemed to sigh and acquiesce.

"So you want us not to take advantage of a good opportunity," Alaricth said.

"I was unaware you'd begun raiding, Father," she said.

He waved her off. "You know I'm not talking about me; I'm talking about others," he said.

"Yes, that is what we're here to ask for," she said.

Her father groaned a little. "Fine, you're obviously more than welcome to ask, and you're more than welcome to stay here."

"Thank you," she said.

Aelis spoke. "This is not the conversation to have now. Come, Fernwen, let me show you around the house," she said. "Branrik, will you be a dear and get some firewood?" she asked.

Branrik grunted and got up, walking out, leaving Hildrana and her father alone.

Her gaze followed her brother, and as soon as he was out of earshot, her father answered the unasked question.

"He's getting worse," he said.

Hildrana's expression darkened. "I can see that. Is it just the limp?"

Alaricth shook his head. "No, it seems to be everything," he said, and she could see how much it was weighing him down.

I wonder if this is why his hair has turned gray, she thought, *or was it just the leadership he faced, having to lead? Perhaps it was both.*

"I take it there's nothing anyone can do," Hildrana said.

Alaricth shook his head. "Never has been, never will be," he said. He sighed. "Honestly, you coming back," he said.

"Bad omen," she said.

He shrugged. "Just an omen. Doesn't mean that it's bad, does it?"

He sat back in his chair, and it creaked.

"I am sorry to come back to you with sad tidings," she said.

He waved her off. "Don't be. I understand why you haven't been home. Believe me. But now that you're here, we'll make the best of it." Then, after a moment, he said, "That daughter of yours," trailing off.

Hildrana smirked. "Has her grandfather's attitude," she said.

Alaricth grinned. "That she does. I guess she'll do alright," he said.

Hildrana chuckled. "I think she will. You're going to like her," she said.

He nodded. "Of course I will. She's my granddaughter. What's there not to like?"

———

THE SKY ABOVE THEM WAS A DEEP GRAY THAT THREATENED RAIN, THOUGH MARIOKOS found it doubtful that it would come. It had been hot as of late and dry. They would see clouds, but rarely would they get a shower. He was standing next to the men of his squad. Around them were Command and the rest of the platoons, along with Caelwen. His Essaerithon was much the same as it had been before, though now it had extra shielding in the form of a covering that was bone-white and hard. It wasn't hard-wearing so much as for show. He had put some colorful flourishes on it, and they had attached emblems from the Empire and the Legion, giving it the appearance of an Essaerite meant for war, not for toiling in the ground and building.

On either side of it were Caelwen's large cats, and behind them, the legionnaires. Alessandros and Theoliano were standing at the head, watching as several messengers from the Legion approached the city. From the walls of the town, Mariokos saw people looking down—men, women, and children. They jeered and shouted things at the messengers, but the men approached the gates, professional as ever. There was a slight crack in the gates, and the men went inside, and then it was time to wait. The messengers were to tell the leaders of the town that they had until nightfall to make their decision. Then, the Legion would attack, though Mariokos knew that it wouldn't attack until the next day. The assumption was that there would be a little back and forth, as there usually was, about the terms of the town's surrender, or if they weren't going to surrender at all. Mariokos hoped that they would.

And so they waited. As per the terms of engagement, both he and Caelwen's Essaerites stayed away from the city. Both of them had a handful of small birds that they were using—nothing major and nothing that took too much of their Essaeris—but he kept them away from the city. Instead, they circled around the area, making sure that the Legion wasn't going to be ambushed or approached from behind, or that the town wasn't evacuating or receiving reinforcements. Neither appeared to be happening. And so they waited. Mariokos found himself thankful for the cloudy day, as the sun wasn't bearing down on him. After a while, Caelwen approached. Her face and neck were covered in a sheen of sweat from the heat, and her expression was hard and concerned.

"How are you holding up?" he asked.

She looked over at him and then back to the gates of the town. "I'm fine. I'm wondering what they're going to do," she said.

He'd wondered that as well. Their play had been a smart one, but the Valfarans were different from the Ulfgarath, and he was beginning to appreciate that. They were much more strong-willed, which was something he didn't think would have been possible, as the Gwenthari they had met in Ulfgarath were extraordinarily hard-headed when it came to most things.

After a few hours, they had lunch and continued to wait. This wasn't new for them, of course. It wasn't uncommon for the leaders of a town or settlement to discuss something amongst themselves. While Mariokos knew that there were plenty in the legions who just wanted to get to work, at the end of the day, this was a business transaction, and the lives of the men around them had value, as did the town.

As dusk approached, Mariokos felt his trepidation rise, and then there was activity at the top of the wall. Everyone perked up, waiting for the gate to open, but it didn't. Instead, over the side of the wall, they saw something come over and then flop against it, held by a rope.

Mariokos squinted and had one of his hawks veer closer, and then he saw it —saw what was against the wall. It was a man, or had once been a man. He still wore his helmet from the Legion, but the man's skin had been removed, as had some of his fingers and toes. There was more activity on the wall, and another one of the men from the Legion who had been part of the messengers was there.

He screamed, and they could see blood on him. He too was thrown over the wall. He jerked and smacked against it, as the rope that had a hook through his abdomen snapped and flung him against it. The man flinched, spluttered, and moaned before going still. The people on the walls cheered loudly.

There was an eerie calm over the gathered Legionnaires, and Mariokos could see Theoliano and Alessandros tense. Theoliano's eyes narrowed in controlled anger. Next to him, he could almost feel and see Alessandros vibrating. The man shifted, his expression darkening. He swore under his breath and started speaking quickly to Theoliano, though Mariokos couldn't hear the words being exchanged.

Theoliano appeared to be trying to talk to Alessandros, trying to talk him down from something. Alessandros made a cutting gesture with his hand and snapped. Theoliano went rigid and nodded. Alessandros turned to Caelwen and Mariokos and bellowed for them to come over. He shared a quick glance with his wife and then walked up to Alessandros.

Mariokos wondered if he was about to be blamed because it had been his idea to try to intimidate the Gwenthari. Alessandros glared at them.

"Well, I think we know their answer," Alessandros said. "Fucking barbarians," he muttered under his breath. Mariokos didn't say anything, and to his relief, neither did Caelwen. Alessandros stared at both of them, his expression hard.

"These people want barbarism, then barbarism we shall give them," Alessandros said, his voice cruel and cold. "Do you have birds that can carry ropes?"

Mariokos was taken aback but answered quickly, "Yes, sir, I do. I have hawks; they can carry small ropes. Why, sir?"

Alessandros nodded. "We are going to take ropes, the ends covered in pitch and on fire, and you are going to drop them on the thatched roofs in the town, and, if there's anything behind that gate holding it closed, on that as well," he said.

Mariokos felt a pit forming in his gut. Alessandros looked at Caelwen. "When this happens, when it is dark, and this town burns, your Essaerites are to attack the men on the gate. Kill them, rip them to pieces, throw them over the edge; I don't care," he said.

He turned to Mariokos. "And while she's doing that, your Essaerithon is to tackle that gate. I want it ripped off its hinges. Do you understand?" Alessandros said. Mariokos could hear a cold, cruel insanity in Alessandros's voice. He didn't dare argue.

He nodded quickly. "Yes, sir," he said.

Alessandros nodded. "Good. Make it happen."

———

CAELWEN'S NOSTRILS FILLED WITH THE NOXIOUS SCENT OF BURNING FLESH, THE ACRID stench clawing at the back of her throat. In the distance, wood cracked and collapsed with eerie finality, while the air buzzed faintly with the moans of the wounded and the low, pitiful weeping of the survivors. Ash drifted down like black snow, clinging to her hair. To her left, columns of smoke rose from the town. A handful of buildings were still on fire, though many were just now blackened cinders. Around her, ash fell from the sky, coating the grass of the fields. The town's living inhabitants were in those same fields. The night had been a long one.

The morning had been likewise. She looked over at a pyre, seeing a group of men on top of it, flames licking up their bodies. They screamed and howled. This had been the scene all morning. These were the town's leaders. They were being burned alive as punishment for what they did to the messengers. First, they had watched as members of their family were brought one by one to be burned alive. Then it was their turn. It made her feel sick. She knew it did Mariokos as well.

The inside of the town was a collection of corpses, and those that were left were beaten and haggard. Many of them were covered in soot and blood as they knelt in the field watching their leaders burn. As further penance, the legion was taking boys and girls of a certain age to be slaves—an entire generation lost to the town. The others had suffered atrocities throughout the evening, and what belongings they had that hadn't burned had been taken by the legions. It was disheartening. She had never seen anything like it before, but Alessandros had almost seemed crazed. *There's something wrong with him,* she thought.

She'd had a small run-in with him early in the morning when he'd asked her to use her Essaerites to shred some children in front of their parents. She'd refused. He'd been irritated, but she'd held her ground, and eventually, he'd given up. She watched him now as the men burned. He seemed to be calming, relaxing, almost happy. She shook her head. She started to walk away and saw Theoliano. He too looked haggard and grim.

"You saved a lot of lives last night," he said to her.

She glanced over at the town and the people in the field and then looked back at him. "Did I?" she said coolly.

"This is war," he said.

She nodded. "And I'm not sure how that saves lives," she said. Then she softened. "Sorry. I'm being difficult. Thank you," she said.

He shook his head. "No. You're right. I understand. And I forget this takes a higher toll on Essaerists than it does on regular people," he said.

She raised an eyebrow.

"You see through your Essaerites. And your Essaerites kill more than any man ever could," he said. "I can understand why that would bother you."

She nodded. "Thank you for understanding. Most don't. They think it's easier to kill with Essaerites, and I suppose the process itself is. And perhaps," she said, thinking, "perhaps the deaths don't feel the same as when you commit them with your own hand, but they weigh on you nonetheless," she said.

He looked thoughtful. "Why do I feel like you're not talking about now?" he said.

She shrank. "Probably because I'm not. I understand what happened last night. And I'm happy that legionnaires didn't die and that I was able to stop them from getting hurt by doing my part, but," she said, "I still don't like it. I would rather be healing people, not killing them," she said, glancing at the fire. "And certainly not this," she said, shaking her head. "Nothing good comes of things like this."

She felt a small wave of nausea hit her. She looked at the pyre one last time, shook her head in disgust, and turned, walking back to camp.

ABOUT THE AUTHOR

Nicholas Taylor is a fantasy and science fiction author. He was born in 1981 in Denver, Colorado, where he lives with his wife and family. Nicholas was an imaginative child who enjoyed writing stories and daydreaming about new worlds and places from a young age.

In his twenties, Nicholas rekindled a love for reading and consuming fantasy and science fiction. The culmination was his decision to write a novel in the winter of 2007. That first novel was Legon Awakening, which ran as a weekly podcast and was later released in print, digital, and audio editions that thousands have enjoyed.

Nicholas enjoys writing fiction that pulls readers into immersive worlds with likable and relatable characters. He strives to draw the reader into the scene with the characters, allowing them to explore magical realms or distant planets.

For more about Nicholas Taylor
Visit:
www.NicholasTaylor.co

www.ingramcontent.com/pod-product-compliance
Lightning Source LLC
Chambersburg PA
CBHW030918260626
47169CB00002B/305